Andrew K. H. Boyd

The Recreations of a Country Parson

Andrew K. H. Boyd

The Recreations of a Country Parson

ISBN/EAN: 9783337227913

Printed in Europe, USA, Canada, Australia, Japan

Cover: Foto ©Andreas Hilbeck / pixelio.de

More available books at **www.hansebooks.com**

THE RECREATIONS OF A COUNTRY PARSON

First Series

ALEXANDER STRAHAN, PUBLISHER

LONDON AND NEW YORK

1866

CONTENTS.

CHAPTER VI.

CHAPTER VII.

CHAPTER VIII.

CHAPTER IX.

THE RECREATIONS OF A COUNTRY PARSON

CHAPTER I.

CONCERNING THE COUNTRY PARSON'S LIFE.

THIS is Monday morning. It is a beautiful sun-shiny morning early in July. I am sitting on the steps that lead to my door, somewhat tired by the duty of yesterday, but feeling very restful and thankful. Before me there is a little expanse of the brightest grass, too little to be called a lawn, very soft and mossy, and very carefully mown. It is shaded by three noble beeches, about two hundred years old. The sunshine around has a green tinge from the reflection of the leaves. Double hedges, thick and tall, the inner one of gleaming beech, shut out all sight of a country lane that runs hard by : a lane into which this gravelled sweep of would-be avenue enters, after winding deftly through evergreens, rich and old, so as to make the utmost of its little length. On the side furthest from the lane, the miniature lawn opens into a garden of no great extent, and beyond the garden you see a green field sloping upwards to a wood which bounds the view. One-half of the front of the house is covered to the roof by a climbing rose-tree, so rich now with cluster roses that you see only the white soft

A

masses of fragrance. Crimson roses and fuchsias cover half-way up the remainder of the front wall; and the sides of the flight of steps are green with large-leaved ivy. If ever there was a dwelling embosomed in great trees and evergreens, it is here. Everything grows beautifully: oaks, horse-chestnuts, beeches; laurels, yews, hollies; lilacs and hawthorn trees. Off a little way on the right, graceful in stem, in branches, in the pale bark, in the light-green leaves, I see my especial pet, a fair acacia. This is the true country; not the poor shadow of it which you have near great and smoky towns. That sapphire air is polluted by no factory chimney. Smoke is a beauty here, there is so little of it: rising thin and blue from the cottage; hospitable and friendly-looking from the rare mansion. The town is five miles distant: there is not even a village near. Green fields are all about; hawthorn hedges and rich hedge-rows; great masses of wood everywhere. But this is Scotland: and there is no lack of hills and rocks, of little streams and waterfalls; and two hundred yards off, winding round that churchyard whose white stones you see by glimpses through old oak branches, a large river glides swiftly by.

It is a quiet and beautiful scene; and it pleases me to think that Britain has thousands and thousands like it. But of course none, in my mind, equal this: for this has been my home for five years.

I have been sitting here for an hour, with a book on my knee; and upon that a piece of paper, whereon

I have been noting down some thoughts for the sermon which I hope to write during this week, and to preach next Sunday in that little parish church of which you can see a corner of a gable through the oaks which surround the churchyard. I have not been able to think very connectedly, indeed: for two little feet have been pattering round me, two little hands pulling at me occasionally, and a little voice entreating that I should come and have a race upon the green. Of course I went: for like most men who are not very great or very bad, I have learned, for the sake of the little owner of the hands and the voice, to love every little child. Several times, too, I have been obliged to get up and make a dash at a very small weed which I discerned just appearing through the gravel; and once or twice my man-servant has come to consult me about matters connected with the garden and the stable. My sermon will be the better for all these interruptions. I do not mean to say that it will be absolutely good, though it will be as good as I can make it: but it will be better for the races with my little girl, and for the thoughts about my horse, than it would have been if I had not been interrupted at all. The Roman Catholic Church meant it well: but it was far mistaken when it thought to make a man a better parish priest by cutting him off from domestic ties, and quite emancipating him from all the little worries of domestic life. *That* might be the way to get men who would preach an unpractical religion, not human in interest, not able to comfort, direct, sustain through daily cares, temptations, and sorrows. But for preaching which will come home to men's business and bosoms, which will not appear to ignore those things which must of necessity occupy the greatest part of an ordinary mortal's thoughts, commend me to the preacher who has learned by experience what are human ties, and what is human worry.

It is a characteristic of country life, that living in the country you have so many cares outside. In town, you have nothing to think of (I mean in the way of little material matters) beyond the walls of your dwelling. It is not your business to see to the paving of the street before your door ; and if you live in a square, you are not individually responsible for the tidiness of the shrubbery in its centre. When you come home, after the absence of a week or a month, you have nothing to look round upon and see that it is right. The space within the house's walls is not a man's proper province. Your library-table and your books are all the domain which comes within the scope of your orderly spirit. But if you live in the country, in a house of your own with even a few acres of land attached to it, you have a host of things to think of when you come home from your week's or month's absence; you have an endless number of little things worrying you to take a turn round and see that they are all as they should be. You can hardly sit down and rest for their tugging at you. Is the grass all trimly mown? Has the pruning been done that you ordered? Has that rose-tree been trained? Has that bit of fence been mended? Are all the walks perfectly free from weeds? Is there not a gap left in box-wood edgings? and are the edges of all walks through grass sharp and clearly defined? Has that nettly corner of a field been made tidy? Has any one been stealing the fruit? Have the neighbouring cows been in your clover? How about the stable?—any fractures of the harness?—any scratches on the carriage?—anything amiss with the horse or horses? All these, and innumerable questions more, press on the man who looks after matters for himself, when he arrives at home.

Still, there is good in all this. That which in a desponding mood you call a worry, in a cheerful mood you think a source of simple, healthful interest in life. And there is one case in particular, in which I doubt not the reader of simple and natural tastes (and such may all my readers be) has experienced, if he be a country parson not too rich or great, the benefit of these gentle counter-irritants. It is when you come home, leaving your wife and children for a little while behind you. It is autumn: you are having your holiday: you have all gone to the sea-side. You have been away two or three weeks; and you begin to think that you ought to let your parishioners see that you have not forgotten them. You resolve to go home for ten days, which shall include two Sundays with their duty. You have to travel a hundred and thirty miles. So on a Friday morning you bid your little circle good bye, and set off alone. It is not, perhaps, an extreme assumption that you are a man of sound sense and feeling, and not a selfish conceited humbug : and, the case being so, you are not ashamed to confess that you are somewhat saddened by even that short parting ; and that various thoughts obtrude themselves of possible accident and sorrow before you meet again. It is only ten days, indeed : but a wise man is recorded to have once advised his fellow-men in words which run as follows, "Boast not thyself of to-morrow, for thou knowest not what a day may bring forth." And as you sail along in the steamer, and sweep along in the train, you are thinking of the little things that not without tears bade their governor farewell. It was early morning when you left : and as you proceed on your solitary journey, the sun ascends to noon, and declines towards evening. You have read your newspaper : there is no one else in that compartment of the carriage : and hour after hour you grow more and more dull and down-hearted. At length, as the sunset is gilding the swept harvest-fields, you reach the quiet little railway station among the hills. It is wonderful to see it. There is no village : hardly a dwelling in sight : there are rocky hills all round ; great trees ; and a fine river, by following which the astute engineer led his railway to this seemingly inaccessible spot. You alight on that primitive platform, with several large trees growing out of it, and with a waterfall at one end of it: and beyond the little palisade, you see your trap, (let me not say carriage,) your man-servant, your horse, perhaps your pair. How kindly and pleasant the expression even of the horse's back! How unlike the bustle of a railway station in a large town! The train goes, the brass of the engine red in the sunset; and you are left in perfect stillness. Your baggage is stowed, and you drive away gently. It takes some piloting to get down the steep slope from this out-of-the-way place. What a change from the thunder of the train to this audible quiet! You interrogate your servant first in the comprehensive question, if all is right. Relieved by his general affirmative answer, you descend into particulars. Any one sick in the parish? how was the church attended on the Sundays you were away? how is Jenny, who had the fever; and John, who had the paralytic stroke? How are the servants? how is the horse; the cow; the pig; the dog? How is the garden progressing? how about fruit? how about flowers? There was an awful thunderstorm on Wednesday: the people thought it was the end of the world. Two bullocks were killed, and thirteen sheep. Widow Wiggins' son had deserted from the army, and had come home. The harvest-home at such a farm is to-night: may Thomas go? What a little quiet world is the country parish:

what a microcosm even the country parsonage! You
are interested and pleased: you are getting over your
stupid feeling of depression. You are interested in
all these little matters, not because you have grown a
gossiping, little-minded man, but because you know
it is fit and right and good for you to be interested in
such things. You have five or six miles to drive:
never less: the scene grows always more homely and
familiar as you draw nearer home. And arrived at
last, what a deal to look at! What a welcome on the
servants' faces: such a contrast to the indifferent
looks of servants in a town. You hasten to your
library-table to see what letters await you: country-
folk are always a little nervous about their letters, as
half expecting, half fearing, half hoping, some vague,
great, undefined event. You see the snug fire: the
chamber so precisely arranged, and so fresh-looking:
you remark it and value it fifty times more amid
country fields and trees than you would turning out
of the manifest life and civilisation of the city street.
You are growing cheerful and thankful now; but
before it grows dark, you must look round out of
doors: and *that* makes you entirely thankful and
cheerful. Surely the place has grown greener and
prettier since you saw it last! You walk about the
garden and the shrubbery: the gravel is right, the
grass is right, the trees are right, the hedges are right,
everything is right. You go to the stable-yard: you
pat your horse, and pull his ears, and enjoy seeing his

snug resting-place for the night. You peep into the cow-house, now growing very dark : you glance into the abode of the pig : the dog has been capering about you all this while. You are not too great a man to take pleasure in these little things. And now when you enter your library again, where your solitary meal is spread, you sit down in the mellow lamplight, and feel quite happy. How different it would have been to have walked out of a street-cab into a town-house, with nothing beyond its walls to think of!

This is so sunshiny a day, and everything is looking so cheerful and beautiful, that I know my present testimony to the happiness of the country parson's life must be received with considerable reservation. Just at the present hour, I am willing to declare that I think the life of a country clergyman, in a pretty parish, with a well-conducted and well-to-do population, and with a fair living, is as happy, useful, and honourable as the life of man can be. Your work is all of a pleasant kind ; you have, generally speaking, not too much of it ; the fault is your own if you do not meet much esteem and regard among your parishioners of all degrees ; you feel you are of some service in your generation : you have intellectual labours and tastes which keep your mind from growing rusty, and which admit you into a wide field of pure enjoyment : you have pleasant country cares to divert your mind from head-work, and to keep you for hours daily in the open air, in a state of pleasurable interest; your little children grow up with green fields about them, and pure air to breathe: and if your heart be in your sacred work, you feel, Sunday by Sunday, and day by day, a solid enjoyment in telling your fellow-creatures the Good News you are commissioned to address to them, which it is hard to describe to another, but which you humbly and thankfully take and keep. You have not, indeed, the excitement and the exhilaration of commanding the attention of a large educated congregation : those are reserved for the popular clergyman of a city parish. But then, you are free from the temptation to attempt the unworthy arts of the clap-trap mob-orator, or to preach mainly to display your own talents and eloquence ; you have striven to exclude all personal ambition ; and, forgetting yourself or what people may think of yourself, to preach simply for the good of your fellow-sinners, and for the glory of that kind Master whom you serve. And around you there are none of those heart-breaking things which must crush the earnest clergyman in a large town : no destitution ; poverty, indeed, but no starvation : and although evil will be wherever man is, nothing of the gross, daring, shocking vice which is matured in the dens of the great city. The cottage children breathe a confined atmosphere while within the cottage ; but they have only to go to the door, and the pure air of heaven is about them, and they live in it most of their waking hours. Very different with the pale children of a like class in the city, who do but exchange the infected chamber for the filthy lane, and whose eyes are hardly ever gladdened by the sight of a green field. And when the diligent country parson walks or drives about his parish, not without a decided feeling of authority and ownership, he knows every man, woman, and child he meets, and all their concerns and cares. Still, even on this charming morning, I do not forget that it depends a good deal upon the parson's present mood, what sort of account he may give of his country parish and his parochial life. If he have been recently cheated by a well-to-do farmer in the price of some farm produce; if he have seen a humble neighbour deliberately forcing his cow through a weak part of the hedge into a rich pasture-field of the glebe, and then have found him ready to swear that the cow trespassed entirely without his knowledge or will; if he meet a hulking fellow carrying in the twilight various rails from a fence to be used as firewood; if, on a warm summer day, the whole congregation falls fast asleep during the sermon; if a farmer tells him what a bad and dishonest man a discharged man-servant was, some weeks after the parson had found that out for himself and packed off the dishonest man; if certain of the cottagers near appear disposed to live entirely, instead of only partially, of the parsonage larder; the poor parson may sometimes be found ready to wish himself in town, compact within a house in a street with no back-door; and not spreading out such a surface, as in the country he must, for petty fraud and peculation. But, after all, the country parson's great worldly cross lies for the most part in his poverty, and in the cares which arise out of that. It is not always so, indeed. In the lot of some the happy medium has been reached; they have found the "neither poverty nor riches" of the wise man's prayer. Would that it were so with all! For how it must cripple a clergyman's usefulness, how abate his energies, how destroy his eloquence, how sicken his heart, how narrow and degrade his mind, how tempt (as it has sometimes done) to unfair and dishonest shifts and expedients, to go about not knowing how to make the ends meet, not seeing how to pay what he owes! If I were a rich man, how it would gladden me to send a fifty-pound note to certain houses I have seen! What a dead weight it would lift from the poor wife's heart! Ah! I can think of the country parson, like poor Sydney Smith, adding his accounts, calculating his little means, wondering where he can pinch or pare any closer, till the poor fellow bends down his stupified head and throbbing temples on his hands, and wishes he could creep into a quiet grave. God tempers the wind to the shorn lamb; or I should wonder how it does not drive some country parsons mad, to think what would become of their children if they were taken away. It is the warm nest upon the rotten bough. They need abundant faith ; let us trust they get it. But in a desponding mood, I can well imagine such a one resolving that no child of his shall ever enter upon a course in life which has brought himself such misery as he has known.

I have been writing down some thoughts, as I have said, for the sermon of next Sunday. To-morrow morning I shall begin to write it fully out. Some individuals, I am aware, have maintained that listening to a sermon is irksome work ; but to a man whose tastes lie in that way, the writing of sermons is most pleasant occupation. It does you good. Unless you are a mere false pretender, you cannot try to impress any truth forcibly upon the hearts of others, without impressing it forcibly upon your own. All that you will ever make other men feel, will be only a subdued reflection of what you yourself have felt. And sermon-writing is a task that is divided into many stages. You begin afresh every week : you come to an end every week. If you are writing a book, the end appears very far away. If you find that although you do your best, you yet treat some part of your subject badly, you know that the bad passage remains as a permanent blot : and you work on under the cross-influence of that recollection. But if, with all your pains, this week's sermon is poor, why, you hope to do better next week. You seek a fresh field : you try again. No doubt, in preaching your sermons you are somewhat annoyed by rustic boorishness and want of thought. Various bumpkins will forget to close the door behind them when they enter church too late, as they not unfrequently do. Various men with great hob-nailed shoes, entering late, instead of quietly slipping into a pew close to the door, will stamp noisily up the passage to the further extremity of the church. Various faces will look up at you week by week, hopelessly blank of all interest or intelligence. Some human beings will not merely sleep, but loudly evince that they are sleeping. Well, you gradually cease to be worried by these little things. At first, they jarred through every nerve; but you grow accustomed to them. And if you be a man of principle and of sense, you know better than to fancy that amid a rustic people your powers are thrown away. Even if you have in past days been able to interest congregations of the refined and cultivated class, you will now shew your talent and your principle at once by accommodating your instructions to the comprehension of the simple souls committed to your care. I confess I have no patience with men who profess to preach sermons carelessly prepared, because they have an uneducated congregation. Nowhere is more careful preparation needed; but of course it must be preparation of the right sort. Let it be received as an axiom, that the very first aim of the preacher should be to interest. He must interest, before he can hope to instruct or improve. And no matter how filled with orthodox doctrine and good advice a sermon may be, if it put the congregation to sleep, it is an abominably bad sermon.

Surely, I go on to think, this kind of life must affect all the productions of the mind of the man who leads it. There must be a smack of the country, its scenes and its cares, about them all. You walk in shady lanes: you stand and look at the rugged bark of old trees: you help to prune evergreens: you devise flower-gardens and winding walks. You talk to pigs, and smooth down the legs of horses. You sit on mossy walls, and saunter by the river side, and through woodland paths. .You grow familiar with the internal arrangements of poor men's dwellings: you see much of men and women in those solemn seasons when all pretences are laid aside ; and they speak with confidence to you of their little cares and fears, for this world and the other. You kneel down and pray by the bedside of many sick ; and you know the look of the dying face well. Young children, whom you have humbly sought to instruct in the best of knowledge, have passed away from this life in your presence, telling you in interrupted sentences whither they trusted they were going, and bidding you not forget to meet them there. You feel the touch of the weak fingers still ; the parting request is not forgotten. You mark the spring blossoms come back ; and you walk among the harvest sheaves in the autumn even-ing. And when you ride up the parish on your duty, you feel the influence of bare and lonely tracts, where, ten miles from home, you sometimes dismount from your horse, and sit down on a grey stone by the way-side, and look for an hour at the heather at your feet, and at the sweeps of purple moorland far away. You go down to the churchyard frequently : you sit on the gravestone of your predecessor who died two hundred years since ; and you count five, six, seven spots where those who served the cure before you sleep. Then, leaning your head upon your hand, you look thirty years into the future, and wonder whether you are to grow old. You read, through moss-covered letters, how a former incumbent of the parish died in the last century, aged twenty-eight. That afternoon, coming from a cottage where you had been seeing a frail old woman, you took a flying leap over a brook near, with precipitous sides ; and you thought that some day, if you lived, you would have to creep quietly round by a smoother way. And now you think you see an aged man, tottering and grey, feebly walking down to the churchyard as of old, and seating himself hard .by where you sit. The garden will have grown weedy and untidy : it will not be the trim, precise dwelling which youthful energy and hopefulness keep it now.

Let it be hoped that the old man's hat is not seerly, nor his coat threadbare : it makes one's heart sore to see *that.* And let it be hoped that he is not alone. But you go home, I think, with a quieter and kindlier heart.

You live in a region, mental and material, that is

very entirely out of the track of worldly ambition.
You do not blame it in others : you have learnt to
blame few things in others severely, except cruelty
and falsehood : but you have outgrown it for yourself.
You hear, now and then, of this and the other school
or college friend becoming a great man. One is an
Indian hero : one is attorney-general : one is a cabinet
minister. You like to see their names in the newspapers. You remember how in college competitions
with them, you did not come off second-best. You
are struck at finding that such a man, whom you
recollect as a fearful dunce, is getting respectably on
through life : you remember how at school you used
to wonder whether the difference between the clever
boy and the booby would be in after days the same
great gulf that it was then. Your life goes on very
regularly, each week much like the last. And, on the
whole, it is very happy. You saunter for a little in
the open air after breakfast : you do so when the
evergreens are beautiful with snow as well as when
the warm sunshine makes the grass white with widely-
opened daisies. Your children go with you wherever
you go. You are growing subdued and sobered ; but
they are not : and when one sits on your knee, and
lays upon your shoulder a little head with golden
ringlets, you do not mind very much though your own
hair (what is left of it) is getting shot with gray. You
sit down in your quiet study to your work : what
thousands of pages you have written at that table !

You cease your task at one o'clock: you read your *Times:* you get on horseback and canter up the parish to see your sick: or you take the ribbons and tool into the county town. You feel the stir of even its quiet existence: you drop into the bookseller's: you grumble at the venerable age of the Reviews that come to you from the club. Generally, you cannot be bothered with calls upon your tattling acquaintances: you leave these to your wife. You drive home again, through the shady lanes, away into the green country: your man-servant in his sober livery tells you with pride, when you go to the stable-yard for a few minutes before dinner, that Mr Snooks, the great judge of horse-flesh, had declared that afternoon in the inn stable in town, that he had not seen a better-kept carriage and harness anywhere, and that your plump steed was a noble creature. It is well when a servant is proud of his belongings: he will be a happier man, and a more faithful and useful. When you next drive out, you will see the silver blazing in the sun with increased brightness. And now you have the pleasant evening before you. Do not, like some slovenly men in remote places, sit down to dinner an unwashed and untidy object: living so quietly as you do, it is especially needful, if you would avoid an encroaching rudeness, to pay careful attention to the little refinements of life. And the great event of the day over, you have music, books, and children; you have the summer saunter in the twilight ; you have the winter evening fireside ; you take perhaps another turn at your sermon for an hour or two. The day has brought its work and its recreation ; you can look back each evening upon something done ; save when you give yourself a holiday which you feel has been fairly toiled for. And what a wonderful amount of work, such as it is, you may, by exertion regular but not excessive, turn off in the course of the ten months and a-half of the working year !

And thus, day by day, and month by month, the life of the country parson passes quietly away. It will be briefly comprehended on his tombstone, in the assurance that he did his duty, simply and faith-fully, through so many years. It is somewhat mono-tonous, but he is too-busy to weary of it : it is varied by not much society, in the sense of conversation with educated men with whom the clergyman has many common feelings. But it is inexpressibly pleas-ing when, either to his own house or to a dwelling near, there comes a visitor with whom an entire sym-pathy is felt, though probably holding very antagon-istic views: then come the "good talks" with delighted Johnson ; genial evenings, and long walks of after-noons. The daily post is a daily strong sensation, sometimes pleasing, sometimes painful, as he brings tidings of the outer world. You have your daily *Times ;* each Monday morning brings your *Saturday*

Review; and the *Illustrated London News* comes not merely for the children's sake. You read all the quarterlies, of course; you skim the monthlies; but it is with tenfold interest and pleasure that month by month you receive that magazine which is edited by a dear friend who sends it to you, and in which sometimes certain pages have the familiar look of a friend's face. You draw it wet from its big envelope: you cut its leaves with care: you enjoy the fragrance of its steam as it dries at the study fire: you glance at the shining backs of that long row of volumes into which the pleasant monthly visitants have accumulated: you think you will have another volume soon. Then there is a great delight in occasionally receiving a large bundle of books which have been ordered from your bookseller in the city a hundred miles off: in reading the address in such big letters that they must have been made with a brush: in stripping off the successive layers of immensely thick brown paper: in reaching the precious hoard within, all such fresh copies (who are they that buy the copies you turn over in the shop, but which you would not on any account take?): such fresh copies, with their brannew bindings and their leaves so pure in a material sense: in cutting the leaves at the rate of two or three volumes an evening, and in seeing the entire accession of literature lying about the other table (not the one you write on) for a few days ere they are given to the shelves. You are not in the least ashamed to confess that you are pleased by all these little things. You regard it as not necessarily proving any special pettiness of mind or heart. You regard it as no proof of greatness in any man, that he should appear to care nothing for anything. Your private belief is that it shews him to be either a humbug or a fool.

In this little volume, the indulgent reader will find certain of those Essays which the writer discovered on cutting the leaves of the magazine which comes to him on the last day of every month. They were written as something which might afford variety of work, which often proves the most restful of all recreation. They are nothing more than that which they are called—a country clergyman's *Recreations.* My solid work, and my first thoughts, are given to that which is the business and the happiness of my life. But these Essays have led me into a field which to myself was fresh and pleasant. And I have always returned from them, with increased interest, to graver themes and trains of thought. I have not forgot, as I wrote them, a certain time, when my little children must go away from their early home; when these evergreens I have planted and these walks I have made shall pass to my successor (may he be a better man !) ; and when I shall perhaps find my resting-place under those ancient oaks. Nor have I wholly failed to remember a coming day, when bishops and archbishops shall be called to render an account of the fashion in which they exercised their solemn and dignified trusts; and when I, who am no more than the minister of a Scotch country parish, must answer for the diligence with which I served my little cure.

CHAPTER II.

CONCERNING THE ART OF PUTTING THINGS:

BEING THOUGHTS ON REPRESENTATION AND MISREPRESENTATION.

LET the reader be assured that the word *Represen-tation*, which has caught his eye on glancing at the title of this essay, has nothing earthly to do with the Elective Franchise, whether in boroughs or counties. Not a syllable will be found upon the following pages bearing directly or indirectly upon any New Reform Bill. I do not care a rush who is member for this county. I have no doubt that all members of Parliament are very much alike. Everybody knows that each individual legislator who pushes his way into the House is actuated solely by a pure patriotic love for his country. No briefless barrister ever got into Parliament in the hope of getting a place of twelve hundred a-year. No barrister in fair practice ever did so in the hope of getting a silk gown, or the Solicitor-Generalship, or a seat on the bench. No merchant or country-gentleman ever did so in the hope of gaining a little accession of dignity and influence in the town or county in which he lives.

All these things are universally understood; and they are mentioned here merely to enable it to be said, that this treatise has nothing to do with them.

Edgar Allan Poe, the miserable genius who died in America a few years ago, declared that he never had the least difficulty in tracing the logical steps by which he chose any subject on which he had ever written, and matured his plan for treating it. And some readers may remember a curious essay, contained in his collected works, in which he gives a minute account of the genesis of his extraordinary poem, *The Raven.* But Poe was a humbug; and it is impossible to place the least faith in anything said by him upon any subject whatever. In his writings we find him repeatedly avowing that he would assert any falsehood, provided it were likely to excite interest and " create a sensation." I believe that most authors could tell us that very frequently the conception and the treatment of their subject have darted on them all at once, they could not tell how. Many clergymen know how strangely texts and topics of discourse have been suggested to them, while it was impossible to trace any link of association with what had occupied their minds the instant before. The late Douglas Jerrold relates how he first conceived the idea of one of his most popular productions. Walking on a winter day, he passed a large enclosure full of romping boys at play. He paused for a minute; and as he looked and mused, a thought flashed upon him.   It was not so beautiful, and you would say not so natural, as the reflections of Gray, as he looked from a distance at Eton College.   As Jerrold gazed at the schoolboys, and listened to their merry shouts, there burst upon him the conception of *Mrs Caudle's Curtain Lectures!*   There seems little enough con- nexion with what he was looking at ; and although Jerrold declared that the sight suggested the idea, he could not pretend to trace the link of association.   It would be very interesting if we could accurately know the process. by which authors, small or great, piece together their grander characters.   How did Milton pile up his Satan ? how did Shakspeare put together Hamlet or Lady Macbeth ? how did Charlotte Brontë imagine Rochester ?   Writers generally keep their secrets, and do not let us see behind the scenes.   We can trace, indeed, in successive pieces by Sheridan, the step-by-step development of his most brilliant jests, and of his most gushing bursts of the feeling of the moment.   No doubt Lord Brougham had tried the woolsack to see how it would do, before he fell on his knees upon it (on the impulse of the instant) at the end of his great speech on the Reform Bill.   But of course Lord Brougham would not tell us; and Sheridan did not intend us to know.   Even Mr Dickens, when, in his preface to the cheap edition of *Pickwick*, he avows his purpose of telling us all about the origin of that amazingly successful serial, gives us no inkling of the process by which he produced the character which we all know so well.   He tells us a great deal about the mere details of the work : the pages of letter-press, the number of illustrations, the price and times ot publication.   But the process of actual authorship remains a mystery.   The great painters would not tell where they got their colours.   The effort which gives a new character to the acquaintance of hundreds of thousands of Englishmen, shall be concealed beneath a decorous veiL   All that Mr Dickens tells us is this: "I thought of Mr Pickwick, and wrote the first number."   And to the natural question of curiosity, "How on earth did you think of Mr Pickwick?" the author's silence replies, "I don't choose to tell you *that!*"

And now, courteous reader, you are humbly asked to suffer the writer's discursive fashion, as he records how the idea of the present discourse, treatise, dissertation, or essay flashed upon his mind.   Yesterday was a most beautiful frosty day.   The air was indescribably exhilarating : the cold was no more than bracing ; and as I fared forth for a walk of some miles, I saw the tower of the ancient church, green with centuries of ivy, looking through the trees which surround it, the green ivy silvered over with hoar-frost.   The hedges on either hand, powdered with rime, were shining in the cold sunshine of the winter afternoon.   First, I passed through a thick pine-wood, bordering the road on both sides.   The stems of the fir-trees had that warm rich colour which is always pleasant to look at ; and the green branches were just touched with frost.

One undervalues the evergreens in summer: their colour is dull when compared with the fresher and brighter green of the deciduous trees; but now, when these gay transients have changed to shivering skeletons, the hearty firs, hollies, and yews warm and cheer the wintry landscape. Not the wintry, I should say, but the *winter* landscape, which conveys quite a different impression. The word *wintry* wakens associations of bleakness, bareness, and bitterness; a hearty evergreen tree never looks wintry, nor does a landscape to which such trees give the tone. Then emerging from the wood, I was in an open country. A great hill rises just ahead, which the road will skirt by and by: on the right, at the foot of a little cliff hard by, runs a shallow, broad, rapid river. Looking across the river, I see a large range of nearly level park, which at a mile's distance rises into upland; the park shews broad green glades, broken and bounded by fine trees, in clumps and in avenues. In summertime you would see only the green leaves: but now, peering through the branches, you can make out the outline of the gray turrets of the baronial dwelling which has stood there—added to, taken from, patched, and altered, but still the same dwelling—for the last four hundred years. And on the left, I am just passing the rustic gateway through which you approach that quaint cottage on the knoll two hundred yards off—one story high, with deep thatch, steep gables, overhanging eaves, and veranda of rough oak—a

sweet little place, where Izaak Walton might successfully have carried out the spirit of his favourite text,
and "studied to be quiet." All this way, three miles
and more, I did not meet a human being. There was
not a breath of air through the spines of the firs, and
not a sound except the ripple of the river. I leant
upon a gate, and looked into a field. Something was
grazing in the field; but I cannot remember whether
it was cows, sheep, oxen, elephants, or camels; for as
I was looking, and thinking how I should begin a
sermon on a certain subject much thought upon for
the last fortnight, my mind resolutely turned away
from it, and said, as plainly as mind could express it,
For several days to come I shall produce material
upon no subject but one,—and *that* shall be the comprehensive, practical, suggestive, and most important
subject of the ART OF PUTTING THINGS !

And, indeed, there is hardly a larger subject, in relation to the social life of the nineteenth century in
England; and there is hardly a practical problem to
the solution of which so great an amount of ingenuity
and industry, honest and dishonest, is daily brought,
as the grand problem of setting forth yourself, your
goods, your horses, your case, your plans, your thoughts
and arguments—all your belongings, in short—to the
best advantage. From the Prime Minister, who exerts
all his wonderful skill and eloquence to put his policy
before Parliament and the country in the most favourable light, and the Chancellor of the Exchequer, who

does his very best to cast a rosy hue even upon an income-tax, down to the shopman who arranges his draperies in the window against market-day in that fashion which he thinks will prove most fascinating to the maid-servant with her newly-paid wages in her pocket, and the nurse who in a most lively and jovial manner assures a young lady of three years old that she will never feel the taste of her castor-oil,—yea, even to the dentist who with a joke and a smiling face approaches you with his forceps in his hand :—from the great Attorney-General seeking to place his view of his case with convincing force before a bewil- dered jury, (that view being flatly opposed to common sense,) down to the schoolboy found out in some mis- chievous trick and trying to throw the blame upon somebody else : almost all civilised beings in Great Britain are from morning to night labouring hard to put things in general or something in particular in the way that they think will lead to the result which best suits their views ;—are, in short, practising the art of representing or misrepresenting things for their own advantage. Great skill, you would say, must result from this constant practice : and indeed it probably does. But then, people are so much in the habit of trying to *put things* themselves, that they are uncom- monly sharp at seeing through the devices of others. "Set a thief to catch a thief," says the ancient adage : and so, set a man who can himself tell a very plausible story without saying anything positively untrue, to discover the real truth under the rainbow tints of the plausible story told by another.

But do not fancy, my kind reader, that I have any purpose of making a misanthropical onslaught upon poor humanity. I am very far from desiring to imply that there is anything essentially wrong or dishonest in trying to put things in the most favourable light for our views and plans. The contrary is the case. It is a noble gift, when a man is able to put great truths or momentous facts before our minds with that vividness and force which shall make us feel these facts and truths in their grand reality. A great evil, to which human beings are by their make subject, is, that they can talk of things, know things, and understand things, without *feeling* them in their true importance—without, in short, *realising* them. There appears to be a certain numbness about the mental organs of perception; and the man who is able to *put things* so strikingly, clearly, pithily, forcibly, glaringly, whether these things are religious, social, or political truths, as to get through that numbness, that crust of insensibility, to the *quick* of the mind and heart, must be a great man, an earnest man, an honest man, a good man. I believe that any great reformer will find less practical discouragement in the opposition of bad people than in the *inertia* of good people. You cannot get them to feel that the need and the danger are so imminent and urgent; you cannot get them to bestir themselves with the activity and energy which the case demands. You cannot get them to take it in that the open sewer and the airless home of the working man are such a very serious matter; you cannot get them to feel that the vast uneducated masses of the British population form a mine beneath our feet which may explode any day, with God knows what devastation. I think that not all the wonderful eloquence, freshness, and pith of Mr Kingsley form a talent so valuable as his power of compelling people to *feel* what they had always known and talked about, but never felt. And wherein lies that power, but just in his skill to *put things*—in his power of truthful representation?

Sydney Smith was once talking with an Irish Roman Catholic priest about the proposal to endow the Romish Church in Ireland. " We would not take the Saxon money," said the worthy priest, quite sincerely; " we would not defile our fingers with it. No matter whether Parliament offered us endowments or not, we would not receive them." "Suppose," replied Sydney Smith, " you were to receive an official letter that on calling at such a bank in the town three miles off, you would hereafter receive a hundred pounds a-quarter, the first quarter's allowance payable in advance on the next day; and suppose that you wanted money to do good, or to buy books, or anything else, do you mean to say you would not drive over to the town and take the hundred pounds out of the bank?" The priest was staggered. He had never looked at the thing in that precise light. He had never had the vague distant question of endowment brought so home to him.   He had been quite sincere in his spirited repudiation of Saxon coin, as recorded above; but he had not exactly understood what he was saying and doing.   "*Oh, Mr Smith*," he replied, "*you have such a way of putting things!*"   What a triumph of the Anglican's art of truthful representation!

One of the latest instances of skill in putting things, which I remember to have struck me, I came upon, where abundance of such skill may be found—in a leading article in the *Times*.   The writer of that article was endeavouring to shew that the work of the country clergy is extremely light.   Of course he is sadly mistaken; but this by the way.   As to sermons, said the lively writer, (I don't pretend to give his exact words,) what work is there in a sermon? Just fancy that you are writing half-a-dozen letters of four pages each, and crossed!   The thing was cleverly put; and it really came on me with the force of a fact, a new and surprising fact.   Many sermons has this thin right hand written; but my impression of a sermon, drawn from some years' experience, is of a composition very different from a letter—something demanding that brain and heart should be worked to the top of their bent for more hours than need be mentioned here; something implying as hard and as exhausting labour as man can well go through. Surely, I thought, I have been working under a sad delusion!   Only half-a-dozen light letters of gossip to a friend: *that* is the amount of work implied in a sermon!   Have I been all these years making a bugbear of such a simple and easy matter as *that?* Here is a new and cheerful way of putting the thing! But unhappily, though the clever representation would no doubt convey to some thousands of readers the impression that to write a sermon was a very simple affair after all, it broke down, it crumpled up, it went to pieces when brought to the test of fact. When next morning I had written my text, I thought to myself, Now here I have just to do the same amount of work which it would cost me to write half-a-dozen letters to half-a-dozen friends, giving them our little news.   Ah, it would not do!   In a little, I was again in the struggle of mapping out my subject, and cutting a straight track through the jungle of the world of mind ; looking about for illustrations, seeking words to put my meaning with clearness and interest before the simple country-folk I preach to.   It was not the least like letter-writing.   The clever writer's way of putting things was wrong ; and though I acquit him of any crime beyond speaking with authority of a thing which he knew nothing about, I must declare that his representation was a misrepresentation.   If you have sufficient skill, you may put what is painful so that it shall sound pleasant ; you may put a wearisome journey by railway in such a connexion with cozy cushions, warm rugs, a review or a new book, storm sweeping the fields without, and

c

warmth and ease within, that it shall seem a delightful thing. You may put work, in short, so that it shall look like play. But actual experiment breaks down the representation. You cannot change the essential nature of things. You cannot make black white, though a clever man may make it seem so.

Still, we all have a great love for trying to put any hard work or any painful business, which it is certain we must go through, in such a light as may make it seem less terrible. And it is not difficult to deceive ourselves when we are eager to be deceived. No one can tell how much comfort poor Damien drew from the way in which he put the case on the morning of his death by horrible tortures: "The day will be long," he said, "but it will have an end." No one can tell what a gleam of light may have darted upon the mind of Charles I. as he knelt to the block, when Bishop Juxon put encouragingly the last trial the monarch had to go through: "One last stage, somewhat turbulent and troublesome, *but still a very short one.*" No one can tell how much it soothed the self-love of Tom Purdie, when Sir Walter Scott ordered him to cut down some trees which Tom wished to stand, and positively commanded that they should go down in spite of all Tom's arguments and expostulations, and all this in the presence of a number of gentlemen before whom Tom could not bear any impeachment of his woodcraft; no one, I say, can tell how much it soothed the worthy forester's self-love when after half-an-hour's sulky meditation he thought of the happy plan of putting the thing on another footing than that of obedience to an order, and looking up cheerfully again, said, "As for those trees, I think I 'll *tak' your advice*, Sir Walter!" Would it be possible, I wonder, thus pleasantly to *put* the writing of an article so as to do away the sense of the exertion which writing an article implies? Have we not all little tricks which we play upon ourselves, to make our labour seem lighter, our dignity greater, our whole position jollier, than in our secret soul we know is the fact! Think, then, thou jaded man, bending over the written page which is one day to attain the dignity of print in *Fraser* or *Blackwood*, how in these words thou art addressing many thousands of thy enlightened countrymen and thy fair countrywomen, and becoming known (as Fielding puts it in one of his simply felicitous sentences) "to numbers who otherwise never saw or knew thee, and whom thou shalt never see or know." Think how thou shalt lie upon massive library-tables, in substantially elegant libraries, side by side perhaps with Helps, Kingsley, or Hazlitt; how thou shalt lighten the cares of middle-aged men, and (if thou art a writer of fiction) be smuggled up to young ladies' chambers; who shall think, as they read thy article, (oh, much mistaken!) what a nice man thou art! Alas! all that way of putting things is mere poetry. It won't do. It still remains, and always must remain, the stretch and

strain of mind and muscle, to write.   Let not the
critic be severe on people who write ill: they deserve
much credit and sympathy because they write at all.
But though these grand and romantic ways of putting
the writing of one's article will not serve, there are
little prosaic material expedients which really avail to
put it in a light in which it looks decidedly less
laborious.   Slowly let the large drawer be pulled out
wherein lies the paper which will serve, if we are
allowed to see them, for many months to come.
There lies the large blue quarto, so thick and substantial; there the massive foolscap, so soft and
smooth, over which the pen so pleasantly and un-
scratchingly glides; *that* is the raw material for the
article.   Draw it forth deliberately: fold it accurately:
then the ivory stridently cuts it through.   Weigh the
paper in your hand; then put the case thus: "Well,
it is only covering these pages with writing, after all;
it is just putting three-and-twenty lines, of so many
words each on the average, upon each of these un-
blotted surfaces."   Surely there is not so much in
that.   Do not think of all the innumerable processes
of mind that go to it; of the weighing of the consequences of general propositions; of the choice of
words; of the pioneering your track right on, not
turning to either hand; of the memory taxed to bring
up old thoughts upon your subject; of the clock striking unheard while you are bent upon your task, so
much harder than carrying any reasonable quantity

of coals, or blacking ever so many boots, or currying ever so many horses. Just stick to this view of the matter, just put the thing this way—that all you have to do is to blacken so many pages, and take the comfort of that way of putting it.

To such people as we human beings are, there is hardly any matter of greater practical importance than what we have called the Art of Putting Things. For, to us, things *are* what they *seem*. They affect us just according to what we think them. Our knowledge of things, and our feeling in regard to things, are all contingent on the way in which these things have been put before us; and what different ways there are of putting every possible doctrine, or opinion, or doing, or thing, or event! And what mischievous results, colouring all our views and feelings, may follow from an important subject having been wrongly, disagreeably, injudiciously put to us when we were children! How many men hate Sunday all their lives because it was put to them so gloomily in their boyhood; and how many Englishmen, on the other hand, fancy a Scotch Sunday the most disagreeable of days because the case has been wrongly put to them, while in truth there is, in intelligent religious Scotch families, no more pleasant, cheerful, genial, restful, happy day. And did not Byron always hate Horace, put to him in youth with the associations of impositions and the birch? There is no more sunshiny inmate of any home than the happy-tempered one who has the art of putting all things in a pleasant light, from the great misfortunes of life down to a broken carriage-spring, a servant's failings, a child's salts and senna. You are extremely indignant at some person who has used you ill; you are worried and annoyed at his misconduct; it is as though you were going about with a mustard blister applied to your mind: when a word or two from some genial friend puts the entire matter in a new light, and your irritation goes, the blister is removed, your anger dies out, you would like to pat the offending being on the head, and say you bear him no malice. And it is wonderful what a little thing sometimes suffices to put a case thus differently. When you are complaining of somebody's ill-usage, it will change your feeling and the look of things, if the friend you are speaking to does no more than say of the peccant brother, "Ah! poor fellow!" I think that every man or woman who has got servants, and who has pretty frequently to observe (I mean to see, not to speak of) some fault on their part, owes a deep debt of gratitude to the man, whoever he was, who thus kindly and wisely gave us a forbearing stand-point from which to regard a servant's failings, by putting the thing in this way, true in itself though new to many, that you cannot expect perfection for fourteen, or even for fifty pounds a-year. Has not that way of putting things sometimes checked you when you meditated a sharp reproof, and allayed anger which otherwise would have been pretty hot? Even when a rogue cheats you, (though that, I confess, is a peculiarly irritating thing,) is not your wrath mollified by putting the thing thus: that the poor wretch probably needed very much the money out of which he cheated you, and would not have cheated you if he could have got it honestly? When a horse-dealer sells you, at a remarkably stiff figure, a broken-winded steed, do not yield to unqualified indignation. True, the horse-dealer is always ready to cheat, but feel for the poor fellow, every man thinks it right to cheat *him;* and with every man's hand against him, what wonder though his hand should be against every man? Everything, you see, turns on the way in which you put things. And it is so from earliest youth to latest age. The old scholar, whose delight is to sit among his books, thus puts his library:—

> "My days among the dead are pass'd:
> Around me I behold,
> Where'er these casual eyes are cast,
> The mighty minds of old:
> My never-failing friends are they,
> With whom I converse night and day." *

You see the library was not mere shelves of books, and the books were not mere printed pages. You remember how Robinson Crusoe, in his cheerful moods, put his island home. He sat down to his lonely meal, but *that* was not how he put things. No. " Here was my majesty, all alone by myself, attended by my

* Southey.

servants :" his servants being the dog, parrot, and cat. I remember how a wealthy merchant, a man quite of the city as opposed to the country, once talked of emigrating to America, and buying an immense tract of land, where he and his family should lead a simple, unartificial, innocent life. He was not in the least cut out for such a life, and would have been miserable in it, but he was fascinated with the notion because he put it thus :—" I shall have great flocks and herds, and live in a tent *like Abraham.*" And *that* way of putting things brought up before the busy man of the nineteenth century I know not what sweet picture of a primevally quiet and happy life. I can remember yet how, when I crept about my father's study, a little boy of three years old, I felt the magic of the art of putting things. All children are restless. It is impossible for them to remain still, and we all know how a child in a study worries the busy scholar. All admonitions to keep quiet failed ; it was really impossible to obey them. Creep, creep about ; upset footstools ; pull off table-covers ; upset ink. But when the thing was put in a different way ; when the kind voice said, " Now, you 'll be my little dog : creep into your house there under the table, and lie quite still," there was no difficulty in obeying *that* command : and, except an occasional bow-wow, there was perfect stillness. The art of putting things had prevailed. It was necessary to keep still ; for a dog in a study, I knew, must keep still, and I was a dog.

It must be a worrying thing for a great warrior or statesman, fighting a great battle, or introducing a great legislative measure, to remember that the estimation in which he is to be held in his own day and country, and in other countries and ages, depends not at all on what his conduct is in itself, but entirely on the way in which it shall be put before mankind— represented, or misrepresented, in newspapers, in rumours, in histories. How very unlikely it is that history will ever put the case on its real merits : the characters of history will either be praised far above their deserts, or abused far beyond their sins. "Do not read history to me," said Sir Robert Walpole, "for *that*, I know, must be false." History could be no more than the record of the way in which men had agreed to put things ; and those behind the scenes, the men who pull the wires which move the puppets, must often have reason to smile at the absurd mistakes into which the history-writing outsiders fall. And even apart from ignorance, or bias, or intention to deceive, what a fearful thought it must be to a great man taking a conspicuous part in some great solemnity, such as the trial of a queen, or the impeachment of a governor-general, to reflect that this great solemnity, and his own share in it, and how he looked, and what he said, may possibly be put before mankind by the great historian Mr Wordy ! One can enter into Johnson's feeling when, on hearing that Boswell intended to write his biography, he exclaimed, in mingled

terror and fury—"If I thought he contemplated writing my life, I should render *that* impossible by taking
his!" It was something to shudder at, the idea of
going down to posterity as represented by a Boswell!
But the great lexicographer was mistaken: the Dutch-
painter-like biography shewed him exactly as he was,
the great, little, mighty, weak, manly, babyish mind
and heart. And not great men alone, historical per-
sonages, have this reason for disquiet and apprehen-
sion. Don't you know, my reader not unversed in
the ways of life, that it depends entirely on how the
story is told, how the thing is represented or misrepresented, whether your conduct on any given occasion
shall appear heroic or ridiculous, reasonable or absurd,
natural or affected, modest or impudent: and don't
you know, too, what a vast number of ill-set people are
always ready to give the story the unfavourable turn,
to put the matter in the bad light; and how many
more, not really ill-set, not really with any malicious
intention, are prompted by their love of fun, in relating
any act of any acquaintance, to try to set it in a ridiculous light? Your domestic establishment is shabby
or unpretending, elegant or tawdry, just as the fancy
of the moment may lead your neighbour to put the
thing. Your equipage is a neat little turn-out or a
shabby attempt, your house is quiet or dull, yourself a
genius or a blockhead, just as it may strike your friend
on the instant to put the thing. And don't we all
know some people—not bad people in the main—who

never by any chance put the thing except in the un favourable way? I have heard the self-same house called a snug little place and a miserable little hole; the same man called a lively talker and an absurd rattlebrain; the same person called a gentlemanlike man and a missy piece of affectation; the same income called competence and starvation; the same horse called a noble animal and an old white cow:— the entire difference, of course, lay in the fashion in which the narrator chose, from inherent *bonhomie* or inherent verjuice, to put the thing. While Mr Bright probably regards it as the most ennobling occupation of humanity to buy in the cheapest and sell in the dearest market, Byron said, as implying the lowest degree of degradation—

> " Trust not for freedom to the Franks—
> They have a king *who buys and sells !*"

And it is just the two opposite ways of putting the same admitted fact, to say that Britain is the first mercantile community of the world, and to say that we are a nation of shopkeepers. One-way of putting the fact is the dignified, the other is the degrading. If a boy plays truant or falls asleep in church, it just depends on how you put it, or how the story is told, whether you are to see in all this the natural thoughtlessness of boyhood, or a first step towards the gallows. "Billy Brown stole some of my apples," says a kind-hearted man; "well, poor fellow, I daresay he seldom gets any." "Billy Brown stole my apples," says the severe man; "ah, the vagabond, he is born to be hanged." Sydney Smith put Catholic Emancipation as common justice and common sense; Dr M'Neile puts it as a great national sin, and the origin of the potato disease. John Foster mentions in his *Diary*, that he once expostulated with a great hulking, stupid bumpkin, as to some gross transgression of which he had been guilty. Little effect was produced on the bumpkin, for dense stupidity is a great duller of the conscience. Foster persisted: "Do not you think," he said, "that the Almighty will be angry at such conduct as yours?" Blockhead as the fellow was, he could take in the idea of my essay; he replied, "That's just as A tak's ut!" But what struck little Paul Dombey as strange, that the same bells rung for weddings and for funerals, and that the same sound was merry or doleful just as we put it, is true of many things besides bells. The character of everything we hear or see is reflected upon it from our own minds. The sun *sees* the earth look bright because it first *made* it so. You go to a public meeting, my friend. You make a speech. You get on, you think, uncommonly well. When your auditor Mr A. or Miss B. goes home, and is asked there what sort of appearance you made, don't you fancy that the reply will be affected in any appreciable degree by the actual fact! It depends entirely on the state of the relator's nerves or digestion, or the passing fancy of the moment, whether you shall be said to have done delightfully or disgustingly ; whether you shall be said to have made a brilliant figure, or to have made a fool of yourself. You never can be sure, though you spoke with the tongue of angels, but that ill-nature, peevishness, prejudice, thoughtlessness, may put the case that your speech was most abominable. Do you fancy that you could ever say or do anything that Mr Snarling could not find fault with, or Miss Limejuice could not misrepresent?

Years ago, I was accustomed to frequent the courts of law, and to listen with much interest to the great advocates of that time, as Follett, Wilde, Thesiger, Kelly. Nowhere in the world, I think, is one so deeply impressed with the value of tact and skill in putting things, as in the Court of Queen's Bench at the trial of an important case by a jury. Does not all the enormous difference, as great as that between a country bumpkin and a hog, between Follett and Mr Briefless, lie simply in their respective powers of putting things? The actual facts, the actual merits of the case, have very little indeed to do with the verdict, compared with the counsel's skill in putting them ; the artful marshalling of circumstances, the casting weak points into shadow, and bringing out strong points into glaring relief. I remember how I used to look with admiration at one of these great men when, in his speech to the jury, he was approaching some circumstance in the case which made dead against him. It was beautiful to see the intellectual gladiator cautiously approaching the hostile fact; coming up to it, tossing and turning it about, and finally shewing that it made strongly in his favour. Now, if that was really so, why did it look as if it made against him? Why should so much depend on the way in which he put it? Or, if the fact was in truth one that made against him, why should it be possible for a man to put it so that it should seem to make in his favour, and all without any direct falsification of facts or arguments, without any of that mere vulgar misrepresentation which can be met by direct contradiction? Surely it is not a desirable state of matters, that a plausible fellow should be able to explain away some very doubtful conduct of his own, and by skilful putting of things should be able to make it seem even to the least discerning that he is the most innocent and injured of human beings. And it is provoking, too, when you feel at once that his defence is a mere intellectual juggle, and yet, with all your logic, when you cannot just on the instant tear it to pieces, and put the thing in the light of truth. Indeed, so well is it understood that by tact and address you may so put things as to make the worse appear the better reason, that the idea generally conveyed, when we talk of putting things, is, that there is something wrong, something to be adroitly concealed, some weak point in regard to which dust is to be thrown into too observant eyes. There is a common impression, not one of unqualified truth, that when

all is above board, there is less need for skilful putting of the case. Many people think, though the case
is by no means so, that truth may always be depended
on to tell its own story and produce its due impression. Not a bit of it. However good my case
might be, I should be sorry to intrust it to Mr Numskull, with Sir Fitzroy Kelly on the other side.

It is a coarse and stupid expedient to have recourse
to anything like falsification in putting things as they
would make best for yourself, reader. And there is
no need for it. Unless you have absolutely killed a
man and taken his watch, or done something equally
decided, you can easily represent circumstances so as
to throw a favourable light upon yourself and your
conduct. It is a mistake to fancy that in this world
a story must be either true or false, a deed either
right or wrong, a man either good or bad. There are
few questions which can be answered by Yes or No.
Almost all actions and events are of mingled character; and there is something to be said on both sides
of almost every subject which can be debated. Who
does not remember how, when he was a boy, and
had done some mischief which he was too honest to
deny, he revolved all he had done over and over,
putting it in many lights, trying it in all possible
points of view, till he had persuaded himself that he
had done quite right, or at least that he had done
nothing that was so very wrong, after all? There
was a lurking feeling, probably, that all this was self-

deception ; and oh ! how our way of putting the case, so favourably to ourselves, vanished into air when our teacher and governor sternly called us to account ! All those jesuitical artifices were forgotten, and we just felt that we had done wrong, and there was no use trying to justify it.

The noble use of the power of putting things, is when a man employs that power to give tenfold force to truth. When you go and hear a great preacher, you sometimes come away wishing heartily that the impression he made on you would last : for you feel that though what struck you so much was not the familiar doctrine which you knew quite well before, but the way in which he put it, still that startling view of things was the right view. Probably in the pulpit more than anywhere else, we feel the difference between a man who talks about and about things, and another man who puts them so that we *feel* them. And when one thinks of all the ignorance, want, and misery which surround us in the wretched dwellings of the poor, which we know all about but take so coolly, it is sad to remember that truth does not make itself felt as it really is, but depends so sadly for the practical effect upon the skill with which it is put—upon the tact, graphic power, and earnest purpose of the man who tells it. A landed proprietor will pass a wretched row of cottages on his estate daily for years, yet never think of making an effort to improve them : who, when the thing is fairly put to him, will forthwith bestir himself to have things brought into a better state. He will wonder how he could have allowed matters to go on in that unhappy style so long; but will tell you truly, that though the thing was before his eyes, he really never before thought of it in that light.

Some people have a happy knack for putting in a pleasant way everything that concerns themselves. Mr A.'s son gets a poor place as a bank clerk; his father goes about saying that the lad has found a fine opening in business. The young man is ordained, and gets a curacy on Salisbury Plain; his father rejoices that there, never seeing a human face, he has abundant leisure for study, and for improving his mind. Or, the curacy is in the most crowded part of Manchester or Bethnal Green; the father now rejoices that his son has opportunities of acquiring clerical experience, and of visiting the homes of the poor. Such a man's house is in a well-wooded country; the situation is delightfully sheltered. He removes to a bare district without a tree,—ah! there he has beautiful pure air and extensive views. It is well for human beings when they have the pleasant art of thus putting things; for many, we all know, have the art of putting things in just the opposite way. They look at all things through jaundiced eyes; and as things appear to themselves, so they put them to others. You remember, reader, how once upon a time David Hume the historian kindly sent Rousseau a present of a dish of beef-steaks. Rousseau fired at this; he discerned in it a deep-laid insult; he *put it* that Hume, by sending the steaks, meant to insinuate that he, Rousseau, could not afford to buy proper food for himself. Ah, I have known various Rousseaus! They had not the genius, indeed, but they had all the wrong-headedness.

Who does not know the contrasted views of mankind and of life that pervade all the writings of Dickens and of Thackeray? It is the same world that lies before both, but how differently they put it! And look at the accounts in the Blue and Yellow newspapers respectively, of the borough member's speech to his constituents' last night in the Corn Exchange. Judge by the account in the one paper, and he is a Burke for eloquence, a Peel for tact, a Shippen for incorruptible integrity. Judge by the account in the other, and you would wonder where the electors caught a mortal who combines so remarkably ignorance, stupidity, carelessness, inefficiency, and dishonesty. As for the speech, one journal declares it was fluent, the other that it was stuttering; one that it was frank, the other that it was trimming; one that it was sense, the other that it was nonsense. Nor need it be supposed that either journal intends deliberate falsehood. Each believes his own way of putting the case to be the right way; and the truth, in most instances, doubtless lies midway between. But in fact, till the end of time, there will be at least two ways of putting everything. Perhaps the M.P. warmed with his subject, and threw himself heart and soul into his speech. Shall we say that he spoke with eloquent energy, or shall we put it that he bellowed like a bull? Was he quiet and correct? Then we may choose between saying that he is a classical speaker, and that he was as stiff as a poker. He made some jokes, perhaps: take your choice whether you shall call him clever or flippant, a wit or a buffoon. And so of everybody else. You know a clever, well-read young woman; you may either call her such, or talk sneeringly of blue-stockings. You meet a lively, merry girl, who laughs and talks with all the frankness of innocence. *You* would say of her, my kindly reader, something like what I have just said; but crabbed Mrs Backbite will have it that she is a romp, a bois-terous hoyden, of most unformed manners. Perhaps Mrs Backbite, spitefully shaking her head, says she trusts, she really hopes, there is no harm in the girl; but certainly no daughter of *hers* should be allowed to associate with her. And not merely does the way, favourable or unfavourable, in which the thing shall be put, depend mainly on the temperament of the person who puts it, so that you shall know before-hand that Mr Snarling will always give the unfavour-able view, and Mr Jollikin the favourable; but a further element of disturbance is introduced by the fact, that often the narrator's mood is such, that it is a toss-up, five minutes before he begins to tell his story, whether he shall put the conduct of his hero as good or bad.

Who needs the art of putting things more than the painter of portraits? Who sees so much of the littleness, the petty vanity, the silliness of mankind? It must be hard for such a man to retain much respect for human nature. The lurking belief in the mind of every man that he is remarkably good-looking, concealed in daily intercourse with his fellows, breaks out in the painter's studio. And without positive falsification, how cleverly the artist often contrives to put the features and figure of his sitter in a satisfactory fashion! Have not you seen the portrait of a plain, and even a very ugly person, which was strikingly like, and still very pleasant-looking and almost pretty? Have not you seen things so skilfully put, that the little snob looked dignified, the vulgar boor gentlemanlike, the plain-featured woman angelic —and all the while the likeness was accurately preserved?

It seems to me that in the case of many of those fine things which stir the heart and bring moisture to the eye, it depends entirely on the way in which they are put, whether they shall strike us as pathetic or silly, as sublime or ridiculous. The venerable aspect of the dethroned monarch, led in the triumphal procession of the Roman emperor, and looking indifferently on the scene, as he repeated often the words of Solomon, " Vanity, vanity, all is vanity!"

depends much for the effect it always produces on the reader upon the stately yet touching fashion in which Gibbon tells the story. So with Hazlitt's often-recurring account of Poussin's celebrated picture, the *Et in Arcadiâ Ego*. As for Burke flinging the dagger upon the floor of the House of Commons, and Brougham falling on his knees in the House of Peers, what a ridiculous representation *Punch* could give of such things! What shall be said of Addison, often tipsy in life, yet passing away with the words addressed to his regardless step-son, "See in what peace a Christian can die!" We need not think of things which are essentially ridiculous, though their perpetrators intended them to be sublime: as Lord Ellenborough's proclamation about the Gates of Somnauth, Sir William Codrington's despatch as to the blowing-up of Sebastopol, and all the grand passages in the writings of Mr Wordy. Let me confess that I think it a very unhealthy sign of the times, this love which now exists of putting grave matters in a ridiculous light, which produces *Comic Histories of England, Comic Blackstones, Comic Parliamentary Debates, Comic Latin Grammars*, and the like. Dreary indeed must be the fun of such books; but *that* is not the worst of them. Yet one cannot seriously object to such a facetious serial as *Punch*, which represents the funny element in our sad insular character. *Punch* lives by the art of putting things, and putting them in a single way; but how wonderfully well, how successfully, how genially, he puts all things funnily! But to burlesque *Macbeth* or *Othello*, to travesty Virgil, to parody the soliloquy in *Hamlet*, though it may be putting things in a novel and amusing way, approaches to the nature of sacrilege. Sometimes, indeed, the ludicrous way of putting things has served an admirable purpose; as in the imitations of Southey's Sapphics and Kotzebue's morality in the *Poetry of the Anti-jacobin.* And the ludicrous way of putting things has sometimes brought them much more vividly home to "men's business and bosoms," as in Sydney Smith's description of the possible results of a French invasion. Nor has it failed to answer the end of most cogent argument, as in his description of Mrs Partington sweeping back the Atlantic Ocean.

Do not fancy, my friend, that you can by possibility so live that ill-natured folk will not be able to put everything you do unfavourably. The old man with the ass was a martyr to the desire so to act that there should be no possibility of putting what he did as wrong. And when John Gilpin's wife, for fear the neighbours should think her proud, caused the chaise to draw up five doors off, rely upon it some of the neighbours would say she did so in the design of making her carriage the more conspicuous. When you give a dinner-party, and after your guests are gone, sit down and review the progress of the entertainment, thinking how nicely everything went on, do you remember, madam, that at that same moment

your guests are seated at their own homes, putting all
the circumstances in quite a different way : laughing
at your hired greengrocer, who (you are just saying)
looked so like a butler ; execrating your champagne,
which (you are this moment flattering yourself) passed
for the product of the grape and not of the gooseberry ; and generally putting yourself, your children,
your house, your dinner, your company, your music,
into such ridiculous lights, that, if you knew it, (which
happily you never will,) you would wish that you had
mingled a little strychnine with the vintage so vilified.
Still, it is pleasant to believe that there is no real
malice in the way in which most people cut up their
friends behind their backs. You really have a very
kindly feeling towards Mr A. or Mrs B., though you
do turn them into ridicule in their absence. After
laughing at Mr A. to Mrs B., you are quite ready to
laugh at Mrs B. to Mr A. The truth appears to be,
that all this is an instance of that reaction which is
necessary to human beings. In people's presence
politeness requires that you should put everything
that concerns them in the most agreeable and favourable way. Impatient of this constraint, you revenge
yourself upon it whenever circumstances permit, by
putting things in the opposite fashion. I feel not the
least enmity towards Mr Snooks for saying behind
my back that my essays are wretched trash. He has
frequently said in my presence that they are far superior to anything ever written by Macaulay, Milton, or

Shakspeare.   I knew that after my dear friend's civility had been subjected to so violent a strain as was implied in his making the latter declaration, it would of necessity fly back, like a released bow, whenever he left me; and that the first mutual acquaintance he met would have the satisfaction of hearing the case put in a very different way.   And no doubt, if my dear friend were put upon his oath, his true opinion of me would transpire as nearly midway between the two ways of putting it respectively before my face and behind my back.

You are a country clergyman, let us say, my reader, with a small parish; and while you do your duty faithfully and zealously, you spend a spare hour now and then upon a review or a magazine article.   You like the thought that thus, from your remote solitude, you are addressing a larger audience than that which you address Sunday by Sunday.   You think that reasonable and candid people would say that this is an improving and pleasant way of employing a little leisure time, instead of rusting into stupidity, or mooning about blankly, or smoking yourself into vacancy, or reading novels, or listening to and retailing gossip, or hanging about the streets of the neighbouring county town, or growing sarcastic and misanthropic.   But don't you remember, my dear friend, that although *you* put the case in this way, it is highly probable that some of your acquaintances, whose proffered contributions to the periodical with which you are supposed to be connected have been "declined with thanks," and whom malignant editors exclude from the opportunity of enlightening an ungrateful world, may put the matter very differently indeed? True, you are always thoroughly prepared with your sermon on Sundays, you are assiduous in your care of the sick and the aged, you have cottage lectures here and there throughout the parish, you teach classes of children and young people, you know familiarly the face and the circumstances of every soul of your population, and you honestly give your heart and strength to your sacred calling, suffering nothing whatever to interfere with *that:* but do you fancy that all this diligence will prevent Miss Lemonjuice and Mr Flyblow from exclaiming, " Ah, see Mr Smith; isn't it dreadful! See how he neglects his proper work, and spends his time, his *whole* time, in writing articles for the *Quarterly Review !* It's disgraceful! The bishop, if he did his duty, would pull him up !"

A striking instance of the effect of skilfully putting things may be found in the diary of Warren Hastings. The great Governor-General always insisted that his conduct of Indian affairs had been just and beneficent, and that the charges brought by Burke and Sheridan were without foundation in truth. He declared that he had that conviction in the centre of his being; that he was as sure of it as of his own existence. But as he listened to the opening speech of Burke, he tells us he saw things in a new light. He felt the spell of the way in which the great orator put things. Could this really be the right way? "For half-an-hour," says Hastings, "I looked up at Burke in a reverie of wonder, and during that time I actually felt myself the most guilty being upon earth!" But Hastings adds that he did what the boy who has played truant does —he took refuge in his own way of putting things. "I recurred to my own heart, and there found what sustained me under all this accusation."

A young lad's choice of a profession depends mainly upon the way in which the life of that profession is put before him. If a boy is to go to the bar, it will be expedient to make the Chancellorship the prominent feature in the picture presented to him. It will be better to keep in the background the lonely evenings in the chambers at the Temple, the weary backbenches in court, the heart-sickening waiting year after year. And the first impression, strongly rooted, will probably last. I love my own profession. I would exchange its life and its work for no other position on earth ; but I feel that I owe part of its fascination to the fragrance of boyish fancies of it which linger yet. Blessed be the kind and judicious parent or preceptor, whose skilful putting of things long ago has given to our vocation, whatever it may be, a charm which can overcome the disgust which might otherwise come of the hard realities, the little daily worries, the discouragements and frustrated hopes ! How much depends on first impressions—on the way in which a man, a place, a book is put to us for the first time! Something of cheerlessness and dreariness will always linger about even the summer aspect of the house which you first approached when the winter afternoon was closing in, dark, gusty, cold, miserable-looking. What a difference it makes to the little man who is to have a tooth pulled out, whether the dentist approaches with a grievous look, in silence, with the big forceps conspicuous in his hand; or comes up cheerfully, with no display of steel, and says, with a smiling face, " Come, my little friend, it will be over in a moment; you will hardly have time to feel it; you will stand it like a brick, and mamma will be proud of having such a brave little boy!" Or, if either man or boy has a long task to go through, how much more easily it will be done if it is put in separate divisions than if it is set before one all in a mass! *Divide et impera* states a grand principle in the art of putting things. If your servant is to clear away a mass of snow, he will do it in half the time and with twice the pleasure if you first mark it out into squares, to be cleared away one after the other. By the make of our being we like to have many starts and many arrivals: it does not do to look too far on without a break. I remember the driver of a mail-coach telling me, as I sat on the box through a sixty-mile drive, that it would weary him to death to drive that road daily if it were as straight as a railway: he liked the turnings and windings, which put the distance in the form of successive bits. It was sound philosophy in Sydney Smith to advise us, whether physically or morally, to "take short views." It would knock you up at once if, when the railway carriage moved out of the station at Edinburgh, you began to trace in your mind's eye the whole route to London. Never do that. Think first of Dunbar, then of Newcastle, then of York, and, putting the thing thus, you will get over the distance without fatigue of mind. What little child would have heart to begin the alphabet, if, before he did so, you put clearly before him all the school and college work of which it is the beginning? The poor little thing would knock up at once, wearied out by your want of skill in putting things. And so it is that Providence, kindly and gradually putting things, wiles us onward, still keeping hope and heart, through the trials and cares of life. Ah, if we had had it put to us at the outset how much we should have to go through, to reach even our present stage in life, we should have been ready to think it the best plan to sit down and die at once! But, in compassion for human weakness, the Great Director and Shower of events practises the Art of Putting Things. Might not we sometimes do so when we do not? When we see some poor fellow grumbling at his lot, and shirking his duty, might not a little skill employed in putting these things in a proper light serve better than merely expressing our contempt or indignation? A single sentence might make him see that what was complaining of was reasonable and right. It is quite wonderful from what odd and perverse points of view people will look at things: and then things look so very different. The hill behind your house, which you have seen a thousand times, you would not know if you approached it from some unwonted quarter. Now, if you see a man afflicted with a perverse twist of mind, making him put things in general or something in particular in a wrong way, you do him a much kinder turn in directing him how to put things rightly, than if you were a skilful surgeon and cured him of the most fearful squint that ever hid behind blue spectacles.

Did not Franklin go to hear Whitefield preach a charity sermon resolved not to give a penny; and was he not so thoroughly overcome by the great preacher's way of putting the claims of the charity which he was advocating, that he ended by emptying his pockets into the plate? I daresay Alexander the Great was somewhat staggered in his plans of conquest by Parmenio's way of putting things. "After you have conquered Persia, what will you do?" "Then I shall conquer India." "After you have conquered India, what will you do?" "Conquer Scythia." "And after you have conquered Scythia, what will you do?" "Sit down and rest." "Well," said Parmenio to the conqueror, "why not sit down and rest now?" I trust young Sheridan was proof against his father's way of putting things, when the young man said he meant to go down a coal-pit. "Why go down a coal-pit?" said Sheridan the elder. "Merely to be able to say I have been there." "You blockhead," replied the high-principled sire, "what is there to keep you from saying so without going?"

I remember witnessing a decided success of the art of putting things. A vulgar rich man who had recently bought an estate in Aberdeenshire, exclaimed, "It is monstrous hard! I have just had this morning to pay forty pounds of stipend to the parish minister for my property. Now I never enter the parish church," (nor any other, he might have added,) "and why should I pay to maintain a church to which I don't belong?" I omit the oaths which served as sauce. Now, that was Mr Oddbody's way of putting things, and you would say his case was a hard one. But a quiet man who was present changed the aspect of matters. "Is it not true, Mr Oddbody," he said, "that when you bought your estate its rental was reckoned after deducting the payment you mention; that the exact value of your annual payment to the minister was calculated, and the amount deducted from the price you paid for the property? And is it not therefore true, that not a penny of that forty pounds really comes out of your pocket?" Mr Oddbody's face elongated. The bystanders unequivocally signified what they thought of him; and as long as he lived he never failed to be remembered as the man who had tried to extort sympathy by false pre-tences.

To no man is tact in putting things more essential than to the clergyman. An injudicious and unskilful preacher may so put the doctrines which he sets forth as to make them appear revolting and absurd. It is a fearful thing to hear a stupid fellow preaching upon the doctrine of Election. He may so put that doctrine that he shall fill every clever young lad who hears him with prejudices against Christianity, which may last through life. And in advising one's parishioners, especially in administering reproof where needful, let the parish priest, if he would do good, call into play all his tact. With the best intentions, through lack of skill in putting things, he may do great mischief. Let the calomel be concealed beneath the jelly. Not that I counsel sneakiness ; *that* is worse than the most indiscreet honesty. There is no need to put things, like the dean immortalised by Pope, who when preaching in the Chapel Royal, said to his hearers that unless they led religious lives they would ultimately reach a place "which he would not men-tion in so polite an assembly." Nor will it be ex-pedient to put things like the contemptible wretch who, preaching before Louis XIV., said, *Nous mour-rons tous;* then, turning to the king, and bowing humbly, *presque tous.* And it is only in addressing quite exceptional congregations that it would now-a-days be regarded as a piece of proper respect for the mighty of the earth, were the preacher, in stating that all who heard him were sinners, to add, by way of reservation, all who have less than a thousand a-year.

Any man who approaches the matter with a candid spirit, must be much struck by the difference between the Protestant and the Roman Catholic ways of putting the points at issue between the two great Churches. The Roman prayers are in Latin, for instance. A violent Protestant says that the purpose is to keep the people in ignorance. A strong Romanist tells you that Latin was the universal language of educated men when these prayers were drawn up; and puts it that it is a fine thing to think that in all Romish churches over Christendom the devotions of the people are expressed in the selfsame words. Take keeping back the Bible from the people. To us nothing appears more flagrant than to deprive any man of God's written Word. Still the Romanist has something to say for himself. He puts it that there is so much difficulty in understanding much of the Bible—that such pernicious errors have followed from false interpretations of it. Think, even, of the dogma of the infallibility of the Church. The Protestant puts that dogma as an instance of unheard of arrogance. The Romanist puts it as an instance of deep humility and earnest faith. He says he does not hold that the Church, in her own wisdom, is able to keep infallibly right; but he says that he has perfect confidence that God will not suffer the Church deliberately to fall into error. Here, certainly, we have two very different ways of putting the same things.

But who shall say that there are no more than two ways of putting any incident, or any opinion, or any character? There are innumerable ways—ways as many as are the idiosyncrasies of the men that put them. You have to describe an event, have you? Then you may put it in the plain matter-of-fact way, like the *Times'* reporter; or in the sublime way, like Milton and Mr Wordy; or in the ridiculous way, like *Punch* (of design) and Mr Wordy (unintentionally); or in the romantic way, like Mr G. P. R. James; or in the minutely circumstantial way, like Defoe or Poe; or in the affectedly simple way, like *Peter Bell;* or in the forcible, knowing way, like Macaulay; or in the genial, manly, good-humoured way, like Sydney Smith; or in the flippant way, like Mr Richard Swiveller, who when he went to ask for an old gentleman, inquired as to the health of the "ancient buffalo;" or in the lackadaisical way, like many young ladies; or in the whining, grumbling way, like many silly people whom it is unnecessary to name; or in the pretentious, lofty way, introducing familiarly many titled names without the least necessity, like many natives of beautiful Erin.

What nonsense it is to say, as it has been said, that the effect of anything spoken or written depends upon the essential thought alone! Why, nine-tenths of the practical power depends on the way in which it is put. Somebody has asserted that any thought which is not eloquent in any words whatever, is not eloquent at all. He might as well have said that black was white. Not to speak of the charm of the mere music of gracefully modulated words, and felicitously arranged phrases, how much there is in beautifully logical treatment, and beautifully clear development, that will interest a cultivated man in a speech or a treatise, quite irrespective of its subject! I have known a very eminent man say that it was a delight to him to hear Follett make a speech, he did not care about what. The matter was no matter; the intellectual treat was to watch how the great advocate put it. And we have all read with delight stories with no incident and little character, yet which derived a nameless fascination from the way in which they were told. Tell me truly, my fair reader, did you not shed some tears over Dickens's story of Richard Doubledick? Could you have read that story aloud without breaking down? And yet, was there ever a story with less in it? But how beautifully Dickens put what little there was, and how the melody of the closing sentences of the successive paragraphs lingers on the ear! And you have not forgotten the exquisite touches with which Mrs Stowe put so simple a matter as a mother looking into her dead baby's drawer. I have known an attempt at the pathetic made on a kindred topic provoke yells of laughter; but I could not bear the woman, and hardly the man, who could read Mrs Stowe's putting of that simple conception without the reverse of smiles. Many readers, too, will not forget how much more sharply they have seen many places and things, from railway-engine sheds to the Britannia Bridge, when put by the graphic pen of Sir Francis Head. That lively baronet is the master of clear, sharp presentment.

I have not hitherto spoken of such ways of putting things as were practised in King Hudson's railway reports, or in those of the Glasgow Western Bank, cooked to make things pleasant by designed misrepre sentation. So far we have been thinking of compara- tively innocent variations in the ways of putting things —of putting the best foot foremost in a comparatively honest way. But how much intentional misrepresen- tation there is in British society! How few people can tell a thing exactly as they saw it! It goes in one colour, and comes out another, like light through tinted glass. It is rather amusing, by the way, when a friend comes and tells you a story which he heard from yourself, but so put that you hardly know it again. Unscrupulous putters of things should have good memories. There is no reckoning the ways in which, by varying the turn of an expression, by a tone or look, an entirely false view may be given of a con- versation, a transaction, or an event. A lady says to her cook, You are by no means overworked. The cook complains in the servants' hall that her mistress said she had nothing to do. Lies, in the sense of pure inventions, are not common, I believe, among people with any claim to respectability; but it is perfectly awful to think how great a part of ordinary conversation, especially in little country towns, consists in putting things quite differently from the actual fact; in short, of wilful misrepresentation. Many people cannot resist the temptation to deepen the colours, and strengthen the lines, of any narration, in order to make it more telling. Unluckily, things usually occur in life in such a manner as just to miss what would give them a point and make a good story of them; and the temptation is strong to make them, by the deflection of a hair's-breadth, what they ought to have been.

It is sad to think, that in ninety-nine out of every hundred cases in which things are thus untruly put, the representation is made worse than the reality. Few old ladies endeavour, by their imaginative putting of things, to exhibit their acquaintances as wiser, better, and more amiable, than the fact. An exception may be made whenever putting her friends and their affairs in a dignified light would reflect credit upon the old lady herself. *Then*, indeed, their income is vast, their house is magnificent, their horses are Eclipses, their conversation is brilliant, their attention to their friends unwearying and indescribable. Alas for our race: that we lean to evil rather than to good, and that it is so much more easy and piquant to pitch into a man than to praise him!

Let us rejoice that there is one happy case in which the way of putting things, though often false, is always favourable. I mean the accounts which are given in country newspapers of the character and the doings of the great men of the district. I often admire the country editor's skill in putting all things (save the speech of the opposition M.P., as already mentioned) in such a rosy light ; nor do I admire his genial *bonhomie* less than his art. If a marquis makes a stammering speech, it is sure to be put as most interesting and eloquent. If the rector preaches a dull and stupid charity sermon, it is put as striking and effective. A public meeting, consisting chiefly of empty benches, is put as most respectably attended. A gift of a little flannel and coals at Christmas-time, is put as seasonable munificence. A bald and seedy building, just erected in the High Street, is put as chaste and classical ; an extravagant display of gingerbread decoration, is put as gorgeous and magnificent. In brief, what other men heartily wish this world were, the conductors of local prints boldly declare that it is. Whatever they think a great man would like to be called, *that* they make haste to call him. Happy fellows, if they really believe that they live in such a world and among such beings as they put ! Their gushing heart is too much for even their sharp head, and they see all things glorified by the sunshine of their own exceeding amiability.

The subject greatens on me, but the paper dwindles :

the five-and-forty fair expanses of foolscap are darkened
at last.   It would need a volume, not an essay, to do
this matter justice.   Sir Bulwer Lytton has declared,
n pages charming but too many, that the world's great
question is, WHAT WILL HE DO WITH IT?   I shall not
debate the point, but simply add, that only second to
that question in comprehensive reach and in practical
importance is the question—How WILL HE PUT IT!

CHAPTER IIL

CONCERNING TWO BLISTERS OF HUMANITY:

BEING THOUGHTS ON PETTY MALIGNITY AND PETTY
TRICKERY.

IT is highly improbable that any reader, of ordinary power of imagination, would guess the particular surface on which the paper is spread whereon I am at the present moment writing. Such is the reflection which flows naturally from my pencil's point as it begins to darken this page. I am seated on a manger, in a very light and snug stable, and my paper is spread upon a horse's face, occupying the flat part between the eyes. You would not think, unless you tried, what an extensive superficies may there be found. If you put a thin book next the horse's skin, you will write with the greater facility: and you will find, as you sit upon the edge of the manger, that the animal's head occupies a position which, as regards height and slope, is sufficiently convenient. His mouth, it may be remarked, is not far from your knees, so that it would be highly inexpedient to attempt the operation with a vicious, biting brute, or indeed with any horse of whose temper you are not well assured. But you, my good Old Boy, (for such is the quadruped's name,) *you* would not bite your master. Too many carrots have you received from his hand; too many pieces of bread have you licked up from his extended palm. A thought has struck me which I wish to preserve in writing, though indeed at this rate it will be a long time before I work my way to it. I am waiting here for five minutes till my man-servant shall return with something for which he has been sent, and wherefore should even five minutes be wasted? Life is not very long, and the minutes in which one can write with ease are not very many. And perhaps the newness of such a place of writing may communicate something of freshness to what is traced by a somewhat jaded hand. You winced a little, Old Boy, as I disposed my book and this scrap of an old letter on your face, but now you stand perfectly still. On either side of this page I see a large eye looking down wistfully; above the page a pair of ears are cocked in quiet curiosity, but with no indication of fear. Not that you are deficient in spirit, my dumb friend; you will do your twelve miles an hour with any steed within some miles of you; but a long course of kindness has gentled you as well as Mr Rarey could have done, though no more than seven summers have passed over your head. Let us ever, kindly reader, look with especial sympathy and regard at any inferior animal on which the doom of man has fallen, and which must eat its food, if not in the sweat of its brow, then in that of its sides.

Curious, that a creature should be called all through life to labour, for which yet there remains no rest! As for us human beings, we can understand and we can bear with much evil, and many trials and sorrows here, because we are taught that all these form the discipline which shall prepare' us for another world, a world that shall set this right. But for you, my poor fellow-creature, I think with sorrow as I write here upon your head, there remains no such immortality as remains for me. What a difference between us! You to your sixteen or eighteen years here, and then oblivion. I to my threescore and ten, and then eternity! Yes, the difference is immense; and it touches me to think of your life and mine, of your doom and mine. I know a house where, at morning and evening prayer, when the household assembles, among the servants there always walks in a certain shaggy little dog, who listens with the deepest attention and the most solemn gravity to all that is said, and then, when prayers are over, goes out again with his friends. I cannot witness that silent procedure without being much moved by the sight. Ah, my fellow-creature, *this* is something in which you have no part! Made by the same Hand, breathing the same air, sustained like us by food and drink, you are witnessing an act of ours which relates to interests that do not concern you, and of which you have no idea. And so, here we are, you standing at the manger, Old Boy, and I sitting upon it; the mortal and the immortal; close together; your nose on my knee, my paper on your head; yet with something between us broader than the broad Atlantic. As for you, if you suffer here, there is no other life to make up for it. Yet it would be well if many of those who are your betters in the scale of creation, fulfilled their Creator's purposes as well as you. He gave you strength and swiftness, and you use these to many a valuable end: not many of the superior race will venture to say that they turn the powers God gave them to account as worthy of their nature. If it come to the question of deserving, you deserve better than me. Forgive me, my fellow-creature, if I have sometimes given you an angry flick, when you shied a little at a pig or a donkey. But I know you bear me no malice; you forget the flicks, (they are not many,) and you think rather of the bread and the carrots, of the times I have pulled your ears, and smoothed your neck, and patted your nose. And forasmuch as this is all your life, I shall do my very best to make it a comfortable one. *Happiness*, of course, is something which you can never know. Yet, my friend and companion through many weary miles, you shall have a deep-littered stall, and store of corn and hay so long as I can give them; and may this hand never write another line if it ever does you wilful injury!

Into this paragraph has my pencil of its own accord rambled, though it was taken up to write about something else. And such is the happiness of the writer of essays : he may wander about the world of thought at his will. The style of the essayist has attained what may be esteemed the perfection of freedom, when it permits him, in writing upon any subject whatsoever, to say whatever may occur to him upon any other subject. And truly it is a pleasing thing for one long trammelled by the requirements of a rigorous logic, and fettered by thoughts of symmetry, connexion, and neatness in the discussion of his topic, to enter upon a fresh field where all these things go for nothing, and to write for readers many of whom would never notice such characteristics if they were present, nor ever miss them if they were absent. There is all the difference between plodding wearily along the dusty highway, and rambling through green fields, and over country stiles, leisurely, saunteringly, going nowhere in particular. You would not wish to be always desultory and rambling, but it is pleasant to be so now and then. And there is a delightful freedom about the feeling that you are producing an entirely unsymmetrical composition. It is fearful work, if you have a thousand thoughts and shades of thought about any subject, to get them all arranged in what a logician would call their proper places. It is like having a dissected puzzle of a thousand pieces given you in confusion, and being required to fit all the little pieces of ivory into their box again. By most men this work of orderly and symmetrical composition can be done well only by its being done comparatively slowly. In the case of ordinary folk the mind is a machine, which may indeed, by putting on extra pressure, be worked faster; but the result is the deterioration of the material which it turns off. It is an extraordinary gift of nature and training, when a man is like Follett, who, after getting the facts of an involved and intricate case into his mind only at one or two o'clock in the morning, could appear in Court at nine A.M., and there proceed to state the case and all his reasonings upon it, with the very perfection of logical method, every thought in its proper place, and all this at the rate of rapid extempore speaking. The difference between the rate of writing and that of speaking, with most men, makes the difference between producing good material and bad. A great many minds can turn off a fair manufacture at the rate of writing, which, when overdriven to keep pace with speaking, will bring forth very poor stuff indeed. And besides this, most people cannot grasp a large subject in all its extent and its bearings, and get their thoughts upon it marshalled and sorted, unless they have at least two or three days to do so. At first all is confusion and indefiniteness, but gradually things settle into order. Hardly any mind, by any effort, can get them into order quickly. If at all, it is by a tremendous exertion; whereas the mind has a curious power, without any perceptible effort, of arranging in order thoughts upon any subject, if you give it time. Who that has ever written his ideas on some involved point but knows this? You begin by getting up information on the subject about which you are to write. You throw into the mind, as it were, a great heap of crude, unordered material. From this book and that book, from this review and that newspaper, you collect the observations of men who have regarded your subject from quite different points of view, and for quite different purposes; you throw into the mind cartload after cartload of facts and opinions, with a despairing wonder how you will ever be able to get that huge, contradictory, vague mass into anything like shape and order. And if, the minute you had all your matter accumulated, you were called on to state what you knew or thought upon the subject, you could not do so for your life in any satisfactory manner. You would not know where to begin, or how to go on; it would be all confusion and bewilderment. Well, do not make the slightest effort. What is impossible now will be quite easy by and by. The peas, which cost a sovereign a pint at Christmas, are quite cheap in their proper season. Go about other things for three or four days: and at the end of that time you will be aware that the machinery of your mind, voluntarily and almost unconsciously playing, has sorted and arranged that mass of matter which you threw into it. Where all was confusion and uncertainty, all is now order and clearness; and you see exactly where to begin, and what to say next, and where and how to leave off.

The probability is, that all this has not been done without an effort, and a considerable amount of labour. But then, instead of the labour having been all at once, it has been very much subdivided. The subject was simmering in your mind all the while, though you were hardly aware of it. Time after time, you ·took a little run at it, and saw your way a little farther through it. But this multitude of little separate and momentary efforts does not count for much ; though in reality, if they were all put together, they would probably be found to have amounted to as much as the prolonged exertion which would at a single heat have attained the end. A large result, attained by innumerable little detached efforts, seems as if it had been attained without any effort at all.

I love a parallel case ; and I must take such cases from my ordinary experience. Yesterday, passing a little cottage by the wayside, I perceived at the door the carcase of a very large pig extended on a table. Approaching, as is my wont, the tenant of the cottage and owner of the pig, I began to converse with him on the size and fatness of the poor creature which had that morning quitted its sty for ever. It had been *shot*, he told me ; for such, in these parts, is at present the most approved way of securing for swine an end as little painful as may be. I admired the humanity of the intention, and hoped that it might be crowned with success. Then my friend the proprietor of the bacon began to discourse on the philosophy of the rearing of pigs by labouring men. No doubt, he said, the four pounds, or thereabout, which he would get for his pig, would be a great help to a hard-working man with five or six little children. But after all, he remarked, it was likely enough that during the months of the pig's life, it had bit by bit consumed and cost him as much as he would get for it now. But then, he went on, it cost us *that* in little sums we hardly felt; while the four pounds it will sell for come all in a lump, and seem to give a very perceptible profit. Successive unfelt sixpences had mounted up to that considerable sum; even as five hundred little unfelt mental efforts had mounted up to the large result of sorting and methodising the mass of crude fact and opinion of which we were thinking a little while ago.

Having worked through this preliminary matter, (which will probably be quite enough for some readers, even as the Solan goose, which does but whet the appetite of the Highlander, annihilates that of the Sassenach,) I now come to the subject which was in my mind when I began to write on the horse's head. I am not in the stable now; for the business which detained me there is long since despatched: and after all, it is more convenient to write at one's study-table. I wish to say something concerning certain evils which press upon humanity; and which are to the feeling of the mind very much what a mustard-blister is to the feeling of the body. To the healthy man or woman they probably do not do much serious harm ; but they maintain a very constant irritation. They worry and annoy. It is extremely interesting, in reading the published diaries of several great and good men, to find them recording on how many days they were put out of sorts, vexed and irritated, and rendered unfit for their work of writing, by some piece of petty malignity or petty trickery. How well one can sympathise with that good and great, and honest and amiable and sterling man, Dr Chalmers, when we find him recording in his diary, when he was a country parish minister, how he was unable to make satisfactory progress with his sermon one whole forenoon, because some tricky and over-reaching farmer in the neighbourhood drove two calves into a field of his glebe, where the great man found them in the morning devouring his fine young clover ! There was something very irritating and annoying in the paltry dishonesty. And the sensitive machinery of the good man's mind could not work sweetly when the gritty grains of the small vexation were fretting its polished surface. Let it be remarked in passing, that the peculiar petty dishonesty of driving cattle into a neighbouring proprietor's field, is far from being an uncommon one. And let me inform such as have suffered from it of a remedy against it which has never been known to fail. If the trespassing animals be cows, wait till the afternoon : then have them well milked, and send them home. If horses, let them instantly be put in carts, and sent off ten miles to fetch lime. A sudden strength will thenceforward invest your fences; and from having been so open that no efforts on the part of your neighbours could keep their cattle from straying into your fields, you will find them all at once become wholly impervious.

But, to return, I maintain that these continual blisters, of petty trickery and petty malignity, produce a very vexatious effect. You are quite put about at finding out one of your servants in some petty piece of dishonesty or deception. You are decidedly worried if you happen to be sitting in a cottage where your coachman does not know that you are; and if you discern from the window that functionary, who never exercises your horses in your presence save at a walk, galloping them furiously over the hard stones; shaking their legs and endangering their wind. It is annoying to find your haymakers working desperately hard and fast when you appear in the field, not aware that from amid a little clump of wood you had discerned them a minute before reposing quietly upon the fragrant heaps, and possibly that you had overheard them saying that they need not work very hard, as they were working for a gentleman. You would not have been displeased had you found them honestly resting on the sultry day: but you are annoyed by the small attempt to deceive you. Such pieces of petty trickery put you more out of sorts than you would like to acknowledge : and you are likewise ashamed to discover that you mind so much as you do, when some good-natured friend comes and informs you how Mr Snarling has been misrepresenting something you have said or done ; and Miss Limejuice has been telling lies to your prejudice. You are a clergyman, perhaps ; and you said in your sermon last Sunday that, strong Protestant as you are, you believed that many good people may be found in the Church of Rome. Well, ever since then, Miss Limejuice has not ceased to rush about the parish, exclaiming in every house she entered, " Is not this awful ? Here, on Sunday morning, the rector said that we ought all to become Roman Catholics ! One comfort is, the Bishop is to have him up directly. I was always sure that he was a Jesuit in disguise." Or you are a country gentleman ; and at an election time you told one of your tenants that such a candidate was your friend, and that you would be happy if he could conscientiously vote for him, but that he was to do just what he thought right. Ever since, Mr Snarling has been spreading a report that you went, drunk, into your tenant's house, that you thrust your fist in his face, that you took him by the collar and shook him, that you told him that, if he did not vote for your friend, you would turn him out of your farm, and send his wife and children to the workhouse. For in such playful exaggerations do people in small communities not unfrequently indulge. Now, you are vexed when you hear of such pieces of petty malignity. They don't do you much harm; for most people whose opinion you value, know how much weight to attach to any statement of Miss Limejuice and Mr Snarling; and if you try to do your duty day by day where God has put you, and to live an honest, Christian life, it will go hard but you will live down such malicious vilification. But these things worry. They act as blisters, in short, without the medicinal value of blisters. And little contemptible worries do a great deal to detract from the enjoyment of life. To meet great misfortunes we gather up our endurance, and pray for Divine support and guidance; but as for small blisters, the *insect cares* (as James Montgomery called them) of daily life, we are very ready to think that they are too little to trouble the Almighty with them, or even to call up our fortitude to face them. This is not a sermon; but let it be said that whosoever would learn how rightly to meet the perpetually-recurring worries of workday existence, should read an admirable little treatise by Mrs Stowe, the authoress of *Uncle Tom's Cabin,* entitled *Earthly Care a Heavenly Discipline.* The price of the work is one penny, but it contains advice which is worth an uncounted number of pence. Nor, as I think, are there to be found many more corroding and vexatious agencies than those which have been already named. To know that your servants, or your humbler neighbours, or your tradespeople, or your tenantry, or your scholars, are practising upon you a system of petty deception; or to be informed (as you are quite sure to be informed) how such and such a mischievous (or perhaps only thoughtless) acquaintance is putting words into your mouth which you never uttered, or abusing your wife and children, or gloating over your failure to get into Parliament, or the lameness of your horses, or the speech you stuck in at the recent public dinner;—all these things are pettily vexatious to many men. No doubt, over-sensitiveness is abundantly foolish. Some folk appear not merely to be thin-skinned, but to have been (morally) deprived of any skin at all; and such folk punish themselves severely enough for their folly. They wince when any one comes near them. The Pope may go wrong, but they cannot. It is treasonable, it is inexpiable sin, to hint that, in judgment, in taste, in conduct, it is possible for them to deviate by a hair's-breadth from the right line of perfection. Indeed, I believe that no immorality, no criminality, would excite such wrath in some men, as to tread upon a corner of their self-conceit. Yet it is curious how little sympathy these over-sensitive people have for the sensitiveness of other people. You would say they fancied that the skin of which they have been denuded has been applied to thicken to rhinoceros callousness the moral hide of other men. They speak their mind freely to their acquaintances of their acquaintances' belongings. They will tell an acquaintance (they have no friends, so I must repeat the word) that he made a very absurd speech, that she sung very badly, that the situation of his house (which he cannot leave) is abominably dull, that his wife is foolish and devoid of accomplishments, that her husband is a man of mediocre abilities, that her little boy has red hair and a squint, that the potatoes he rears are abominably bad, that he is getting unwieldily stout, that his riding-horse has no hair on his tail. All these things, and a hundred more, such people say with that mixture of dulness of perception and small malignity of nature which go to make what is vulgarly called a person who "speaks his mind." The right way to meet such folk is by an instant reciprocal action. Just begin to speak your mind to them, and see how they look. Tell them, with calm politeness, that before expressing their opinion so confidently, they should have considered what their opinion was worth. Tell them that civility requires that you should listen to their opinion, but that they may be assured that you will act upon your own. Téll them what you think of their spelling, their punctuation, their features, their house, their carpets, their window-curtains, their general standing as members of the human race. How blue they will look ! They are quite taken aback when the same petty malignity and insolence which they have been accustomed for years to carry into their neighbours' territory is suddenly directed against their own. And you will find that not only

are they themselves skinlessly sensitive, but that their
sensitiveness is not bounded by their own mental and
corporeal being ; and that it extends to the extreme
limits ot their horses' legs, to the very top of their
chimney-pots, to every member of the profession
which was honoured by the choice of their great-
grandfather.

You have observed, no doubt, that the mention of
over-sensitive people acted upon the writer's train of
thought as a pair of *points* in the rails act upon a
railway train.   It shunted me off the main line ; and
in these remarks on people who talk their mind, I
have been, so to speak, running along a siding.   To
go back to the point where I left the line, I observe,
that although it is very foolish to mind much about
such small matters as being a little cheated day by
day, and a good deal misrepresented now and then
by amiable acquaintances, still it is the fact that even
upon people of a healthful temperament such things
act as moral blisters, as moral pebbles in one's boots.
The petty malignity which occasionally annoys you is
generally to be found among your acquaintances, and
people of the same standing with yourself; while the
petty trickery for the most part exists in the case of
your inferiors.   I think one always feels the better
for looking any small evil of life straight in the face.
To define a thing, to fix its precise dimensions, almost
invariably makes it look a good deal smaller.   Indefiniteness much increases apparent size ; so let us now

examine the size and the operation of these blisters of humanity.

As for petty malignity, my reader, have you not seen a great deal of it? There are not many men who appear to love their neighbours as themselves. No one enjoys a misfortune or disappointment which befals himself: but there is too much truth in the smart Frenchman's saying, that there is something not entirely disagreeable to us in the misfortunes of even our very best friends. The malignity, indeed, is petty. It is only in small matters. And it is rather in feeling than in action. Even that sour Miss Limejuice, though she would be very glad if your horse fell lame or your carriage upset, would not see you drowning without doing her very best to save you. Ah, poor thing! she is not so bad, after all. This has been to her but a bitter world; and no wonder if she is, on the surface, a little embittered by it. But when you get fairly through the surface of her nature, as real misfortunes and trials do, there is kindliness about that withered heart yet. She would laugh at you if you broke down in your speech on the hustings; but she would throw herself in the path of a pair of furious runaway horses, to save a little child from their trampling feet. I do not believe that among ordinary people, even in a gossiping little country town, there is much real and serious malice in this world. I cling to that belief; for if many

men were truly as mischievous as you would sometimes think when you hear them talk, one might turn
misanthrope and hermit at once. There is hardly a
person you know who would do you any material
injury; not one who would cut down your roses, or
splash your entrance-gate with mud; not one who
would not gladly do you a kind turn if it lay within
his power. Yet there are a good many who would
with satisfaction repeat any story which might be a
little to your disadvantage; which might tend to
prove that you are rather silly, rather conceited,
rather ill-informed. You have various friends who
would not object to shew up any ridiculous mistake
you might happen to make; who would never forget
the occasion on which it appeared that you had never
heard of the *Spectator* or Sir Roger de Coverley, or
that you thought that Mary Queen of Scots was the
mother of George III. You have various friends who
would preserve the remembrance of the day on which
the rector rebuked you for talking in church; or on
which your partner and yourself fell flat on the floor
of the ball-room at the county town of Oatmealshire,
in the midst of a galop. You have various good-
natured friends to whom it would be a positive enjoyment to come and tell you what a very unfavourable
opinion Mr A. and Mrs B. and Miss C. had been
expressing of your talents, character, and general conduct. How true was the remark of Sir Fretful Pla-
giary, that it is quite unnecessary for any man to take

pains to learn anything bad that has been said about him, inasmuch as it is quite sure to be told him by some good-natured friend or other!   You have various acquaintances who will be very much gratified when a rainy day spoils the pic-nic to which you have invited a large party; and who will be perfectly enraptured, if you have hired a steamboat for the occasion, and if the day proves so stormy that every soul on board is deadly sick.   And indeed it is satisfactory to think that in our uncertain climate, where so many festal days are marred as to their enjoyment by drenching showers, there is compensation for the sufferings of the people who are ducked, in the enjoyment which that fact affords to very many of their friends.   By taking a larger view of things, you discover that there is good in everything.   You were Senior Wrangler: you just miss being made a Bishop at forty-two.   No doubt that was a great disappointment to yourself; but think what a joy it was to some scores of fellows whom you beat at College, and who hate you accordingly.   Some months ago a proprietor in this county was raised to the peerage.   His tenantry were entertained at a public dinner in honour of the event. The dinner was held in a large canvas pavilion.   The day came.   It was fearfully stormy, and torrents of rain fell.   A perfect shower-bath was the portion of many of the guests; and finally the canvas walls and roof broke loose, smashed the crockery, and whelmed the feast in fearful ruin.   During the nine days which followed, the first remark made by every one you met was, "What a sad pity about the storm spoiling the dinner at Stuckup Place!" And the countenance of every one who thus expressed his sorrow was radiant with joy! And quite natural too. They would have felt real regret had the new peer been drowned or shot: but the petty malignity which dwells in the human bosom made them rejoice at the small but irritating misfortune which had befallen. Shall I confess it, *mea culpa, mea maxima culpa*, I rejoiced in common with all my fellow-creatures! I was ashamed of the feeling. I wished to ignore it and extinguish it; but there was no doubt that it was there. And if Lord Newman was a person of en-larged and philosophic mind, he would have rejoiced that a small evil, which merely mortified himself and gave bad colds to his tenantry, afforded sensible plea-sure to several thousands of his fellow-men. Yes, my reader: it is well that a certain measure of small malice is ingrained in our fallen nature. For thus some pleasure comes out of almost all pain; some good from almost all evil. Your little troubles vex you, but they gratify your friends. Your horse comes down and smashes his knees. No doubt, to you and your groom it is unmingled bitterness. But every man within several miles, whose horse's knees have already been smashed, hails the event as a real blessing to himself. You signally fail of getting into Parliament, though you stood for a county in which you fancied that your own influence and that of your connexions was all-powerful. No doubt, you are sadly mortified. No doubt, you do not look like yourself for several weeks. But what chuckles of joy pervade the hearts and faces of five hundred fellows who have no chance of getting into the House themselves, and who dislike you for your huge fortune, your grand house, your countless thoroughbreds, your insufferable dignity, and your general forgetfulness of the place where you grew, which by those around you is perfectly well remembered. And while it is true that even people of a tolerably benevolent nature do not really feel any great regret at any mortification or disappointment which befals a wealthy and pretentious neighbour, it is also certain that a greater number of folk do actually gloat over any event which humbles the wealthy and pretentious man. You find them, with a malignant look, putting the case on a benevolent footing. " This taking-down will do him a great deal of good : he will be much the wiser and better for it." It is not uncharitable to believe, that in many cases in which such sentiments are expressed, the true feeling of the speaker is rather one of satisfaction at the pain which the disappointment certainly gives, than of satisfaction at the beneficial discipline which may possibly result from it. The thing *said* amounts to this : " I am glad that Mr Richman has got a taking-down, because the taking-down, though painful at the time, is in fact a blessing." The thing *felt* amounts to this : " I am glad that Mr Richman has got a taking-down, because I know it will make him very miserable." Every one who reads this page knows that this is so. Ah, my malicious acquaintances, if you know that the sentiment you entertain is one that would provoke universal execration if it were expressed, does not *that* shew that you ought not to entertain it ?

I have said that I do not believe there is much real malignity among ordinary men and women. It is only at the petty misfortunes of men's friends that they ever feel this unamiable satisfaction. When great sorrow befals a friend, all this unworthy feeling goes ; and the heart is filled with true sympathy and kindness. A man must be very bad indeed if this is not the case. It strikes me as something fiend-like rather than human, Byron's savage exultation over the melancholy end of the great and amiable Sir Samuel Romilly. Romilly had given him offence by acting as legal adviser to some whom Byron regarded as his enemies. But it was babyish to cherish enmity for such a cause as that ; and it was diabolical to re-joice at the sad close of that life of usefulness and honour. It was not good in James Watt, writing in old age an account of one of his many great inventions, to name very bitterly a man who had pirated it ; and to add, with a vengeful chuckle, that the poor man was " afterwards hanged." No private ground of offence should make you rejoice that your fellow-creature was hanged. You may justifiably rejoice in such a case only when the man hanged was a public offender, and an enemy of the race. Throw up your hat, if you please, when Nana Sahib stretches the hemp at last! *That* is all right. He never did harm to you individually: but you think of Cawnpore; and it is quite fit that there should be a bitter, burning satisfaction felt at the condign punishment of one whose punishment eternal justice demands. What is the use of the gallows, if not for that incarnate demon? I think of the poor sailors who were present at the trial of a bloodthirsty pirate of the Cuban coast. "I suppose," said the one doubtingly to the other, "the devil will get that fellow." "I should hope so," was the unhesitating reply; "or what would be the use of having any devil!"

But some real mischievous malice there is, even among people who bear a creditable character. I have occasionally heard old ladies (very few) tearing up the character of a friend with looks as deadly as though their weapon had been a stiletto, instead of that less immediately fatal instrument of offence, concerning which a very high authority informs us, that in some cases it is "set on fire of hell." Ah, you poor girl, who danced three times (they call it nine) with Mr A. at the Assembly last night, happily you do not know the venomous way in which certain spiteful tabbies are pitching into you this morning! And you, my friend, who drove along Belvidere Place (the fashionable quarter of the county town) yesterday, in your new drag with the new harness and the pair of thoroughbreds, and fancied that you were charming every eye and heart, if you could but hear how your equipage and yourself were scarified last evening, as several of your elderly female acquaintances sipped together the cup that cheers! How they brought up the time that you were flogged at the public school, and the term you were rusticated at Oxford! Even the occasion was not forgotten on which your grand-father was believed, forty years since, to have rather done Mr Softly in the matter of a glandered steed. And the peculiar theological tenets of your grand-mother were set forth in a fashion that would have astounded that good old lady. And you, who are so happily occupied in building in that beautiful wood-land spot that graceful Elizabethan house, little you know how bitterly some folk, dwelling in hideous seedy mansions, sneer at you, and your gimcracks, and your Gothic style in which you "go back to bar-barism." You, too, my friend, lately made a Queen's counsel, or a judge, or a bishop, if the shafts of envy could kill you, you would not live long. It is curious, by the way, how detraction follows a man when he first attains to any eminent place in State or Church; how keenly his qualifications are canvassed; how loudly his unfitness for his situation is proclaimed; and how, when a few months have passed, everybody gets quite reconciled to the appointment, and accepts it as one of the conditions of human affairs. Sometimes, indeed, the right man, by emphasis, is put in the right place ; so unquestionably the right man that even envy is silenced : as when Lord St Leonards was made Lord Chancellor, or when Mr Melvill was appointed to preach before the House of Commons. But even when men who have been plucked at the University were made bishops, or princes who had never seen a gun fired in anger field-marshals, or briefless barristers judges, although a general outcry arose at the time, it very speedily died away. When you find a man actually in a place, you do not weigh his claims to be there so keenly as if you were about to appoint him to it. If a resolute premier made Tom Spring a chief-justice, I doubt not that in six weeks the country would be quite accustomed to the fact, and accept it as a part of the order of nature. How else is it that the nation is content to have blind and deaf generals placed in high command, and infirm old admirals going to sea who ought to be going to bed ?

It is a sad fact that there are men and women who will, without much investigation as to its truth, repeat a story to the prejudice of some man or woman whom they know. They are much more critical in weighing the evidence in support of a tale to a friend's credit and advantage. I do not think they would absolutely invent such a calumnious narrative ; but they will repeat, if it has been told them, what, if they do not know it to be false, they also do not know to be true, and strongly suspect to be false.

My friend Mr C., rector of a parish in Hampshire, has a living of about five hundred a year. Some months ago he bought a horse for which he paid fifty pounds. Soon after he did so, I met a certain malicious woman who lived in his neighbourhood. "So," said she, with a look far from benevolent, "Mr C. has gone and paid a hundred pounds for a horse! Monstrous extravagance for a man with his means and with a family." "No, Miss Verjuice," I replied: "Mr C. did not pay nearly the sum you mention for his horse: he paid no more for it than a man of his means could afford." Miss Verjuice was not in the least discomfited by the failure of her first shaft of petty malignity. She had another in her quiver which she instantly discharged. "Well," said she, with a face of deadly ferocity, "if Mr C. did not pay a hundred pounds for his horse, *at all events he said he did!*" This was the drop too much. I told Miss Verjuice, with considerable asperity, that my friend was incapable of petty vapouring and petty falsehood; and in my book, from that day forward, there has stood a black cross against the individual's name.

Egypt, it seems, is the country where malevolence, in the sense of pure envy of people who are better off, is most prevalent and is most feared. People there believe that the envious eye does harm to those on whom it rests. Thus, they are afraid to possess fine

houses, furniture, and horses, lest they should excite
envy and bring misfortune. And when they allow
their children to go out for a walk, they send them
dirty and ill-dressed, for fear the covetous eye should
injure them :—

" At the bottom of this superstition is an enormous prevalence
of envy among the lower Egyptians. You see it in all their
fictions. Half of the stories told' in the coffee-shops by the
professional story-tellers, of which the *Arabian Nights* are a
specimen, turn on malevolence. Malevolence, not attributed,
as it would be in European fiction, to some insult or injury
inflicted by the person who is its object, but to mere envy :
envy of wealth, or of the other means of enjoyment, honourably
acquired and liberally used." *

A similar envy, no doubt, occasionally exists in this
country ; but people here are too enlightened to fancy
that it can do them any harm. Indeed, so far from
standing in fear of exciting envy by their display of
possessions and advantages, some people feel much
gratified at the thought of the amount of envy and
malignity which they are likely to excite. " Won't old
Hunks turn green with fury," said a friend to me, " the
first time I drive up to his door with those horses ? "
They were indeed beautiful animals ; but their proprietor appeared to prize them less for the pleasure
they afforded himself, than for the mortification they
would inflict on certain of his neighbours. " Won't
Mrs Grundy burst with spite when she sees this
drawing-room ? " was the remark of my lately-married

* Archbishop Whately's *Bacon*, p. 97.

cousin Henrietta, when she shewed me that very pretty apartment for the first time. "Won't Snooks be ferocious," said Mr Dryasdust the book-collector, "when he hears that I have got this almost unique edition?" Ah, my fellow-creatures, we are indeed a fallen race!

Hazlitt maintains that the petty malignity of mortals finds its most striking field in the matter of will-making. He says—

"The last act of our lives seldom belies the former tenor of them for stupidity, caprice, and unmeaning spite. All that we seem to think of is to manage matters so (in settling accounts with those who are so unmannerly as to survive us) as to do as little good and plague and disappoint as many people as possible."[*]

Every one knows that this brilliant essayist was accustomed to deal in sweeping assertions; and it is to be hoped that such cases as that which he here describes form the exception to the rule. But it must be admitted that most of us have heard of wills at whose reading we might almost imagine their malicious maker fancied he might be invisibly present to chuckle over the disappointment and mortification which he was dealing even from his grave. Cases are also recorded in which rich old bachelors have played upon the hopes of half-a-dozen poor relations, by dropping hints to each separately that *he* was to be the fortunate heir of all their wealth; and then have

[*] *Table-Talk*, vol. i., p. 171. "Essay on Will-making."

left their fortune to an hospital, or have departed from this world intestate, leaving an inheritance mainly of quarrels, heart-burnings, and Chancery suits. How often the cringing, tale-bearing toady, who has borne the ill-humours of a rich sour old maid for thirty years, in the hope of a legacy, is cut off with nineteen guineas for a mourning ring! You would say perhaps, "Serve her right." I differ from you. If any one likes to be toadied, he ought in honesty to pay for it. He knows quite well he would never have got it save for the hope of payment; and you have no more right to swindle some poor creature out of years of cringing and flattering than out of pounds of money. A very odd case of petty malice in will-making was that of a man who, not having a penny in this world, left a will in which he bequeathed to his friends and acquaintance large estates in various parts of England, money in the funds, rings, jewels, and plate. His inducement was the prospect of the delight of his friends at first learning about the rich possessions which were to be theirs, and then the bitter disappointment at finding how they had been hoaxed. Such deceptions and hoaxes are very cruel. Who does not feel for poor Moore and his wife, receiving a lawyer's letter just at a season of special embarrassment, to say that some deceased admirer of the poet had left him five hundred pounds, and after being buoyed up with hope for a few days, finding that some malicious rascal had been playing upon them! No; poor people know that want of money is too serious a matter to be joked about.

Let me conclude what I have to say about petty malignity by observing that I am very far from maintaining that all unfavourable remark about people you know proceeds from this unamiable motive. Some folk appear to fancy that if you speak of any man in any terms but those of superlative praise, this must be because you bear him some ill-will; they cannot understand that you may merely wish to speak truth and do justice. Every person who writes a stupid book and finds it unfavourably noticed in any review, instantly concludes that the reviewer must be actuated by some petty spite. The author entirely overlooks the alternative that his book may be said to be bad because it *is* bad, and because it is the reviewer's duty to say so if he thinks so. I remember to have heard the friend of a lady who had published a bitterly bad and unbecoming work speaking of the notice of it which had appeared in a periodical of the very highest class. The notice was of course unfavourable. "Oh," said the writer's friend, "I know why the review was so disgraceful; the man who wrote it was lately jilted, and he hates all women in consequence!" It happened that I had very good reason to know who wrote the depreciatory article, and I could declare that the motive assigned to the reviewer had not the least existence in fact.

Unfavourable remark has frequently no earthly connexion with malignity great or petty. It is quite fit that as in people's presence politeness requires that you should not say what you think of them, you should have an opportunity of doing so in their absence ; and every one feels when the limits of fair criticism are passed. What *could* you do if, after listening with every appearance of interest to some old lady's wearisome vapouring, you felt bound to pretend, after you had made your escape, that you thought her conversation was exceedingly interesting? What a relief it is to tell what you have suffered to some sympathetic friend ! I have heard injudicious people say, as something much to a man's credit, that he never speaks of any mortal except in his praise. I do not think the fact is to the man's advantage. It appears to prove either that the man is so silly that he thinks everything he hears and sees to be good, or that he is so crafty and reserved that he will not commit himself by saying what he thinks. Outspoken good-nature will sometimes get into scrapes from which self-contained craft will keep free ; but the man who, to use Miss Edgeworth's phrase, " thinks it best in general not to speak of things," will be liked by nobody.

By petty trickery I mean that small deception which annoys and worries you without doing you material harm. Thus it passes petty trickery when a bank publishes a swindling report, on the strength of whose false representations of prosperity you invest your hard-won savings in its stock and lose them all. It passes petty trickery when your clerk absconds with some hundreds of pounds. It indicates petty trickery when you find your servants writing their letters on your crested note-paper, and enclosing them in your crested envelopes. It indicates that at some time or other a successful raid has been made upon your paper-drawer. It indicates petty trickery when you find your horses' ribs beginning to be conspicuous, though they are only half worked, and are allowed three feeds of corn a day. Observe your coachman then, my friend. Some of your corn is going where it should not. It indicates petty trickery when your horses' coats are full of dust, though whenever you happen to be present they are groomed with incredible vigour: they are not so in your absence. It indicates petty trickery when, suddenly turning a corner, you find your coachman galloping the horses along the turnpike-road at the rate of twenty-three miles an hour. It indicates petty trickery when you find your neighbours' cows among your clover. It indicates petty trickery when you find amid a cottager's stock of firewood several palisades taken from your park-fence. It indicates petty trickery when you discern in the morning the traces of very large hobnailed shoes crossing your wife's flower garden towards the tree where the magnum bonums are nearly ripe. But why extend the catalogue? Every man can add to it a hundred instances. Says Bacon, "The small wares ind petty points of cunning are infinite, and it were a good deed to make a list of them." Who could make such a list? What numbers of people are practising petty trickery at every hour of the day! Yet, forasmuch as these tricks are small and pretty frequently seen through, they form only a blister: they are irritating but not dangerous: and it *is* very irritating to know that you have been cheated, to however small an extent. How inestimable is a thoroughly honest servant! Apart from anything like principle, if servants did but know it, it is well worth their while to be strictly truthful and reliable: they are then valued so much. It is highly expedient, besides being right. And not only is it extremely vexatious to find out any domestic in dishonesty of any kind, not only does it act as a blister at the moment, but it fosters in one's self a suspicious habit of mind which has in it something degrading. It is painful to be obliged to feel that you must keep a strict watch upon your stable or your granary. You have somewhat of the feeling of a spy; yet you cannot, if you have ordinary powers of observation, shut your eyes to what passes round you.

There is, indeed, some petty trickery which is highly venial, not to say pleasing. When a little child, on being offered a third plate of plum-pudding, says, with a wistful and half-ashamed look, "No, thank you," well you know that the statement is not entirely candid, and that the poor little thing would be sadly disappointed if you took him at his word.

Think of your own childish days; think what plum-pudding was then, and instantly send the little man a third plate, larger than the previous two. So if your gardener gets wet to the skin in mowing a little bit of turf, in a drenching summer-shower, which turns it, parched for the last fortnight, to emerald green, tell him he must be very wet, and give him a glass of whisky; never mind, though he, in his politeness, declares that he does not want the whisky, and is perfectly dry and comfortable. You will find him very readily dispose of the proffered refreshment. So if you go into a poor, but spotlessly-clean little cottage, where a lonely widow of eighty sits by her spinning-wheel. Her husband and her children are dead, and there she is, all alone, waiting till she goes to rejoin them. A poor, dog's-eared, ill-printed Bible lies on the rickety deal-table near. You take a large parcel which you have brought, wrapped in brown paper; and as you talk with the good old Christian, you gradually untie it. A well-sized volume appears; it is the Volume which is worth all the rest that ever were written; and you tell your aged friend that you have brought her a Bible, with great, clear type, which will be easily read by her failing eyes, and you ask her to accept it. You see the flush of joy and gratitude on her face, and you do not mind though she says something which is not strictly true—that it was too kind of you, that she did not need it, that she could manage with the old one yet. Nor would you severely blame the brave fellow who jumped off a bridge forty feet high, and pulled out your brother when he was just sinking in a flooded river, if, when you thanked him with a full heart for the risk he had run, he replied, in a careless, good-humoured way, that he had really done nothing worth the speaking of. The brave man is pained by your thanks : but he thought of his wife and children when he leaped from the parapet, and he knew well that he was hazarding his life. And he is perfectly aware that the statement which he makes is not consistent with fact—but surely you would never call him a trickster !

Mr J. S. Mill, unquestionably a very courageous as well as a very able writer, has declared in a recent publication, that, in Great Britain, the higher classes, for the most part, speak the truth, while the lower classes, almost without exception, have frequent recourse to falsehood. I think Mr Mill must have been unfortunate in his experience of the poor. I have seen much of them, and I have found among them much honesty and truthfulness, along with great kindness of heart. They have little to give away in the form of money, but will cheerfully give their time and strength in the service of a sick neighbour. I have known a shepherd who had come in from the hills in the twilight of a cold December afternoon, weary and worn out, find that the little child of a poor widow in the next cottage had suddenly been taken ill, and without sitting down, take his stick, and walk away through the dark to the town nine miles off, to fetch the doctor.   And when I told the fine fellow how much I respected his manly kindness, I found he was quite unaware that he had done anything remarkable ; "it was just what ony neibour wad do for anither !"   And I could mention scores of similar cases.   And as for truthfulness, I have known men and women among the peasantry, both of England and Scotland, whom I would have trusted with untold gold,—or even with what the Highland laird thought a more searching test of rectitude—with unmeasured whisky.   Still I must sorrowfully admit that I have found in many people a strong tendency, when they had done anything wrong, to justify themselves by falsehood.   It is not impossible that over-severe masters and mistresses, by undue scoldings administered for faults of no great moment, foster this unhappy tendency.   It was not, however, of one class more than another, that the quaint old minister of a parish in Lanarkshire was speaking, when one Sunday morning he read as his text the verse in the Psalms, "I said in my haste, All men are liars," and began his sermon by thoughtfully saying—

"Ay, David, ye said it in your haste, did you ?   If ye had lived in this parish, ye might have said it at your leisure !"

There is hardly a sadder manifestation of the spirit of petty trickery than that which has been pressed on the attention of the public by recent accounts of the adulteration of food.   It is, indeed, sad enough,

"When chalk, and alum, and plaster, are sold to the poor for
    bread,
And the spirit of murder works in the very means of life : "

and when the luxuries of the rich are in many cases quite as much tampered with ; while, when medical appliances become needful to correct the evil effects of red-lead, plaster of Paris, cantharides, and oil of vitriol, the physician is quite uncertain as to the practical power of the medicine he prescribes, inasmuch as drugs are as much adulterated as food.   Still, there seems reason to hope that, more frequently than the *Lancet* Commission would lead one to think, you really get in the shops the thing you ask and pay for. I firmly believe that, in this remote district of the world, such petty dishonesty is unknown : and I cannot refrain from saying that, notwithstanding all I have read of late years in tracts, sermons, poems, and leading articles, of the frequency of fraud in the dealings of tradesmen in towns, I never in my own experience have seen the least trace of it.

Most human beings, however, will tell you that day by day they witness a good deal of indirectness, insincerity, and want of straightforwardness—in fact, of petty trickery.   There are many people who appear incapable of doing anything without going round about the bush, as Caledonians say.   There are many people who always try to disguise the real

motive for what they do.   They will tell you of anything but the consideration that actually weighs with
them, though that is in most cases perfectly well
known to the person they are talking to.   Some men
will tell you that they travel second-class by railway
because it is warmer, cooler, airier, pleasanter than
the first-class.   They suppress all mention of the consideration that obviously weighs with them, viz., that
it is cheaper.   Mr Squeers gave the boys at Dothe-
boys Hall treacle and sulphur one morning in the
week.   The reason he assigned was that it was good
for their health : but his more outspoken wife stated
the true reason, which was that, by sickening the
children, it made breakfast unnecessary upon that
day.   Some Dissenters pretend that they want to
abolish Church-rates, with a view to the good of the
Church : of course everybody knows that their real
wish is to do the Church harm.   Very soft indeed
would the members of the Church be, if they believed
that its avowed enemies are extremely anxious for
its welfare.   But the forms of petty trickery are endless.   Bacon mentions in one of his *Essays* that he
knew a statesman who, when he came to Queen
Elizabeth with bills to sign, always engaged her in
conversation about something else, to distract her
attention from the papers she was signing.   And
when some impudent acquaintance asks you, reader,
to put your name to another kind of bill, for his ad·
vantage, does he not always think to delude you into

doing so by saying that your signing is a mere form, intended only for the fuller satisfaction of the bank that is to lend him the money? He does not tell you that he is just asking you to give him the sum named on that stamped paper. Don't believe a word he says, and shew him the door. Signing a promise to pay money is never a form; if it be a form, why does he ask you to do it? Bacon mentions another man, who "when he came to have speech, would pass over that he intended most, and go forth, and come back again, and speak of it as a thing he had almost forgot." I have known such men too. We have all known men who would come and talk about many indifferent things, and then at the end bring in, as if accidentally, the thing they came for. Always pull such men sharply up. Let them understand that you see through them. When they sit down, and begin to talk of the weather, the affairs of the district, the new railway, and so forth, say at once, "Now, Mr Pawky, I know you did not come to talk to me about these things. What is it that you want to speak of? I am busy, and have no time to waste." It is wonderful how this will beat down Mr Pawky's guard. He is prepared for sly finesse, but he is quite taken aback by downright honesty. If you try to do him, he will easily do you: but perfect candour foils the crafty man, as the sturdy Highlander's broadsword at once cut down the French master of fence, vapouring away with his rapier. *You* cannot beat a rogue with his own weapons.   Try him with truth : like David, he "has not proved" that armour ; he is quite unaccustomed to it, and he goes down.

Men in towns know that time is valuable to them, and by long experience they are assured that there is no use in trying to overreach a neighbour in a bargain, because he is so sharp that they will not succeed. But in agricultural districts some persons may be found who appear to regard it as a fond delusion that "honesty is the best policy;" and who never deal with a stranger without feeling their way, and trying how far it may be possible to cheat him. I am glad to infer, from the universal contempt in which such persons are held, that they form base, though by no means infrequent, exceptions to the general rule. The course which such individuals follow in buying and selling is quite marked and invariable. If they wish to buy a cow or rent a field, they begin by declaring with frequency and vehemence that they don't want the thing,—that, in fact, they would rather not have it,—that it would be inconvenient for them to become possessors of it. They then go on to say that still, if they can get it at a fair price, they may be induced to think of it. They next declare that the cow is the very worst that ever was seen, and that very few men would have such a creature in their possession. The seller of the cow, if he knows his customer, meanwhile listens with entire indifference to Mr

Pawky's asseverations, and after a while proceeds to name his price. Fifteen pounds for the cow. "Oh," says Mr Pawky, getting up hastily and putting on his hat, "I see you don't want to sell it. I was just going to have offered you five pounds. I see I need not spend longer time here." Mr Pawky, however, does not leave the room: sometimes, indeed, if dealing with a green hand, he may actually depart for half-an-hour; but then he returns and resumes the negotiation. A friend of his has told him that possibly the cow was better than it looked. It looked very bad indeed; but it might be a fair cow after all. So the proceedings go on: and after an hour's haggling, and several scores of falsehoods told by Mr Pawky, he becomes the purchaser of the animal for the sum originally named. Even now he is not exhausted. He assures the former owner of the cow that it is the custom of the district always to give back half-a-crown in the pound, and refuses to hand over more than £13, 2s. 6d. The cow is by this time on its way to Mr Pawky's farm. If dealing with a soft man, this final trick possibly succeeds. If with an experienced person, it wholly fails. And Mr Pawky, after wasting two hours, telling sixty-five lies, and stamping himself as a cheat in the estimation of the person with whom he was dealing, ends by taking nothing by all his petty trickery. Oh, poor Pawky, why not be honest and straightforward at once? You would get just as much money, in five cases out of six; and you would save your time and breath, and miss running up that fearful score in the book of the recording angel!

After any transaction with Mr Pawky, how delightful it is to meet with a downright honest man! I know several men—farmers, labourers, country gentlemen—of that noble class, whose "word is as good as their bond!" I know men whom you could not even imagine as taking a petty advantage of any mortal. They are probably far from being pieces of perfection. They are crotchety in temper; they are rough in address; their clothes were never made by Stultz; possibly they do not shave every morning. But as I look at the open, manly face, and feel the strong gripe of the vigorous hand, and rejoice to think that the world goes well with them, and that they find it pay to speak the truth, I feel for the minute as if the somewhat over-strained sentiment had truth in it, that

"An honest man's the noblest work of God!"

I am firmly convinced that no man, in the long run, gains by petty trickery. Honesty *is* the best policy. You remember how the roguish Ephraim Jenkinson, in the *Vicar of Wakefield*, mentioned that he contrived to cheat honest Farmer Flamborough about once a year; but still the honest farmer grew rich, and the rogue grew poor, and so Jenkinson began to bethink him that he was in the wrong track after all. A man who with many oaths declares a broken-winded nag is sound as a bell, and thus gets fifty pounds for an animal he bought for ten, and then declares with many more oaths that he never warranted the horse, may indeed gain forty pounds in money by that transaction, but he loses much more than he gains. The man whom he cheated, and the friends of the man whom he cheated, will never trust him again; and he soon acquires such a character that every one who is compelled to have any dealings with him stands on his guard, and does not believe a syllable he says. I do not mention here the solemn consideration of how the gain and loss may be adjusted in the view of another world; nor do more than allude to a certain solemn question as to the profit which would follow the gain of much more than forty pounds, by means which would damage something possessed by every man. All trickery is folly. Every rogue is a fool. The publisher who advertises a book he has brought out, and appends a flattering criticism of it as from the *Times* or *Fraser's Magazine* which never appeared in either periodical, does not gain on the whole by such petty deception; neither does the publisher who appends highly recommendatory notices, marked with inverted commas as quotations, though with the name of no periodical attached, the fact being that he composed these notices himself. You will say that Mr Barnum is an instance of a man who made a large fortune by the greater and lesser arts of trickery; but would you, my honest and honourable friend, have taken that fortune on the same terms? I hope not.

And no blessing seems to have rested on Barnum's gains. Where are they now? The trickster has been tricked—the doer done. There is a hollowness about all prosperity which is the result of unfair and underhand means. Even if a man who has grown rich through trickery seems to be going on quite comfortably, depend upon it he cannot feel happy. The sword of Damocles is hanging over his head. Let no man be called happy before he dies.

I believe, indeed, that in some cases the conscience grows quite callous, and the notorious cheat fancies himself a highly moral and religious man ; and although it is always extremely irritating to be cheated, it is more irritating than usual to think that the man who has cheated you is not even made uneasy by the checks of his own conscience. I would gladly think that in most cases,

> "Doubtless the pleasure is as great
> Of being cheated as to cheat."

I would gladly think that the man who has done another feels it as blistering to remember the fact as the man who has been done does. It would gratify me much if I were able to conclude that every man who is a knave knows that he is one. I doubt it. Probably he merely thinks himself a sharp, clever fellow. Only this morning I was cheated out of four and sixpence by a man of very decent appearance. He obtained that sum by making three statements, which I found on inquiring, after he had gone, were false. The gain, you see, was small. He obtained just eighteenpence a lie. Yet he went off, looking extremely honest. And no doubt he will be at his parish church next Sunday, shaking his head sympathetically at the more solemn parts of the sermon. And probably when he reflects upon the transaction, he merely thinks that he was sharp and I was soft. The analogy between these small tricks and a blister holds in several respects. Each is irritating, and the irritation caused by each gradually departs. You are very indignant at first learning that you have been taken in ; you are rather sore, even the day after—but the day after *that* you are less sore at having been done than sorry for the rogue who was fool enough to do you.

I am writing only of that petty trickery which acts as a blister of humanity ; as I need say nothing of those numerous forms of petty trickery which do not irritate, but merely amuse. Such are those silly arts by which some people try to represent themselves to their fellow-creatures as richer, wiser, better-informed, more highly connected, more influential, and more successful than the fact. I felt no irritation at the schoolboy who sat opposite me the other day in a railway carriage, and pretended that he was reading a Greek play. I allowed him to fancy his trick had succeeded, and conversed with him of the characteristics of Æschylus. He did not know much about them. A friend of mine, a clergyman, went to the house of a weaver in his parish.   As he was about to knock at the door, he heard a solemn voice within ; and he listened in silence as the weaver asked God's blessing upon his food.   Then he lifted the latch and entered : and thereupon the weaver, resolved that the clergyman should know he said grace before meat, *began and repeated his grace over again.*   My friend was not angry ; but he was very, very sorry.   And never, till the man had been years in his grave, did he mention the fact.   As for the fashion in which some people fire off, in conversation with a new acquaintance, every titled name they know, it is to be recorded that the trick is invariably as unsuccessful as it is contemptible.   And is not a state dinner, given by poor people, in resolute imitation of people with five times their income, with its sham champagne, its disguised greengrocers, and its general turning the house topsy-turvy,—is not such a dinner one great trick, and a very transparent one ?

The writer is extremely tired.   Is it not curious that to write for four or five hours a day for four or five successive days, wearies a man to a degree that ten or twelve daily hours of ploughing does not weary the man whose work is physical ?   Mental work is much the greater stretch : and it is strain, not time, that kills.   A horse that walks at two miles and a-half an hour, ploughing, will work twelve hours out of the twenty-four.   A horse that runs in the mail at twelve miles an hour, works an hour and a-half and rests twenty-two and a half; and with all that rest soon breaks down. The bearing of all this is that it is time to stop; and so, my long black goosequill, lie down!

CHAPTER IV.

NOBODY likes to work. I should never work at all if I could help it. I mean, when I say that nobody likes work, that nobody does so whose tastes and likings are in a natural and unsophisticated condition. Some men, by long training and by the force of various circumstances, do, I am aware, come to have an actual craving, a morbid appetite for work; but it is a morbid appetite, just as truly as that which impels a lady to eat chalk, or a child to prefer pickles to sugar-plums. Or if my reader quarrels with the word *morbid*, and insists that a liking for brisk, hard work is a healthy taste and not a diseased one, I will give up that phrase, and substitute for it the less strong one, that a liking for work is an *acquired taste*, like that which leads you and me, my friend, to like bitter beer. Such a man, for instance, as Lord Campbell, has brought himself to that state that I have no doubt he actually enjoys the thought of the enormous quantity of work which he goes through; but when he does so, he does a thing as completely out of nature as is done by the Indian fakir, who feels a gloomy satisfaction as he reflects on the success with which he has laboured to weed out all but bitterness from life. I know quite well that we can bring ourselves to such a state of mind that we shall feel a sad sort of pleasure in thinking how much we are taking out of ourselves, and how much we are denying ourselves. What college man who ever worked himself to death but knows well the curious condition of mind? He begins to toil, induced by the love of knowledge, or by the desire of distinction; but after he has toiled on for some weeks or months, there gradually steals in such a feeling as that which I have been describing. I have felt it myself, and so know all about it. I do not believe that any student ever worked harder than I did. And I remember well the gloomy kind of satisfaction I used to feel, as all day, and much of the night, I bent over my books, in thinking how much I was foregoing. The sky never seemed so blue and so inviting as when I looked at it for a moment now and then, and so back to the weary page. And never did the green woodland walks picture themselves to my mind so freshly and delightfully as when I thought of them as of something which I was resolutely denying myself. I remember even now, when I went to bed at half-past four in the morning, having risen at half-past six the previous morning, and having done nearly as much for months, how I was positively pleased to see in the glass the ghastly cheeks, and the deep black circles round the eyes. There is, I repeat, a certain pleasure in thinking one is working desperately hard, and taking a great deal out of one's-self; but it is a pleasure which is unnatural, which is factitious, which is mor bid. It is not in the healthy, unsophisticated human animal. We know, of course, that Lord Chief-Justice Ellenborough said when he was about seventy, that the greatest pleasure that remained to him in life, was to hear a young barrister, named Follett, argue a point of law ; but it was a highly artificial state of mind, the result of very long train-ing, which enabled the eminent judge to enjoy the gratification which he described: and to ordinary men a legal argument, however ably conducted, would be sickeningly tiresome. If you want to know the natural feeling of humanity towards work, see what children think of it. Is not the task always a dis-agreeable necessity, even to the very best boy ? How I used to hate mine ! Of course, my friendly reader, if you knew who I am, I should talk of myself less freely ; but as you do not know, and could not pos-sibly guess, I may ostensibly do what every man tacitly does—make myself the standard of average human nature, the first meridian from which all dis-tances and deflections are to be measured. Well, my feeling towards my school tasks was nothing short of hatred. And yet I was not a dunce. No, I was a clever boy. I was at the head of all my classes. Not more than once or twice have I competed at school or college for a prize which I did not get. And I hated work all the while. Therefore I believe that all unsophisti-cated mortals hate it. I have seen silly parents trying to get their children to say that they liked school-time better than holiday-time ; that they liked work better than play. I have seen, with joy, manly little fellows repudiating the odious and unnatural sentiment ; and declaring manfully that they preferred cricket to Ovid. And if any boy ever tells you that he would rather learn his lessons than go out to the play-ground, beware of that boy. Either his health is drooping, and his mind becoming prematurely and unnaturally developed; or he is a little humbug. He is an impostor. He is seeking to obtain credit under false pretences. Depend upon it, unless it really be that he is a poor little spiritless man, deficient in nerve and muscle, and un-healthily precocious in intellect, he has in him the elements of a sneak ; and he wants nothing but time to ripen him into a pickpocket, a swindler, a horse-dealer, or a British Bank director.

Every one, then, naturally hates work, and loves its opposite, play. And let it be remarked that not idleness, but play, is the opposite of work. But some people are so happy, as to be able to idealise their work into play : or they have so great a liking for their work, that they do not feel their work as effort, and thus the element is eliminated which makes work a pain. How I envy those human beings who have such enjoyment in their work that it ceases to be work at all ! There is my friend Mr Tinto the painter ; he is never so happy as when he is busy at his canvas, drawing forth from it forms of beauty: he is up at his work almost as soon as he has daylight for it; he paints all day, and he is sorry when the twilight compels him to stop. He delights in his work, and so his work becomes play. I suppose the kind of work which, in the case of ordinary men, never ceases to be work, never loses the conscious feeling of strain and effort, is that of composition. A great poet, possibly, may find much pleasure in writing, and there have been exceptional men who said they never were so happy as when they had the pen in their hand. Buffon, I think, tells us that once he wrote for fourteen hours at a stretch, and all that time was in a state of positive enjoyment; and Lord Macaulay, in the preface to his recently published *Speeches*, assures us that the writing of his *History* is the occupation and the happiness of his life. Well, I am glad to hear it. Ordinary mortals cannot sympathise with the feeling. To *them*, composition is simply hard work, and hard work is pain. Of course, even commonplace men have occasionally had their moments of inspiration, when thoughts present themselves vividly, and clothe themselves in felicitous expressions, without much or any conscious effort. But these seasons are short and far between; and although while they last, it becomes comparatively pleasant to write, it never becomes so pleasant as it would be to lay down the pen, to lean back in the easy-chair, to take up the *Times* or *Fraser*, and enjoy the luxury of being carried easily along that track of thought which cost its writer so much labour to pioneer through the trackless jungle of the world of mind. Ah, how easy it is to read what it was so difficult to write! There is all the difference between running down from London to Manchester by the railway after it has been made, and of making the railway from London to Manchester. You, my intelligent reader, who begin to read a chapter of Mr Froude's eloquent *History*, and get on with it so fluently, are like the snug old gentleman, travelling-capped, railway-rugged, great-coated, and plaided, who leans back in the corner of the softly-cushioned carriage as it flits over Chat Moss; while the writer of the chapter is like George Stephenson, toiling month after month to make the track along which you speed, in the face of difficulties and discouragements which you never think of. And so I say, it may sometimes be somewhat easy and pleasant to write, but never so easy and pleasant as it is not to write. The odd thing, too, about the work of the pen is this: that it is often done best by the men who like it least and shrink from it most, and that it is often the most laborious writing along which the reader's mind glides most easily and pleasurably. It is not so in other matters. As the general rule, no man does well the work which he dislikes. No man will be a good preacher who dislikes preaching. No man will be a good anatomist who hates dissecting. Sir Charles

Napier, it must be confessed, was a great soldier, though he hated fighting; and as for writing, some men have been the best writers who hated writing, and who would never have penned a line but under the pressure of necessity. There is John Foster; what a great writer he was: and yet his biography tells us, in his own words too, scores of times, how he shrunk away from the intense mental effort of composition; how he abhorred it and dreaded it, though he did it so admirably well. There is Coleridge: how that great mind ran to waste, because Coleridge shrank from the painful labour of formal composition: and so *Christabel* must remain unfinished: and so, instead of volumes of hoarded wisdom and wit, we have but the fading remembrances of hours of marvellous talk. I do not by any means intend to assert that there are not worse things than work, even than very hard work; but I say that work, as work, is a bad thing. It may once have been otherwise, but the curse is in it now. We do it because we must: it is our duty: we live by it; it is the Creator's intention that we should; it makes us enjoy leisure and recreation and rest; it stands between us and the pure misery of idleness; it is dignified and honourable; it is the soil and the atmosphere in which grow cheerfulness, hopefulness, health of body and mind. But still, if we could get all these good ends without it, we should be glad.

We do not care for exertion for its own sake. Even Mr Kingsley does not love the north-east wind for itself, but because of the good things that come with it and from it. Work is not an end in itself. "The end of work," said Aristotle, "is to enjoy leisure;" or, as *The Minstrel* hath it, "the end and the reward of toil is rest." I do not wish to draw from too sacred a source the confirmation of these summer-day fancies; but I think, as I write, of the descriptions which we find in a certain Volume of the happiness of another world. Has not many an over-wrought and wearied-out worker found comfort in an assurance of which I shall here speak no further, that "there remaineth a rest to the people of God?"

And so, my reader, if it be true that nobody, any-where, would (in his sober senses) work if he could help it, how especially true is that great principle on this beautiful July day! It is truly a day on which to do nothing. I am here, far in the country, and when I this moment went to the window, and looked out upon a rich summer landscape, everything seemed asleep. The sky is sapphire-blue, without a cloud; the sun is pouring down a flood of splendour upon all things; there is not a breath stirring, hardly the twitter of a bird. All the air is filled with the fragrance of the young clover. The landscape is richly wooded; I never saw the trees more thickly covered with leaves, and now they are perfectly still. I am writing north of the Tweed, and the horizon is of blue hills, which some Southrons would call mountains. The wheat fields are beginning to have a little of the harvest-tinge, and they contrast beautifully with the deep green of the hedge-rows. The roses are almost over, but I can see plenty of honeysuckle in the hedges still, and a perfect blaze of it has covered one projecting branch of a young oak. I am looking at a little well-shaven green (I shall not call it a lawn, because it is not one ;) it has not been mown for nearly a fortnight, and it is perfectly white with daisies. Beyond, at a very short distance, through the branches of many oaks, I can see a gable of the church, and a few large gravestones shining white among the green grass and leaves. I do not find all these things any great temptation now, for I have got interested in my work, and I like to write of them. But I found it uncommonly hard to sit down this morning to my work. Indeed, I found it impossible, and thus it is that at five o'clock P.M. I have got no further than the present line. I had quite resolved that this morning I would sit doggedly down to my essay, in which I have really (though the reader may find it hard to believe it) got something to say; but when I walked out after breakfast, I felt that all nature was saying that this was not a day for work. Come forth and look at me, seemed the message breathed from her beautiful face. And then I thought of Wordsworth's ballad, which sets out so pleasing an excuse for idleness :—

Books ! 'tis a dull and endless strife,
  Come, hear the woodland linnet !
How sweet his music ! on my life
  There 's more of wisdom in it.

" And hark ! how blithe the throstle sings !
  He, too, is no mean preacher :
Come forth into the light of things,
  Let Nature be your teacher.

" She has a world of ready wealth,
  Our minds and hearts to bless,—
Spontaneous wisdom breathed by health,
  Truth breathed by cheerfulness.

" One impulse from a vernal wood
  May teach you more of man,
Of moral evil and of good,
  Than all the sages can !"

Just at my gate, the man who keeps in order the roads of the parish was hard at work. How pleasant, I thought, to work amid the pure air and the sweet-smelling clover ! And how pleasant, too, to have work to do of such a nature that when you go to it every morning you can make quite sure that, barring accident, you will accomplish a certain amount before the sun shall set ; while as for the man whose work is that of the brain and the pen, he never can be certain in the morning how much his day's labour may amount to. He may sit down at his desk, spread out his paper, have his ink in the right place, and his favourite pen, and yet he may find that he cannot *get on*, that thoughts will not come, that his mind is utterly sterile, that he cannot see his way through his subject, or that if he can produce anything at all it is poor miserable stuff, whose poorness no one knows better than himself. And so, after hours of effort and discouragement, he may have to lay his work aside, having accomplished nothing, having made no progress at all—wearied, stupified, disheartened, thinking himself a mere blockhead. Thus musing, I approached the roadman. I inquired how his wife and children were. I asked how he liked the new cottage he had lately moved into. Well, he said; but it was far from his work : he had walked eight miles and a half that morning to his work ; he had to walk the same distance home again in the evening after labouring all day; and for this his wages were thirteen shillings a-week, with a deduction for such days as he might be unable to work. He did not mention all this by way of complaint ; he was comfortably off, he said ; he should be thankful he was so much better off than many. He had got a little pony lately very cheap, which would carry himself and his tools to and from his employment, and that would be very nice. In all likelihood, my friendly reader, the roadman would not have been so communicative to you ; but as for me, it is my duty and my happiness to be the sympathising friend of every man, woman, and child in this parish, and it pleases me much to believe that there is no one throughout its little population who does not think of me and speak to me as a friend. I talked a little longer to the roadman about parish affairs. We mutually agreed in remarking the incongruous colours of a pair of ponies which passed in a little phaeton, of which one was cream-coloured and the other dapple-grey. The phaeton came from a friend's house a little way off, and I wondered if it were going to the railway to bring some one who (I knew) was expected ; for in such simple matters do we simple country-folk find something to maintain the interest of life. I need not go on to describe what other things I did ; how I looked with pleasure at a field of oats and another of potatoes in which I am concerned, and held several short conversations with passers-by ; but the result of the whole was a conviction that, after all, it was best to set to work at once, though well remembering how much by indoor work in the country on such a day as this one is missing. And the thought of the road-man's seventeen miles of walking, in addition to his day's work, was something of a reproof and a stimulus. And thus, determined at least to make a beginning, did I write this much *Concerning Work and Play.*

I find a great want in all that is written on the subject of recreation. People tell me that I need recreation, that I cannot do without it, that mind and body alike demand it. I know all that, but they do not tell me how to recreate myself. They fight shy of all practical details. Now it is just these I want. All working men must have play ; but what sort of play can we have? I envy schoolboys their facility of being amused, and of finding recreation which entirely changes the current of their thoughts. A boy flying his kite or whipping his top is pursued by no remembrance of the knotty line of Virgil which puzzled him a little while ago in school; but when the grown-up man takes his sober afternoon walk— perhaps the only relaxation which he has during the day—he is thinking still of the book which he is writing and of the cares which he has left at home. Then, and all the worse for myself, I can feel no interest in flying a kite, or rigging and sailing a little ship, or making a mill-wheel and setting it going, or in marbles, or ball, or running races, or playing at leap-frog. And even if they did feel interest in athletic sports, the lungs and sinews of most educated men of middle age would forbid their joining in them. I need not therefore suggest the doubt which would probably be cast upon a man's sanity were he found eagerly knuckling down (how stiff it would soon make him!), or wildly chasing the flying football, or making a rush at a friend and taking a flying leap over his head. Now what recreation, I want to know, is open to the middle-aged man of literary tastes? Shooting, coursing, fishing, says one; but he does not care for shooting, or coursing, or fishing. Gardening, says another; but he does not care for gardening. Watching ferns, caterpillars, frogs, and other " common objects of the country ;" well, but he lives in town, and if he did not he does not feel the least interest in ferns and caterpillars. Music is suggested; well, he has no great ear, and he may dwell where he can have little or none of it. Society! pray what is society? No doubt the conversation of intelligent men and women is a most grateful and stimulating recreation; but is there any recreation in dreary dinner-parties, where one listens to the twaddle of silly old gentlemen and emptier young ones, or in the hothouse atmosphere and crush of most evening parties? These are not play; they are very hard work, and a treadmill work producing no beneficial results, but rather provocative of all manner of ill-tempers. Then, no doubt, there is most agreeable recreation for some people in the excitement of a polka or galop and its attendant light and cheerful talk, not to say flirtation; but then our representative man has got beyond these things: these are for young people—he is married now and sobered down; he probably was never the man to make himself eminently agreeable in such a scene, and he is less so now than ever. Besides, if play be something from which you are to return with renewed strength and interest to work, I doubt whether the ball-room is the place where it is to be found. Late hours, a feverish atmosphere, and excessive exercise, tend to morning slumbers, headaches, crossness, and laziness. To find dancing which answers the end of recreation, we must go to less fashionable places. I like the pictures which Goldsmith gives us of the sunny summer evenings of France, where the whole population of the village danced to his flute in the shade ; and even the soured Childe Harold melted somewhat into sympathy with the Spanish peasants as they twirled their casta- nets in the twilight.   Southey's picture is a pretty one, but its description sounds somewhat unreal :—

> " But peace was on the cottage, and the fold
>   From court intrigue, from bickering faction far :
>   Beneath the chestnut-tree love's tale was told,
>   And to the tinkling of the light guitar,
>   Sweet stoop'd the western sun, sweet rose the evening star !"

Nor let it be fancied that such a scene cannot be ıepresented except in countries to which distance and strangeness give their interest.   This very season, on a beautiful summer evening, I saw a happy party of eighty country-folk dancing upon a greener little bit of turf than Goldsmith ever saw in France.   And I wished such things were more common ; though the grave Saxon spirit, equal to the enjoyment of such gaiety now and then, might perhaps flag under it did it come too often.   But on the occasion to which I refer, there was no lack of innocent cheerfulness ; the enjoy- ment seemed real ; and though there were no castanets and no guitars, but a fiddle for music and reels for dances, there were as pretty faces and as graceful figures among the girls, I warrant, as you would find from the Rhine to the Pyrenees.

But, to resume the somewhat ravelled thread of our discussion,—if a man has come to this, that he can feel no interest in such recreations as those which we have mentioned, what is he to do? And let it be remembered that I am putting no fanciful case: be sorry, if you will, for the man who from taste and habit cannot be easily amused; but remember that such is the lot of a very large proportion of the intellectual labourers of the race. ·And what is such a man to do? After using his eyes and exerting his brain all the forenoon in reading and writing by way of work, must he just use his eyes and exert his brain all the evening in reading and writing by way of play? Has it come to this, that he must find the only recreation that remains for him in the *Times,* the *Quarterly Review,* and *Fraser's Magazine?* All these things are indeed excellent in their way. They relax and interest the mind: but then they wear out the eyes, they contract the chest, and render the muscles flabby, they ruin the ganglionic apparatus; they make the mind, but unmake the body. Now that will not do. Does nothing remain, in the way of play, but the afternoon walk or drive: the vacant period between dinner and tea, when no one works, notwithstanding Johnson's warning, that he who resolves that he cannot work between dinner and tea, will probably proceed to the conclusion that he cannot work between breakfast and dinner; a little quiet gossip with your wife, a little romping with your children, if you have a wife and children; and then back again to the weary books?

Think of the elder Disraeli, who looked at printed pages so long, that by and by, wherever he looked, he saw nothing but printed pages, and then became blind. Think what poor specimens of the human animal, physically, many of our noblest and ablest men are. Do not men, by their beautiful, touching, and far-reaching thoughts, reach the heart and form the mind of thousands, who could not run a hundred yards without panting for breath, who could not jump over a five-feet wall though a mad bull were after them, who could not dig in the garden for ten minutes without having their brain throbbing and their entire frame trembling, who could not carry in a sack of coals though they should never see a fire again, who could never find a day's employment as porters, labourers, grooms, or anything but tailors? Educated and cultivated men, I tell you that you make a terrible mistake; and a mistake which, before the end of the twentieth century, will sadly deteriorate the Anglo-Saxon race. You make your recreation purely mental. You give a little play to your minds after their day's work; but you give no play to your eyes, to your brains, to your hearts, to your digestion,—in short, to your bodies. And therefore you grow weak, unmuscular, nervous, dyspeptic, near-sighted, out-of-breath, neuralgic, pressure-on-the-brain, thin-haired men. And in time, not only does all the train of evils that follows your not providing proper recreation for your physical nature, come miserably to affect your spirits; but, besides that, it comes to jaundice and pervert and distort all your views of men and things. I have heard of those who, though suffering almost ceaseless pain, could yet think hopefully of the prospects of humanity, and take an unprejudiced view of some political question that appealed strongly to prejudice, and give kindly sympathy and sound advice to a poor man who came to seek advice in some little trouble which is great to him. But I fear that in the majority of instances, the human being whose liver is in a bad way, whose digestion is ruined, or even who is suffering from violent toothache, is prone to snub the servants, to box the children's ears, to think that Britain is going to destruction, and that the world is coming to an end.

It may be said, that the class of intellectual workers have their yearly holiday. August and September in each year bring with them the "Long Vacation." And it is well, indeed, that most men whose work is brain-work have that blessed period of relief, wherein, amid the Swiss snows, or the Highland heather, or out upon the Mediterranean waves, they seek to reinvigorate the jaded body and mind, and to lay in a store of health and strength with which to face the winter work again. But this is not enough. A man might just as well say that he would eat in August or September all the food which is to support him through the year, as think in that time to take the whole year's recreation, the whole year's play, in one *bonne bouche.* Recreation must be a daily thing. Every day must have its play, as well as its work. There is much sound, practical sense in Sir Thomas More's *Utopia;* and nowhere sounder than where he tells us that in his model country he would have "half the day allotted for work, and half for honest recreation." Every day, bringing, as it does, work to every man who is worth his salt in this world, ought likewise to bring its play: play which will turn the thoughts into quite new and cheerful channels; which will recreate the body as well as the mind; and tell me, Great Father of Waters, to whom Rasselas appealed upon a question of equal difficulty, or tell me, anybody else, what that play shall be! Practically, in the case of most educated men, of most intellectual workers, heavy reading and writing stand for work, and light reading and writing stand for play.

I can well imagine what a delightful thing it must be for a toil-worn barrister to throw briefs, and cases, and reports aside, and quitting the pestilential air of Westminster Hall, laden with odours from the Thames which are not the least like those of Araby the Blest, to set off to the Highlands for a few weeks among the moors. No schoolboy at holiday-time is lighter-hearted than he, as he settles down into his corner in that fearfully fast express train on the Great Northern Railway. And when he reaches his box in the North at last, what a fresh and happy sensation it must be to get up in the morning in that pure unbreathed air, with the feeling that he has nothing to do,—nothing, at any rate, except what he chooses; and after the deliberately-eaten breakfast, to saunter forth with the delightful sense of leisure,—to know that he has time to breathe and think after the ceaseless hurry of the past months,—and to know that nothing will go wrong although he should sit down on the mossy parapet of the little one-arched bridge that spans the brawling mountain-stream, and there rest, and muse, and dream just as long as he likes! Two or three such men come to this neighbourhood yearly; and I enjoy the sight of them, they look so happy. Every little thing, if they indeed be genial, true, unstiffened men, is a source of interest to them. The total change makes them grow rapturous about matters which we, who are quite accustomed to them, take more coolly. I think, when I look at them, of the truthful lines of Gray :—

> See the wretch, that long has tost
>   On the thorny bed of pain, '
> At length repair his vigour lost,
>   And breathe and walk again :
> The meanest flow'ret of the vale,
> The simplest note that swells the gale,
> The common sun, the air, the skies,
> To him are opening paradise.

Equidem invideo, a little. I feel somewhat vexed when I think how much more beautiful these pleasant scenes around me really are, than what, by any effort,

I can make them seem to me. You hard-wrought town-folk, when you come to rural regions, have the advantage of us leisurely country-people.

But, much as that great Queen's Counsel enjoys his long vacation's play, you see it is not enough. Look how thin his hair is, how pale his cheeks are, how fleshless those long fingers, how unmuscular those arms. What he needs, in addition to the autumn holiday, is some *bonâ fide* play every day of his life. What is his amusement when in town? Why, mainly it consists of going into society, where he gains nothing of elasticity and vigour, but merely injures his diges-tive organs. Why does he not rather have half-an-hour's lively bodily exercise,—rowing, or quoits, or tennis, or skating, or anything he may have taste for? And if it be foolish to take all the year's play at once, as so many intellectual workers think to do, much more foolish is it to keep all the play of life till the work is over : to toil and moil at business through all the better years of our time in this world, in the hope that at length we shall be able to retire from business, and make the evening of life all holiday, all play. In all likelihood the man who takes this course will never retire at all, except into an untimely grave ; and if he should live to reach the long-coveted retreat, he will find that all play and no work makes life quite as wearisome and as little enjoyable as all work and no play. *Ennui* will make him miserable ; and body and mind, deprived of their wonted occupation, will soon break down. After very hard and long-continued work, there is indeed a pleasure in merely sitting still and doing nothing.   But after the feeling of pure exhaustion is gone, *that* will not suffice. A boy enjoys play, but he is miserable in enforced idleness.   In writing about retiring from the task-work of life, one naturally thinks of that letter to Wordsworth, in which Charles Lamb told what he felt when he was finally emancipated from his drudgery in the India House :—

"I came home FOR EVER on Tuesday week. The incomprehensibleness of my condition overwhelmed me. It was like passing from life into eternity. Every year to be as long as three ; that is, to have three times as much real time—time that is my own—in it ! I wandered about thinking I was happy, and feeling I was not. But that tumultuousness is passing off, and I begin to understand the nature of the gift. Holidays, even the annual month, were always uneasy joys, with their conscious fugitiveness, the craving after making the most of them. Now, when all is holiday, there are no holidays. I can sit at home, in rain or shine, without a restless impulse for walkings."

There are unhappy beings in the world, who secretly stand in fear of all play, on the hateful and wicked notion, which I believe some men regard as being of the essence of Christianity, though in truth it is its contradiction, that everything pleasant is sinful,—that God dislikes to see His creatures cheerful and happy. I think it is the author of *Friends in Council* who says something to the effect, that many people, infected with that Puritan falsehood, slink about creation, afraid to confess that they ever are enjoying themselves. It is a sad thing when such a belief is entertained by even grown-up men; but it stirs me to absolute fury when I know of it being impressed upon poor little children, to repress their natural gaiety of heart. Did you ever, my reader, read that dreary and preposterous book in which Thomas Clarkson sought to shew that Quakerism is not inconsistent with common sense? Probably not; but perhaps you may have met with Jeffrey's review of it. Nothing short of a vehement kicking could relieve my feelings if I heard some sly, money-making old rascal impressing upon some merry children that

"Stillness and quietness both of spirit and body are necessary, as far as they can be obtained. Hence, Quaker children are rebuked for all expressions of anger, as tending to raise those feelings which ought to be suppressed; a raising even of the voice beyond due bounds is discouraged, as leading to the disturbance of their minds. They are taught to rise in the morning in quietness; to go about their ordinary occupations with quietness; and with quietness to retire to their beds."

Can you think of more complete flying in the face of the purposes of the kind Creator? Is it not His manifest intention that childhood should be the time of merry laughter, of gaiety, and shouts, and noise? There is not a sadder sight than that of a little child prematurely subdued and "quiet." Let me know of any drab-coated humbug impressing such ideas on any child of mine; and though from circumstances I cannot personally see him put under the pump, I know certain quarters in which it is only needful to drop a very faint hint, in order to have him first pumped upon, and then tarred and feathered.

But there is another class of mortals, who are free from the Puritan principle, and who have no objection to amusement for themselves, but who seem to have no notion that their inferiors and their servants ought ever to do anything but work. The reader will remember the fashionable governess in *The Old Curiosity Shop*, who insisted that only genteel children should ever be permitted to play. The well-known lines of Dr Isaac Watts,—

> "In books, or work, or healthful play,
> Let my first years be pass'd,"—

were applicable, she maintained, only to the children of families of the wealthier sort : while for poor children there must be a new reading, which she improvised as follows :—

> "In work, work, work. In work alway,
> Let my first years be pass'd,
> That I may give, for every day,
> Some good account at last."

And as for domestic servants, poor creatures, I fear there is many a house in which there is no provision whatever made for play for them. There can be no drearier round of life than that to which their employers destine them. From the moment they rise, hours before any member of the family, to the moment when they return to bed, it is one constant push of sordid labour,—often in chambers to which air and light and cheerfulness can never come. And if they ask a rare holiday, what a fuss is made about it! Now, what is the result of all this? Some poor solitary beings do actually sink into the spiritless drudges which such a life tends to make them: but the greater number feel that they cannot live with all work and no play; and as they cannot get play openly, they get it secretly: they go out at night, when you, their mistress, are asleep; or they bring in their friends at those unseasonable hours: they get that amusement and recreation on the sly, and with the sense that they are doing wrong and deceiving, which they ought to be permitted to have openly and honestly: and thus you break down their moral principle, you train them to cheat you, you educate them into liars and thieves. Of course, your servants thus regard you as their natural enemy: it is fair to take any advantage you can of a gaoler: you are their task-imposer, their driver, their gaoler,—anything but their friend; and if they can take advantage of you in any way, they will. And serve you right.

I have known injudicious clergymen who did all they could to discourage the games and sports of their parishioners. They could not prevent them; but one thing they did,—they made them disreputable. They made sure that the poor man who ran in a sack, or climbed a greased pole, felt that thereby he was forfeiting his character, perhaps imperilling his salvation:

and so he thought that having gone so far, he might go the full length: and thus he got drunk, got into a fight, thrashed his wife, smashed his crockery, and went to the lock-up. How much better it would have been had the clergyman sought to regulate these amusements; and since they *would* go on, try to make sure that they should go creditably and decently! Thus, poor folk might have been cheerful without having their conscience stinging them all the time: and let it be remembered, that if you pervert a man's moral sense (which you may quite readily do with the uneducated classes) into fancying that it is wicked to use the right hand or the right foot, while the man still goes on using the right hand and the right foot, you do him an irreparable mischief: you bring on a temper of moral recklessness; and help him a considerable step toward the gallows. Since people must have amusement, and will have amusement, for any sake do not get them to think that amusement is wicked. You cannot keep them from finding recreation of some sort: you may drive them to find it at a lower level, and to partake of it soured by remorse, and by the wretched resolution that they will have it right or wrong. Instead of anathematising all play, sympathise with it genially and heartily; and say, with kind-hearted old Burton—

"Let the world have their May-games, wakes, Whitsunales; their dancings and concerts; their puppet-shows, hobby-horses, tabors, bagpipes, balls, barley-breaks, and whatever sports and recreations please them best, provided they be followed with discretion."

Let it be here remarked, that recreation can be fully enjoyed only by the man who has some earnest occupation. The end of work is to enjoy leisure; but to enjoy leisure you must have gone through work. Play-time must come after school-time, otherwise it loses its savour. Play, after all, is a relative thing; it is not a thing which has an absolute existence. There is no such thing as play, except to the worker. It comes out by contrast. Put white upon white, and you can hardly see it: put white upon black, and how plain it is. Light your lamp in the sunshine, and it is nothing: you must have darkness round it to make its presence felt. And besides this, a great part of the enjoyment of recreation consists in the feeling that we have earned it by previous hard work. One goes out for the afternoon walk with a light heart when one has done a good task since breakfast. It is one thing for a dawdling idler to set off to the Continent or to the Highlands, just because he is sick of everything around him; and quite another thing when a hard-wrought man, who is of some use in life, sets off, as gay as a lark, with the pleasant feeling that he has brought some worthy work to an end, on the selfsame tour. And then a busy man finds a relish in simple recreations; while a man who has nothing to do finds all things wearisome, and thinks that life is "used up:" it takes something quite out of the way to tickle that indurated palate : you might as well think to prick the hide of a hippopotamus with a needle, as to excite the interest of that *blasé* being by any amusement which is not highly spiced with the cayenne of vice. And *that*, certainly, has a powerful effect. It was a glass of water the wicked old Frenchwoman was drinking when she said, " Oh that this were a sin, to give it a relish !"

So it is worth while to work, if it were only that we might enjoy play. Thus doth Mr Heliogabalus, my next neighbour, who is a lazy man and an immense glutton, walk four miles every afternoon of his life. It is not that he hates exertion less, but that he loves dinner more ; and the latter cannot be enjoyed unless the former is endured. And the man whose disposition is the idlest may be led to labour when he finds that labour is his only chance of finding any enjoyment in life. James Montgomery sums up much truth in a couple of lines in his *Pelican Island*, which run thus :—

> "Labour, the symbol of man's punishment ;
> Labour, the secret of man's happiness."

Why on earth do people think it fine to be idle and useless ? Fancy a drone superciliously desiring a working bee to stand aside, and saying, " Out of the way, you miserable drudge ; *I* never made a drop of honey in all my life !" I have observed too, that some silly people are ashamed that it should be known that they are so useful as they really are, and take pains to represent themselves as more helpless, ignorant, and incapable than the fact. I have heard a weak old lady boast that her grown-up daughters were quite unable to fold up their own dresses ; and that as for ordering dinner, they had not a notion of such a thing. This and many similar particulars were stated with no small exultation, and that by a person far from rich, and equally far from aristocratic. "What a silly old woman you are!" was my silent reflection ; " and if your daughters really are what you represent them, woe betide the poor man who shall marry one of the incapable young noodles!" Give me the man, I say, who can turn his hand to all things, and who is not ashamed to confess that he can do so ; who can preach a sermon, nail up a paling, prune a fruit-tree, make a water-wheel or a kite for his little boy, write an article for *Fraser* or a leader for the *Times* or the *Saturday Review*. What a fine, genial, many-sided life did Sydney Smith lead at his Yorkshire parish! I should have liked, I own, to have found in it more traces of the clergyman ; but perhaps the biographer thought it better not to parade these. And in the regard of facing all difficulties with a cheerful heart, and nobly resolving to be useful and helpful in little matters as well as big, I think that life was as good a sermon as ever was preached from pulpit.

I have already said, in the course of this rambling discussion, that recreation must be such as shall turn the thoughts into a new channel, otherwise it is no recreation at all. And walking, which is the most usual physical exercise, here completely fails. Walking has grown by long habit a purely automatic act, demanding no attention : we think all the time we are walking ; Southey even read while he took his daily walk. But Southey's story is a fearful warning. It will do a clergyman no good whatever to leave his desk and to go forth for his *constitutional,* if he is still thinking of his sermon, and trying to see his way through the treatment of his text. You see in Gray's famous poem how little use is the mere walk to the contemplative man, how thoroughly it falls short of the end of play.. You see how the hectic lad who is supposed to have written the *Elegy* employed himself when he wandered abroad :—

> "There, at the foot of yonder nodding beech,
>   That wreathes its old fantastic roots so high,
> His listless length at noontide would he stretch,
>   And pore upon the brook that babbles by.
>
> "Hard by yon wood, now smiling as in scorn,
>   Muttering his wayward fancies, he would rove ;
> Now drooping, woful, wan, like one forlorn,
>   Or crazed with care, or cross'd in hopeless love."

That was the fashion in which the poor fellow took his daily recreation and exercise! His mother no doubt packed him out to take a bracing walk ; she ought to have set him to saw wood for the fire, or to dig in the garden, or to clean the door-handles if he had muscle for nothing more. These things would have distracted his thoughts from their grand flights, and prevented his mooning about in that listless manner. Of course while walking he was bothering away about the poetical trash he had in his desk at home ; and so he knocked up his ganglionic functions, he encouraged tubercles on his lungs, and came to furnish matter for the "hoary-headed swain's" narrative, the silly fellow !

Riding is better than walking, especially if you have a rather skittish steed, who compels you to attend to him on pain of being landed in the ditch, or sent, meteor-like, over the hedge. The elder Disraeli has preserved the memory of the diversions in which various hard thinkers found relaxation. Petavius, who wrote a deeply learned book, which I never saw, and which no one I ever saw ever heard of, twirled round his chair for five minutes every two hours that he was at work. Samuel Clarke used to leap over the tables and chairs. It was a rule which Ignatius Loyola imposed on his followers, that after two hours of work, the mind should always be unbent by some recreation. Every one has heard of Paley's remarkable feats of rapid horsemanship. Hundreds of times did that great man fall off. The Sultan Mahomet, who conquered Greece, unbent his mind by carving wooden spoons. In all these things you see, kindly reader, that true recreation was aimed at: that is, entire change of thought and occupation. Izaak Walton, again, who sets forth so pleasantly the praise of angling as the "Contemplative Man's Recreation," wrongly thinks to recommend the gentle craft by telling us that the angler may think all the while he plies it. I do not care for angling; I never caught a minnow; but still I joy in good old Izaak's pleasant pages, like thousands who do not care a pin for fishing, but who feel it like a cool retreat into green fields and trees to turn to his genial feeling and hearty pictures of quiet English scenery. He, however, had a vast opinion of the joys of angling in a pleasant country: only let him go quietly a-fishing—

> "And if contentment be a stranger then,
>   I'll ne'er look for it, but in heaven, again."

And he repeats with much approval the sentiments of "Jo. Davors, Esq.," in whose lines we may see much more of scenery than of the actual fishing :—

> "Let me live harmlessly; and near the brink
>   Of Trent or Avon have a dwelling-place,
> Where I may see my quill or cork down sink,
>   With eager bite of perch, or bleak, or dace :
> And on the world and my Creator think :
>   While some men strive ill-gotten goods to embrace ;
> And others spend their time in base excess
> Of wine, or worse, in war and wantonness.

> "Let them that list, these pastimes still pursue,
>   And on such pleasing fancies feed their fill ;
> So I the fields and meadows green may view,
>   And daily by fresh rivers walk at will,
> Among the daisies and the violets blue,
>   Red hyacinth and yellow daffodil ;
> Purple narcissus like the morning's rays,
> Pale gander-grass, and azure culver-keys.

> "All these, and many more of His creation,
>   That made the heavens, the angler oft doth see;
> Taking therein no little delectation,
>   To think how strange, how wonderful they be!
> Framing thereof an inward contemplation,
>   To set his heart from other fancies free:
> And whilst he looks on these with joyful eye,
> His mind is rapt above the starry sky."

Who shall say that the *terza-rima* stanza was not written in English fluently and gracefully, before the days of Whistlecraft and *Don Juan?*

If thou desirest, reader, to find a catalogue of sports from which thou mayest select that which likes thee best, turn up Burton's *Anatomy of Melancholy*, or Joseph Strutt's *Sports and Pastimes of the People of England.* There mayest thou read of *Rural Exercises practised by Persons of Rank*, of *Rural Exercises Generally practised:* (note how ingeniously Strutt puts the case: he does not say practised by Snobs, or the Lower Orders, or the Mobocracy.) Next are *Pastimes Exercised in Towns and Cities;* and finally, *Domestic Amusements*, and *Pastimes Appropriated to particular Seasons.* Were it not that my paper is verging to its close, I could surprise thee with a vast display of curious erudition; but I must content myself with having laid down the conditions which all true play must fulfil; and let every man choose the kind of play which hits his peculiar taste. There never has been in England any lack of sports in nominal existence: I heartily wish they were all (except the cruel ones of baiting and torturing animals) still kept up. The following lines are from a little book published in the reign of James I. :—

> "Man, I dare challenge thee to Throw the Sledge,
>   To Jump or Leape over ditch or hedge :
>   To Wrastle, play at Stooleball, or to Runne,
>   To Pitch the Barre, or to shoote off a Gunne :
>   To play at Loggetts, Nine Holes, or Ten Pinnes,
>   To try it out at Football by the shinnes :
>   At Ticktack, Irish Noddie, Maw, and Ruffe,
>   At Hot Cockles, Leapfrog, or Blindmanbuffe :
>   To drink half-pots, or deale at the whole canne,
>   To play at Base, or Pen and ynkhorne Sir Jan :
>   To daunce the Morris, play at Barley-breake,
>   At all exploytes a man can think or speak :
>   At Shove-Groate, Venterpoynt, or Crosse and Pile,
>   At Beshrow him that's last at yonder Style :
>   At leaping o'er a Midsommer-bon-fier,
>   Or at the Drawing Dun out of the Myer."

In most agricultural districts it is wonderful how little play there is in the life of the labouring class. Well may the agricultural labourer be called a "working man," for truly he does little else than work. His eating and sleeping are cut down to the *minimum* that shall suffice to keep him in trim for working. And the consequence is, that when he does get a holiday, he does not know what to make of himself; and in too many cases he spends it in getting drunk. I know places where the working men have no idea of any play, of any recreation, except getting drunk. And if their overwrought wives, who must nurse five or six children, prepare the meals, tidy the house,—

in fact, do the work which occupies three or four servants in the house of the poorest gentleman,—if the poor overwrought creatures can contrive to find a blink of leisure through their waking hours, they know how to make no nobler use of it than to gossip, rather ill-naturedly, about their neighbours' affairs, and especially to discuss the domestic arrangements of the squire and the parson.   Working men and women too frequently have forgotten how to play.   It is so long since they did it, and they have so little heart for it. And God knows that the pressure of constant care, and the wolf kept barely at arm's length from the door, do leave little heart for it: O wealthy proprietors of land, you who have so much in your power, try to infuse something of joy and cheerfulness into the lot of your humble neighbours!   Read and ponder the essay and the conversation on *Recreation*, which you will find in the first volume of *Friends in Council.* And read again, I trust for the hundredth time, the poem from which I quote the lines which follow.   Let me say here, that I verily believe some of my readers will not know the source whence I draw these lines. More is the shame : but longer experience of life is giving me a deep conviction of the astonishing ignorance of my fellow-creatures.   I shall not tell them. They shall have the mortification of asking their friends the question.   Only let it be added, that the poem where the passage stands contains others more sweet and touching by far,—so sweet and touching that in

all the range of English poetry they have never been
surpassed :—

> "How often have I blest the coming day,
>   When toil remitting lent its turn to play;
>   And all the village train, from labour free,
>   Led up their sports beneath the spreading tree,
>   While many a pastime circled in the shade,
>   The young contending as the old survey'd;
>   And many a gambol frolick'd o'er the ground,
>   And sleights of art and feats of strength went round.
>   And still, as each repeated pleasure tired,
>   Succeeding sports the mirthful band inspired :
>   The dancing pair that simply sought renown,
>   By holding out to tire each other down,—
>   The swain mistrustless of his smutted face,
>   While secret laughter titter'd round the place,—
>   The bashful virgin's sidelong looks of love,
>   The matron's glance that would those looks reprove;—
>   These were thy charms, sweet village, sports like these,
>   With sweet succession, taught even toil to please."

CHAPTER V.

ONCE upon a time, I lived in the very heart of London : absolutely in Threadneedle Street. I lived in the house of a near relation, an opulent lawyer, who, after he had become a rich man, chose still to dwell in the locality where he had made his fortune. All around, for miles in every direction, there were nothing but piles of houses—streets and lanes of dingy brick houses everywhere. Not a vestige of nature could be seen, except in the sky above, in the stunted vegetation of a few little City gardens, and in the foul and discoloured river. The very surface of the earth, for yards in depth, was the work of generations that had lived and died centuries before amid the narrow lanes of the ancient city. There, for months together, I, a boy without youth, under the care of one who, though substantially kind, had not a vestige of sympathy with nature or with home affections, wearily counted the days which were to pass before the yearly visit to a home far away. I cannot by any words express the thirst and craving which I then felt for green fields and trees. The very name of *the country* was like music in my ear; and when I heard any man say he was *going down to the country*, how I envied him! It was not so bad in winter: though even then the clear frosty days called up many pictures of cheerful winter skies away from those weary streets ;—of boughs bending beneath the quiet snow ;—of the beautiful fretwork of the frost upon the hedges and the grass, and of its exhilarating crispness in the air ;—of the stretches of the frozen river, seen through the leafless boughs, covered with happy groups whose merry faces were like a good-natured defiance of the wintry weather. But when the spring revival began to make itself felt, when the days began to lengthen, and the poor shrubs in the squares to bud, and when there was that accession of light during the day which is so cheerful after the winter gloom, then the longing for the country grew painfully strong, like the seaman's calenture, or the Swiss exile's yearning for his native hills. When I knew that the hawthorn hedges were white, and the fruit-trees laden with blossoms, how I longed to be among them! I well remember the kindly feeling I bore to a dingy hostelry in a narrow lane off Cheapside, for the sake of its name. It was called *Blossom's Inn;* and many a time I turned out of my way, and stood looking up at its sign, with eyes that saw a very different scene from the blackened walls. I remember how I used to rise at early morning, and take long walks in whatever direction I thought it possible that a glimpse of anything like the country could be seen : away up the New North Road there were some trees, and some little plots of grass.   There was something at once pleasing and sad about those curious little gardens which still exist here and there in the heart of London, consisting generally of a plot of grass of a dozen yards in length and breadth, surrounded by a walk of yellow gravel, stared at on every side by the back windows of tall brick houses, and containing a few little trees, whose leaves in spring look so strangely fresh against the smoke-blackened branches.   I do not wish to be egotistical ; and I describe all these feelings merely because I believe that honestly to tell exactly what one has himself felt, is the true way to describe the common feelings of most people in like circumstances. I dare say that if any youth of sixteen, pent up in Threadneedle Street now, should happen to read what I have written, he will understand it all with a hearty sympathy which I shall not succeed in exciting in the minds of many of my readers.   But such a one will know, thoroughly and completely, what pictures rise before the mind's eye of one pent up amid miles of brick walls and stone pavements, at the mention of the country, of trees, hedge-rows, fields, quiet lanes and footpaths, and simple rustic people.

I wish to assure the man, shut up in a great city, that he has compensations and advantages of which he probably does not think.   The keenness of his relish for country scenes, the intensity of his enjoyment of his occasional glimpses of them, counter-balance in a great degree the fact that his glimpses of them are but few. I live in the country now, and have done so for several years. It is a beautiful district of country too, and amid a quiet and simple population; yet I must confess that my youthful notion of rural bliss is a good deal abated. "Use lessons marvel," it is said: one cannot be always in raptures about what one sees every hour of every day. It is the man in populous cities pent, who knows the value of green fields. It is your Cockney (I mean your educated Londoner) who reads *Bracebridge Hall* with the keenest delight, and luxuriates in the thought of country scenes, country houses, country life. He has not come close enough to discern the flaws and blemishes of the picture; and he has not learned by experience that in whatever scenes led, human life is always much the same thing. I have long since found that the country, in this nineteenth century, is by no means a scene of Arcadian innocence;—that its apparent simplicity is sometimes dogged stupidity;—that men lie and cheat in the country just as much as in the town, and that the country has even more of mischievous tittle-tattle;—that sorrow and care and anxiety may quite well live in Elizabethan cottages grown over with honeysuckle and jasmine, and that very sad eyes may look forth from windows round which roses twine. The poets (town poets, no doubt) were drawing upon their imagination, when they told how "Virtue lives in Irwan's Vale," and how "with peace and plenty there, lives the happy villager." Virtue and religion are plants of difficult growth, even in the country; and notwithstanding Cowper's exquisite poem, I am not sure that "the calm retreat, the silent shade, with prayer and praise agree" better than the closet into which the weary man may enter, in the quiet evening, after the business and bustle of the town. People may pace up and down a country lane, between fragrant hedges of blossoming hawthorn, and tear their neighbours' characters to very shreds. And the eye that is sharp to see the minutest object on the hillside far away, may be blind to the beauty which is spread over all the landscape. Nor is the country always in the trim holiday dress which delights the summer wayfarer. Country roads are not all nicely grávelled walks between edges of clipped box, or through velvety turf, shaven by weekly mowings. There are many days on which the country looks, to any one without a most decided taste for it, extremely bleak and drear. The roads are puddles of mud, which will search its way through boots to which art has supplied soles of two inches' thickness. The deciduous trees are shivering skeletons, bending before the howling blast. The sheep paddle about the brown fields, eating turnips mingled with clay. Now, for myself, I like all that: but a man from the town would not. I positively enjoy the wet, blustering afternoon, with its raw wind, its driving sleet, its roads of mud. How delightful the rapid "constitutional" from half-past two till half-past four, with the comfortable feeling that we have accomplished a good forenoon's work at our desk, (sermon or article, as the case may be,) and with the cheerful prospect of getting rid of all these sloppy garments, and feeling so snug and clean ere we sit down to dinner, when we shall hear the rain and wind softened into music through the warm crimson drapery of our windows; and then the evening of leisure amid books and music, with the *placens uxor* on the other easy-chair by the fireside, and the little children, screaming with delight, tumbling about one's knees. So I like even the gusty, rainy afternoon, for the sake of all that it suggests to me. Nor will the true inhabitant of the country forget the delight with which he has hailed a gloomy, drizzling November day, when he has evergreen shrubs to transplant. Have I not stood for hours, in a state of active and sensible enjoyment, watching how the hollies and yews and laurels gradually clothed some bare spot or unsightly corner, rejoicing that the calm air and ceaseless mizzle, which made my attendants and myself like soaked sponges, was life to these stout shoots and these bright hearty green leaves! But a town man does not understand all these things; and I have no doubt that on one of these January days, when the entire distant prospect—hills, sky, trees, fields—might be faithfully depicted on canvas by different shades of Indian ink, he would see nothing in the prospect but gloom and desolation.

Then it is very picturesque to see the ploughman at work on a soft, mild winter day. It is a beautiful contrast, that light brown of the turned-over earth, and the fresh green of the remainder of the field ; and what more pleasing than these lines of furrow, so beautifully straight and regular? But go up and walk by the ploughman's side, you man from town, and see how you like it. You will find it awfully dirty work. In a few minutes you will find it difficult to drag along your feet, laden with some pounds weight to each of adherent earth ; and you will have formed some idea of the physical exertion, and the constant attention, which the ploughman needs, to keep his furrow straight and even, to retain the plough the right depth in the ground, and to manage his horses. Hard work for that poor fellow ; and ill-paid work. No horse, mule, donkey, camel, or other beast of labour in the world, goes through so much exertion, in proportion to his strength, between sunrise and sunset, as does that rational being, all to earn the humblest shelter and the poorest fare that will maintain bare life. You walk beside him, and see how poorly he is dressed. His feet have been wet since six o'clock A.M., when he went half-a-mile from his cottage up to the stables of the farm to dress his horses; he has had a little tea and coarse bread, and nothing more, for his dinner at twelve o'clock, (I speak from personal knowledge :) he will have nothing more till his twelve (I have known it fifteen) hours of work are finished, when he will have his scanty supper: and while he is walking backwards and forwards all day, his mind is not so engaged but that he has abundant time to think of his little home anxieties, which are not little to him, though they may be nothing, my reader, to you—of the ailing wife at home, for whom the doctor orders wine which he cannot buy, and of the children, poorly fed, and barely clad, and hardly at all educated, born to the same life of toil and penury as himself. I know nothing about political economy; I have not understanding for it ; and I feel glad, when I think of the social evils I see, that the responsibility of treating them rests upon abler heads than mine. Neither do I know how much truth there may be in the stories. of which I hear the echoes from afar, of the occasional privation and oppression of the manufacturing poor, against which, as it seems to me, these unhappy strikes and trades' unions are their helpless and frantic appeal. But I can say, from my own knowledge of the condition of our agricultural population, that sometimes men bearing the character of reputable farmers practise as great tyranny and cruelty towards their labourers and cottars, under a pure sky and amid beautiful scenery, as ever disgraced the ugly and smoky factory town, where such things seem more in keeping with the locality.

Yet, though in a gloomy mood, one can easily make out a long catalogue of country evils,—evils which I know cannot be escaped in a fallen world, and among a sinful race,—still I thank God that my lot is cast in the country. I know, indeed, that the town contains at once the best and the worst of mankind. In the country, we are, intellectually and morally, a sort of middling species; we do not present the extremes, either in good or evil, which are to be found in the hot-house atmosphere of great cities. There is no reasoning with tastes, as every one knows; but to some men there is, at every season, an indescribable charm about a country life. I like to know all about the people around me; and I do not care though in return they know all, and more than all, about me. I like the audible stillness in which one lives on autumn days; the murmur of the wind through trees even when leafless, and the brawl of the rivulet even when swollen and brown. There is a constant source of innocent pleasure and interest in little country cares, in planting and tending trees and flowers, in sympathising with one's horses and dogs,—even with pigs and poultry. And although one may have lived beyond middle age without the least idea that he had any taste for such matters, it is amazing how soon he will find, when he comes to call a country home his own, that the taste has only been latent, kept down by circumstances, and ready to spring into vigorous existence whenever the repressing circumstances are removed. Men in whom this is not so, are the exception to the universal rule. Take the Senior Wrangler from his college, and put him down in a pretty country parsonage; and in a few weeks he will take kindly to training honeysuckle and climbing roses, he will find scope for his mathematics in laying out a flower-garden, and he will be all excitement in planning and carrying out an evergreen shrubbery, a primrose bank, a winding walk, a little stream with a tiny waterfall, spanned by a rustic bridge. Proud he will be of that piece of engineering, as ever was Robert Stephenson when he had spanned the stormy Menai. There is something in all this simple work that makes a man kind-hearted: out-of-door occupation of this sort gives one much more cheerful views of men and things, and disposes one to sympathise heartily with the cottager proud of his little rose-plots, and of his enormous gooseberry that attained to renown in the pages of the county newspaper. I do not say anything of the incalculable advantage to health which arises from this pleasant intermingling of mental and physical occupation in the case of the recluse scholar; nor of the animated rebound with which one lays down the pen or closes the volume, and hastens out to the total change of interest which is found in the open air; nor of the evening at mental work again, but with the lungs that play so freely, the head that feels so cool and clear, the hand so firm and ready, testifying that we have not forgotten the grand truth that to care for bodily health and condition is a Christian duty, bringing with its due discharge an immediate and sensible blessing. I am sure that the poor man who comes to ask a favour of his parish clergyman, has a far better chance of finding a kind and unhurried hearing, if he finds him of an afternoon superintending his labourers, rosy with healthful exercise, delighted with the good effect which has been produced by some little improvement—the deviation of a walk, the placing of an araucaria—than if he found the parson a bilious, dyspeptic, splenetic, gloomy, desponding, morose, misanthropic, horrible animal, with knitted brow and jarring nerves, lounging in his easy-chair before the fire, and afraid to go out into the fine clear air, for fear (unhappy wretch) of getting a sore throat or a bad cough. I remember to have read somewhere of an humble philanthropist who undertook the reformation of a number of juvenile thieves; and for that end employed them in a large garden somewhere near London, to raise vegetables and flowers for the market. There did the youthful prig concentrate his thoughts on the planting of cabbage, and find the unwonted delight of a day spent in innocent labour; there did the area-sneak bud the rose and set the potato; and there, as days passed on, under the gentle influence of vegetable nature, did a healthier, happier, purer tone come over the spiritual nature, even as a healthier blood came to heart and veins. The philanthropist was a true philosopher. There is not a more elevating and purifying occupation than that of tending the plants of the earth. I should never be afraid of finding a man revengeful, malignant, or cruel, whom I knew to be fond of his shrubs and flowers. And I believe that in the mind of most men of cultivation, there is some vague, undefined sense that the country is the scene where human life attains its happiest development. I believe that the great proportion of such men cherish the hope, perhaps a distant and faint one, that at some time they shall possess a country home, where they may pass the last years tranquilly, far from the tumult of cities. Many of those who cherish such a hope will never realise it; and many more are quite unsuited for enjoying a country life were it within their reach. But all this is founded upon the instinctive desire there is in human nature to possess some portion of the earth's suface. You look with indescribable interest at an acre of ground which is your own. There is something quite remarkable about your own trees. You have a sense of property in the sunset over your own hills. And there is a perpetual pleasure in the sight of a fair landscape, seen from your own door. Do not believe people who say that all scenes soon become indifferent, through being constantly seen. An ugly street may cease to be a vexation, when you get accustomed to it; but a pleasant prospect becomes even more pleasant, when the beauty which arises from your own associations with it is added to that which is properly its own. No doubt, you do grow weary of the landscape before your windows, when you are spending a month at some place of temporary sojourn, seaside or inland; but it is quite different with that which surrounds your own home. You do not try *that* by so exacting a standard. You never think of calling your constant residence dull, though it may be quiet to a degree which would make you think a place insupportably dull, to which you were paying a week's visit.

What an immense variety of human dwellings are comprised within the general name of the Country Home! We begin with such places as Chatsworth and Belvoir, Arundel and Alnwick, Hamilton and Drumlanrig: houses standing far withdrawn within encircling woods, approached by avenues of miles in length, which debouch on public highways in districts of country quite remote from one another; with acres of conservatory, and scores of miles of walks; and shutting in their sacred precincts by great park walls from the approach and the view of an obtrusive world beyond. We think of the old Edwardian Castle, weather-worn and grim, with drawbridge and portcullis and moat and oak-roofed hall and storied windows; of the huge, square, corniced, many-chimneyed, ugly building of the renaissance, which never has anything to recommend its aspect except when it gains a dignity

from enormous size; then down through the classes
of manor-houses, abbeys, and halls, high-gabled, oriel-
windowed, turret-staired, long-corridored, haunted-
chambered; with their parks, greater or less, their oaken
clumps, their spreading horse-chestnuts, their sunshiny
glades, their startled deer; till we come to the villa
with a few acres of ground, such as Dean Swift wished
for himself, with its modest conservatory, its neat little
shrubbery, its short carriage drive, its brougham or
phaeton drawn by one stout horse. Then, upon the
outskirts of the country town, we find a class of less
ambitious dwellings, which yet struggle for the title of
villa—cheap would-be Gothic houses, with overhanging eaves and latticed windows, standing in a half-acre
plot of ground, which yet is large enough to give a
new direction to the tradesman's thoughts, by giving
him space to cultivate a few shrubs and flowers. Last
comes the wayside cottage, sometimes neat and pretty,
often cold, damp, and ugly; sometimes gay with its
little plot of flowers, sometimes odorous with its neighbouring dung-heap; the difference depending not half
so much upon the income enjoyed by its tenant, as
upon his having a tidy, active wife, and a kindly, improving, generous landlord.

And various as the varied dwellings are the scenes
amid which they stand. In rich English dales, in
wild Highland glens, on the bank of quiet inland
rivers, and on windy cliffs frowning over the ocean—
there, and in a thousand other places, we have still

the country home, with its peculiar characteristics. Thither comes the postman only once a day, always anxiously, often nervously expected: and thither the box of books, the magazines of last month, and the reviews of last quarter, sent from the reading-club in the High Street of the town five miles off. How truly, by the way, has somebody or other stated that the next town and the railway station are always five miles away from every country house! Thither the carrier, three times a-week, brings the wicker-woven box of bread; there does the managing housewife have her store-room, round whose shelves are arranged groceries of every sort and degree; and there, at uncertain intervals, dies the home-fed sheep or pig, which yieldeth joints which are pronounced far superior to any which the butcher's shop ever supplied. There, sometimes, is found the cheerful, modest establishment, calculated rather within the income, with everything comfortable, neat, and even elegant; where family dinners may be enjoyed which afford real satisfaction to all, and win the approval of even the most refined *gourmet;* and there sometimes, especially when the mistress of the house is a fool, is found the unhappy scramble of the *ménage* that, with a thousand a-year, aims at aping five thousand; where there is a French ladies'-maid of cracked reputation, and a lady who talks largely of "what she has been accustomed to," and "what she regards herself as entitled to;" where every-day comfort is sacrificed to occasional attempts at showy entertainments, to which the neighbouring peer goes under the pressure of a most urgent invitation ; where gooseberry champagne and very acid claret flow in hospitable profusion ; and where dressed-up stable-boys and ploughmen dash wildly up against each other, as the uneasy banquet strains anxiously along.

Very incomplete would be any attempt at classifying the country homes of Britain, in which no mention should be made of the dwellings of the clergy. In this country, the parish priest is not isolated from all sympathy with the members of his flock by an enforced celibacy ; he is not only the spiritual guide of his parishioners, but he is in most instances the head of a family, the cultivator of the ground, the owner of horses, cows, sheep, pigs, and dogs. I do not deny that in theory, and once perhaps in a thousand times in practice, it is a finer thing that the clergyman should be one given exclusively to his sacred calling, standing apart from and elevated above the little prosaic cares of life, and "having his conversation in heaven." It seems at first as if it better befitted one who has to be much exercised in sacred thoughts and duties—whose hands are to dispense the sacred emblems of Communion, and whose voice is to breathe direction and comfort into dying ears—to have nothing to do with such sublunary matters as seeing a cold bandage put upon a horse's foreleg, or arranging for the winter supply of hay, or considering as to laying in store of coals at the setting in of snowy weather. It jars somewhat upon our imagination of the even run of that holy calling, to think of the parson (like Sydney Smith) proudly producing his lemon-bag, or devising his patent Tantalus and his universal scratcher. But surely all this is a wrong view of things. Surely it is Platonism rather than Christianity to hold that there is anything necessarily debasing or materialising about the cares of daily life. All these cares take their character from the spirit with which we pass through them. The simple French monk, five hundred years since, who acted as cook to his brethren, indicated the clergyman's true path when he wrote, "I put my little egg-cake on the fire for the sake of Christ;" and George Herbert, more gracefully, has shewn how, as the eye may either look *on* glass, or look *through* it, we may look no further than the daily task, or may look through it to something nobler beyond :

> "Teach me, my God and King,
>   In all things Thee to see :
> And what I do in anything,
>   To do it as for Thee.
>
> "A servant with this clause
>   Makes drudgery divine :
> Who sweeps a room, as for Thy laws,
>   Makes that, and the action, fine."

We have all in our mind some abstracted and idealised picture of what the country parsonage, as well as the country parson, should be : the latter, the clergyman and the gentleman : the former, the fit abode for him and his; near the church, not too much retired from the public way, old and ivied, of course Gothic, with bay windows, fantastic gables, wreathed chimneys, and overhanging eaves; with many evergreens, with ancient trees; with peaches ripening on the sunny garden wall, with an indescribable calm and peacefulness over the whole, deepened by the chime of the passing river, and the windy caw of the distant rookery; such should the country parsonage be. But the best of anything is not the commonest of the class : and I can only add that I believe it would afford unmingled satisfaction to the tenant of rectory, vicarage, parsonage, deanery, or manse, if his dwelling were all that the writer would wish to see it.

It is pleasant to think over what we may call the poetry of country house-making,—the historical cases in which men have sought to idealise to the utmost the scene around them, and to live in a more ambitious or a humbler fairyland. Yet the instances that first occur to us do not encourage the belief that happiness is more certainly to be found in fairyland than in Man-. chester or in Siberia. One thinks of Beckford, the master of almost unlimited wealth, "commanding his fairy palace to glitter amid the orange groves, and aloes, and palms of Cintra :" and after he had formed his paradise, wearying of it, and abandoning it, to move the gloomy moralising of *Childe Harold.* One thinks of him, not yet content with his experience, spending twenty years upon the turrets and gardens of Fonthill, that "cathedral turned into a toyshop;" whose magnificence was yet but a faint and distant attempt to equal the picture drawn by the prodigal imagination of the author of *Vathek*. One thinks of Horace Walpole, amid the gimcrackery of Strawberry Hill; of Sir Walter Scott, building year by year that "romance in stone and lime," and idealising the bleakest and ugliest portion of the banks of the Tweed, till the neglected Clartyhole became the charming but costly Abbotsford. One thinks of Shenstone, devoting his life to making a little paradise of the Leasowes, where, as Johnson tells us in his grand resounding prose, he set himself "to point his prospects, to diversify his surface, to entangle his walks, and to wind his waters; which he did with such judgment and fancy as made his little domain the envy of the great and the admiration of the skilful; a place to be visited by travellers and copied by designers." Nor must we forget how the bitter little Pope, by the taste with which he laid out his five acres at Twickenham, did much to banish the stiff Dutch style, and to encourage the modern fashion of landscape-gardening in imitation of nature, which was so successfully carried out by the well-known Capability Brown. It is putting too extreme a case, when we pass to that which in our boyish days we all thought the perfection and delight of country residences, the island-cave of Robinson Crusoe: with its barricade of stakes which took root and grew into trees, and its impenetrable wilderness of wood, all planted by the exile's hand, which went down to the margin of the sea. It is coming nearer home, to pass to the French château ; the tower perched upon the rock above the Rhine ; and the German castle, which of course is somewhere in the Black Forest, frequented by robbers and haunted by ghosts. And we ascend to the sublime in human abodes, when we think of the magnificent Alhambra, looking down proudly upon Moorish Granada : that miracle of barbaric beauty, which Washington Irving has so finely described : with its countless courts and halls, its enchanted gateways, its graceful pillars of marble of different hues, and its fountains that once made cool music for the delight of Moslem prince and peer.

We pass, by an easy transition, to the literature of country houses, of which there are two well-marked classes. We have the real and the ideal schools of the literature of country houses and country life : or perhaps, as both are in a great degree ideal, we should rather call them the would-be real, and the avowedly romantic. We have the former charmingly exemplified in *Bracebridge Hall;* charmingly in the Spectator's account of Sir Roger de Coverley, amid his primitive tenantry ; with a little characteristic coarseness, in Swift's poem, beginning,

> I 've often wish'd that I had clear,
> For life, six hundred pounds a year,—

which, by the way, is an imitation of that graceful Latin poet who delighted, so many centuries since, in his little Sabine farm. Then there are Miss Mitford's quiet pleasing delineations of English country life ; many delightful touches of it in *Friends in Council* and its sequel ; and Samuel Rogers, though essentially a man of the town, has given a very complete picture of cottage life in his little poem, which thus sets out—

> Mine be a cot beside the hill ;
> A beehive's hum shall soothe my ear :
> A willowy brook, that turns a mill,
> With many a fall, shall linger near.

We mention all these, not, of course, as a thousandth part of what our literature contains of country houses and life, but as a sample of that mode of treating these subjects which we have termed the would-be real : and as specimens of the avowedly romantic way of describing such things, we refer to Poe's gorgeous picture of the " Domain of Arnheim," where his affluent imagination has run riot, under the stimulus of fancied boundless wealth ; and the same author's " Landor's Cottage," a scene of sweet simplicity, which is somewhat spoiled by just the smallest infusion of the theatrical. The writings of Poe, with all their extraordinary characteristics, are so little known in this country, that we dare say our readers will feel obliged to us for a short account of the former piece.

A certain man, named Ellison, suddenly came into

the possession of a fortune of a hundred millions sterling. Poe, you see, being wretchedly poor, did not do things by halves. Ellison resolved that he would find occupation and happiness in making the finest place in the world ; and he made it. The approach to Arnheim was by the river. After intricate windings, pursued for some hours through wild chasms and rocks, the vessel suddenly entered a circular basin of water, of two hundred yards' diameter : this basin was surrounded by hills of considerable height :—

" Their sides sloped from the water's edge at an angle of some forty-five degrees, and they were clothed from base to summit, not a perceptible point escaping, in a drapery of the most gorgeous flower-blossoms : scarcely a green leaf being visible among the sea of odorous and fluctuating colour. This basin was of great depth, but so transparent was the water that the bottom, which seemed to consist of a thick mass of small round alabaster pebbles, was distinctly visible by glimpses,—that is to say, whenever the eye could permit itself *not* to see, far down in the inverted heaven, the duplicate blooming of the hills. On these latter there were no trees, nor even shrubs of any size. . . . . . As the eye traced upwards the myriad-shaped slope, from its sharp junction with the water to its vague termination amid the folds of overhanging cloud, it became, indeed, difficult not to fancy a panoramic cataract of rubies, sapphires, opals, and golden onyxes, rolling silently out of the sky."

Here the visitor quits the vessel which has borne him so far, and enters a light canoe of ivory, which is wafted by unseen machinery :—

" The canoe steadily proceeds, and the rocky gate of the vista is approached, so that its depths can be more distinctly seen. To the right arise a chain of lofty hills, rudely and luxuriantly wooded. It is observed, however, that the trait of exquisite *cleanness* where the bank dips into the water still prevails. There is not one token of the usual river *débris*. To the left, the character of the scene is softer and more obviously artificial. Here the bank slopes upward from the stream in a very gentle ascent, forming a broad sward of grass of a texture resembling nothing so much as velvet, and of a brilliancy of green which would bear comparison with the tint of the purest emerald. This plateau varies in breadth from ten to three hundred yards ; reaching from the river bank to a wall, fifty feet high, which extends in an infinity of curves, but following the general direction of the river, until lost in the distance to the westward. This wall is of one continuous rock, and has been formed by cutting perpendicularly the once rugged precipice of the stream's southern bank ; but no trace of the labour has been suffered to remain. The chiselled stone has the hue of ages, and is profusely hung and overspread with the ivy, the coral honeysuckle, the eglantine, and the clematis. . . . .

"Floating gently onward, the voyager, after many short turns, finds his progress apparently barred by a gigantic gate, or rather door, of burnished gold, elaborately carved and fretted, and reflecting the direct rays of the now sinking sun with an effulgence that seems to wreathe the whole surrounding forest in flames. . . . . The canoe approaches the gate. Its ponderous wings are slowly and musically unfolded. The boat glides between them, and commences a rapid descent into a vast amphitheatre entirely begirt with purple mountains, whose bases are laved by a gleaming river throughout the full extent of their circuit. Meantime the whole Paradise of Arnheim bursts upon the view. There is a gush of entrancing melody : there is an oppressive sense of strange sweet odour : there is a dream like intermingling to the eye of tall, slender Eastern trees,—bosky shrubberies,— flocks of golden and crimson birds,—lily-fringed lakes,—meadows of violets, tulips, poppies, hyacinths, and tuberoses,—long intertangled lines of silver streamlets,—and, upspringing confusedly from amid all, a mass of semi-Gothic, semi-Saracenic architecture, sustaining itself as if by miracle in mid-air,—glittering in the red sunlight with a hundred oriels, minarets, and pinnacles; and seeming the phantom handiwork, conjointly, of the Sylphs, the Fairies, the Genii, and the Gnomes." *

This is certainly landscape-gardening on a grand scale : but the whole thing is a shade too immediately suggestive of the *Arabian Nights.* Why not, we are disposed to say, go the entire length of Aladdin's palace at once, and give us walls of alternate blocks of silver and gold; gardens, whose trees bear fruits of diamond, emerald, ruby, and sapphire; and a roc's egg hung up in the entrance-hall? Fancy a man driving up in a post-chaise from the railway-station to a house like that! Why, the only permissible way of arriving at its front door would be on an enchanted horse, that has brought one from Bagdad through the air; and instead of a footman in spruce livery coming out to take in one's portmanteau, 1 should look to be received by a porter with an elephant's head, or an afrit with bat's wings. I could not go up comfortably to my room to dress for dinner : and only fancy coming down to the drawing-room in a coat by Stultz and dress boots by Hoby! Rather should we wreathe our brow with flowers, endue a purple robe, the gift of Noureddin, and perfume our handkerchief with odours which had formed part of the last freight of Sinbad the Sailor. If we made any remark, political or critical, which happened to be

* *Works of Edgar Allan Poe.* Vol. I., pp. 400-403. American Edition.

disagreeable to our host, of course he would immediately change us into an ape, and transport us a thousand leagues in a second to the Dry Mountains.

But to return to the sober daylight in which ordinary mortals live, and to the sort of country in which a man may live whose fortune is less than a hundred millions, we have abundance of the literature of the country in one shape or another: poetry and poetic prose which profess to depict country life, and books of detail which profess to instruct us how to manage country concerns. We breathe a clear, cool atmosphere for which we are the better, when we turn over the pages of *The Seasons: that* is a book which never will become stale. Cowper's poetry is redolent of the country: and though it is all nonsense to say that "God made the country and man made the town," yet *The Winter Walk at Noon* almost leads us to think so. You see the Cockney's fancy that the country is a paradise, always in holiday guise, in poor Keats's lines—

> "Oh for a drop of vintage that hath been
>   Cool'd for a long age in the deep-delved earth,
>   Tasting of Flora and the country green,
>   Dance, and Provençal song, and sun-burnt mirth!"

And there are several books whose titles are sure to awaken pleasant thoughts in the mind of the lover of nature, who knows that, notwithstanding Dr Johnson's axiom, one green field is not just like any other green field, and who prefers a country lane to Fleet

Street. There is Mr Jesse's *Country Life*, which is mainly occupied in describing, with a minute and kindly accuracy, the ways and doings of bird, beast, and insect; and thus calling forth a feeling of interest in all our humble fellow-creatures; for in the case of inferior animals the principle holds good, that all that is needed to make one like almost any of them is just to come to know them. And on this track one need do no more than name White's delightful *Natural History of Selbourne*. There is Mr William Howitt's *Boy's Country Book*, which sets out the sports and occupations of childhood and rural scenes, with a fulness of sympathy which makes us lament that its author should ever exchange these genial topics for the briars of polemical controversy. There is Mr Wilmott's *Summer-time in the Country;* a disappointing book; for notwithstanding the melody of its name, it is mainly a string of criticisms, good, bad, and indifferent: with a slight surrounding atmosphere, indeed, of country life; but most of the production might have been written in Threadneedle Street. There is a pleasant and well-informed little anonymous volume, called *The Flower Garden*, which contains the substance of two articles originally published in the *Quarterly Review;* and every one knows Bacon's *Essay of Gardens*, in which the writer gives the reins to his fancy, and pictures out a little paradise of thirty acres in extent, including in it some specimen of all schools of landscape-gardening. Mrs

Loudon's various publications have done much to foster a taste for gardening among ladies. An exceedingly pleasing and genial book, called *The Manse Garden*, which has had a large circulation in Scotland, is intended to stimulate the Scottish clergy to neatness and taste in the arrangement of their gardens and glebes. A handsome work entitled *Rustic Adornments for Homes of Taste*, lately published, contains many practical instructions for the decoration of the country home. And an elegantly-illustrated volume, which appeared a few months ago, is given to *Rhymes and Roundelays in Praise of a Country Life*. Sir Joseph Paxton has not thought it unworthy of him to write a little tract, called *The Cottager's Calendar of Garden Operations*, the purpose of which is to shew how much may be done in the most limited space in the way of growing vegetables for profit and flowers for ornament; and in these days, when happily the social and sanitary elevation of the masses is beginning to attract something of the notice which it deserves, I trust that reformers will not forget the powerful influence of the garden, and a taste for gardening concerns, in elevating and purifying the working man's mind, and adding interest and beauty to the working man's home. And in truth, we shall never succeed in inducing working men to spend their evenings at home rather than in the alehouse till we have succeeded in rendering their own homes tidy, comfortable, and inviting to a degree that shall at least equal the neatly-sanded floor and the well-scrubbed benches which they can enjoy for a few pence elsewhere.

If there be any among my readers who have it in view to build a country house, I strongly recommend them to have it done by Mr George Gilbert Scott, whose pleasantly-written book on *Secular and Domestic Architecture* will be read with delight by many who are condemned to live in towns, or who must put up with such a country home as their means permit, but who can luxuriate in imagining what kind of a house they would have if they could have exactly such a house as they wish. Mr Scott is an out and out supporter of Gothic architecture as the best style for every possible building, large or small, in town or country, from the nobleman's palace to the labourer's cottage, from a cathedral or a town-house to a barn or a pigsty. But Mr Scott gives a judicious view of Gothic architecture, as a style capable of unlimited expansion and adaptation, having in its nature the power to accommodate itself to every requirement of modern life and progress, and capable, without surrendering its distinctive character, of modification, development, addition, and subtraction, to a degree which renders it the true architecture of the nineteenth century no less than of the thirteenth. It is doing Gothic architecture great injustice to speak of it as the mediæval architecture. Such a description vaguely suggests that it is a style especially suited to the requirements of life in the Middle Ages : and, by consequence, not well adapted to the exigencies of life at a period when life is very different from what it was in the Middle Ages. And the notion has been countenanced by the injudicious fashion in which houses were built at the beginning of the great reaction in favour of Gothic. When people grew wearied and disgusted at the ugly Grecian houses which disfigure so many fine old English parks, paltry and pitiful importations of a foreign style into a country which had an indigenous style incomparably superior in beauty, in comfort, in every requisite of the country house, the reaction ran into excess ; and instead of building Gothic *houses*, that is, instead of trying to produce buildings which should be noble and picturesque, and at the same time commodious and convenient to live in, architects built abbeys and castles ; and in those cases where they did not produce specimens of mere confectioner's Gothic, they produced buildings utterly unsuited to the exigencies and conditions of modern English life, however beautiful they might be. Now, nothing could be a more flagrant violation of the *spirit* of Gothic, than this scrupulous conformity to the *letter* of Gothic. The true Gothic architect must hold fitness and use in view as his primary end ; and his skill is shewn when upon these he superinduces beauty. A fortified castle, with moat and drawbridge, arrow-slits, and donjon-keep, was a convenient and suitable building in an unsettled and lawless age. It is a most inconvenient and unsuitable building in England in the nineteenth century ; and while we should prize and cherish the noble specimens of the Edwardian castle which we possess, for their beauty and their associations, we ought to remember that if the architects who built them were living now, they would be the first to lay that style aside, as no longer suitable ; and they would shew the true Gothic taste and spirit in devising dwellings as noble, as picturesque, as interesting, as thoroughly Gothic in character, but fitted for the present age, and the present age's modes of life. It was not because the Edwardian castle was grand and beautiful, that the Edwardian architects built it as they did ; they built it as they did because *that* was the most suitable and convenient fashion ; and upon fitness and use they engrafted grandeur and beauty. And it is not by a slavish imitation of ancient details and forms that we shall succeed in producing, at the present day, what is justly entitled to be called Gothic architecture. It is rather by a free development and carrying out of old principles applied to new circumstances and requirements. And it is the glory of Gothic, that you cannot make a new demand upon it for increased or altered accommodations and appliances, which may not, in the hand of a worthy architect, be complied with, not only without diminution of beauty, but even with increase of beauty. It is beyond comparison the most squeezable of all styles ; and, provided the squeezing be effected by a master's hand, the style will look all the better for it.

There is a floating belief, entirely without reason, that Gothic is exclusively an ecclesiastical fashion of building. Many people fancy that Gothic architecture suits a church; but is desecrated, or at least becomes unsuitable, when applied to secular and domestic buildings. There can be no doubt, indeed, that to every person who possesses any taste, it is a self-evident axiom that Gothic is the true church architecture : but in the age during which the noblest Gothic churches were built, it was never fancied that churches must be built in one style, and secular buildings in a style essentialy dissimilar. The belief which is entertained by the true lover of Gothic architecture is this : that Gothic is essentially the most beautiful architecture ; that, properly treated, it is the most commodious architecture ; and that, therefore, the Gothic is the style in which all buildings, sacred or secular, public or domestic, ought to be built ; with such modifications in the style of each separate building as its special purpose and use shall suggest. It must be admitted, however, that Gothic architecture has one disadvantage as compared with that architecture which is exhibited in Baker Street, in the London suburban terraces, and in the Manchester cotton-mills. Gothic architecture costs more money ; but, in judicious hands, not so very much more.

As to the capacity of Gothic architecture to accommodate itself to houses of all classes, let the reader ponder the following words :—

"It seems to be generally imagined that the merits of the Elizabethan style are most displayed in its grand baronial residences, such as Burleigh or Hatfield. I think quite the contrary. A style is best tested by reducing it to its humblest conditions ; and the great glory of this style is, not that it produced gorgeous and costly mansions for the nobles, but that it produced beautifully simple, yet perfectly architectural, cottages for the poor ; appropriate and comfortable farmhouses ; and pleasant-looking residences for the smaller country-gentlemen, and for the inhabitants of country towns and villages."

Following up the same idea, Mr Scott somewhere else says :—

"What we want is a style which will stand this test, which will be pleasing in its most normal forms, yet be susceptible of every gradation of beauty, till it reach the noblest and most exalted objects to which art can aspire."

Let it be accepted as an indubitable axiom, that Gothic building is the best building for the town as well as for the country. But I am not called to enter upon that controversial ground, for we are dealing with country houses, in regard to which I believe there is no difference of opinion among people of taste and sense. The country house, as of course, must be Gothic. Tasteless blockheads will no doubt say that the Gothic house is all frippery and ginger-bread, (as indeed houses of confectioner's Gothic very often are ;) they will chuckle with delight whenever they hear that the rain has penetrated where the roof of a bay-window joins the wall, or through some ill-contrived gutter in the irregular roof of the house; they will maintain, in the face of fact, that Gothic windows will not admit sufficient light, and cannot exclude draughts; and they will praise the unpretending square-built house "with no nonsense about it." Let us leave such tasteless people to the contemplation of the monstrosities they love: when the question is one of grace or beauty, *their* opinion is (as Coleridge used to say) "neither here nor there." Granting (which we do not grant) that Gothic architecture is out of place in the town, and congenial and suitable in the country, I do not know that we could pay to that style any higher tribute than to say that it is the most seemly and suitable to be placed in conjunction with the fairest scenes of nature. I do not think we could say better of any work of man, than that it bears with advantage to be set side by side with the noblest works of God. Yet, though a worthy Gothic building looks beautiful anywhere, it has a special charm in a sweet country landscape. It seems just what was wanted to render the scene perfect. It is in harmony with the trees and flowers and hills around, and with the blue sky overhead. It is a perpetual pleasure to look at it. I do not believe that any mortal can find real enjoyment in standing and gazing at a huge square house, with a great waggon roof, and with square holes cut in a great level blank wall for windows. It may draw a certain grandeur from vast size : and it may possess fine accessories,—be shadowed by noble trees, backed by wild or wooded hills, and *shaded off* into the fields and lawns by courtly terraces ; but the big square box is in itself ugly, and never can be anything but ugly. But how long and delightedly one can contemplate the worthy Gothic house of similar pretension—with its lights and shadows, its irregular sky-line, its great mullioned bay-windows and its graceful oriels perched aloft, its many gables, its wreathed chimneys, its towers and pinnacles, its hall and chapel boldly shewn on the external outline :—for the characteristic of Gothic is, that it frankly exhibits construction, and makes a beauty of the exhibition ; while the square-box architecture aims at concealing construction,—producing the four walls, pierced with the regular rows of windows, quite irrespective of internal requirements, and then considering how to fit in the requisite apartments, like the pieces of a child's dissected puzzle, into the square case made for them. Then Gothic admits, and indeed invites, the use of external colouring : and if *that* were only accomplished by the judicious employment of those bricks of different colours which have lately been brought to great perfection, the charm which the entire building possesses to please the eye is indefinitely increased. Only let it be remembered by every man who builds a Gothic country house, that it must be built with much taste and judgment. Gothic is an ambitious style ; and it is especially so in the present state of feeling in England with regard to it. We do not think of criticising a common square house. The taste is never called into play when we look at it. It is taken for granted, *à priori*, that it must be ugly. Not so with a Gothic house. There is a pretension about *that*. The Gothic house invites us to look at it; and, of course, to form an opinion of it. And therefore, if it be ugly, it is offensively ugly. It aims high, and it must expect severity in case of failure. The square-box house comes forward humbly: it is a goose, and does not pretend to fly. And even a goose is respectable while it keeps to its own line. But the ugly Gothic house is a goose that hath essayed the eagle's flight; and if it come down ignominiously to the earth, it is deservedly laughed at. And so, let no man presume to build a country house without securing the services of a thoroughly good architect. And for myself I can say, that whenever I grow a rich man and build a Gothic house, the architect shall be Mr Scott. Indeed a person of moderate means would be safe in seeking the advice of that accomplished gentleman: for he would, it is evident, take pains to render even a very small house a pleasing picture. He holds that a building of the smallest extent affords as decided if not as abundant scope for fine taste and careful treatment as the grandest baronial dwelling in Britain. A cottage may be quite as pretty and pleasing as a castle or a palace could be in their more ambitious style.

Although Gothic architecture has an unlimited

capacity of adapting itself to all circumstances and exigencies, yet there is a freedom about a country site which suits it bravely. In the country the architect is not hampered by want of space : he is not tied to a street-line beyond which he must not project, nor fettered by municipal regulations as to the height or sky-outline of his building. He may spread over as much ground as he pleases. And the only restrictions by which he is confined are thus set out by Mr Scott, in terms which will commend themselves to the common sense of all readers :—

"The grand principle of planning is, that every room should be in its right position—both positively and relatively to each other—to the approaches, views, and aspect ; and that this should be so effected as not only to avoid disturbing architectural beauty, either within or without, but to be in the highest degree conducive to it."

In treating of *Buildings in the Country*, Mr Scott gives us some account of his ideal of houses suited to all ranks and degrees of men. Let us look at his picture of what a villa ought to be :—

"To begin, then, with the ordinary villa. Its characteristics should be quiet cheerfulness and unpretending comfort ; it should, both within and without, be the very embodiment of innocent and simple enjoyment. No foolish affectation of rusticity, but the reality of everything which tends to the appreciation of country pleasures in their more refined form. The external design should so unite itself with the natural objects around, that they should appear necessary to one another, and that neither could be very different without the other suffering. The architecture should be quiet and simple ; the material that most suited to the neighbourhood—neither too formal and highly finished,

nor yet too rustic. The interior should partake of the same
general feeling. It should bear no resemblance to the formality
of a town house ; the rooms should be moderate in height, and
not too rigidly regular in form ; some of the ceilings should shew
their timbers wholly or in part ; some of the windows should, if
it suits the position, open out upon the garden or into conservatories. In most situations the house should spread wide rather
than run up high ; but circumstances may vary this."

I ask my readers' attention to the paragraph which
follows ; it contains sound social philosophy :—

"In this, as in other classes of house-building, the servants'
apartments should be well cared for. They should be allowed
a fair share in the enjoyments provided for their masters. I have
seen houses replete with comfort and surrounded with beauty,
where, when you once get into the servants' rooms, you might
as well be in a prison. This is morally wrong ; let us give our
dependents a share in our pleasures, and they will serve us none
the less efficiently for it."

Every one can see how pleasant and cheerful a
home a villa would be which should successfully em-
body Mr Scott's views of what a villa ought to be.
Such a dwelling would be quite within the reach of
all who possess such a measure of income as in this
country now-a-days will suffice to provide those things
which are the necessaries of life to people brought up
as ladies and gentlemen. And with what heart and
vigour a man would set himself to laying out the
little piece of land around his house—to making
walks, planting clumps of evergreens, and perhaps
leading a little brooklet through his domain—if the
house, seen from every point, were such as to be a

perpetual feast to the eye and the taste! I heartily wish that the poorest clergyman in Britain had just such a parsonage as Mr Scott has depicted, and the means of living in it without undue pinching and paring.

Then, leaving the villa, Mr Scott points out with great taste and moderation what the cottage should be. Judiciously, he does not aim at too much. It serves no good end to represent the *beau-idéal* cottage as a building so costly to erect and to maintain, that landlords of ordinary means get frightened at the mention of so expensive a toy. Cottages may be built so as to be very tasteful and pleasing, while yet the expense of their erection is so moderate that labourers tolerably well off can afford to pay such a rent for them as shall render their erection by no means an unprofitable investment of money. Not, indeed, that a landlord who feels his responsibility as he ought, will ever desire to screw a profit out of his cottagers; but it is well that it should be known that it need not entail any loss whatever to provide for the working class in the country, dwellings in which the requirements of comfort and decency shall be fulfilled. The merest touch from an artistic hand is often all that is needed to convert an ugly, though comfortable, cottage into a pretty and comfortable one. A cottage built of flint, dressed and reticulated with brick, with wood frames and mullions, and the gables of timber, will look exceedingly pleasing. Even of such inexpensive material as mud, thatched with reeds, a very pretty cottage may be built. The truth is, that nowhere is taste so much needed as in building with cheap materials. A good architect will produce a building which will form a pleasing picture, at as small a cost as it is possible to enclose a like space from the external air in the very ugliest way. Gracefulness of form adds nothing to the cost of material. And there is scope for the finest taste in disposing the very cheapest materials in the most effective and graceful fashion. I have seen a church (built, indeed, by a first-rate architect) which was a beautiful picture, both without and within, while yet it cost so little, that I should (if I were a betting man) be content to lay any odds that no mortal could produce a building which would protect an equal number of people from the weather for less money, though with unlimited licence as to ugliness.

The material *mud* is one's ideal of the very shabbiest material for building which is within human reach. *Hovel* is the word that naturally goes with *mud*. Yet Mr Scott once built a large parsonage, which cost between two and three thousand pounds, of mud, thatched with reeds. Warmth was the end in view. I have no doubt the parsonage proved a most picturesque and quaint affair; and if I could find out where it is, I would go some distance to see it.

Having given us his idea of what a country villa and a country cottage ought to be, Mr Scott proceeds

to set out his ideal of the home of the nobleman or
great landed proprietor :—

"The proper expressions for a country mansion of the higher
class—the residence of a landed proprietor—beyond that degree
of dignity suited to the condition of the owner, are, perhaps,
first, a friendly, unforbidding air, giving the idea of a kind of
patriarchal hospitality; a look that seems to invite approach
rather than repel it. Secondly, an air which appears to connect
it with the history of the country, and a style which belongs to it.
Thirdly, a character which harmonises well with the surrounding
scenery, and unites itself with it, as if not only were the best
spot chosen for the house, and its natural beauties fostered and
increased so as to render this the central focus, but further, that
the house itself should seem to be the very thing which was
necessary to give the last touch and finish to the scene—the
object for which nature had prepared the site, and without which
its charms would be incomplete."

It is not too much to say that a very great proportion of the more ambitious dwellings of this country
signally fail of coming up to these conditions, and
serve only to disfigure the beautiful parks in which
they stand. A huge Palladian house entirely lacks
the genial, hearty, inviting look of the Elizabethan or
Gothic house. Instead of having a look of that hospitality and welcome which we are proud to think of
as especially English, the Palladian mansion is merely
suggestive, as Mr Scott remarks, of gamekeepers and
parkrangers on the watch to turn all intruders out.
Our author would have the architect who is intrusted
with the building of a house of this class retain in its
design all that is practically useful and noble in the
Elizabethan mansion—at the same time remembering

that Elizabethan architecture is Gothic somewhat
debased, and that its details, where faulty, should be
set aside, and their place supplied by those of an
earlier and purer period. Nor should it be forgotten
that the purest and noblest Gothic is the most willing
to bend itself to the requirements of altered circumstances : and it is therefore needful that the architect,
in forming his plan, should hold it steadily in view
that he is building a house which is to be inhabited
by a nobleman or gentleman of the latter half of the
nineteenth century; and which must therefore be
thoroughly suited to the demands of our own day,
and our own day's modes and habits of thought and
life. And the castle and the abbey, though both
quite unfit to be taken as models out-and-out, may
yet supply hints for noble and dignified details in the
designing of a modern English home. Thus, borrow-
ing ideas from all quarters, Mr Scott would produce
a noble dwelling—strictly Gothic in design—thoroughly English in its entire character—at once
majestic and comfortable—at once dignified and inviting—with a mediæval nobility of aspect, and with
the reality of every arrangement which our advanced
civilisation and increased refinement can require or
suggest. As for lesser details, is there not something
in the following passage which makes an architectural
epicure's mouth water?—

"The chapel and corridors perhaps richly vaulted in stone—
the hall nobly roofed with oak—the ceilings of the rooms either

boldly shewing their timbers, partially or throughout, or richly panelled with wood; or if plastered, treated genuinely and truthfully, without aping ideas borrowed from other materials; the floors of halls and passages paved with stone, tile, marble, enriched with incised or tesselated work, or a union of all; those of the leading apartments of polished oak and parqueterie (the rendering of mosaïc into wood); rich wainscoting used where suitable, and the woodwork throughout honestly treated, and of character proportioned to its position, not neglecting the use of inlaying in the richer woods; marble liberally used in suitable positions, the plainer kinds inlaid and studiously contrasted with the richer; the coloured decorations, whether of walls or ceilings, or in stained glass, delicately and artistically treated, and of the highest art we can obtain, and everywhere proportioned to their position; historical and fresco painting freely used, and in a style at once suited to the architecture, and thoroughly free from what may be called mediævalism, in the sense in which the term is misused to imply an antiquated, grotesque, or imperfect mode of drawing; all of these, and an infinity of other modes of ornamentation, are open to the architect in this class of building."

It is pleasant to read well-written descriptions of human dwellings in which art has done all it can do towards providing a pleasant and beautiful setting for human life. Such is Mr Loudon's account of what he calls the *beau-idéal English Villa*, in his *Cyclopædia of Rural Architecture*. Such is Mr Scott's sketch of the *beau-idéal* of a nobleman's house at the present day. The latter forms a pleasing companion picture to that long since drawn by the affluent imagination of Bacon. All who have a taste for such things will read it with great delight; nor will it tend in the least degree to make the true lover of the country envious or discontented.   I can turn with perfect satisfaction from that grand description to my own little parsonage.   There is a peculiar comfort and interest about a little place, which vanishes with increasing magnitude and magnificence.   And it is a law of all healthy mind, that what is one's own has an attraction for one's self far beyond that possessed by much finer things which belong to another.   A man with one little country abode, may have more real delight in it, than a duke has in his wide demesnes.   Indeed I heartily pity a duke with half-a-score of noble houses.   He can never have a *home feeling* in any one of them.   While the possessor of a few acres knows every corner and every tree and shrub in his little realm; and knows what is the aspect of each upon every day of the year.   I speak from experience.   I am the possessor of twelve acres of mother earth; and I know well what pleasure and interest are to be found in the little affairs of that limited tract.   My study-window looks out upon a corner of the garden; a blank wall faces it at a distance of five-and-twenty feet.   When I came here, I found that corner sown with potatoes, and that wall a dead expanse of stone and mortar.   But I resolved to make the most of my narrow view, and so contrive that it should look cheerful at every season.   And now the corner is a little square of as soft and well-shaven green turf as can be seen; through which snowdrops and crocuses peep in early spring; its surface is broken by two clumps of evergreens, laurels, hollies, cedars, yews, which look warm and pleasant all the winter time; and over one clump rises a standard rose of ten feet in height, which, as I look up from my desk through my window, shews like a crimson cloud in summer. The blank wall is blank no more, but beautiful with climbing roses, honeysuckle, fuchsias, and variegated ivy. What a pleasure it was to me, the making of this little improvement; and what a pleasure it is still every time I look at it. No one can sympathise justly with the feeling till he tries something of the sort for himself. And not merely is such occupation as that which I speak of a most wholesome diversity from mental work. It has many other advantages. It leads to a more intelligent delight in the fairest works of the Creator; and though it might be hard to explain the logical steps of the process, it leads a man to a more kindly and sympathetic feeling towards all his fellow-men. Have not I, unfaithful that I am, spent the forenoon in writing a very sharp review of some foolish book; and then, having gone out to the garden for two or three hours, come in, thinking that after all it would be cruel to give pain to the poor fellow who wrote it; and so proceeded to weed out everything severe, and give the entire article a rather complimentary turn.

It is a vain fancy to try to sketch out the kind of

life which is to be led in the country house after we get it. For almost every man gradually settles into a habitude of being which is rather formed by circumstances than adopted of purpose and by choice. Only let it be remembered, that pleasure disappears when it is sought as an end. Happiness is a thing that is come upon incidentally, while we are looking for something else. The man who would enjoy country life in a country home, must have an earnest occupation besides the making and delighting in his home, and the sweet scenes which surround it. If *that* be all he has to do, he will soon turn weary, and find that life, and the interest of life, have stagnated and scummed over. The end of work is to enjoy leisure ; but to enjoy leisure one must have performed work. It will not do to make the recreation of life the business of life. But I believe, that to the man who has a worthy occupation to fill up his busy hours, there is no purer or more happy recreation than may be found in the cares and interests of the country home.

CHAPTER VI

CONCERNING TIDINESS:

BEING THOUGHTS UPON AN OVERLOOKED SOURCE OF HUMAN CONTENT.

SAID Sydney Smith to a lady who asked him to recommend a remedy for low spirits,—Always have a cheerful, bright fire, a kettle simmering on the hob, and a paper of sugar-plums on the mantelpiece.

Modern grates, it is known, have no hobs: nor does it clearly appear for what purpose the kettle was recommended. If for the production of frequent cups of tea, I am not sure that the abundant use of that somewhat nervous and vaporous liquid is likely to conduce to an equable cheerfulness. And Sydney Smith, although he must have become well acquainted with whisky-toddy during his years in Edinburgh, would hardly have advised a lady to have recourse to alcoholic exhilaration, with its perilous tendencies and its subsequent depression. Sugar-plums, again, damage the teeth, and produce an effect the reverse of salutary upon a most important organ, whose condition directly affects the spirits. As for the bright fire, *there* the genial theologian was certainly right:

for when we talk, as we naturally do, of a *cheerful* fire, we testify that long experience has proved that this peculiarly British institution tends to make people cheerful. But, without committing myself to any approval of the particular things recommended by Sydney Smith, I heartily assent to the principle which is implied in his advice to the nervous lady: to wit, that cheerfulness and content are to a great degree the result of outward and physical conditions; let me add, the result of very little things.

Time was, in which happiness was regarded as being, perhaps, too much a matter of one's outward lot. Such is the belief of a primitive age and an untutored race. Every one was to be happy, whatever his mental condition, who could but find admittance to Rasselas's *Happy Valley.* The popular belief that there might be a scene so fair that it would make blest any human being who should be allowed to dwell in it, is strongly shewn in the name universally given to the spot which was inhabited by the parents of the race before evil was known. It was the *Garden of Delight:* and the name describes not the beauty of the scene itself, but the effect it would produce upon the mind of its tenants. The paradises of all rude nations are places which profess to make every one happy who enters them, quite apart from any consideration of the world which he might bear within his own breast. And the pleasures of these paradises are mainly addressed to sense. The gross Esquimaux went direct to eating and drinking: and so his heaven (if we may believe Dr Johnson) is a place where "oil is always fresh and provisions always warm." He could conceive nothing loftier than the absence of cold meat, and the presence of unlimited blubber. Quite as gross was the Paradise of the Moslem, with its black-eyed houris, and its musk-sealed wine: and the same principle, that the outward scene and circumstances in which a man is placed are able to make him perfectly and unfailingly happy, whatever he himself may be, is taken for granted in all we are told of the Scandinavian Valhalla, the Amenti of the old Egyptian, the Peruvian's Spirit-World, and the Red Man's Land of Souls. But the Christian Heaven, with deeper truth, is less a locality than a character: its happiness being a relation between the employments provided, and the mental condition of those who engage in them. It was a grand and a noble thing, too, when a Creed came forth, which utterly repudiated the notion of a Fortunate Island, into which, after any life you liked, you had only to smuggle yourself, and all was well. It was a grand thing, and an intensely practical thing, to point to an unseen world, which will make happy the man who is prepared for it, and who is fit for it; and no one else.

And, to come down to the enjoyments of daily life, the time was when happiness was too much made a thing of a quiet home, of a comfortable competence, of climbing roses and honeysuckle, of daisies and but-

tercups, of new milk and fresh eggs, of evening bells
and mist stealing up from the river in the twilight, of
warm firesides, and close-drawn curtains, and mellow
lamps, and hissing urns, and cups of tea, and easy-
chairs, and old songs, and plenty of books, and laughing girls, and perhaps a gentle wife and a limited number of peculiarly well-behaved children. And indeed
it cannot be denied that if these things, with health
and a good conscience, do not necessarily make a man
contented, they are very likely to do so. One cannot
but sympathise with the spirit of snugness and comfort which breathes from Cowper's often-quoted lines,
though there is something of a fallacy in them. Here
they are again : they are pleasant to look at :—

> Now stir the fire, and close the shutters fast,
> Let fall the curtains, wheel the sofa round,
> And, while the bubbling and loud-hissing urn
> Throws up a steamy column, and the cups,
> That cheer but not inebriate, wait on each,
> So let us welcome peaceful evening in.

I have said there is a fallacy in these lines. It is
not that they state anything which is not quite correct,
but that they contain a *suggestio falsi.* Although
Cowper does not directly say so, you see he leaves
on your mind the impression that if all these arrangements are made,—the fire stirred, the curtains drawn,
the sofa wheeled round, and so forth,—you are quite
sure to be extremely jolly, and to spend a remarkably
pleasant evening. Now the fact is quite otherwise.
You may have so much anxiety and care at your

heart, as shall entirely neutralise the natural tendency of all these little bits of outward comfort ; and no one knew that better than the poor poet himself. But that which Cowper does but insinuate, an unknown verse-writer boldly asserts : to wit, that outward conditions are able to make a man as happy as it is possible for man to be. He writes in the style which was common a couple of generations back : but he really makes a pleasant homely picture :—

> The hearth was clean, the fire was clear,
>   The kettle on for tea ;
> Palemon in his elbow-chair,
>   As blest as man could be.
>
> Clarinda, who his heart possess'd,
>   And was his new-made bride,
> With head reclined upon his breast,
>   Sat toying by his side.
>
> Stretch'd at his feet, in happy state,
>   A favourite dog was laid,
> By whom a little sportive cat
>   In wanton humour play'd.
>
> Clarinda's hand he gently press'd :
>   She stole a silent kiss ;
> And, blushing, modestly confess'd
>   The fulness of her bliss.
>
> Palemon, with a heart elate,
>   Pray'd to Almighty Jove,
> That it might ever be his fate
>   Just so to live and love.
>
> Be this eternity, he cried,
>   And let no more be given ;
> Continue thus my loved fireside,—
>   I ask no other heaven !

Poor fellow! It is very evident that he had not been married long. And it is charitable to attribute the wonderful extravagance of his sentiments to temporary excitement and obfuscation. But without saying anything of his concluding wish, which appears to border on the profane, we see in his verses the expression of the rude belief that, given certain outward circumstances, a man is sure to be happy.

Perhaps the pendulum has of late years swung rather too far in the opposite direction, and we have learned to make too little of external things. No doubt the true causes of happiness are *inter præcordia*. No doubt it touches us most closely, whether the world within the breast is bright or dark. No doubt content, happiness, our being's end and aim, call it what you will, is an inward thing, as was said long ago by the Latin poet, in words which old Lord Auchinleck (the father of Johnson's Boswell) inscribed high on the front of the mansion which he built amid the Scottish woods and rocks "where Lugar flows :"—

> "Quod petis, hic est ;
> Est Ulubris : animus si te non deficit æquus."

But then the question is, how to get the *animus æquus:* and I think that now-a-days there is with some a disposition to push the principle of

> "My mind to me a kingdom is,"

too far. Happiness is indeed a mental condition, but we are not to forget that mental states are very strongly, very directly, and very regularly affected and produced by outward causes. In the vast majority of men outward circumstances are the great causes of inward feelings; and you can count almost as certainly upon making a man jolly by placing him in happy circumstances, as upon making a man wet by dipping him in water. And I believe a life which is too subjective is a morbid thing. It is not healthy nor desirable that the mind's shadow and sunshine should come too much from the mind itself. I believe that when this is so, it is generally the result of a weak physical constitution: and it goes along with a poor appetite and.shaky nerves: and so I hail Sydney Smith's recommendation of sugar-plums, bright fires, and simmering kettles, as the recognition of the grand principle that mental moods are to a vast extent the result of outward conditions and of physical state. If Macbeth had asked Dr Forbes Winslow the question—

"Canst thou not minister to a mind diseased ?"

that eminent physician would instantly have replied, —"Of course I can, by ministering to a body diseased." No doubt such mental disease as Macbeth's is beyond the reach of opiate or purgative, and neither sin nor remorse can be cured by sugar-plums. But as for the little depressions and troubles of daily life, I believe that Sydney Smith proposed to treat them soundly. Treat them physically. Treat them *ab extra.* Don't expect the mind to originate much

good for itself. With commonplace people it is mainly
dependent upon external influences. It is not a perennial fountain, but a tank which must be replenished
from external springs. For myself, I never found my
mind to be to me a kingdom. If a kingdom at all,
it was a very sterile one, and a very unruly one. I
have generally found myself, as my readers have no
doubt sometimes done, a most wearisome and stupid
companion. If any man wishes to know the consequence of being left to his own mental resources, let
him shut himself up for a week, without books or
writing materials or companions, in a chamber lighted
from the roof. He will be very sick of himself before
the week is over: he will (I speak of commonplace
men) be in tolerably low spirits. The effect of
solitary confinement, we know, upon uneducated
prisoners, is to drive them mad. And not only do
outward circumstances mainly make and unmake our
cheerfulness, but they affect our intellectual powers
just as powerfully. They spur or they dull us. Till
you enjoy, after long deprivation, the blessing of converse with a man of high intellect and cultivation,
you do not know how much there is in you. Your
powers are stimulated to produce thought of which
you would not have believed yourself capable. And
have not you felt, dear reader, when in the society of
a blockhead, that you became a blockhead too? Did
you not feel your mind sensibly contracting, like a ball
of india-rubber, when compressed by the dead weight

of the surrounding atmosphere of stupidity? But when you had a quiet evening with your friend Dr Smith, or Mr Jones, a brilliant talker, did not he make you talk too with (comparative) brilliancy? You found yourself saying much cleverer things than you had been able to say for months past. The machinery of your mind played fervidly; words came fittingly, and thoughts came crowding. The friction of two minds of a superior class, will educe from each much finer thought than either could have produced when alone.

And now, my friendly reader, the upshot of all this which I have been saying is, that I desire to recommend to you a certain overlooked and undervalued thing, which I believe to be a great source of content and a great keeper-off of depression. I desire to recommend something which I think ought to supplant Sydney Smith's kettle and sugar-plums, and which may co-exist nicely with his cheerful fire. And I beg the reader to remark what the end is towards which I am to prescribe a means. It is not *suprema felicitas :* it is quiet content. The happiness which we expect at middle age is a calm, homely thing. We don't want raptures : they weary us, they wear us out, they shatter us. We want quiet content ; and above all, we want to be kept clear of over-anxiety and of causeless depression. As for such buoyancy as that of Sydney Smith himself, who tells us that when a man of forty he often longed to jump over the tables and chairs in pure glee and light-heartedness,—why, if

nature has not given you *that*, you must just do without it.   Art cannot give it you : it must come spontaneous if it come at all.   But what a precious thing
it is !   Very truly did David Hume say, that for a
man to be born with a fixed disposition always to look
at the bright side of things, was a far happier thing
than to be born to a fortune of ten thousand a-year.
But Hume was right, too, when he talked of *being
born with* such a disposition.   The hopeful, unanxious
man, quite as truly as the poet, *nascitur, non fit.*   No
training could ever have made the nervous, shrinking,
evil-foreboding Charlotte Brontë like the gleeful,
boisterous, life-enjoying Christopher North.   There
were not pounds enough in that little body to keep
up a spirit like that which dwelt in the Scotch Professor's stalwart frame.   And to indicate a royal road
to constant light-heartedness is what no man in his
senses will pretend to do.   But we may attain to
something humbler.   Sober content is, I believe,
within the reach of all who have nothing graver to vex
them than what James Montgomery the poet called
the "insect cares" of daily life.   There may be, of
course, lots which are darkened over by misfortunes
so deep that to brighten *them* all human skill would be
unavailing.   But ye who are commonplace people,—
commonplace in understanding, in feeling, in circumstances ; ye who are not very clever, not extraor-
dinarily excitable, not extremely unlucky ; ye who
desire to be, day by day, equably content and even

passably cheerful; listen to me while I recommend, in subordination of course to something too serious to discuss upon this half-earnest page, the maintenance of a constant, pervading, active, all-reaching, energetic TIDINESS!

No fire that ever blazed, no kettle that ever simmered, no sugar-plums that ever corroded the teeth and soothed to tranquil stupidity, could do half as much to maintain a human being in a condition of moderate jollity and satisfaction, as a daily resolute carrying out of the resolution, that everything about us,—our house, our wardrobe, our books, our papers, our study-table, our garden-walks, our carriage, our harness, our park-fences, our children, our lamps, our gloves, yea, our walking-stick and our umbrella, shall be in perfectly accurate order; that is, shall be, to a hair's-breadth, RIGHT!

If you, my reader, get up in the morning, as you are very likely to do in this age of late dinners, somewhat out of spirits, and feeling (as boys expressively phrase it) rather *down in the mouth,* you cannot tell why; if you take your bath and dress, having still the feeling as if the day had come too soon, before you had gathered up heart to face it and its duties and troubles; and if, on coming down stairs, you find your breakfast-parlour all in the highest degree snug and tidy,—the fire blazing brightly and warmly, the fire-irons accurately arranged, the hearth clean, the carpet swept, the chairs dusted, the breakfast equipage neatly arranged upon the snow-white cloth,—it is perfectly wonderful how all this will brighten you up. You will feel that you would be a growling humbug if you did not become thankful and content. "Order is Heaven's first law:" and there is a sensible pleasure attending the carrying of it faithfully out to the very smallest things. Tidiness is nothing else than the carrying into the hundreds of little matters which meet us and touch us hour by hour the same grand principle which directs the sublimest magnitudes and affairs of the universe. Tidiness is, in short, the being right in thousands of small concerns in which most men are slovenly satisfied to be wrong. And though a hair's-breadth may make the difference between right and wrong, the difference between right and wrong is not a little difference. An untidy person is a person who is wrong, and is doing wrong, for several hours every day; and though the wrong may not be grave enough to be indicated by a power so solemn as conscience, (as the current through the Atlantic cable after it had been injured, though a magnetic current, was too faint to be indicated by the machines now in use,) still, constant wrong-doing, in however slight a degree, cannot be without a jar of the entire moral nature. It cannot be without putting us out of harmony with the entire economy under which we live. And thus it is that the most particular old bachelor, or the most precise old maid, who insists upon everything about the house being in perfect order, is, in so far, co-operating with the great plan of Providence; and, like every one who does so, finds an innocent pleasure result from that unintended harmony. Tidiness is a great source of cheerfulness. It is cheering, I have said, even to come into one's breakfast room and find it spotlessly tidy; but still more certainly will this cheerfulness come if the tidiness is the result of our own exertion.

And so I counsel you, my friend, if you are ever disheartened about some example which has been pressed upon you of the evil which there is in this world; if you get vexed and worried and depressed about some evil in the government of your country, or of your county, or of your parish; if you have done all you can to think how the evil may be remedied, and if you know that further brooding over the subject would only vex and sting and do no good;—if all this should ever be so, then I counsel you to have resort to the great refuge of Tidiness. Don't sit over your library fire, brooding and bothering; don't fly to sugar-plums; they will not avail. There is a corner of one of your fields that is grown up with nettles; there is a bit of wall or of palisade out of repair; there is a yard of the edging of a shrubbery walk where an overhanging laurel has killed the turf; there is a bed in the garden which is not so scrupulously tidy as it ought to be; there is a branch of a peach-tree that has pulled out its fastenings to the wall, and that is flapping about in the wind. Or there is a drawer of papers which has for weeks been in great confusion ; or a division of your bookcase where the books might be better arranged.   See to these things forthwith : the out-of-door matters are the best.   Get your man-servant—all your people, if you have half-a-dozen—and go forth and see things made tidy : and see that they are done thoroughly ; work half done will not serve for our present purpose.   Let every nettle be cut down and carried off from the neglected corner ; then let the ground be dug up and levelled, and sown with grass seed.   If it rains, so much the better : it will make the seed take root at once.   Let the wall or fence be made better than when it was new ;   let a wheelbarrowful of fresh green turf be brought ;   let it be laid down in place of the decayed edging ;   let it be cut accurately as a watch's machinery ; let the gravel beside it be raked and rolled : then put your hands in your pockets and survey the effect with delight.   All this will occupy you, interest you, dirty you, for a couple of hours, and you will come in again to your library fireside quite hopeful and cheerful.   The worry and depression will be entirely gone ; you will see your course beautifully : you have sacrificed to the good genius of Tidiness, and you are rewarded accordingly. I am simply stating phenomena, my reader.   I don't pretend to explain causes ; but I hesitate not to assert, that to put things *right*, and to know that things are put right, has a wonderful effect in enlivening and cheering.   You cannot tell why it is so ; but you come in a very different man from what you were when you went out. You see things in quite another way. You wonder how you could have plagued yourself so much before. We all know that powerful effects are often produced upon our minds by causes which have no logical connexion with these effects. Change of scene helps people to get over losses and disappointments, though not by any process of logic. If the fact that Anna Maria cruelly jilted you, thus consigning you to your present state of single misery, was good reason why you should be snappish and sulky in Portland Place, is it not just as good reason now, when, in the midst of a tag-rag procession, you are walking into Chamouni after having climbed Mont Blanc? The state of the facts remains precisely as before. Anna Maria is married to Mr Dunderhead, the retired ironmonger with ten thousand a-year. Nor have any new arguments been suggested to you beyond those which Smith good-naturedly addressed to you in Lincoln's Inn Square, when you threatened to punch his head. But you have been up Mont Blanc; you have nearly fallen into a crevasse; your eyes are almost burnt out of your head. You have looked over that sea of mountains which no one that has seen will ever forget: here is your alpen-stock, and you shall carry it home with you as an ancient palmer his faded branch from the Holy Land. And though all this has nothing earthly to do with your disappointment, you feel that somehow all this has tided you over it. You are quite content. You don't grudge Anna Maria her ferruginous happiness. You are extremely satisfied that things have turned out as they did. The sale of nails, pots, and gridirons is a legitimate and honourable branch of commercial enterprise. And Mr Dunderhead, with all that money, must be a worthy and able man.

I am writing, I need hardly say, for ordinary people when I suggest Tidiness as a constant source of temperate satisfaction. Of course great and heroic men are above so prosaic a means of content. Such amiable characters as Roderick Dhu, in the *Lady of the Lake*, as Byron's Giaour and Lara, not to name Childe Harold, as the heroes of *Locksley Hall* and *Maud*, and as Mr Bailey's *Festus*, would no doubt receive my humble suggestions very much as Mynheer Van Dunk, who disposed of his two quarts of brandy daily, might be supposed to receive the advice to substitute for his favourite liquor an equal quantity of skimmed milk. And possibly Mr Disraeli would not be content out of office, however orderly and tidy everything about his estate and his mansion might be. Yet it is upon record that a certain ancient emperor, who had ruled the greatest empire this world ever saw, found it a pleasant change to lay the sceptre and the crown aside, and, descending from the throne, to take to cultivating cabbages. And as he looked at the tidy rows and the bunchy heads, he declared that he had changed his condition for the better; that tidiness in a cabbage-garden could make a man happier than the imperial throne of the Roman empire. It is well that it should be so, as in this world there are many more cabbage-gardens than imperial thrones; and tidiness is attainable by many by whom empire is not attainable.

A disposition towards energetic tidiness is a perennial source of quiet satisfaction. It always provides us with something to think of and to do: it affords scope for a little ingenuity and contrivance: it carries us out of ourselves: and prevents our leading an unhealthily subjective life. It gratifies the instinctive love of seeing things *right* which is in the healthy human being. And it is founded upon the philosophical fact, that there is a peculiar satisfaction in having a thing, great or small, which was wrong, put right. You have greater pleasure in such a thing, when it has been fairly set to rights, than if it never had been wrong. Had Brummell been a philosopher instead of a conceited and empty-pated coxcomb, I should at once have understood, when he talked of "his favourite leg," that he meant a leg which had been fractured, and then restored as good as ever. Is it a suggestion too grave for this place, that this principle of the peculiar interest and pleasure which are felt in an evil remedied, a spoiled thing mended, a wrong righted, may cast some light upon the Divine dealing with this world? It is fallen, indeed, and evil: but it will be set right.　And *then*, perhaps, it may seem better to its Almighty Maker than even on the First Day of Rest.　And the human being who systematically keeps right, and sets right, all things, even the smallest, within his own little dominion, enjoys a pleasure which has a dignified foundation ; which is real, simple, innocent, and lasting.　Never say that it is merely the fidgety particularity of an old bachelor which makes him impatient of suffering a weed or a withered leaf on his garden walk, a speck of dust on his library table, or a volume turned upside down on his shelves.　He is testifying, perhaps unconsciously, to the grand, sublime, impassable difference between Right and Wrong.　He is a humble combatant on the side of Right.　He is maintaining a little outpost of the lines of that great army which is advancing with steady pace, conquering and to conquer.　And if the quiet satisfaction he feels comes from an unexciting and simple source—why, it is just from such sources that the quiet content of daily life must come. We cannot, from the make of our being, be always or be long in an excitement.　Such things wear us and themselves out : and they cannot last.　·The really and substantially happy people of this world are always calm and quiet.　In feverish youth, of course, young people get violently spoony, and are violently ambitious.　*Then*, life is to be all romance.　They are to live in a world over which there spreads a light such as never was on land or sea.　They think that

Thekla was right when she said, as one meaning that life, for her, was done, "I have lived and loved!" Mistaken she! The solid work of life was then just beginning. She had just passed through the moral scarlet-fever; and the noblest, greatest, and happiest part of life was to come. And as for the dream of ambition, *that* soon passes away. A man learns to work, not to make himself a famous name, but to provide the wherewithal to pay his butcher's and his grocer's bills. Still, who does not look back on that time with interest! Was it indeed ourselves, now so sobered, grave, and matter-of-fact, whom we see as we look back?

> Make me feel the wild pulsation that I felt before the strife,
> When I heard my days before me, and the tumult of my life ;
>
> Yearning for the large excitement which the coming years
>   would yield,
> Eager-heartéd as a boy when first he leaves his father's field,
>
> And at night along the dusky highway near and nearer drawn,
> Sees in heaven the light of London flaring like a dreary dawn.

But just what London proves to the eager-hearted boy, life proves to the man. He intended to be Lord Chancellor: he is glad by and by to get made an Insolvent Commissioner. He intended to be a millionaire: he is glad, after some toiling years, to be able to pay his house-rent and make the ends meet. He intended to startle the quiet district of his birth, and make his mother's heart proud with the story of his fame: he learns to be glad if he does his home no discredit, and can now and then send his sisters a ten-pound note :—

> So sleeps the pride of former days,
>   So glory's thrill is o'er :
> And hearts that once beat high for praise,
>   Now feel that pulse no more !

But though these excitements be gone, there still remains to the middle-aged man the calm pleasure of looking at the backs of the well-arranged volumes on his book-shelves; of seeing that his gravel-walks are nicely raked, and his grass-plots smoothly mown; of having his carriage, his horses, and his harness in scrupulous order; the harness with the silver so very bright and the leather so extremely black, and the horses with their coats so shiny, their ribs so invisible, and all their corners so round. Now, my reader, all these little things will appear little only to very un-thinking people. From such little things comes the quiet content of commonplace middle life, of matter-of-fact old age. I never admired or liked anything about Lord Melbourne so much as that which I shall now tell you in much better words than my own :—

"He went one night to a minor theatre, in company with two ladies and a fashionable young fellow about town—a sort of man not easy to be pleased.

"The performance was dull and trashy enough, I daresay. The next day Lord Melbourne called upon the ladies. The fashionable young gentleman had been there before his lordship, and had been complaining of the dreadfully dull evening they had all passed. The ladies mentioned this to Lord Melbourne.

'Not pleased! Not pleased! Confound the man! Didn't he see the fishmongers' shops, and the gas-lights flashing from the lobsters' backs, as we drove along? Wasn't that happiness enough for him?'

"Lord Melbourne had then ceased to be Prime Minister, but you see he had not ceased to take pleasure in any little thing that could give it." *

Now, is not all this an admirable illustration of my great principle, that the tranquil enjoyment of life comes to be drawn a good deal from external sources, and a great deal more from very little things? An ex-Prime Minister thought that the sight of lobsters' backs shining in the gas-light was quite enough to make a reasonable man content for one evening. But give me, say I, not the fleeting joy of the lobsters' backs, any more than Sydney Smith's sugar-plums, lazy satisfactions partaken in passiveness. Give me the perennial, calm, active, stimulating moral and intellectual content which comes of living amid hundreds of objects and events which are all scrupulously RIGHT; and thus, let us all (as Wordsworth would no doubt have written had I pressed the matter upon him)

> "feed this mind of ours,
> In a wise TIDINESS!"

I have long wished to write an essay on Tidiness; for it appears to me that the absence of this simple and humble quality is the cause of a considerable part

---

* "Friends in Council Abroad." *Fraser's Magazine*, vol. liii. p. 2. (January, 1856.)

of all the evil and suffering, physical and moral, which exist among ordinary folk in this world. Most of us, my readers, are little people; and so it is not surprising that our earthly comfort should be at the mercy of little things. But even if we were, as some of us probably think ourselves, very great and eminent people, not the less would our content be liable to be disturbed by very small matters. A few gritty grains of sand finding their way amid the polished shafts and axles of some great piece of machinery, will suffice to send a jar through it all; and a single drop of a corroding acid falling ceaselessly upon a bright surface will speedily ruin its brightness. And in the life of many men and women, the presence of that physical and mental confusion and discomfort which result from the absence of tidiness, is just that dropping acid, those gritty particles. I do not know why it is that, by the constitution of this universe, evil has so much more power than good to produce its effect and to propagate its nature. One drop of foul will pollute a whole cup of fair water; but one drop of fair water has no power to appreciably improve a cup of foul. Sharp pain, present in a tooth or a toe, will make the whole man miserable, though all the rest of his body be easy; but if all the rest of the body be suffering, an easy toe or tooth will cause no perceptible alleviation. And so a man with an easy income, with a pretty house in a pleasant neighbourhood, with a good-tempered wife and healthy children, may quite

well have some little drop of bitterness day by day in-
fused into his cup, which will take away the relish of it
all. And this bitter drop, I believe, in the lot of many
men, is the constant existence of a domestic muddle.

And yet, practically important as I believe the subject to be, still one rather shrinks from the formal discussion of it. It is not a dignified matter to write
about. The name is naturally suggestive of a sour old
maid, a precise old bachelor, a vinegar-faced school-
mistress, or at best a plump and bustling housemaid.
To some minds the name is redolent of worry, fault-
finding, and bother. Every one can see that it is a
fine thing to discuss the laws and order of great
things,—such as comets, planets, empires, and great
cities ; things, in short, with which we have very little
to do. And why should law and order appear contemptible just where they touch ourselves? Is it as
the ocean, clear and clean in its distant depths,
grows foul and turbid just where it touches the
shore? That which we call law and order when
affecting things far away, becomes tidiness where it
reaches us. Yet it is not a dignified topic for an
essay.

This is a beautiful morning. It is the morning of
one of the last days of September, but the trees, with
the exception of some of the sycamores and limes, are
as green and thick-leaved as ever. The dew lies
thick upon the grass, and the bright morning sun
turns it to glancing gems. The threads of gossamer

among the evergreen leaves look like necklaces for Titania. The crisp air, just touched with frostiness, is exhilarating. The dahlias and hollyhocks are bright, but the frost will soon make an end of the former. The swept harvest-fields look trim, and the outline of the distant hills shews sharp against the blue sky. Taking advantage of the moisture on the grass, the gardener is busy mowing it. Curious, that though it sets people's teeth on edge to listen to the sharpening of edge-tools in general, yet there is something that is extremely pleasing in the whetting of a scythe. It had better be a little way off. But it is suggestive of fresh, pleasant things; of dewy grass and bracing morning air; of clumps of trees standing still in the early mistiness; of "milkmaids singing blithe." Let us thank Milton for the last association: we did not get it from daily life. I never heard a milkmaid singing; in this part of the country I don't think they do sing; and I believe cows are invariably milked within doors. But now, how pleasant the trim look of that newly-mown lawn, so carefully swept and rolled; there is not a dandelion in it all,—no weed whatsoever. There are indeed abundant daisies, for though I am assured that daisies in a lawn are weeds, I never shall recognise them as such. To me they shall always be flowers, and welcome everywhere. Look too, at the well-defined outline of the grass against the gravel. I feel the joy of tidiness, and I gladly write in its praise.

Looking at this grass and gravel, I think of Mr Tennyson. I remember a little poem of his which contains some description of his home. There, he tells us, the sunset falls

> "All round a careless-order'd garden,
>   Close by the ridge of a noble down."

I lament a defect in that illustrious man. Great is my reverence for the author of *Maud;* great for the author of *Locksley Hall* and the *May Queen;* greatest of all for the author of *In Memoriam :* but is it possible that the Laureate should be able to elaborate his verses to that last and most exquisite perfection, while thinking of weedy walks outside his windows, of unpruned shrubs, and fruit-trees fallen from the walls? Must the thought be admitted to the mind, that Mr Tennyson is not tidy? I know not. I never saw his garden. Rather let me believe that these lines only shew how tidy he is. Perhaps his garden would appear in perfect order to the visitor; perhaps it seems "careless-ordered" only to his own sharp eye. Perhaps he discerns a weed here and there; a blank of an inch length in a box-wood edging. Perhaps, like lesser men, he cannot get his servants to be as tidy as himself. No doubt such is the state of matters.

There are, indeed, many degrees in the scale of tidiness. It is a disposition that grows upon one, and sometimes becomes almost a bondage. Some great musical composer said, shortly before he died, that he was only then beginning to get an insight into the capabilities of his art; and I dare say a similar idea has occasionally occurred to most persons endowed with a very keen sense of order. In matters external, tidiness may go to the length of what we read of Broek, that Dutch paradise of scrubbing-brushes and new paint; in matters metaphysical, it may go the length of what John Foster tells us of himself, when his fastidious sense of the exact sequence of every shade of thought compelled him to make some thousands of corrections and improvements in revising a dozen printed pages of his own composition. Tidiness is in some measure a matter of natural temperament; there are human beings who never could by possibility sit down contentedly, as some can, in a chamber where everything is topsy-turvy, and who never could by possibility have their affairs, their accounts, their books and papers, in that inextricable confusion in which some people are quite satisfied to have theirs. There may, indeed, be such a thing as that a man shall be keenly alive to the presence or absence of order in his belongings, but at the same time so nerveless and washy that he cannot bestir himself and set things to rights; but as a general rule, the man who enjoys order and exactness will take care to have them about him. There are people who never go into a room but they see at a glance if any of its appointments are awry; and the impression is precisely that which a discordant note leaves on a musical ear. A friend of mine, not an ecclesiastical architect, never enters any church without devising various alterations in it. The same person, when he enters his library in the morning, cannot be easy until he has surveyed it minutely, and seen that everything is right to a hair's-breadth. Taught by long experience, the servants have done their part, and all appears perfect already to the casual observer. Not so to his eye. The hearth-rug needs a touch of the foot: the library-table becomes a marvel of collocation. Inkstands, pen-trays, letter-weighers, pamphlets, books, are marshalled more accurately than Frederick the Great's grenadiers. A chair out of its place, a corner of a crumb-cloth turned up, and my friend could no more get on with his task of composition than he could fly. I can hardly understand how Dr Johnson was able to write the *Rambler* and to balance the periods of his sonorous prose while his books were lying upstairs dog's-eared, battered, covered with dust, strewed in heaps on the floor. But I do not wonder that Sydney Smith could go through so much and so varied work, and do it all cheerfully, when I read how he thought it no unworthy employment of the intellect which slashed respectable humbug in the *Edinburgh Review*, to arrange that wonderful store-room in his rectory at Foston, where every article of domestic consumption was allotted its place by the genial, clear-headed, active-minded man : where was the lemon-bag, where was the soap of different prices (the cheapest placed in the wrappings marked with the dearest price): where were salt, pickles, hams, butter, cheese, onions, and medicines of every degree, from the "gentle jog" of ordinary life to the fearfully-named preparations reserved for extremity. Of course it was only because the kind reviewer's wife was a confirmed invalid that it became a man's duty to intermeddle with such womanly household cares: let masculine tidiness find its sphere out of doors, and feminine within. It is curious how some men, of whom we should not have expected it, had a strong tendency to a certain orderliness. Byron, for example, led a very irregular life, morally speaking; yet there was a curious tidiness about it too. He liked to spend certain hours of the forenoon daily in writing; then, always at the same hour, his horses came to the door; he rode along the same road to the same spot; there he daily fired his pistols, turned, and rode home again. He liked to fall into a kind of mill-horse round: there was an imperfectly-developed tidiness about the man. And even Johnson himself, though he used to kick his books savagely about, and had his study floor littered with fragments of manuscript, shewed hopeful symptom of what he might have been made, when he daily walked up Bolt Court, carefully placing his feet upon the self-same stones, in the self-same order.

Great men, to be sure, may do what they please, and if they choose to dress like beggars and to have their houses as frowsy as themselves, why, we must excuse it for the sake of all that we owe them. But Wesley was philosophically right when he insisted on the necessity, for ordinary men, of neatness and tidiness in dress; and we cannot help making a moral estimate of people from what we see of their conformity to the great law of rightness in little things. I cannot tolerate a harum-scarum fellow who never knows where to find anything he wants, whose boots and handkerchiefs and gloves are everywhere but where they are needed. And who would marry a slatternly girl, whose dress is frayed at the edges and whose fingers are through her gloves? The Latin poet wrote, *Nulla fronti fides;* but I have considerable faith in a front-door. If, when I go to the house of a man of moderate means, I find the steps scrupulously clean, and the brass about the door shining like gold; and if, when the door is opened by a perfectly neat servant, (I don't suppose a footman,) I find the hall trim as it should be, the oil-cloth shiny without being slippery, the stair-carpet laid straight as an arrow, the brass rods which hold it gleaming, I cannot but think that things are going well in that house; that it is the home of cheerfulness, hopefulness, and reasonable prosperity; that the people in it speak truth and hate whiggery. Especially I respect the mistress of that house; and conclude that she is doing her duty in that station in life to which it has pleased God to call her.

But if tidiness be thus important everywhere, what

must it be in the dwellings of the poor? In these, so
far as my experience has gone, tidiness and morality
are always in direct proportion.   You can see at once
when you enter a poor man's cottage (always with
your hat off, my friend) how his circumstances are,
and generally how his character is. If the world is
going against him ; if hard work and constant pinching will hardly get food and clothing for the children,
you see the fact in the untidy house : the poor mistress
of it has no heart for that constant effort which is
needful in the cottage to keep things right ; she has
no heart for the constant stitching which is needful
to keep the poor little children's clothes on their backs.
Many a time it has made my heart sore to see, in the
relaxation of wonted tidiness, the first indication that
things are going amiss, that hope is dying, that the
poor struggling pair are feeling that their heads are
getting under water at last. Ah, there is often a sad
significance in the hearth no longer so cleanly swept,
in the handle wanting from the chest of drawers, in
little Jamie's torn jacket, which a few stitches would
mend, but which I remember torn for these ten days
past !   And remember, my reader, that to keep a
poor man's cottage tidy his wife must always have
spirit and heart to work. If *you* choose, when you
feel unstrung by some depression, to sit all day by the
fire, the house will be kept tidy by the servants without
your interference. And indeed the inmates of a house
of the better sort are putting things out of order from

morning till night, and would leave the house in a sad mess if the servants were not constantly following in their wake and setting things to rights again. But if the labourer's wife, anxious and weak and sick at heart as she may rise from her poor bed, do not yet wash and dress the little children, they will not be either washed or dressed at all; if she do not kindle her fire, there will be no fire at all; if she do not prepare her husband's breakfast, he must go out to his hard work without any; if she do not make the beds and dust the chairs and tables and wash the linen, and do a host of other things, they will not be done at all. And then in the forenoon Mrs Bouncer, the retired manufacturer's wife, (Mr Bouncer has just bought the estate,) enters the cottage with an air of extreme condescension and patronage, and if everything about the cottage be not in tidy order, Mrs Bouncer rebukes the poor down-hearted creature for laziness and neglect. I should like to choke Mrs Bouncer for her heartless insolence. I think some of the hatefullest phases of human nature are exhibited in the visits paid by newly rich folk to the dwellings of the poor. You, Mrs Bouncer, and people like you, have no more right to enter a poor man's house and insult his wife than that poor man has to enter your drawing-room and give you a piece of his mind upon matters in general and yourself in particular. We hear much now-a-days about the distinctive characteristics of ladies and gentlemen, as contrasted with those of people who are well-dressed and live in fine houses, but whom no house and no dress will ever make gentlemen and ladies. It seems to me that the very first and finest characteristic of all who are justly entitled to these names of honour, is a most delicate, scrupulous, chivalrous consideration for the feelings of the poor. Without *that* the cottage-visitor will do no good to the cottager. If you, my lady friend, who are accustomed to visit the dwellings of the poor in your neighbourhood, convey by your entire demeanour the impression that you are, socially and intellectually, coming a great way down stairs in order to make yourself agreeable and intelligible to the people you find there, you had better have stayed at home. You will irritate, you will rasp, you will embitter, you will excite a disposition to let fly at your head. You may sometimes gratify your vanity and folly by meeting with a servile and crawling adulation, but it is a hypocritical adulation that grovels in your presence and shakes the fist at you after the door has closed on your retreating steps. Don't fancy I am exaggerating: I describe nothing which I have not myself seen and known.

I like to think of the effect which tidiness has in equalising the real content of the rich and poor. If even you, my reader, find it pleasant to go into the humblest little dwelling where perfect neatness reigns, think what pleasure the inmates (perhaps the solitary inmate) of that dwelling must have in daily maintaining that speckless tidiness, and living in the midst of it. There is to me a perfect charm about a sanded floor, and about deal furniture scrubbed into the perfection of cleanliness. How nice the table and the chairs look; how inviting that solitary big arm-chair by the little fire!. The fireplace indeed consists of two blocks of stone washed over with pipeclay, and connected by half a dozen bars of iron; but no register grate of polished steel ever pleased me better. God has made us so that there is a racy enjoyment, a delightful smack, about extreme simplicity co-existing with extreme tidiness. I don't mean to say that I should prefer that sanded floor and those chairs of deal to a Turkey carpet and carved oak or walnut; but I assert that there is a certain indefinable relish about the simpler furniture which the grander wants. In a handsome apartment you don't think of looking at the upholstery in detail; you remark whether the general effect be good or bad; but in the little cottage you look with separate enjoyment on each separate simple contrivance. Do you think that a rich man, sitting in his sumptuous library, all oak and morocco, glittering backs of splendid volumes, lounges and sofas of every degree, which he merely paid for, has half the enjoyment that Robinson Crusoe had when he looked round his cave with its rude shelves and bulkheads, its clumsy arm-chair and its rough pottery, all contrived and made by his own hands? Now the poor cottager has a good deal of the Robinson Crusoe enjoyment; something of the pleasure which Sandford and Merton felt when they had built and thatched their house, and then sat within it, gravely proud and happy, whilst the pelting shower came down but could not reach them. When a man gets the length of considering the architectural character of his house, the imposing effect which the great entrance-hall will have upon visitors, the vista of drawing-room retiring within drawing-room, he loses the relish which accompanies the original idea of a house as a something which is to keep us snug and warm from wind and rain and cold. So if you gain something by having a grand house, you lose something too, and something which is the more constantly and sensibly felt—you lose the joy of simple tidiness ; and your life grows so artificial, that many days you never think of your dwelling at all, nor remember what it looks like.

I have not space to say anything of the importance of tidiness in the poor man's dwelling in a sanitary point of view. Untidiness *there* is the direct cause of disease and death. And it is the thing, too, which drives the husband and father to the alehouse. All this has been so often said, that it is needless to repeat it ; but there is another thing which is not so generally understood, and which deserves to be mentioned. Let me then say to all landed proprietors, it depends very much upon you whether the poor man's home shall be tidy or not. Give a poor man a decent cottage, and he has some heart to keep tidiness about the door, and his wife has some heart to maintain tidiness within. Many of the dwellings which the rich provide for the poor are such that the poor inmates must just sit down in despair, feeling that it is vain to try to be tidy, either without doors or within. If the cottage floor is of clay, which becomes a damp puddle in rainy weather; if the roof be of very old thatch, full of insects, and open to the apartment below; if you go *down* one or two steps below the level of the surrounding earth when you enter the house; if there be no proper chimney, but merely a hole in the roof, to which the smoke seems not to find its way till it has visited every other nook; if swarms of parasitic vermin have established themselves beyond expulsion through fifty years of neglect and filth; if a dung-heap be by ancient usage established under the window;* then how can a poor overwrought man or woman (and energy and activity die out in the atmosphere of constant anxiety and care) find spirit to try to tidy a place like that? They do not know where to begin the hopeless task. A little encouragement will do wonders to develop a spirit of tidiness. The love of order and neatness, and the capacity of enjoying order and neatness, are latent in all human hearts. A man who has lived for a dozen

* The writer describes nothing which he has not seen a hundred times. He has seen a cottage, the approach to which was a narrow passage, about two feet in breadth, cut through a large dung-heap, which rose more than a yard on either side of the narrow passage, and which was piled up to a fathom's height against the cottage wall. This was *not* in Ireland.

years in a filthy hovel, without once making a resolute endeavour to amend it, will, when you put him
down in a neat pretty cottage, astonish you by the
spirit of tidiness he will exhibit; and his wife will
astonish you as much. They feel that now there is
some use in trying. There was none before. The
good that is in most of us needs to be encouraged and
fostered. In few human beings is tidiness, or any
other virtue, so energetic that it will force its way in
spite of extreme opposition. Anything good usually
sets out with timid, weakly beginnings; and it may
easily be crushed then. And the love of tidiness is
crushed in many a poor man and woman by the kind
of dwelling in which they are placed by their landlords. Let us thank God that better times are beginning; but times are still bad enough. I don't
envy the man, commoner or peer, whom I see in his
carriage-and-four, when I think how a score or two
families of his fellow-creatures upon his property are
living in places where he would not put his horses or
his dogs. I am conservatively enough inclined; but
I sometimes think I could join in a Chartist rising.

Experience has shewn that healthy, cheerful, airy
cottages for the poor, in which something like decency
is possible, entail no pecuniary loss upon the philan-
thropic proprietor who builds them. But even if
they did, it is his bounden duty to provide such
dwellings. If he do not, he is disloyal to his country,
an enemy to his race, a traitor to the God who

intrusted him with so much. And surely, in the judgment of all whose opinion is worth a rush, it is a finer thing to have the cottages on a man's estate places fit for human habitation,—with the climbing roses covering them, the little gravel-walk to the door, the little potato-plot cultivated at after-hours, with windows that can open and doors that can shut; with little children not pallid and lean, but plump and rosy (and fresh air has as much to do with that as abundant food has),—surely, I say, it is better a thousand times to have one's estate dotted with scenes such as *that*, than to have a dozen more paintings on one's walls, or a score of additional horses in one's stables.

And now, having said so much in praise of tidiness, let me conclude by remarking that it is possible to carry even this virtue to excess. It is foolish to keep houses merely to be cleaned, as some Dutch house-wives are said to do. Nor is it fit to clip the graceful forms of Nature into unnatural trimness and formality, as Dutch gardeners do. Among ourselves, however, I am not aware that there exists any tendency to either error; so it is needless to argue against either. The perfection of Dutch tidiness is to be found, I have said, at Broek, a few miles from Amsterdam. Here is some account of it from Washington Irving's ever-pleasing pen :—

" What renders Broek so perfect an Elysium in the eyes of all true Hollanders, is the matchless height to which the spirit of cleanliness is carried there. It amounts almost to a religion among the inhabitants, who pass the greater part of their time rubbing and scrubbing, and painting and varnishing : each house-wife vies with her neighbour in devotion to the scrubbing-brush, as zealous Catholics do in their devotion to the Cross.

" I alighted outside the village, for no horse or vehicle is permitted to enter its precincts, lest it should cause defilement of the well-scoured pavements. Shaking the dust off my feet, then, I prepared to enter, with due reverence and circumspection, this *sanctum sanctorum* of Dutch cleanliness. I entered by a narrow street, paved with yellow bricks, laid edgewise, and so clean that one might eat from them. Indeed, they were actually worn deep, not by the tread of feet, but by the friction of the scrubbing-brush.

" The houses were built of wood, and all appeared to have been freshly painted, of green, yellow, and other bright colours. They were separated from each other by gardens and orchards, and stood at some little distance from the street, with wide areas or courtyards, paved in mosaic with variegated stones, polished by frequent rubbing. The areas were divided from the streets by curiously-wrought railings or balustrades of iron, surmounted with brass and copper balls, scoured into dazzling effulgence. The very trunks of the trees in front of the houses were by the same process made to look as if they had been varnished. The porches, doors, and window-frames of the houses were of exotic woods, curiously carved, and polished like costly furniture. The front doors are never opened, except on christenings, marriages, and funerals ; on all ordinary occasions, visitors enter by the back-doors. In former times, persons when admitted had to put on slippers, but this oriental ceremony is no longer insisted on."

We are assured by the same authority, that such is the love of tidiness which prevails at Broek, that the good people there can imagine no greater felicity than to be ever surrounded by the very perfection of it. And it seems that the *prediger*, or preacher of the place, accommodates his doctrine to the views of his hearers; and in his weekly discourses, when he would describe that Happy Place where, as I trust, my readers and I will one day meet the quiet burghers of Broek, he strongly insists that it is the very tidiest place in the universe: a place where all things (I trust he says *within* as well as *around*) are spotlessly pure and clean; and where all disorder, confusion, and dirt, are done with for ever!

CHAPTER VII.

HOW I MUSED IN THE RAILWAY TRAIN;

BEING THOUGHTS ON RISING BY CANDLE-LIGHT; ON NERVOUS FEARS; AND ON VAPOURING.

NOT entirely awake, I am standing on the platform of a large railway terminus in a certain great city, at 7.20 A.M., on a foggy morning early in January. I am about to set out on a journey of a hundred miles by the 7.30 train, which is a slow one, stopping at all the stations. I am alone; for more than human would that friendship be which would bring out mortal man to see one off at such an hour in winter. It is a dreamy sort of scene; I can hardly feel that it substantially exists. Who has not sometimes, on a still autumn afternoon, suddenly stopped on a path winding through sere, motionless woods, and felt within himself, Now, I can hardly believe in all this. You talk of the difficulty of realising the unseen and spiritual; is it not sometimes, in certain mental moods, and in certain aspects of external nature, quite as difficult to feel the substantial existence of things which we can see and touch ? Extreme stillness and loneliness, perhaps, are the usual conditions of this peculiar feeling. Sometimes most men have thought to themselves that it would be well for them if they could but have the evidence of sense to assure them of certain great realities which while we live in this world we never can touch or see ; but I think that many readers will agree with me when I say, that very often the evidence of sense comes no nearer to producing the solid conviction of reality than does that widely different evidence on which we believe the existence of all that is not material. You have climbed, alone, on an autumn day, to the top of a great hill ; a river runs at its base unheard ; a champaign country spreads beyond the river ; cornfields swept and bare ; hedgerows dusky green against the yellow ground ; a little farmhouse here and there, over which the smoke stagnates in the breezeless air. It is heather that you are standing on. And as you stand there alone, and look away over that scene, you have felt as though sense, and the convictions of sense, were partially paralysed : you have been aware that you could not *feel* that the landscape before you was solid reality. I am not talking to blockheads, who never thought or felt anything particularly ; of course *they* could not understand my meaning. But as for you, thoughtful reader, have you not sometimes, in such a scene, thought to yourself, not without a certain startled pleasure,—Now, I realise it no more substantially that there spreads a landscape beyond that river, than that there spreads a country beyond the grave !

There are many curious moods of mind, of which you will find no mention in books of metaphysics. The writers of works of mental philosophy keep by the bread and butter of the world of mind. And every one who knows by personal experience how great a part of the actual phases of thought and feeling lies beyond the reach of logical explanation, and can hardly be fixed and represented by any words, will rejoice when he meets with any account of intellectual moods which he himself has often known, but which are not to be classified or explained. And people are shy about talking of such things. I felt indebted to a friend, a man of high talent and cultivation, whom I met on the street of a large city on a snowy winter day. The streets were covered with unmelted snow ; so were the housetops ; how black and dirty the walls looked, contrasting with the snow. Great flakes were falling thickly, and making a curtain which at a few yards' distance shut out all objects more effectually than the thickest fog. " It is a day," said my friend, " I don't believe in ;" and then he went away. And I know he would not believe in the day, and he would not feel that he was in a world of reality, till he had escaped from the eerie scene out of doors, and sat down by his library fire. But has not the mood found a more beautiful description in Coleridge's tragedy of *Remorse ?* Opium, no doubt, may have in-

creased such phases of mind in his case ; but they are
well known by numbers who never tasted opium :—

<pre>
                On a rude rock,
     A rock, methought, fast by a grove of firs,
     Whose thready leaves to the low-breathing gale,
     Made a soft sound most like the distant ocean,
     I staid, as though the hour of death were pass'd.
 ·   And I were sitting in the world of spirits—
     For all things seem'd unreal.
</pre>

And there can be no doubt that the long vaulted
vistas through a pine wood, the motionless trunks, dark
and ghostly, and the surgy swell of the wind through
the spines, are conditions very likely to bring on, if you
are alone, this particular mental state.

But to return to the railway station which suggested
all this ; it is a dreamy scene, and I look at it with
sleepy eyes. There are not many people going by
the train, though it is a long one. Daylight is an
hour or more distant yet ; and the directors, either
with the design of producing picturesque lights and
shadows in their shed, or with the design of econo-
mising gas, have resorted to the expedient of lighting
only every second lamp. There are no lamps, too,
in the carriages ; and the blank abysses seen through
the open doors remind one of the cells in some
feudal dungeon. A little child would assuredly howl
if it were brought to this place this morning. Away
in the gloom, at the end of the train, the sombre
engine that is to take us is hissing furiously, and
throwing a lurid glare upon the ground underneath

it. Nobody's wits have fully arrived. The clerk who gave me my ticket was yawning tremendously; the porters on the platform are yawning; the guard, who is standing two yards off, looking very neat and trimly dressed through the gloom, is yawning; the stoker who was shovelling coke into the engine fire was yawning awfully as he did so. We are away through the fog, through the mist, over the black country, which is slowly turning gray in the morning twilight. I have with me various newspapers; but for an hour or more it will be impossible to see to read them. Two fellow-travellers, whose forms I dimly trace, I hear expressing indignation that the railway company give no lamps in the carriages. I lean back and try to think.

It is most depressing and miserable work, getting up by candlelight. It is impossible to shave comfortably; it is impossible to have a satisfactory bath; it is impossible to find anything you want. Sleep, says Sancho Panza, covers a man all over like a mantle of comfort; but rising before daylight envelops the entire being in petty misery. An indescribable vacuity makes itself felt in the epigastric regions, and a leaden heaviness weighs upon heart and spirits. It must be a considerable item in the hard lot of domestic servants, to have to get up through all the winter months in the cold dark house : let us be thankful to them through whose humble labours and self-denial we find the cheerful fire blazing in the tidy breakfast parlour when we find our way downstairs. That same apartment looked cheerless enough when the housemaid entered it two hours ago. It is sad when you are lying in bed of a morning, lazily conscious of that circling amplitude of comfort, to hear the chilly cry of the poor sweep outside; or the tread of the factory hands shivering by in their thin garments towards the great cotton mill, glaring spectral out of its many windows, but at least with a cosy suggestion of warmth and light. Think of the baker, too, who rose in the dark of midnight that those hot rolls might appear on your breakfast table; and of the printer, intelligent, active, accurate to a degree that you careless folk who put no points in your letters have little idea of, whose labours have given you that damp sheet which in a little will feel so crisp and firm after it has been duly dried, and which will tell you all that is going on over all the world, down to the opera which closed at twelve, and the parliamentary debate which was not over till half-past four. It is good occasionally to rise at five on a December morning, that you may feel how much you are indebted to some who do so for your sake all the winter through. No doubt they get accustomed to it: but so may you by doing it always. A great many people living easy lives, have no idea of the discomfort of rising by candlelight. Probably they hardly ever did it: when they did it, they had a blazing fire and abundant light to dress by; and even with these advantages, which essentially change the nature of the enterprise, they have not done it for very long. What an aggregate of misery is the result of that inveterate usage in the University of Glasgow. that the early lectures begin at 7.30 A.M. from November till May! How utterly miserable the dark, dirty streets look, as the unhappy student splashes through mud and smoke to the black archway that admits to those groves of Academe! And what a blear-eyed, unwashed, unshaven, blinking, ill-natured, wretched set it is that fills the benches of the lecture-room! The design of the authorities in maintaining that early hour has been much misunderstood. Philosophers have taught that the professors, in bringing out their unhappy students at that period, had it in view to turn to use an hour of the day which otherwise would have been wasted in bed, and thus set free an hour at a better season of the day. Another school of metaphysicians, among whom may be reckoned the eminent authors, Brown, Jones, and Robinson, have maintained with considerable force of argument that the authorities of the University, eager to advance those under their charge in health, wealth, and wisdom, have resorted to an observance which has for many ages been regarded as conducive to that end. Others, again, the most eminent among whom is Smith, have taken up the ground that the professors have fixed on the early hour for no reason in particular; but that, as the classes must meet at some hour of each day, they might just as well meet at that hour as at any other. All these theories are erroneous. There is more in the system than meets the eye. It originated in Roman Catholic days; and something of the philosophy of the stoic and of the faith of the anchorite is involved in it. Grim lessons of endurance; dark hints of penance; extensive disgust at matters in general, and a disposition to punch the head of humanity; are mystically connected with the lectures at 7.30 A.M. in winter. It is quite different in summer, when everything is bright and inviting; if you are up and forth by five or six o'clock any morning then, you feel ashamed as you look at the drawn blinds and the closed shutters of the house in the broad daylight. There is something curious in the contrast between the stillness and shut-up look of a country-house in the early summer morning, and the blaze of light, the dew sparkling life-like on the grass, the birds singing, and all nature plainly awake though man is asleep. You feel that at 7.30 in June, Nature intends you to be astir; but believe it, ye learned doctors of Glasgow College, at 7.30 in December her intention is quite the reverse. And if you·fly in Nature's face, and persist in getting up at unseasonable hours, she will take it out of you by making you horribly uncomfortable.

There is, indeed, one fashion in which rising by candlelight, under the most uncomfortable circumstances, may turn to a source of positive enjoyment.

And the more dreary and wretched you feel, as you wearily drag yourself out of bed into the searching cold, the greater will that peculiar enjoyment be. Have you not, my reader, learned by your own experience that the machinery of the human mind and heart may be *worked backwards*, just as a steam-engine is reversed, so that a result may be produced which is exactly the opposite of the normal one? The fundamental principle on which the working of the human constitution, as regards pleasure and pain, goes, may be stated in the following formula, which will not appear a truism except to those who have not brains to understand it—

THE MORE JOLLY YOU ARE, THE JOLLIER YOU ARE.

But by reversing the poles, or by working the machine backwards, many human beings, such as Indian fakirs, mediæval monks and hermits, Simeon Stylites, very early risers, very hard students, Childe Harold, men who fall in love and then go off to Australia without telling the young woman, and the like, bring themselves to this :—that their fundamental principle, as regards pleasure and pain, takes the following form—

THE MORE MISERABLE YOU ARE, THE JOLLIER YOU ARE.

Don't you know that all *that* is true? A man may bring himself to this point, that it shall be to him a positive satisfaction to think how much he is denying himself, and how much he is taking out of himself.

And all this satisfaction may be felt quite irrespective of any worthy end to be attained by all this pain, toil, endurance, self-denial. I believe indeed that the taste for suffering as a source of enjoyment is an acquired taste; it takes some time to bring any human being to it. It is not natural, in the obvious meaning of the word; but assuredly it is natural in the sense that it founds on something which is of the essence of human nature. You must penetrate through the upper stratum of the heart, so to speak—that stratum which finds enjoyment in enjoyment—then you reach to a deeper *sensorium,* one whose sensibility is as keen, one whose sensibility is longer in getting dulled—that *sensorium* which finds enjoyment in endurance. Nor have many years to pass over us before we come to feel that this peculiar sensibility has been in some measure developed. If you, my friend, are now a man, it is probable (alas! not certain) that you were once a boy. Perhaps you were a clever boy; perhaps you were at the head of your class; perhaps you were a hard-working boy. And now tell me, when on a fine summer evening you heard the shouts and merriment of your companions in the playground, while you were toiling away with your lexicon and your Livy, or turning a passage from Shakspeare into Greek iambics (a hardly-acquired accomplishment, which has proved so useful in after-life), did you not feel a certain satisfaction—it was rather a sad one, but still a satisfaction—as you thought how pleasant it would be to be out in the beautiful sunshine, and yet felt resolved that out you would not go! Well for you if your father and mother set themselves stoutly against this dangerous feeling; well for you if you never overheard them relating with pride to their acquaintances what a laborious, self-denying, wonderful boy thou wast! For the sad satisfaction which has been described is the self-same feeling which makes the poor Hindoo swing himself on a large hook stuck through his skin, and the fakir pleased when he finds that his arm, stretched out for twenty years, cannot now be drawn back. It is precisely the feeling which led the saints of the Middle Ages to starve themselves till their palate grew insensible to the taste of food, or to flagellate themselves as badly as Legree did Uncle Tom, or to refrain wholly from the use of soap and water for forty years. It is a most dangerous thing to indulge in, this enjoyment arising from the principle of the greatest jollity from the greatest suffering; for although we ought to feel thankful that God has so ordered things, that in a world where little that is good can be done except by painful exertion and resolute self-denial, a certain satisfaction is linked even with that exertion and self-denial in themselves, apart from the good results to which they lead; it seems to me that we have no right to add needless bitterness to life that our morbid spirit may draw from it a morbid enjoyment. No doubt self-denial, and struggle against our nature for the right, is a noble thing: but I think that in the present day there is a tendency unduly to exalt both work and self-denial, as though these things were excellent in themselves apart from any excellent ends which follow from them. Work merely as work is not a good thing: it is a good thing because of the excellent things that come with it and of it. And so with self-denial, whether it appear in swinging on a hook or in rising at five on a winter morning. It is a noble thing if it is to do some good; but very many people appear to think it a noble thing in itself, though it do no good whatever. The man deserves canonisation who swings on a hook to save his country; but the man is affected with a morbid reversal of the constitution of human nature who swings on a hook because he finds a strange satisfaction in doing something which is terribly painful and abhorrent. The true nobility of labour and self-denial is reflected back on them from a noble end: there is nothing fine in accumulating suffering upon ourselves merely because we hate it, but feel a certain secondary pleasure in resolutely submitting to what primarily we hate. There is nothing fine in going into a monastery merely because you would much rather stay out. There is nothing fine in going off to America, and never asking a woman to be your wife, merely because you are very fond of her, and know that all this will be a fearful trial to go through. You will be in truth ridiculous, though you may fancy yourself sublime, when you are sitting at the door of your log-hut away in backwoods lonely as those loved by Daniel Boone, and sadly priding yourself on the terrible sacrifice you have made. That sacrifice would have been grand if it had been your solemn duty to make it; it is silly, and it is selfish, if it be made for mere self-denial's sake.

Now a great many people do not remember this. David Copperfield was pleased in thinking that he was taking so much out of himself. He was pleased in thinking so, even though no earthly good came of his doing all that. His kind aunt was ruined, and he was determined that he would deny himself in every way that he might not be a burden upon her; and so when he was walking to any place he walked at a furious pace, and was glad to find himself growing fagged and out of breath, because surely it must be a good thing to feel so jaded and miserable. It was self-sacrifice; it was self-denial. And if to walk at five miles and a half an hour had had any tendency to restore his aunt's little fortune, it could not have been praised too much; and the less David liked it, the more praise it would have deserved. And I venture to think that a good deal of the present talk about Muscular Christianity is based upon this error. I do not know that exertion of the muscles, as such, is necessarily a good or an essentially Christian thing. It is good because it promotes health of body and of mind; but you find many books which appear to teach that it is a fine thing in itself to leap a horse over a five-barred gate, or to crumple up a silver jug, or to thrash a prize-fighter. It is very well to thrash the prize-fighter if it becomes necessary, but surely it would be better to escape the necessity of thrashing the prize-fighter.* Certain of the poems of Long-fellow, much admired and quoted by young ladies, are instinct with the mischievous notion that self-denial for mere self-denial's sake is a grand, heroic, and religious thing. The *Psalm of Life* is extremely vague, and somewhat unintelligible. It is philosophically false to say that

> "Not enjoyment, and not sorrow,
> Is our destined end or way."

For, rightly understood, happiness not only *is* our aim, but is plainly intended to be such by our Creator. He made us to be happy: the whole bearing of re-vealed religion is to make us happy. Of course, the man who grasps at selfish enjoyment turns his back on happiness. Self-sacrifice and exertion, where

---

* To prevent misconception, let me say that I do not allude to the doctrine of what is (perhaps foolishly, but expressively) called *Muscular Christianity*, as taught by Mr Kingsley; but to the absurd caricatures of the doctrine set forth by several writers who teach the excellence of *Unchristian Muscularity*. With the views of Mr Kingsley on this subject I heartily agree: and I know that there is not a word bearing upon it in the essay to which he would not say "Amen." But it must ever be the lot of men who teach doctrines which, though true and sober, sound at first mention new and strange, to have them misrepresented by their opponents, and (what is worse) carica-tured by their imitators.

needful, are the way to happiness; and the main thing which we know of the Christian heaven is, that it is a state of happiness. But Longfellow, talking in that fashion (no doubt sitting in a large easy-chair by a warm fire in a snug study when he did so) wants to convey the utterly false notion that there is something fine in doing what is disagreeable, merely for the sake of doing it. Now, that notion is Bhuddism, but it is not Christianity. Christianity says to us, Suffer, labour, endure up to martyrdom, when duty calls you; but never fancy that there is anything noble in throwing yourself in martyrdom's way. "Thou shalt not tempt the Lord thy God." And as for Longfellow's conception of the fellow who went up the Alps, bellowing out *Excelsior*, it is nothing better than childish. Any one whose mind is matured enough to discern that Childe Harold was a humbug, will see that the lad was a fool. What on earth was he to do when he got to the top of the Alps? The poet does not even pretend to answer that question. He never pretends that the lad whose brow was sad, and his eye like a falchion, &c., had anything useful or excellent to accomplish when he reached the mountain-top at last. Longfellow wishes us to understand that it was a noble thing to push onward and upward through the snow, merely because it is a very difficult and dangerous thing. He wishes us to understand that it was a noble thing to turn away from warm household fires to spectral glaciers, and to resist the invitations of the maiden, who, if the lad was a stranger in those parts, as seems to be implied, must have been a remarkably free-and easy style of young lady—merely because average human nature would have liked extremely to get out of the storm to the bright fireside, and to have had a quiet chat with the maiden. I don't mean to say that about ten years ago I did not think that *Excelsior* was a wonderful poem, setting out a true and noble principle. A young person is captivated with the notion of self-sacrifice, with or without a reason for it; but self-sacrifice, uncalled for and useless, is stark folly. It was very good of Curtius to jump into the large hole in the Forum; no doubt he saved the Senate great expense in filling it up, though probably it would have been easier to do so than to carry the Liverpool and Manchester Railway through Chatmoss. And we cannot think even yet, of Leonidas and his three hundred at Thermopylæ, without some stir of heart; but would not the gallant Lacedæmonians have been silly and not heroic, had not their self-sacrifice served a great end, by gaining for their countrymen certain precious days? Even Dickens, though not much of a philosopher, is more philosophic than Longfellow. He wrote a little book one Christmas-time, *The Battle of Life*, whose plot turns entirely upon an extraordinary act of self-sacrifice; and which contains many sentences which sound like the cant of the day. Witness the following:—

It is a world on which the sun never rises, but it looks upon a thousand bloodless battles, that are some set-off against the miseries and wickedness of battle-fields.

There are victories gained every day in struggling hearts, to which these fields of battle are as nothing.

But although the book contains such sentences, which seem to teach that struggle and self-conquest are noble in themselves, apart from their aim or their necessity, the lesson taught by the entire story is the true and just one, that there is no nobler thing than self-sacrifice and self-conquest, when they are right, when they are needful, when a noble end is to be gained by them.   As some dramatist or other says—

> "That's truly great!   What, think ye, 'twas set up
> The Greek and Roman names in such a lustre,
> But doing right, in stern despite of nature!
> Shutting their ears 'gainst all her little cries,
> When great, august, and godlike virtue call'd!"

The author, you see, very justly remarks that you are not called to fly in the face of nature, unless when there is good reason for it.   And therefore, my friend, don't get up at seven o'clock on a winter morning, if you can possibly help it.   If virtue calls, it will indeed be noble to rise by candlelight; but not otherwise. If you are the engine-driver of an early train, if you are a factory-hand, if you are a Glasgow student of philosophy, get up at an unseasonable period, and accept the writer's sympathy and admiration.   Poor fellow, you cannot help it!   But if you are a Glasgow professor, I have no veneration for that needless act of self-denial.   *You* need not get up so early unless you like.   *You* do the thing of your free choice.

And *your* heroism is only that of the Brahmin who swings on the hook, when nobody asks him to do so.

Having mused in this fashion, I look out of the carriage window. The morning is breaking, cold and dismal. There is a thick white mist. We are flying on, across gray fields, by spectral houses and trees, shewing indistinct through the uncertain light. It is light enough to read, by making an effort. I draw from my pocket a letter, which came late last night: it is from a friend, who is an eminent Editor. I do not choose to remember the name of the periodical which he conducts. I have had time to do no more than glance over it; and I have not yet arrived at its full meaning. I feel as Tony Lumpkin felt, who never had the least difficulty in reading the outside of his letters, but who found it very hard work to decipher the inside. The circumstance was the more annoying, he justly observed, inasmuch as the inside of a letter generally contains the cream of the correspondence.

When I receive a letter from my friend the Editor, I am able, by an intense application of attention for a few minutes, to make out its general drift and meaning. The difficulty in the· way of grasping the entire sense does not arise from any obscurity of style, but wholly from the remarkable nature of the penmanship. And after gaining the general bearing of the document, I am well aware that there are many recesses and nooks of meaning which will not be reached but after repeated perusals. What appeared at first a flourish of the pen may gradually assume the form of an important clause of a sentence, materially modifying its force. What appears at present a blot may turn out to be anything whatever ; what at present looks like No may prove to have stood for Yes. I think sympathetically of the worthy father of Dr Chalmers. When he received his weekly or fortnightly letter from his distinguished son, he carefully locked it up. By the time a little store had accumulated, his son came to pay him a visit ; and then he broke all the seals and got the writer of the letters to read them. I read my letter over ; several shades of thought break upon me, of whose existence in it I was previously unaware. That handwriting is like *In Memoriam.* Read it for the twentieth time, and you will find something new in it. I fold the letter up ; and I begin to think of a matter concerning which I have thought a good deal of late.

Surely, I think to myself, there is a respect in which the more refined and cultivated portion of the human race in Britain is suffering a rapid deterioration, and getting into a morbid state. I mean in the matter of nervous irritability or excitability. Surely people are far more *nervous* now than they used to be some generations back. The mental cultivation and the mental wear which we have to go through, tends to make that strange and inexplicable portion of our physical constitution a very great deal too sensitive for the work and trial of daily life. A few days ago I drove a friend who had been paying us a visit over to our railway station. He is a man of fifty, a remarkably able and accomplished man. Before the train started the guard came round to look at the tickets. My friend could not find his; he searched his pockets everywhere, and although the entire evil consequence, had the ticket not turned up, could not possibly have been more than the payment a second time of four or five shillings, he got into a nervous tremor painful to see. He shook from head to foot; his hand trembled so that he could not prosecute his search rightly, and finally he found the missing ticket in a pocket which he had already searched half-a-dozen times. Now contrast the condition of this highly-civilised man, thrown into a painful flurry and confusion at the demand of a railway ticket, with the impassive coolness of a savage who would not move a muscle if you hacked him in pieces. Is it not a dear price we pay for our superior cultivation, this morbid sensitiveness which makes us so keenly alive to influences which are painful and distressing? I have known very highly educated people who were positively trembling with anxiety and undefined fear every day before the post came in. Yet they had no reason to anticipate bad news; they could conjure up indeed a hundred gloomy forebodings of evil, but no one knew better than themselves how vain and weak were their fears. Surely the knights of old must have been quite dif ferent.   They had great stalwart bodies, and no minds to speak of.   They had no doubt a high sense of honour—not a very enlightened sense—but their purely intellectual nature was hardly developed at all.   They never read anything.   There were not many knights or squires like Fitz Eustace, who

> "Much had pored
> Upon a huge romantic tome,
> In the hall window of his home,
> Imprinted at the antique dome
> Of Caxton or De Worde."

They never speculated upon any abstract subject: and although in their long rides from place to place they might have had time for thinking, I suppose their attention was engrossed by the necessity of having a sharp look-out around them for the appearance of a foe.   And we all know that *that* kind of sharpness—the hunter's sharpness, the guerilla's sharpness—may coexist with the densest stupidity in all matters beyond the little range that is familiar.   The aboriginal Australian can trace friend or foe with the keenness almost of brute instinct: so can the Red Indian, so can the Wild Bushman ; yet the intellectual and moral nature in all these races is not very many degrees above the elephant or the shepherd's dog. And stupidity is a great preservative against nervous excitability or anxiety.   A dull man cannot think of the thousand sad possibilities which the quicker mind sees are brooding over human life.   Nor does this friendly stupidity only dull the understanding ; it gives *inertia*, immobility, to the emotional nature.   Compare a pure thoroughbred horse with a huge heavy cart-horse without a trace of breeding.   The thoroughbred is a beautiful creature indeed : but look at the startled eye, look at the quick ears, look at the blood coursing through those great veins so close to the surface, look how tremblingly alive the creature is to any sudden sight or sound.   Why, there you have got the perfection of equine nature, but you have paid for it just the same price that you pay for the perfection of human nature—what a *nervous* creature you have there ! Then look at the cart-horse. · It is clumsy in shape, ungraceful in movement, rough in skin, dull of eye ; in short, it is à great ugly brute.   But what a placid equanimity there is about it !   How composed, how immovable it looks, standing with its head hanging down, and its eyes half closed.   It is a low type of its race no doubt, but it enjoys the blessing which is en-joyed by the dull, stupid, unrefined woman or man , it is not nervous.   Let something fall with a whack, *it* does not start as if it had been shot.   Throw a little pebble at its flank, it turns round tranquilly to see what is the matter.   Why, the thoroughbred would have been over that hedge at much less provocation. ·

The morbid nervousness of the present day appears in several ways.   It brings a man sometimes to that startled state that the sudden opening of a door, the clash of the falling fire-irons, or any little accident, puts him in a flutter.   How nervous the late Sir

Robert Peel must have been when, a few weeks before his death, he went to the Zoological Gardens, and when a monkey suddenly sprang upon his arm, the great and worthy man fainted! Another phase of nervousness is when a man is brought to that state that the least noise or cross-occurrence seems to jar through the entire nervous system—to upset him, as we say; when he cannot command his mental powers except in perfect stillness, or in the chamber and at the writing-table to which he is accustomed; when, in short, he gets fidgety, easily worried, full of whims and fancies which must be indulged and considered, or he is quite out of sorts. Another phase of the same morbid condition is, when a human being is always oppressed with vague undefined fears that things are going wrong; that his income will not meet the demands upon it, that his child's lungs are affected, that his mental powers are leaving him—a state of feeling which shades rapidly off into positive insanity. Indeed, when matters remain long in any of the fashions which have been described, I suppose the natural termination must be disease of the heart, or a shock of paralysis, or insanity in the form either of mania or idiocy. Numbers of commonplace people who could feel very acutely, but who could not tell what they felt, have been worried into fatal heart-disease by prolonged anxiety and misery. Every one knows how paralysis laid its hand upon Sir Walter Scott, always great, lastly heroic. Protracted anxiety how to make the ends meet, with a large family and an uncertain income, drove Southey's first wife into the lunatic asylum : and there is hardly a more touching story than that of her fears and forebodings through nervous year after year. Not less sad was the end of her overwrought husband, in blank vacuity; nor the like end of Thomas Moore. And perhaps the saddest instance of the result of an over-driven nervous system, in recent days, was the end of that rugged, honest, wonderful genius, Hugh Miller.

Is it a reaction, a desperate rally against something that is felt to be a powerful invader, that makes it so much a point of honour with Englishmen at this day to retain, or appear to retain, a perfect immobility under all circumstances? It is pretty and interesting for a lady, at all events for a young lady, to exhibit her nervous tremors ; a man sternly represses the exhibition of these. Stoic philosophy centuries since, and modern refinement in its last polish of manner, alike recognise the Red Indian's principle, that there is something manly, something fine, in the repression of human feeling. Here is a respect in which the extreme of civilisation and the extreme of barbarism closely approach one another. The Red Indian really did not care for anything; the modern fine gentleman, the youthful exquisite, though really pretty nervous, wishes to convey by his entire deportment the impression, that he does not care for anything. A man is to exhibit no strong emotion. It is unmanly.

If he is glad, he must not look it.   If he loses a great deal more money than he can afford on the Derby, he must take it coolly.   Everything is to be taken coolly: and some indurated folk no doubt are truly as cool as they look.   Let me have nothing to do with such. *Nil admirari* is not a good maxim for a man.   The coolest individual who occurs to me at this moment is Mephistopheles in Goethe's *Faust*.   *He* was not a pleasant character.   That coolness is not human.   It is essentially Satanic.   But in many people in modern days the apparent coolness covers a most painful nervousness.   Indeed, as a general rule, whenever any one does anything which is (socially speaking) outrageously daring, it is because he is nervous ; and struggling with the feeling, and striving to conceal the fact.   A speaker who is too forward, who is jauntily free and easy, is certainly very nervous.   And though I have said that perfect coolness in all circumstances is not amiable or desirable, still one cannot look but with interest, if not with sympathy, at Campbell's fine description of the Red Indian :—

> He said,—and strain'd unto his heart the boy :—
> Far differently, the mute Oneyda took
> His calumet of peace and cup of joy :
> As monumental bronze unchanged his look ;
> A soul that pity touch'd, but never shook ;
> Train'd from his tree-rock'd cradle to his bier
> The fierce extremes of good and ill to brook
> Impassive,—fearing but the shame of fear,—
> A Stoic of the woods,—a man without a tear!

The writings of Mr Dickens furnish me with a com-

panion picture adapted to modern times. I confess
that, upon reflection, I doubt whether a considerable
portion of the interest of Outalissi's peculiar manner
may not be derived from distance in time and space.
Indian immobility and stoical philosophy are not
sublime in the servants' hall of modern society :—

" I don't know anything," said Britain, with a leaden eye and
an immovable visage. " I don't care for anything. I don't make
out anything. I don't believe anything. And I don't want
anything." *

Nervous people should live in large towns. The
houses are so big, and afford such impervious shadow,
that the nervous man, very little when compared with
them, does not feel himself pushed into painful pro-
minence. It is a comfort, too, to see many other
people going about. It carries the nervous man out
of himself. It reminds him that multitudes more have
their cares as well as he. It dispels the uncomfortable
feeling which grows on such people in the country, that
everybody is thinking and talking of them,—to see
numbers of men and women, all quite occupied with
their own concerns, and evidently never thinking of
them at all.

I have known one of these shrinking and evil-foreboding persons say, that he could not have lived in
the country (as he did) had not the district where his
home was been very thickly wooded with large trees.
It was a comfort to a man who wished to shrink out

* *The Battle of Life ; Christmas Books,* p. 169.

of sight and get quietly by when the road along which he was walking wound into a thick wood. The trees were so big and so old, and they seemed to make a shelter from the outer world. In walking over a vast bare level down, a man is the most conspicuous figure in the landscape. There is nothing taller than himself, and he can be seen from miles away. Now, to be pushed into notice—to be made a conspicuous figure —is intensely painful to the nervous man. You and I, my reader, no doubt think such a state of feeling morbid, but it is probably a state to which circumstances might bring most people. And we can quite well understand, that when pressed by care, sorrow, or fear, there is something friendly in the shade of trees —in anything that dims the light, and hides from public view. You remember the poor fellow (a very silly fellow indeed, but very silly fellows can suffer) who asked Little Dorrit to marry him, and met a decided though a kind refusal. He lived somewhere over in Southwark, in a street of poor houses, which had little back-greens, but of course no trees in them. But the poor fellow felt the instinctive longing of the stricken heart for shadow; and so, when his mother hung out the clothes from the wash on ropes crossing and re-crossing the little green, he used to go out and sit amid the flapping sheets, and say that "he felt it *like groves!*" Was not that a testimony to the friendly congeniality of trees to the sad or timorous human being? And when Cowper wearied to get away from a turbulent world to some quiet retreat, he did not wish that that retreat should be in an open country. No, he says—

> Oh, for a lodge in some vast wilderness,
> Some boundless *contiguity of shade,*
> Where rumour of oppression and deceit,
> Of unsuccessful or successful war,
> Might never reach me more !

To the same effect did the same shrinking poet express himself in lines equally familiar :—

> I was a stricken deer that left the herd
> Long since : with many an arrow deep infix'd
> My panting side was charged, when I withdrew
> To seek a tranquil death in *distant shades.*

I suppose that if some heavy blow had fallen upon any of us, we should not choose the open field or the bare hillside as the place to which we should go to think about it. We should rather choose some low-lying, sheltered, shaded spot. Great sorrow does not parade itself. It wishes to get out of sight.

As to the question how this nervousness may be got rid of, it is difficult to know what to think. It is in great measure a physical condition, and not under the control of the will. Some people would treat it physically—send the nervous man to the water-cure,—put him in training like a prize-fighter or a pedestrian, and the like. These are excellent things ; still I have greater confidence in mental remedies. Give the evil-foreboding man plenty to do ; push him out of his quiet course of life into the turmoil which he shrinks away from, and the turmoil will lose its fears. Work is the healthy atmosphere for a human being. The soul of man is a machine with this great peculiarity about it,—that we cannot stop it from motion when we will. Perhaps *that* is a defect. Many a man, through a weary sleepless night, has longed for the power to push some lever or catch into the swift-running engine that was whirring away within him, and bring it to a stand. However, it cannot be. And as the machine *will* go on, we must provide it with grist to grind, we must give it work to do, or it will knock itself in pieces ; or if not *that*, then get all warped and twisted, so that it never shall go without creaking, and straining, and trembling. And so, if you find a man or woman, young or old, vexed with ceaseless fears, worried with all kinds of odd ideas, doubts upon religious matters, and the like, don't argue with them ; *that* is not the treatment that is necessary in the meantime. There is something else to be done first. It would do no good to blister a horse's legs till the previous inflammation has gone down. It will do no good to present the soundest views to a nervous, idle man. Set him to hard work. Give him lots to do. And then that invisible machine, which has been turning off misery and delusion, will begin to turn off content and sound views of all things. After two or three weeks of this healthful treatment you may proceed to argue with your friend. In all likelihood you will find that argument will not be necessary. He has arrived at truth and sense already. There is a wonderfully close connexion between work and sound views; between doing and knowing. It is in life as it is in religion: "If any man will do His will, he shall know of the doctrine whether it be of God."

Looking out now, I see it has grown quite light, though the day is gloomy, and will be so to its close. The train is speeding round the base of a great hill. Far below us a narrow little river is dashing on, all in foam. Its sound is faintly heard at this height. I said to myself, by way of winding up my musing upon nervousness: After all, is not this painful fact just an over-degree of that which makes us living beings? Is it not just *life* too sensitively present in every atom of even the dull flesh? There is that gray rock which we are passing; how still and immovable *it* is! All the stoicism of Greece, all the impassiveness of the mute Oneyda, all the indifference of the *poco-curante* Englishman, how far they fall short of that sublime stillness! But it is still because it is senseless. It looks as if it felt nothing, because it really feels nothing. I compare it with Lord Derby before he gets up to make a great speech; fidgeting on his seat; watching every movement and word of the man he is going to smash; his wonderfully ready mind working with a whirr like wheel-work revolving unseen through its speed; *living intensely*, in fact, in every fibre of his frame. Well, *that* is the finer thing,

after all.   The big cart-horse, already thought of,
is something midway between the Premier and the
granite.   The stupid blockhead is cooler than the
Premier, indeed ; but he is not so cool as the granite.
If coolness be so fine a thing, of course the perfection
of coolness must be the finest thing ; and *that* we
find in the lifeless rock.   What is life but that which
makes us more sensitive than the rock : what is the
highest type of life but that which makes us most sensitive ? It is better to be the warm, trembling, foreboad-
ing, human being, than to be Ben Nevis, knowing nothing, feeling nothing, fearing nothing, cold and lifeless.

It is natural enough to pass from thinking of one
human weakness to thinking of another ; and certain
remarks of a fellow-traveller, not addressed to me,
suggest the inveterate tendency to vapouring and big
talking which dwells in many men and women.   Who
is there who desires to appear to his fellow-creatures
precisely what he is ?   I have known such people and
admired them, for they are comparatively few.   Why
does Mr Smith, when some hundreds of miles from
home, talk of his *place in the country?*   In the ety-
mological sense of the words it certainly is a place
in the country, for it is a seedy one-storied cottage
without a tree near it, standing bleakly on a hillside.
But *a place in the country* suggests to the mind long
avenues, great shrubberies, extensive greenhouses, fine
conservatories, lots of horses, abundance of servants ;

and *that* is the picture which Mr Smith desires to
call up before the mind's eye of those whom he
addresses. When Mr Robinson talks with dignity
about the political discussions which take place in his
servants' hall, the impression conveyed is that
Robinson has a vast establishment of domestics. A
vision rises of ancient retainers, of a dignified house-
keeper, of a bishop-like butler, of Jeamses without
number, of unstinted October. A man of strong
imagination may even think of huntsmen, falconers,
couriers—of a grand baronial *ménage*, in fact. You
would not think that Robinson's establishment consists of a cook, a housemaid, and a stable-boy. Very
well for the fellow too ; but why will he vapour ?
When Mr Jones told me the other day that something or other happened to him when he was going
out " to *the stables* to look at *the horses*," I naturally
thought, as one fond of horseflesh, that it would be a
fine sight to see Jones's *stables*, as he called them. I
thought of three handsome carriage-horses sixteen
hands high, a pair of pretty ponies for his wife to
drive, some hunters, beauties to look at and tremendous fellows to go. The words used might even have
justified the supposition of two or three racehorses,
and several lads with remarkably long jackets walking
about the yard. I was filled with fury when I learned
that Jones's *horses* consisted of a large brougham-
horse, broken-winded, and a spavined pony. I have
known a man who had a couple of moorland farms

habitually talk of his *estate.* One of the commonest
and weakest ways of vapouring is by introducing into
your conversation, very familiarly, the names of
people of rank whom you know nothing earthly
about. "How sad it is," said Mrs Jenkins to me the
other day, "about the duchess being so ill! Poor
dear thing! *We are all in such great distress about
her!*" "*We all*" meant, of course, the landed aristocracy of the district, of which Mrs Jenkins had lately
become a member, Jenkins having retired from the
hardware line and bought a small tract of quagmire.
Some time ago a man told me that he had been down
to Oatmealshire to see his *tenantry.* Of course he
was not aware that I knew that he was the owner of
just one farm. "This is my parish we have entered,"
said a youth of clerical appearance to me in a railway
carriage. In one sense it was; but he would not
have said so had he been aware that I knew he was
the curate, not the rector. "How can Brown and his
wife get on," a certain person observed to me; "they
cannot possibly live: they will starve. Think of
people getting married with not more than *eight or
nine hundred a-year!*" How dignified the man
thought he looked as he made the remark! It was
a fine thing to represent that he could not understand
how human beings could do what he was well aware
was done by multitudes of wiser people than himself.
"It is a cheap horse that of Wiggins's," remarked Mr
Figgins; "it did not cost more than seventy or eighty

pounds." Poor silly Figgins fancies that all who hear him will conclude that his own broken-kneed hack (bought for £25) cost at least £150. Oh, silly folk who talk big, and then think you are adding to your importance, don't you know that you are merely making fools of yourselves? In nine cases out of ten the person to whom you are relating your exaggerated story knows what the precise fact is. He is too polite to contradict you and to tell you the truth, but rely on it he *knows* it. No one believes the vapouring story told by another man; no, not even the man who fancies that his own vapouring story is believed. Every one who knows anything of the world knows how, by an accompanying process of mental arithmetic, to make the deductions from the big story told, which will bring it down to something near the truth. Frequently has my friend Mr Snooks told me of the crushing retort by which he shut up Jeffrey upon a memorable occasion. I can honestly declare that I never gave credence to a syllable of what he said. Repeatedly has my friend Mr. Longbow told me of his remarkable adventure in the Bay of Biscay, when a whale very nearly swallowed him. Never once did I fail to listen with every mark of implicit belief to my friend's narrative, but do you think I believed it? And more than once has Mrs O'Callaghan assured me that the hothouses on her fawther's esteet were three miles in length, and that each cluster of grapes grown on that favoured spot weighed above a hundredweight.   With profound respect I gave ear to all she said ; but, gentle daughter of Erin, did you think I was as soft as I seemed ? You may just as well tell the truth at once, ye big talkers, for every-body will know it, at any rate.

It is a sad pity when parents, by a long course of big talking, and silly pretension, bring up their children with ideas of their own importance which make them appear ridiculous, and which are rudely dissipated on their entering into life. The mother of poor Lollipop, when he went to Cambridge, told me that his genius was such that he was sure to be Senior Wrangler. And possibly he might have been if he had not been plucked.

It is peculiarly irritating to be obliged to listen to a vapouring person pouring out a string of silly ex-aggerated stories, all tending to shew how great the vapouring person is. Politeness forbids your stating that you don't believe them. I have sometimes de-rived comfort under such an infliction from making a memorandum, mentally, and then, like Captain Cuttle, "making a note" on the earliest opportunity. By taking this course, instead of being irritated by each successive stretch, you are rather gratified by the number and the enormity of them. I hereby give notice to all ladies and gentlemen whose conscience tells them that they are accustomed to vapour, that it is not improbable that I have in my possession a written list of remarkable statements made by them.

It is possible that they would look rather blue if they were permitted to see it.

Let me add, that it is not always vapouring to talk of one's self, even in terms which imply a compliment. It was not vapouring when Lord Tenterden, being Lord Chief-Justice of England, standing by Canterbury Cathedral with his son by his side, pointed to a little barber's shop, and said to the boy, "I never feel proud except when I remember that in that shop your grandfather shaved for a penny!" It was not vapouring when Burke wrote, "I was not rocked, and swaddled, and dandled into a legislator: *Nitor in adversum* is the motto for a man like me!" It was not vapouring when Milton wrote that he had in himself a conviction that "by labour and intent study, which he took to be his portion in this life, he might leave to after ages something so written as that men should not willingly let it die." Nor was it vapouring, but a pleasing touch of nature, when the King of Siam begged our ambassador to assure Queen Victoria that a letter which he sent to her, in the English language, was composed and written entirely by himself. It is not vapouring, kindly reader, when upon your return home after two or three days' absence, your little son, aged four years, climbs upon your knee, and begs you to ask his mother if he has not been a very good boy when you were away; nor when he shews you, with great pride, the medal which he has won a few years later. It is not vapouring when the gallant man who heroically jeoparded life and limb for the women's and children's sake at Lucknow, wears the Victoria Cross over his brave heart. Nor is it a piece of national vapouring, though it is, sure enough, an appeal to proud remembrances, when England preserves religiously the stout old *Victory*, and points strangers to the spot where Nelson fell and died.

But a shrieking whistle yells in my ear: my musings are suddenly pulled up. The hundred miles are traversed: the train is slackening its speed. It was half-past seven when we started: it is now about half-past eleven. We draw alongside the platform: *there* are faces I know. I see a black head over the palisade: *that* is my horse. It would be vapouring to say that my *carriage* awaits me: for though it has four wheels, it is drawn by no more than four legs. Drag out a portmanteau from under the seat, exchange a cap for a hat, open the door, jump out, bundle away home. And then, perhaps, I may tell some unknown friends who have the patience to read my essays, *How I mused in the railway train.*

CHAPTER V.

CONCERNING THE MORAL INFLUENCES OF THE DWELLING.

WHEN the great Emperor Napoleon was packed off to Elba, he had, as was usual with him, a sharp eye to theatrical effect. Indeed, that distinguished man, during the period of his great elevation as well as of his great downfall, was subject, in a degree almost unexampled, to the tyranny of a principle which in the case of commonplace people finds expression in the representative inquiry, " What will Mrs Grundy say ? " Whenever Napoleon was about to do anything particular, or was actually doing anything particular, he was always thinking to himself, " What will Mrs Grundy say ? " Of course *his* Mrs Grundy was a much bigger and much more important individual than *your* Mrs Grundy, my reader. *Your* Mrs Grundy is the ill-natured, tattling old tabby who lives round the corner, and whose window you feel as much afraid to pass as if it were a battery commanding the pavement, and as if the ugly old woman's baleful eyes were so many Lancaster guns. Or perhaps your Mrs Grundy is the good-natured friend (as described by Mr Sheridan) who is always ready to tell you of anything he has heard to your disadvantage, but who would not for the world repeat to you any kind or pleasant remark, lest the vanity thereby fostered should injuriously affect your moral development. But Napoleon's Mrs Grundy consisted of Great Britain and Ireland, Russia, Prussia, Austria, Italy, Spain, Denmark, Sweden, Norway, Switzerland, the United States ; in brief, to Napoleon, Mrs Grundy meant Europe, Asia, Africa, and America. And really when a man is asking himself what the whole civilised world will think and say about what he is doing, and when he feels quite sure that it will think and say *something*, it is excusable if in what he does he has an eye to what Mrs Grundy will think and say.

Accordingly, when the great Emperor was forced to exchange the imperial throne of France for the sovereignty of that little speck in the Mediterranean, his first and most engrossing reflection on his journey to Elba was, What will Mrs Grundy say? And many thoughts not very pleasant to an ambitious man of unphilosophical temperament would be suggested by the question. He would naturally think, Mrs Grundy will be chuckling over my downfall . Mrs Grundy will be saying that I, and all my aspirations and hopes, have been fearfully smashed. Mrs Grundy will be saying that it serves me right for my impudence. Mrs Grundy will be saying (kindly) that it will do me a great deal of good. Amiable and benevolent old lady ! Mrs Grundy will be saying that I am now going away to my exile in very low spirits, feeling very bitter, very much disappointed, very thoroughly humbled,—going away (only Napoleon had not read Swift) in the extremity of impotent fury, to " die in a rage, like a poisoned rat in a hole." Mrs Grundy will be saying that when I get to Elba finally, I shall lead a poor life there ; kicking about the dogs and cats, swearing at the servants, whacking the horses viciously, perhaps even throwing plates at the attendants' heads. Such, the Emperor would think, will be the sayings of Mrs Grundy. And the Emperor, not a man of resigned or philosophical temper, would know that in all this Mrs Grundy would be nearly right. But at all events, says Napoleon to himself, she shall not have the satisfaction of thinking that she is so. I shall mortify Mrs Grundy by making her think that I am perfectly jolly. I shall get her to believe that all this humiliation which she has heaped upon me is impotent to touch me where I can really feel. She shall think that she has not found the raw. And so, when Napoleon settled at Elba,—stamped upon his coin, engraven upon his silver plate, emblazoned on his carriage panels, written upon his very china and crockery,—there blazed forth in Mrs Grundy's view the defiant words, *Ubicunque felix !*

Now, had Mrs Grundy had much philosophic insight into human conduct and motives, she would have known that her purpose of humilation and embitterment was attained, and that all her ill-set sayings had proved right. It was because in Elba the great exile was a bitterly disappointed man, that he so ostentatiously paraded before the world the assurance that he was "happy anywhere." It was because he thought so much of Mrs Grundy, and attached so much importance to what she might say, that he hung out this flag of defiance. If he had really been as happy and as independent of outward circumstances as he said he was, he would not have taken the trouble to say so. Had Napoleon said nothing about himself, but begun to grow cabbages and train flowers, and grown fat and rosy, we should not have needed the motto. But if any man, Emperor or not, trumpet forth on the housetops that he is *ubicunque felix;* and if we find him walking moodily by the sea-shore, with a knitted brow and absent air, and a very poor appetite; why, my reader, the answer to his statement may be conveyed, inarticulately, by a low and prolonged whistle; or articulately, by an advice to address that statement to the marines.

If there be a thing which I detest, it is a diffuse and rambling style. Let any writer always treat his subject in a manner terse and severely logical. My own model is Tacitus, and the earlier writings of Bacon. Let a man say in a straightforward way what he has got to say; and the more briefly the better. And above all, young writer, avoid that fashion which is set by the leading articles of the *Times*, of beginning your observations upon a subject with something which to the ordinary mind appears to have nothing earthly to do with it. By carefully carrying out the advices here tendered to you, you may ultimately, after several years of practice, attain to a limited success as an obscure third-rate essayist.

Napoleon, then (to resume our argument after this little *excursus*), paraded before the world the declaration that it did not matter to him where he might be ; he would be "happy anywhere." What tremendous nonsense he talked! Why, setting aside altogether such great causes of difference as an unhealthy climate, stupid society or no society at all, usefulness or uselessness, honour or degradation,—I do not hesitate to say that the scenery amid which a man lives, and the house in which he lives, have a vast deal to do with making him what he is. The same man (to use an expression which is only seemingly Hibernian) is an entirely different man when put in a different place. Life is in itself a neutral thing, colourless and tasteless; it takes its colour and its flavour from the scenes amid which we lead it. It is like water, which external influences may make the dirtiest or cleanest, the bitterest or sweetest, of all things. Life, character, feeling, are things very greatly dependent on external influences. In a larger sense than the common saying is usually understood, we are "the creatures of circumstances." Only very stolid people are not affected by the scenes in which they live. I do not mean to say that an appreciable difference will be produced on a man's character by varied *classes* of scenery; that is, that the same man will be appreciably different, morally, according as you place him for days on a rocky, stormy coast; on a level sandy shore; inland in a fertile wooded country; inland among bleak wild hills; among Scotch firs with their long bare poles; horse-chestnuts blazing with their June blossoms; or thick full laurels, and yews, and hollies, thick to the ground, and shutting an external world out. I do not mean to say that ordinary people will feel any appreciable variation of the moral and spiritual atmosphere, traceable for its cause to such variety of scene. A man must be fashioned of very delicate clay, he must have a nervous system very sensitive, morbidly sensitive, perhaps, if such things as these very decidedly determine what he shall be, morally and intellectually, for the time. Yet no doubt such matters have upon many human beings a real effect. If you live in a country house into whose grounds you enter through a battlemented gateway under a lofty arch; if the great leaves of the massive oak and iron gate are swung back to admit you, as you pass from the road outside to the sequestered pleasance within, where the grass, the gravel, the evergreens, the flowers, the winding paths, the little pond, the noisy little brook that passes beneath the rustic bridge, are all cut off from the outer world by a tall battlemented wall, too tall for leaping or looking over,—I think that, at first at least, you will have a different feeling all day, you will be a different man all day, for that arched gateway and that battlemented wall. You will not feel as if you had come in by a common five-bar gate, painted green, hung from freestone pillars five or six feet high, and shaded with laurels. It is wonderful what an effect is produced upon many minds by even a single external circumstance such as that ; nor can I admit that there is anything morbid in the mind which is affected by such things. A very little thing, a solitary outward fact, may, by the influence of associations not necessarily personal, become idealised into something whose flavour reaches, like salt in cookery, perceptibly through all life. "You may laugh as you please," says one of the most thoughtful and delightful of English essayists, "but life seems somewhat insupportable to me without a pond—a squarish pond, not over clean." You and I do not know, my readers, what early recollections may have made such a little piece of water something whose presence shall appreciably affect the genial philosopher's feeling day by day, and hour by hour. The savour of its presence (I don't speak materially) may reach everywhere. And if there be anything which that writer is *not*, he is not morbid ; and he is not fanciful in the sense in which a fanciful person means a chronicler of morbid impressions. And we all remember the little child in Wordsworth's poem, who persisted in express·ing a decided preference for one place in the country above another which appeared likely to have greater attractions; and who, when pressed for his reasons, did, after much reflection, fix upon a single fact as the cause of his preference :—

> At Kilve there was no weathercock;
> And that's the reason why.

No one can tell how that weathercock may have obtruded itself upon the little man's dreams, or how thoroughly its presence may have permeated all his life.   I know a little child, three years and a half old, whose entire life for many weeks appeared embittered by the presence of a dinner-bell upon the hall-table of her home.   She could not be induced to go near it; she trembled with terror when she heard it rung : it fulfilled for her the part of Mr Thackeray's famous skeleton.   And I am very sure that we have all of us dinner-bells and weathercocks which haunt and worry us, and squarish ponds which give a savour to our life. And for any ordinary mortal to say that he is *ubicunque felix* is pure nonsense.   Napoleon found it was nonsense even at Elba; and at St Helena he found it yet more distinctly.   No man can say truly that he is the same wherever he goes.   That sublime elevation above outward circumstances is not attainable by beings all of whom are half, and a great many of whom are a good deal more than half, material.   We are all moral chameleons; and we take the colour of the objects among which we are placed.

Here am I this morning, writing on busily.   I am

all alone in a quiet little study. The prevailing colour around me is green—the chairs, tables, couches, bookcases, are all of oak, rich in colour, and growing dark through age, but green predominates: window-curtains, table-covers, carpet, rug, covers of chairs and couches, are green. I look through the window, which is some distance off, right before me. The window is set in a frame of green leaves: it looks out on a quiet corner of the garden. There is a wall not far off green with ivy and other climbing plants; there is a bright little bit of turf like emerald, and a clump of evergreens varying in shade. Over the wall I see a round green hill, crowned by oaks which autumn has not begun to make sere. How quiet everything is! I am in a comparatively remote part of the house, and there is no sound of household life; no pattering of little feet; no voices of servants in discussion less logical and calm than might be desired. The timepiece above the fireplace ticks audibly; the fire looks sleepy; and I know that I may sit here all day if I please, no one interrupting me. No man worth speaking of will spend his ordinary day in idleness; but it is pleasant to think that one may divide one's time and portion out one's day at one's own will and pleasure. Such a mode of life is still possible in this country: we do not all as yet need to live in a ceaseless hurry, ever drive, driving on till the worn-out machine breaks down. By and by this life of unfeverish industry, and of work whose results are tangible only to people of cultivation, will no doubt cease ; and it will tend materially to hasten that consummation when the views of the *Times* are carried out, and all the country clergy are required to keep a diary like a rural policeman, shewing how each hour of their time is spent, and open to the inspection of their employers. Now, in a quiet scene like this, where there is not even the little noise of a village near, though I can hear the murmur of a pretty large river, must not the ordinary human being be a very different being from what he would be were he sitting in some gas-lighted counting-house in Manchester, turning over large vellum-bound volumes, adding long rows of figures, talking on sales and prices to a hundred and fifty people in the course of the day, looking out through the window upon a foggy atmosphere, a muddy pavement, a crowded street, huge drays lumbering by with their great horses, with a general impression of noise, hurry, smoke, dirt, confusion, and no rest or peace? It would be an interesting thing for some one equal to the task to go over Addison's papers in the *Spectator*, and try to make out the shade of difference in them which might be conceived as resulting from the influences of the place where they were severally written. It is generally understood that the well-known letters by which Addison distinguished his essays referred to the places where they were composed ; the letters in the Clio indicating Chelsea, London, Islington, and the

Office. Did the sensitive, shy genius feel that in the production dated from each scene there would be some trace of what Yankees call the surroundings amid which it was produced? No doubt a mind like Addison's, impassive as he was, would turn off very different material according to the conditions in which the machine was working. As for Dick Steele, probably it made very little difference to him where he was: at the coffee-house table, with noise and bustle all about him, he would write as quietly as though he had been quietly at home. *He* was indurated by long usage; the hide of a hippopotamus is not sensitive to gentle influences which would be felt by your soft hand, my fair friend. But in the case of ordinary educated men there is no greater fallacy than that suggested by that vile old subject for Latin themes, that *cælum, non animum mutant, qui trans mare currunt.* Ordinary people, in changing the *cælum,* undergo a great change of the *animus* too. A judicious man would be extremely afraid of marrying any girl in England, and forthwith taking her out to India with him; for it would be quite certain that she would be a very different person *there* from what she had been *here;* and how different and in what mode altered and varied only experience could shew. So one might marry one woman in Yorkshire, and live with quite another at Boggley-wollah; and in marriage it is at least desirable to know what it is you are getting. Every one knows people who are

quite different people according as they are in town
or country. I know a man—an exceedingly clever
and learned man—who in town is sharp, severe,
hasty, a very little bitter, and just a shade ill-
tempered, who on going to the country becomes
instantly genial, frank, playful, kind, and jolly : you
would not know him for the same man if his face and
form changed only half as much as his intellectual
and moral nature. Many men, when they go to the
country, just as they put off frock coats and stiff
stocks, and put on loose shooting suits, big thick
shoes, a loose soft handkerchief round their neck ;
just as they pitch away the vile hard hat of city
propriety that pinches, cramps, and cuts the hapless
head, and replace it by the light yielding wide-awake ;
do mentally pass through a like process of relief:
their whole spiritual being is looser, freer, less tied up.
Such changes as that from town to country must, I
should think, be felt by all educated people, and
make an appreciable difference in the moral condition of all educated people. Few men would feel
the same amid the purple moors round Haworth, and
amid the soft English scenery that you see from
Richmond Hill. Some individuals, indeed, whose
mind is not merely torpid, may carry the same
animus with them wherever they go ; but their *animus*
must be a very bad one. Mr Scrooge, before his
change of nature, was no doubt quite independent of
external circumstances, and would no doubt have

thought it proof of great weakness had he not been so. Nor was it a being of an amiable character in whose mouth Milton has put the words, "No matter where, so *I* be still the same." And even in *his* mouth the sentiment was rather vapouring than true. But a dull, heavy, prosaic, miserly, cantankerous, cynical, suspicious, bitter old rascal would probably be much the same anywhere. Such a man's nature is indurated against all the influences of scenery, as much as the granite rock against sunshine and showers.

I dare say there are few people who do not unconsciously admit the principle of which so much has been said. Few people can look at a pretty tasteful villa, all gables, turrets, bay windows, twisted chimneys, verandahs, and balconies, set in a pleasant little expanse of shrubbery, with some fine forest-trees, a green bit of open lawn, and some winding walks through clumps of evergreens, without tacitly concluding that the people who live there must lead a very different life from that which is led in a dull smoky street, and a blackened, gardenless, grassless, treeless house in town; very different even from the life of the people in the tasteless square stuccoed box, with a stiff gravel walk going up to its door, a few hundred yards off. If you are having a day's sail in a steamer, along a pretty coast dotted with pleasant villages, you cannot repress some notion that the human beings whom you see loitering about there upon the rocks, in that pure air and genial idleness, are beings of a different order from those around you. You feel that to set foot on that pier, and to mingle with that throng, would carry you away a thousand miles in a moment; and make you as different from what you are as though you had suddenly dropt from the sky into that quiet voluptuous valley of Typee, where Hermann Melville was so perfectly happy till he discovered that all the kindness of the natives was intended to make him the fatter and more palatable against that festival at which he was to be eaten. And no wonder that he felt comfortable, if that happy valley was indeed what he assures us it was :—

There were no cares, griefs, troubles, or vexations, in all Typee. There were none of those thousand sources of irritation that the ingenuity of civilised man has created to mar his own felicity. There were no foreclosures of mortgages, no protested notes, no bills payable, no debts of honour, in Typee ; no unreasonable tailors or shoemakers perversely bent on being paid, no duns of any description ; no assault and battery attorneys to foment discord, backing their clients up to a quarrel, and then knocking their heads together ; no poor relations everlastingly occupying the spare bedchamber, and diminishing the elbow-room at the family-table ; no destitute widows, with their children starving on the cold charities of the world ; no beggars, no debtors' prisons, no proud and hard-hearted nabobs in Typee ; or, to sum up all in one word—no Money ! That root of all evil was not to be found in the valley.

In this secluded abode of happiness there were no cross old women, no cruel step-dames, no withered spinsters, no love-sick maidens, no sour old bachelors, no inattentive husbands, no melancholy young men, no blubbering youngsters, and no squalling brats. All was mirth, fun, and high good humour.

It is pleasant to read such a description. It is like being carried suddenly from the Royal Exchange on a crowded afternoon, to a grassy, shady bank by the side of a country river. Probably most of us have travelled by railway through a wild country; and when we stopped at some remote station among the hills, have wondered how the people there live, and thought how different their life must be from ours. Nor is it a mere fancy that takes possession of us when we look at the pretty Elizabethan dwelling, the thought of which carried us all the way to the South Pacific. If people are calm enough to be susceptible of external impressions, life really *is* very different there. I do not say it is necessarily happier; but it is very different. Habit, indeed, equalises the practical enjoyment of all lots, excepting only those of extreme suffering and degradation. Whatever level you get to in the scale of advantage, you soon get so accustomed to it that you do not mind much about it. When I used to study metaphysical philosophy, I remember that it appeared to me that this thought supplies by far the most serious of all objections to the doctrine (as taught by nature) of the Divine benevolence. It is a graver objection than the existenco of positive evil. *That* may be conceived to be in some way inevitable; but why should it be that to get a thing instantly diminishes its value to half? I can think of a reason why; and a good reason too: but it is not drawn from the domain of philosophy. A poor fellow, toiling wearily along the dusty road, thinks how happy that man must be who is just now passing him, leaning back upon the cushions of that luxurious carriage, swept along by that pair of smoking thorough-breds. Of course the poor fellow is mistaken. The man in the carriage is no happier than he. And, indeed, I can say conscientiously that the very saddest, most peevish, most irritable, and most discontented faces I have ever seen, I have seen looking out of extremely handsome carriage windows. Luxury destroys real enjoyment. There is more real enjoyment in riding in a wheelbarrow than in driving in a carriage and four. Who does not remember the keen relish of the rapid run in the wheelbarrow of early youth, bumping and rolling about, and finally turning a corner at full speed and upsetting? Who does not remember the delight of the little springless carriage that threatened to dislocate and grind down the bones? But it is indeed much to be lamented, that merely to get near the possession of any coveted thing instantly changes the entire look of it: it may still appear very good and desirable : but the romance is gone. When Mr John Campbell, Student of Theology in St Mary's College, St Andrews, N.B., was working away at his Hebrew, or drilling the lads to whom he acted as tutor, and living sparingly on a few pounds a-year, he would no doubt have thought it a tremendous thing if he had been told that he would yet be a peer—that he would be, first Lord Chief-

Justice and then Lord High Chancellor of England—
and that he would, upon more than one great occasion,
preside over the assembled aristocracy of Britain.
But as he got on step by step, the gradation took off
the force of contrast: each successive step appeared
natural enough, no doubt: and now, when he is fairly
at the top of the tree, if that most amiable and able
judge should ever wish to realise his elevation, I suppose he can do so only by recurring in thought to the
links of St Andrews, and to the days when he drilled
his pupils in Latin and Greek. Student of divinity,
newspaper reporter, utter barrister, King's Counsel,
Solicitor-General, Member for Edinburgh, Attorney-
General, Baron Campbell of St Andrews, Chief-Justice
of England, Lord Chancellor of Great Britain—each
successive point was natural enough when won,
though the end made a great change from the Manse
of Cupar. And when another Scotch clergyman's son,
from a parish adjoining that of Lord Campbell's father,
also went up to London about the same time, a poor
struggling artist, he and all his family would doubtless
have thought it a grand elevation, had they been told
that he was to become one of the most distinguished
members of the Royal Academy. There is something
intensely affecting in the letters which the minister of
Cults (it was a very poor living) sent to his boy in
London, saying that he could, by pinching, send him,
if needful, four or five pounds. But before Sir David
became the great man he grew, old Mr Wilkie was in

his grave : "his son came to honour, and he knew it not." No doubt it was better as it was; but if you or I, kindly reader, had had the ordering of things, the worthy man should have lived to see what would have gladdened his simple heart at last.

Still, making every deduction for the levelling result of getting used to things, a great deal of the enjoyment of life, high or low, depends on the scenery amid which one dwells, and the house in which one lives—I mean the house regarded even in a merely æsthetic point of view. It needs no argument to prove that if one's abode is subject to the grosser physical disadvantages of smoky chimneys, damp walls, neighbouring bogs, incurable draughts, rattling windows, unfitting doors, and the like, the result upon the temper and the views of the man thus afflicted will not be a pleasing one. A constant succession of little contemptible worries tends to foster a querulous, grumbling disposition, which renders a human being disagreeable to himself and intolerable to his friends. Real, great misfortunes and trials may serve to ennoble the character; but ever-recurring petty annoyances produce a littleness and irritability of mind. And while great misfortune at once engages our sympathy, petty annoyances ill borne make the sufferer a laughing-stock. There is something dignified in Napoleon smashed at Waterloo; there is nothing fine about Napoleon at St Helena, swearing at his ill-made soup, and cursing up and down stairs at his insufficient allowance of clean shirts.

But I am not now talking of abodes pressed by physical inconveniences. It is somewhat of a truism to say a man cannot be comfortable when he is uncomfortable; and *that* is the sum of what is to be said on that head. I mean now that one's home, æsthetically regarded, has much influence upon our enjoyment of life. It is a great matter towards making the best of this world, (and possibly, too, of the next,) that our dwelling shall be a pretty one, a pleasant one, and placed amid pleasant scenes. It is a constant pleasure to live in such a home; and it is a still greater pleasure to make it. I do not think I have ever seen happier people, or people who appeared more thoroughly enviable, than people who have been building a pretty residence in the country. Of course they must be building it for themselves to have the full satisfaction of it; also it must not be too large; and finally, it must not be bigger nor grander than they can afford. The last-named point is essential. A duke inherits his castle—he did not build it; and it is too large and splendid for the peculiar feeling which I am describing. It has its own peculiar charms: the charm of vastness of dwelling and domain; the charm of hoary age and historic memories, and of connexion with departed ancestors, and of associations which the millions of the *parvenu* cannot buy. But it lacks the especial charm which Scott felt when he was building Abbotsford; and which lesser men feel when sitting on a stone on a summer morning, and watching the walls going up, listening to the clinking of the chisel, planning out the few acres of ground, and idealising the life which is to be led there ; seeing with half-closed eyes that muddy wheel-cut expanse all green and trim ; and little Jamie running about the walk which will be there in after-days ; and little Lucy diligently planting weeds in the corner where her garden will be. Here, surely, we think, the last days or years may peacefully go by ; and here may we, though somewhat scarred in the battle of life, and somewhat worn with its cares, find a quiet haven at last. To me it is always pleasant reading when I fall in with books about planning and building such homes as these. At the mention of the *Cottage*, and even of the *Villa*, (though I don't like that latter word, it sounds vulgar and cockneyfied and affected ; but I fear we must accept it, for there is no other which conveys the idea of the modest yet elegant country-house for people of refinement, but not of great means,) there rises up before the mind's eye, as if by an enchanter's wand, a whole life of quiet enjoyment. Surely, life in the cottage or the country-house might be made a very pleasing, pure, and happy thing. In that unbreathed air, amid those beautiful scenes, surrounded by the gentle processes and teachings of nature, it is but that outward nature and human life should, on some fair summer-day, be wrought into a happy conformity ; and we should need no other heaven. Take the outward creation at her best, and for all the thorns and thistles of the Fall, *she* would do yet!

I find a great pleasure in reading books of practical architecture : and I have lately found out one by an American architect, one Mr Calvert Vaux, which carries one into fresh fields. It is a large handsome volume, luxurious in the size of its type, and admirable for the excellence of its abundant illustrations. I have more to say of its contents by and by, and shall here say only, that to read such a book with pleasure, the reader must have some little imagination and a good deal of sympathy, so as not to rest on mere architects' designs and builders' specifications, but to picture out and enter into the quiet life which these suggest. Everything depends upon *that.* Therein lies the salt of such a book. The enjoyment of all things beyond eating and drinking arises out of our idealising them. Do you think that a child who will spend an hour delightedly in galloping round the garden on his horse, which horse is a stick, regards that stick as the mere bit of wood? No : that stick is to him instinct with imaginings of a pony's pattering feet and shaggy mane, and erect little ears. It is not so long since the writer was accustomed to ride on horseback in that inexpensive fashion, but what he can remember all that the stick was ; and remember too how sometimes fancy would flag, the idealising power would break down, and from being a horse the stick became merely a stick, a dull, wearisome, stupid thing. And of what little things imagination, thus elevating and enchanting them, can make how much ! You remember the poor little solitary girl, in the wretched kitchen of Sally Brass, in the *Old Curiosity Shop*. Never was there life more bare of anything like enjoyment than the life which that poor creature led. Think, you folk who grumble at your lot, of a life whose features are sketched by such lines as a dark cellar, utter solitude, black beetles, cold potatoes, cuffs, and kicks. Yet the idealising power could convey some faint tinge of enjoyment even into the cellar of House of Brass. The poor little thing, when she made the acquaintance of Mr Richard Swiveller, inquired of him had he ever tasted orange-peel wine. How was it made, he asked. The recipe was simple : take a tumbler of cold water, put a little bit of orange peel into it, and the beverage is ready for use. It has not much taste, added the little solitary, unless you *make believe very much*. Sound and deep little philosopher ! We must apply the same prescription to life, and all by which life is surrounded. You are not to accept them as bare prosaic facts : you must make believe very much. Scott made believe very much at Abbotsford ; we all make believe very much at Christmas-time. Likewise at sight of the first snowdrop in springs after we have begun to grow old ; also when hawthorn blossoms and lilacs come again. And what a bare, cold, savourless life is sketched by the memorable lines which set before us the entire character of a man who could not make believe :—

> In vain, through every changing year,
>   Did nature lead him as before ;
> A primrose by a river's brim,
> A yellow primrose was to him,—
>   And it was nothing more !

Let me recommend to the man with a taste for such subjects, Mr Sanderson's *Rural Architecture,* a neat little manual of a hundred pages, with a number of drawings and ground-plans of labourers' cottages, pretty little villas, village schools, and farm-steadings. And any reader may call it his upon payment of one shilling. ·To the man who has learned to make believe, there will be more than a shilling's worth of enjoyment in the frontispiece, which is a plain but pretty Gothic cottage, surrounded with trees, a little retired from the road, which is reached through a neat rustic gateway, and with the spire of a village church two hundred yards off, peeping through trees and backed by quiet fields rising into hills of no more than English height. A footpath winds through the field towards the clump of wood in which stands the church. The book is a sensible and well-informed one. Its author tells us, but not till the seventieth page of his hundred, that he is "simply desirous of having an agreeable half-hour's chat with the reader, who may take a fancy to indulge in the instructive pastime of building his own house, and who does not

please to appear thoroughly ignorant of the matter he
is about."

Mr Sanderson appears from his book to have but
a poor opinion of human nature. He is by no means
a "confidence-man." The book is full of cautions as
to the necessity of closely watching work-people lest
they should cheat you, and do their work in a dishonest and insufficient manner. I lament to say that
my own little experience leads me to think that these
cautions are by no means unnecessary. I do not
think that builders and carpenters are as bad as horse-
dealers, whose word no man in his senses should regard as of the worth of a pin; but it is extremely
advisable to keep a sharp eye upon them while their
work is progressing. Work improperly done, or done
with insufficient materials, will certainly cause much
expense and annoyance at a future day; still, the con-
stantly-recurring statements as to the likelihood of
fraud, leave on one's mind an uncomfortable impression. Our race is not in a sound state. But perhaps
it is too severe to judge that a decent-looking and
well-to-do individual is a dishonest man, merely because he will at any time tell a lie to make a little
money by it.

There is a satisfaction in finding confirmation of
one's own views in the writings of other men ; and so
I quote with pleasure the following from Dr South-
wood Smith :—

A clean, fresh, and well-ordered house exercises over its

inmates a moral, no less than a physical influence, and has a direct tendency to make the members of the family sober, peaceable, and considerate of the feelings and happiness of each other; nor is it difficult to trace a connexion between habitual feelings of this sort and the formation of habits of respect for property, for the laws in general, and even for those higher duties and obligations the observance of which no laws can enforce. Whereas, a filthy, squalid, unwholesome dwelling, in which none of the decencies common to society—even in the lowest stage of civilisation—are or can be observed, tends to make every dweller in such a hovel regardless of the feelings and happiness of each other, selfish, and sensual. And the connexion is obvious between the constant indulgence of appetites and passions of this class, and the formation of habits of idleness, dishonesty, debauchery, and violence.

There is something very touching in a description in *Household Words* of the moral results of wretched dwellings, such as those in parts of Bethnal Green, in the eastern region of London. Misery and anxiety have here crushed energy out; the people are honest, but they are palsied by despair:—

The people of this district are not criminal. A lady might walk unharmed at midnight through their wretched lanes. Crime demands a certain degree of energy; but if there were ever any harm in these well-disposed people, it has been tamed out of them by sheer want. They have been sinking for years. Ten years ago, or less, the men were politicians; now, they have sunk below that stage of discontent. They are generally very still and hopeless; cherishing each other; tender not only towards their own kin, but towards their neighbours; and they are subdued by sorrow to a manner strangely resembling the quiet and refined tone of the most polished circles.

Very true to nature! How well one can understand the state of mind of a poor man quite crushed and spirit-broken: poisoned by ceaseless anxiety; with no heart to do anything; many a time wishing that he might but creep into a quiet grave; and meanwhile trying to shrink out of sight and slip by unnoticed! Despair nerves for a little while, but constant care saps, and poisons, and palsies. Nor does it do so in Bethnal Green alone, or only in dwellings which are undrained and unventilated, and which cannot exclude rain and cold. Elsewhere, as many of my readers have perhaps learned for themselves, it has shattered many a nervous system, unstrung many a once vigorous mind, crushed down many a once hopeful spirit, and aged many a man who should have been young by his years.

I suppose it is now coming to be acknowledged by all men of sense, that it is a Christian duty to care for our fellow-creatures' bodies as well as for their souls; and that it is hateful cant and hypocrisy to pray for the removal of diseases which God by the revelations of Nature has taught us may be averted by the use of physical means, while these means have not been faithfully employed. When cholera or typhus comes, let us whitewash blackened walls, flush obstructed sewers, clear away intermural pigsties, abolish cesspools, admit abundant air and light, and supply unstinted water:—and having done all we can, let us then pray for God's blessing upon what we have done and for His protection from the plague which by these means we are seeking to hold away from us. Prayers and pains must go together alike in the physical and in the spiritual world. And I think it is now coming to be acknowledged by most rational beings, that houses ought to be pretty as well as healthy ; and that houses, even of the humblest class, *may* be pretty as well as healthy. By the Creator's kind arrangement, beauty and use go together ; the prettiest house will be the healthiest, the most convenient, and the most comfortable. And I am persuaded that great moral results follow from people's houses being pretty as well as healthy. Every one understands at once that a wretched hovel, dirty, ruinous, stifling, bug-infested, dunghill-surrounded, will destroy any latent love of neatness and orderliness in a poor man ; will destroy the love of home, that preservative against temptation which ranks next after religion in the heart, and send the poor man to the public-house, with all its ruinous temptations. But probably it is less remembered than it ought to be, that the home of poor man or well-to-do man ought to be pleasing and inviting, as well as healthy. If not, he will not and cannot have the feeling towards it that it is desirable he should have. And all this is not less to be sought after in the case of people who are so well off that though their home afford no gratification of taste, and even lack the comfort which does not necessarily come with mere abundance, they are not likely to seek refuge at the alehouse, or to take to sottish or immoral courses of any kind.　It makes an educated man domestic, it makes him a lover of neatness and accuracy, it makes him gentle and amiable, (I mean in all but very extreme cases,) to give him a pretty home.　I wish it were generally understood that it does not of necessity cost a shilling more to build a pretty house of a certain size, than to build a hideous one yielding the like accommodation.　Taste costs nothing.　If you have a given quantity of building materials to arrange in order, it is just as easy and just as cheap to arrange them in a tasteful and graceful order and collocation, as in a tasteless, irritating, offensive, and disgusting one.　Elaborate ornament, of course, costs dear: but it does not need elaborate ornament to make a pleasing house which every man of taste will feel enjoyment in looking at.　Simple gracefulness is all that is essentially needful in cottage and villa architecture.　And in this æsthetic age, when there is a general demand for greater beauty in all physical appliances; when we are getting rid of the vile old willow-pattern, when bedroom crockery must be of graceful form and embellishment, when grates and fenders, chairs and couches, window-curtains and carpets, oilcloth for lobby floors and paper for covering walls, must all be designed in conformity with the dictates of an elevated taste, it is not too much to hope that the day will come when every human dwelling that shall be built shall be so built and so placed that it shall form a picture pleasant to all men to look at. It is not necessary to say that this implies a considerable change from the state of matters at present existing in most districts of this country. And I trust it is equally unnecessary to say what school of domestic architecture must predominate if the day we wish for is ever to come. I trust that all my readers (excepting of course the one impracticable man in each hundred, who always thinks differently from everybody else, and always thinks wrong) will agree with me in holding it as an axiom needing no argument to support it, that every building which ranks under the class of villa or cottage, must, if intended to be tasteful or pleasing, be built in some variety of that grand school which is commonly styled the GOTHIC.

I know quite well that there are many persons in this world who would scout the idea that there is any necessity or any use for people who are not rich to make any provision for their ideal life, for their taste for the beautiful. I can picture to myself some utilitarian old hunks, sharp-nosed, shrivelled-faced, with contracted brow, narrow intellect, and no feeling or taste at all, who would be ready (so far as he was able) to ridicule my assertion that it is desirable and possible to provide something to gratify taste and to elevate and refine feeling, in the aspect and arrangement of even the humblest human dwellings. Beauty, some donkeys think, is the right and inheritance of the wealthy alone ; food to eat, clothes to wear, a roof to shelter from the weather, are all that working men should pretend to. And indeed, if the secret belief of such dull grovellers were told, it would be that all people with less than a good many hundreds a-year are stepping out of their sphere and encroach ing on the demesne of their betters, when they aim at making their dwelling such that it shall please the cultivated eye as well as keep off wind and wet. Such mortals cannot understand or sympathise with the gratification arising from the contemplation of objects which are graceful and beautiful; and they think that if there be such a gratification at all, it is a piece of impudence in a poor man to aim at it. It is, they consider, a luxury to which he has no right; it is as though a ploughman should think to have champagne on his simple dinner-table. I verily believe that there are numbers of wealthy men, especially in the ranks of those who have made their own wealth, and who received little education in youth, who think that the supply of animal necessities is all that any mortal (but themselves, perhaps) can need. I have known of such a man, who said with amazement of a youth whose health and life premature care was sapping, " He is well-fed, and well-dressed, and well-lodged, and what the capital D more can the fellow want ?" Why, if he had been a horse or a pig, he would have wanted nothing more ; but the possession of a rational soul brings with it pressing wants which are not of a material nature, which are not to be supplied by material things, and which are not felt by pigs and horses. And the craving for surrounding objects of grace and beauty is one of these; and it cannot be killed out but by many years of sordid money-making, or racking anxiety, or grinding want. The man whose whole being is given to finding food and raiment and sleep, is but a somewhat more intelligent horse. We have something besides a body, whose needs must be supplied; or if not supplied, then crushed out, and we be brought thus nearer to the condition of being mere soulless bodies. Mr Vaux has some just remarks on the importance of a pleasant home to the young. It is indeed a wretched thing when, whether from selfish heedlessness or mistaken principle, the cravings of youthful imagination and feeling are systematically ignored, and life toned down to the last and most prosaic level. Says Mr Vaux—

It is not for ourselves alone, but for the sake of our children, that we should love to build our homes, whether they be villas, cottages, or log-houses, beautifully and well. The young people are mostly at home : it is their storehouse for amusement, their opportunity for relaxation, their main resource ; and thus they are exposed to its influence for good or evil unceasingly : their pliable, susceptible minds take in its whole expression with the fullest possible force, and with unerring accuracy. It is only by degrees that the young hungry soul, born and bred in a hard, unlovely home, accepts the coarse fate to which not the poverty but the indifference of its parents condemns it. It is many many years before the irrepressible longing becomes utterly hopeless : perhaps it is never crushed out entirely ; but it is so stupified by slow degrees into despairing stagnation, if a perpetually-recurring blank surrounds it, that it often seems to die, and to make no sign : the meagre, joyless, torpid home-atmosphere in which it is forced to vegetate absolutely starves it out ; and thus the good intention that the all-wise Creator had in view, when instilling a desire for the beautiful into the life of the infant, is painfully frustrated. It is frequently from this cause, and from this alone, that an impulsive, high-spirited, light-hearted boy will dwindle by degrees into a sharp, shrewd, narrow-minded, and selfish youth ; from thence again into a prudent, hard, and horny manhood ; and at last into a covetous, unloving, and unloved old age. This single explanation is all-sufficient : he never had a pleasant home.*

I trust my readers will conclude from this brief specimen of Mr Vaux's quality, that if he be as thoroughly *up* in the practice of pleasant rural architecture as he is in the philosophy of it, he will be a very agreeable architect indeed. And, in truth, he is so, and his book is a very pleasant one. It is a handsome royal octavo volume of above three hundred pages ; it is prodigally illustrated with excellent wood-engravings, which shew the man who intends building a country-house an abundance of engaging examples from which to choose one. Nor are we shewn merely a number of taking views in perspective ; we have likewise the ground-plan of each floor, shewing the size and height of each chamber ; and further we are furnished with a careful calculation of the probable expense of each cottage or villa. Nor does Mr Vaux's care extend only to the house proper : he shews some good designs for rustic gateways and fences, and some pretty plans for laying out and planting the piece of shrubbery and lawn which sur-

* *Villas and Cottages*, pp. 115, 116.

rounds the abode. America, every one knows, is a country where a man must *push* if he wishes to get on ; he must not be held back by any false modesty ; and Mr Vaux's book is not free from the suspicion of being a kind of advertisement of its author, who is described on the title-page as " Calvert Vaux, Architect, late Downing and Vaux, of Newburgh, on the Hudson." Then, on an otherwise blank page at the end of the volume, we find in large capitals the significant inscription, which renders it impossible for any one who reads the book to say that he does not know where to find Mr Vaux when he wants him :—

> *" Calvert Vaux, Architect,*
> *Appleton's Building,*
> *348 Broadway."*

American architecture appears to stand in sad need of improvement. Mr Vaux tells us, no doubt very truly, that "ugly buildings are the almost invariable rule." In that land of measureless forests there is a building material common, which is little used now in Britain—to wit, wood. Still, wood will furnish the material for very graceful and picturesque houses, even when in the rude form of logs ; and the true blight of housebuilding in America was less the poverty and the hurry of the early colonists, than their Puritan hatred and contempt of art, and of everything beautiful. Further, the democratic spirit could not tolerate the notion of anything being suffered to flourish which, as was wrongly thought, was to minister to the delight of only a select few.

There is something amusing in reading the introductory discourse upon the construction of country-houses, with which Mr Vaux's book sets out. It is odd to witness the trimming, we had almost said the sneaky fashion, in which your Yankee writes about "my country," when he has anything to say in its dispraise. He dares not say what he thinks about America and its people. He must mingle a great deal of insincere compliment with anything in the nature of fault-finding. He writes in mortal terror of the blackguard portion of the press, and he never forgets the great principle, as laid down by Colonel Chollop to Martin Chuzzlewit, that "we air a great people, and we must be cracked up." Mr Vaux is manifestly of opinion, that Yankee bigotry, stupidity, dollar-worship, want of education, want of taste, and vulgar jealousy of people who are so well off as to be able to cultivate art, have prevented and are preventing any great improvement in domestic or any other architecture. But whenever he has timidly ventured to hint as much, he instantly backs out with every appearance of trepidation, and hastens to make up for his delinquency by some extravagant eulogy of "our people and our institutions." It should seem that there is in America a cry for an original and purely American style of architecture; some bold spirits object to the notion of being indebted to the Old World

for anything whatsoever, and thus modestly does Mr
Vaux suggest to such that they are talking nonsense :—

Webster and Clay were orators of originality, but their
words were all old. Their stock-in-trade is common property
in the form of a dictionary, and the boundary lines over which
neither ever ventured to pass are fairly set forth in a good
grammar. Any desire on their part to invent a bran-new language would have been absurd, and any wish to produce a bran-
new style of building is, without doubt, an equally senseless
chimera.

It is not, by the way, entirely true that the Yankees
have been content to take the old words of England,
and aim at originality only by the new arrangement of
these hackneyed materials. They have really made
some progress in the invention of a "bran-new language," but it may be doubted whether it is as good as
the old.

It appears that there are various respects in which
American houses differ materially from those of Britain.
A most uncomfortable and unpleasant arrangement is
that dining-rooms are generally in the basement story ;
that is, they are a sort of cellars underground, lighted
solely by area windows. In town or country, but even
more in the country, a more cheerless and disgusting
plan could hardly be conceived. It comes of the
essentially Yankee belief that a dining-room is merely
a place of shelter into which people are to rush wildly,
bolt huge blocks of food with breathless haste and in
total silence, and then rush out again whenever the
necessities of nature have been supplied. They have

no notion over there of the social, genial, refined, and elevating "Art of Dining."   And not knowing how to dine, of course they do not know how to provide a fitting scene for that civilised and civilising usage. Well says Mr Vaux :—

The fact is, that the art of eating and drinking wisely and well is so important to our social happiness, that it deserves to be developed under somewhat more favourable circumstances than is possible in a basement dining-room.

Another peculiarity of the domestic architecture of the States is, that the houses must be very compact, and the distances within the walls short, on account of the extreme badness, inefficiency, and insolence of the servants.   Not servants, by the by; they repudiate any such title of subjection—they are " helps." Great pains must be taken to consult their feelings and lighten their work, otherwise they are likely to remind you of the fundamental principle of the American constitution, that all men (except niggers) are equal (equal, of course, in stature, in strength, in speed, in talent, in education, in good luck, in dollars); and so to walk off and leave you to do your house-work for yourself.   Then it appears that various appliances essential to comfort, which in England are found in the residence of the poorest gentleman, are in America comparatively rare.   They would probably cause a man to be suspected of aristocratic tendencies, and lead to his being scarified in the *New York Key-hole Listener*, or the *New York Daily Stabber*.   In what country but

America would it have been regarded as a noble spectacle, when the President lately, on reaching a hotel at the end of a journey, declined to wash in a private bed-room, and insisted on taking his turn at a spout in the hall, and his share of the common soap and the grimy towel? Would not the disgusting clap-trap have anywhere else met the contempt which it richly deserved? Again, a peculiar influence is exerted on architecture and architects by the fact that when a spry Yankee wishes to build a house, he very generally thinks to overreach his architect and builder by pretending that he wants much less accommodation than he is resolved to have ; thinking that, the contract once made, and begun to be executed, he will be able to squeeze more work out for the same price. It is gratifying to know that in such cases he usually meets his match, and has to pay smartly; and then for the remainder of his life he goes about grumbling that architects' plans cost much more money to execute than their employers are led in the first instance to believe will be necessary. How lamentable that the exercise of a noble art should ever be degraded into a conflict between a couple of rogues, each trying to outwit the other !

American houses are for the most part square boxes, with no character at all. They are generally painted white, with bright green blinds : the effect is staring and ugly. In America, a perfectly straight line is esteemed the line of beauty, and a cube the most graceful of forms. Two large gridirons, laid across one another, exhibit the ground-plan of the large towns. Two smaller gridirons represent the villages. Mr Vaux is strong for the use of graceful curves, and for laying out roads with some regard to the formation of the ground, and the natural features of interest. But a man of taste must meet many mortifications in a country where the following barbarity could be perpetrated :—

In a case that recently occurred near a country town at some distance from New York, a road was run through a very beautiful estate, one agreeable feature of which was a pretty though small pond, that, even in the dryest seasons, was always full of water, and would have formed an agreeable adjunct to a country-seat. A single straight pencil line on the plan doubtless marked out the direction of the road : and as this line happened to go straight through the pond, straight through the pond was the road accordingly carried, the owner of the estate personally superintending the operation, and thus spoiling his sheet of water, diminishing the value of his lands, and incurring expense by the cost of filling-in, without any advantage whatever ; for a winding road so laid out as to skirt the pond would have been far more attractive and agreeable than the harsh, straight line that is now scored like a railway track clear through the undulating surface of the property ; and such barbarisms are of constant occurrence.

No doubt they are, and they are of frequent recurrence nearer home. I have known places where, if you are anxious to get a body of men to make any improvement upon a church or school-house, it is necessary that you should support your plan solely by considerations of utility. Even to suggest the increase of beauty which would result would be quite certain to knock the entire scheme on the head.

Some features of American house-building follow from the country and climate. Such are the verandahs, and the hooded windows which form part of the design of every villa and every cottage represented in Mr Vaux's book. The climate makes these desirable, and even essential. Such, too, is the abundance of houses built of wood, several designs for such houses being of considerable pretension. And only a hurried and hasty people, with little notion of building for posterity, would accept the statement, that in building with brick, eight inches thick are quite enough for the walls of any country-house, however large. The very slightest brick walls run up in England are, I believe, at least twelve inches thick. The materials for roofing are very different from those to which we are accustomed. Slates are little used, having to be brought from England ; tin is not uncommon. Thick canvas is thought to make a good roof when the surface is not great ; zinc is a good deal employed ; but the favourite roofing material is shingle, which makes a roof pleasing to American eyes.

It is agreeably varied in surface, and assumes by age a soft, pleasant, neutral tint that harmonises with any colour that may be used in the building.

I am not much captivated by Mr Vaux's description of the representative American drawing-room, which, it appears, is entitled the *best parlour :—*

The walls are hard-finished white, the woodwork is white, and a white marble mantelpiece is fitted over a fire-place which is never used. The floor is covered with a carpet of excellent quality, and of a large and decidedly sprawling pattern, made up of scrolls and flowers in gay and vivid colours. A round table with a cloth on it, and a thin layer of books in smart bindings, occupies the centre of the room, and furnishes about accommodation enough for one rather small person to sit and write a note at. A gilt mirror finds a place between the windows. A sofa occupies irrevocably a well-defined space against the wall, but it is just too short to lie down on, and too high and slippery with its spring convex seat to sit on with any comfort. It is also cleverly managed that points or knobs (of course ornamental and French-polished) shall occur at all those places towards which a wearied head would naturally tend, if leaning back to snatch a few moments' repose from fatigue. There is also a row of black walnut chairs, with horse-hair (!) seats, all ranged against the white wall. A console-table, too, under the mirror, with a white marble top and thin gilt brackets. I think there is a piano. There is certainly a tri-angular stand for knick-knacks, china, &c., and this, with some chimney ornaments, completes the furniture, which is all ar-ranged according to stiff, immutable law. The windows and Venetian blinds are tightly closed, the door is tightly shut, and the best room is in consequence always ready—for what? For daily use? Oh, no; it is in every way too good for that. For weekly use? Not even for that; but for *company* use. And thus the choice room, with the pretty view, is sacrificed to keep up a conventional show of finery which pleases no one, and is a great, though unacknowledged, bore to the proprietors.

I am not sure that we in this country have much right to laugh at the folly which maintains such chilly and comfortless apartments. Even so uninhabited and useless is many a drawing-room which I could name on this side of the Atlantic. What an embodiment of all that is stiff, repellent, and uneasy, are the drawing-rooms of most widow ladies of limited means! My space does not permit another extract from Mr Vaux, in which he explains his ideal of the way in which a cottage parlour should be arranged and furnished. Very pleasantly he sketches an unpretending picture, in which snugness and elegance, the *utile* and the *dulce*, are happily and inexpensively combined. But even here Mr Vaux feels himself pulled up by a vision of a hard-headed and close-fisted old Yankee, listening with indignation, and bursting out with "This will never do!"

I may remark, in passing, that Mr Vaux has no earthly idea of the way to build a church. He says, no doubt with truth, that nothing can be more revolting to any man of taste than the meeting-houses which are found throughout the States, which are generally in the shape of "a wooden caricature of a Grecian temple." He insists, very justly, that the house of God ought to be "the purest, the noblest, and the *best* architectural work our minds can conceive and our hands execute." And then he gives a view of a design for a church which strikes me as being the ugliest and most unmeaning I have seen for a long time. I can say honestly that, after the deepest meditation, I cannot for my life guess whether Mr Vaux intends his church to be Gothic or Grecian. The truth is, Mr Vaux knows no more how to design a church than I do how to find the longitude. It is impossible that any man in the United States should know how to build a church, for no man who has lived there all his life has ever seen a decent church. In America, unhappily, there is no National Church, and accordingly the means are lacking which should cover the land with solemn and beautiful ecclesiastical buildings, whose existence should be a spur even to the erectors of dissenting meeting-houses to struggle at some cheap imitation of them. And do you think that a thrifty republican would give his dollars to build York Minster or Canterbury Cathedral! No ; he would flare up at such monstrous waste, as Judas grumbled at the waste of the ointment.

We talk about houses, my friend; we look at houses; but how little the stranger knows of what they are I Search from cellar to garret some old country-house, in which successive generations of boys and girls have grown up, but be sure that the least part of it is that which you can see, and not the most accurate inventory that ever was drawn up by appraiser will include half its belongings. There are old memories crowding about every corner of that home unknown to us : and to minds and hearts far away in India and Australia everything about it is sublimed, saddened, transfigured into something different from what it is to you and me. You know for yourself, my reader, whether there be not something not present elsewhere about the window where you sat when a child and learned your lessons, the table once surrounded by many merry young faces which will not surround it again in this world, the fireside where your father sat, the chamber where your sister died. Very little indeed can sense do towards shewing us the Home, or towards shewing us any scene which has been associated with human life and feeling and embalmed in human memories. The same few hundred yards along the sea-shore, which are nothing to one man but so much ribbed sea-sand and so much murmuring water, may be to another something to quicken the heart's beating and bring the blood to the cheek. The same green path through the spring-clad trees, with the primroses growing beneath them, which lives in one's memory year after year with its fresh vividness undiminished, may be in another merely a vague recollection, recalled with difficulty or not at all.

> Each in his hidden sphere of joy or woe,
>> Our hermit spirits dwell and range apart;
> Our eyes see all around in gloom or glow,
>> Hues of their own, fresh borrow'd from the heart.

CHAPTER IX.

CONCERNING HURRY AND LEISURE.

OH what a blessing it is to have time to breathe,
and think, and look around one! I mean, of
course, that all this is a blessing to the man who has
been overdriven: who has been living for many days
in a breathless hurry, pushing and driving on, trying
to get through his work, yet never seeing the end of
it, not knowing to what task he ought to turn first, so
many are pressing upon him all together. Some folk, I
am informed, like to live in a fever of excitement, and
in a ceaseless crowd of occupations: but such folk
form the minority of the race. Most human beings
will agree in the assertion that it is a horrible feeling
to be in a hurry. It wastes the tissues of the body;
it fevers the fine mechanism of the brain; it renders
it impossible for one to enjoy the scenes of nature.
Trees, fields, sunsets, rivers, breezes, and the like,
must all be enjoyed at leisure, if enjoyed at all. There
is not the slightest use in a man's paying a hurried
visit to the country. He may as well go there blind-
fold, as go in a hurry. He will never see the country.
He will have a perception, no doubt, of hedgerows
and grass, of green lanes and silent cottages, perhaps

of great hills and rocks, of various items which go towards making the country; but the country itself he will never see. That feverish atmosphere which he carries with him will distort and transform even individual objects; but it will utterly exclude the view of the whole. A circling London fog could not do so more completely. For quiet is the great characteristic and the great charm of country scenes; and you cannot see or feel quiet when you are not quiet yourself. A man flying through this peaceful valley in an express train at the rate of fifty miles an hour might just as reasonably fancy that to us, its inhabitants, the trees and hedges seem always dancing, rushing, and circling about, as they seem to him in looking from the window of the flying carriage; as imagine that, when he comes for a day or two's visit, he sees these landscapes as they are in themselves, and as they look to their ordinary inhabitants. The quick pulse of London keeps with him: he cannot, for a long time, feel sensibly an influence so little startling, as faintly flavoured, as that of our simple country life. We have all beheld some country scenes, pleasing but not very striking, while driving hastily to catch a train for which we feared we should be too late; and afterwards, when we came to know them well, how different they looked!

I have been in a hurry. I have been tremendously busy. I have got through an amazing amount of work in the last few weeks, as I ascertain by looking over the recent pages of my diary. You can never be sure whether you have been working hard or not, except by consulting your diary. Sometimes you have an oppressed and worn-out feeling of having been overdriven, of having done a vast deal during many days past; when lo! you turn to the uncompromising record, you test the accuracy of your feeling by that unimpeachable standard; and you find that, after all, you have accomplished very little. The discovery is mortifying, but it does you good; and besides other results, it enables you to see how very idle and useless people, who keep no diary, may easily bring themselves to believe that they are among the hardest-wrought of mortals. They know they feel weary; they know they have been in a bustle and worry; they think they have been in it much longer than is the fact. For it is curious how readily we believe that any strongly-felt state of mind or outward condition—strongly felt at the present moment—has been lasting for a very long time. You have been in very low spirits: you fancy now that you have been so for a great portion of your life, or at any rate for weeks past: you turn to your diary,—why, eight-and-forty hours ago you were as merry as a cricket during the pleasant drive with Smith, or the cheerful evening that you spent with Snarling. I can well imagine that when some heavy misfortune befalls a man, he soon begins to feel as if it had befallen him a long, long time ago: he can hardly remember days which were not darkened by it : it seems to have been the condition of his being almost since his birth. And so, if you have been toiling very hard for three days—your pen in your hand almost from morning to night perhaps—rely upon it that at the end of those days, save for the uncompromising diary that keeps you right, you would have in your mind a general impression that you had been labouring desperately for a very long period—for many days, for several weeks, for a month or two. After heavy rain has fallen for four or five days, all persons who do not keep diaries invariably think that it has rained for a fortnight. If keen frost lasts in winter for a fortnight, all persons without diaries have a vague belief that there has been frost for a month or six weeks. You resolve to read Mr Wordy's valuable *History of the Entire Human Race throughout the whole of Time* (I take for granted you are a young person) : you go at it every evening for a week. At the end of that period you have a vague uneasy impression, that you have been soaked in a sea of platitudes, or weighed down by an incubus of words, for about a hundred years. For even such is life.

Every human being, then, who is desirous of knowing for certain whether he is doing much work or little, ought to preserve a record of what he does. And such a record, I believe, will in most cases serve to humble him who keeps it, and to spur on to more and harder work. It will seldom flatter vanity, or encourage a tendency to rest on the oars, as though

enough had been done.   You must have laboured
very hard and very constantly indeed, if it looks
much in black and white.   And how much work
may be expressed by a very few words in the diary !
Think of Elihu Burrit's "forged fourteen hours, then
Hebrew Bible three hours."   Think of Sir Walter's
short memorial of his eight pages before breakfast,—
and what large and closely-written pages they were !
And how much stretch of such minds as they have
got—how many quick and laborious processes of the
mental machinery—are briefly embalmed in the diaries
of humbler and smaller men, in such entries as,
"After breakfast, walk in garden with children for
ten minutes; then Sermon on 10 pp. ; working hard
from 10 till 1 P.M.; then left off with bad headache,
and very weary?"   The truth is, you can't represent
work by any record of it.   As yet, there is no way
known of photographing the mind's exertion, and
thus preserving an accurate memorial of it.   You
might as well expect to find in such a general phrase
as a *stormy sea* the delineation of the countless shapes
and transformations of the waves throughout several
hours in several miles of ocean, as think to see in Sir
Walter Scott's *eight pages before breakfast* an adequate
representation of the hard, varied, wearing-out work
that went to turn them off.   And so it is, that the
diary which records the work of a very hard-wrought
man, may very likely appear to careless, unsympathis-
ing readers, to express not such a very laborious life

after all. Who has not felt this, in reading the biography of that amiable, able, indefatigable, and over-wrought man, Dr Kitto? He worked himself to death by labour at his desk: but only the reader who has learned by personal experience to feel for him, is likely to see how he did it.

But besides such reasons as these, there are strong arguments why every man should keep a diary. I cannot imagine how many reflective men do not. How narrow and small a thing their actual life must be! They live merely in the present; and the present is only a shifting point, a constantly-progressing mathematical line, which parts the future from the past. If a man keeps no diary, the path crumbles away behind him as his feet leave it; and days gone by are little more than a blank, broken by a few distorted shadows. His life is all confined within the limits of to-day. Who does not know how imperfect a thing memory is? It not merely forgets; it misleads. Things in memory do not merely fade away, preserving as they fade their own lineaments so long as they can be seen: they change their aspect, they change their place, they turn to something quite different from the fact. In the picture of the past, which memory unaided by any written record sets before us, the perspective is entirely wrong. How capriciously some events seem quite recent, which the diary shews are really far away; and how unaccountably many things look far away, which in truth are not left many weeks behind us! A man might almost as well not have lived at all as entirely forget that he has lived, and entirely forget what he did on those departed days. But I think that almost every person would feel a great interest in looking back, day by day, upon what he did and thought upon that day twelvemonths, that day three or five years. The trouble of writing the diary is very small. A few lines, a few words, written at the time, suffice, when you look at them, to bring all (what Yankees call) the *surroundings* of that season before you. Many little things come up again, which you know quite well you never would have thought of again but for your glance at those words, and still which you feel you would be sorry to have forgotten. There must be a richness about the life of a person who keeps a diary, unknown to other men. And a million more little links and ties must bind him to the members of his family circle, and to all among whom he lives. Life, to him, looking back, is not a bare line, stringing together his personal identity ; it is surrounded, intertwined, entangled, with thousands and thousands of slight incidents, which give it beauty, kindliness, reality. Some folk's life is like an oak walking-stick, straight and varnished ; useful, but hard and bare. Other men's life (and such may yours and mine, kindly reader, ever be) is like that oak when it was not a stick but a branch, and waved, leaf-enveloped, and with lots of little twigs growing out of it, upon the summer tree. And yet more precious than the power of the diary to call up again a host of little circumstances and facts, is its power to bring back the indescribable but keenly-felt atmosphere of those departed days. The old time comes over you. It is not merely a collection, an aggregate of facts, that comes back; it is something far more excellent than *that:* it is the soul of days long ago ; it is the dear *auld lang syne* itself ! The perfume of hawthorn-hedges faded is there ; the breath of breezes that fanned our gray hair when it made sunny curls, often smoothed down by hands that are gone ; the sunshine on the grass where these old fingers made daisy chains ; and snatches of music, compared with which anything you hear at the Opera is extremely poor. Therefore keep your diary, my friend. Begin at ten years old, if you have not yet attained that age. It will be a curious link between the altered seasons of your life ; there will be something very touching about even the changes which will pass upon your handwriting. You will look back at it occasionally, and shed several tears of which you have not the least reason to be ashamed. No doubt when you look back, you will find many very silly things in it ; well, you did not think them silly at the time ; and possibly you may be humbler, wiser, and more sympathetic, for the fact that your diary will convince you (if you are a sensible person now) that probably you yourself, a few years or a great many years since, were the greatest fool you ever knew. Possibly at some future time you may look back with similar feelings on your present self: so you will see that it is very fit that meanwhile you should avoid self-confidence and cultivate humility ; that you should not be bumptious in any way ; and that you should bear, with great patience and kindliness, the follies of the young. Therefore, my reader, write up your diary daily. You may do so at either of two times : 1st, After breakfast, whenever you sit down to your work, and before you begin your work ; 2nd, After you have done your indoors work, which ought not to be later than two P.M., and before you go out to your external duties. Some good men, as Dr Arnold, have in addition to this brought up their history to the present period before retiring for the night. This is a good plan ; it preserves the record of the day as it appears to us in two different moods : the record is therefore more likely to be a true one, uncoloured by any temporary mental state. Write down briefly what you have been doing. Never mind that the events are very little. Of course they must be ; but you remember what Pope said of little things. State what work you did. Record the progress of matters in the garden. Mention where you took your walk, or ride, or drive. State anything particular concerning the horses, cows, dogs, and pigs. Preserve some memorial of the progress of the children. Relate the occasions on which you made a kite or a water-wheel for any of them ; also the stories you told them, and the hymns you heard them repeat.

You may preserve some mention of their more remarkable and old-fashioned sayings. *Forsitan et olim
hæc meminisse juvabit:* all these things may bring
back more plainly a little life when it has ceased;
and set before you a rosy little face and a curly little
head when they have mouldered into clay. Or if you
go, as you would rather have it, before them, why,
when one of your boys is Archbishop of Canterbury
and the other Lord Chancellor, they may turn over
the faded leaves, and be the better for reading those
early records, and not impossibly think some kindly
thoughts of their governor who is far away. Record
when the first snow-drop came, and the earliest primrose. Of course you will mention the books you read,
and those (if any) which you write. Preserve some
memorial, in short, of everything that interests you
and yours; and look back each day, after you have
written the few lines of your little chronicle, to see
what you were about that day the preceding year.
No one who in this simple spirit keeps a diary, can
possibly be a bad, unfeeling, or cruel man. No scape-
grace or blackguard could keep a diary such as that
which has been described. I am not forgetting that
various blackguards, and extremely dirty ones, *have*
kept diaries; but they have been diaries to match
their own character. Even in reading Byron's diary,
you can see that he was not so much a very bad
fellow, as a very silly fellow, who thought it a grand
thing to be esteemed very bad. When, by the way,

will the day come when young men will cease to regard it as the perfection of youthful humanity to be a reckless, swaggering fellow, who never knows how much money he has or spends, who darkly hints that he has done many wicked things which he never did, who makes it a boast that he never reads anything, and thus who affects to be even a more ignorant numskull than he actually is? When will young men cease to be ashamed of doing right, and to boast of doing wrong (which they never did)? "Thank God," said poor Milksop to me the other day, "although I have done a great many bad things, I never did, &c. &c. &c." The silly fellow fancied that I should think a vast deal of one who had gone through so much, and sown such a large crop of wild oats. I looked at him with much pity. Ah! thought I to myself, there *are* fellows who actually do the things you absurdly pretend to have done; but if you had been one of those, I should not have shaken hands with you five minutes since. With great difficulty did I refrain from patting his empty head, and saying, "Oh, poor Milksop, you are a tremendous fool!"

It is indeed to be admitted that by keeping a diary you are providing what is quite sure in days to come to be an occasional cause of sadness. Probably it will never conduce to cheerfulness to look back over those leaves. Well, you will be much the better for being sad occasionally. There are other things in this life than to put things in a ludicrous light, and laugh at them. *That*, too, is excellent in its time and place: but even Douglas Jerrold sickened of the forced fun of *Punch*, and thought this world had better ends 'than jesting. Don't let your diary fall behind: write it up day by day: or you will shrink from going back to it and continuing it, as Sir Walter Scott tells us he did. You will feel a double unhappiness in thinking you are neglecting something you ought to do, and in knowing that to repair your omission demands an exertion attended with especial pain and sorrow. Avoid at all events *that* discomfort of diary-keeping, by scrupulous regularity: there are others which you cannot avoid, if you keep a diary at all, and occasionally look back upon it. It must tend to make thoughtful people sad, to be reminded of things concerning which we feel that we cannot think of them ; that they have gone wrong, and cannot now be set right; that the evil is irremediable, and must just remain, and fret and worry whenever thought of; and life go on under that condition. It is like making up one's mind to live on under some incurable disease, not to be alleviated, not to be remedied, only if possible to be forgotten. Ordinary people have all some of these things : tangles in their life and affairs that cannot be unravelled and must be left alone : sorrowful things which they think cannot be helped. I think it highly inexpedient to give way to such a feeling ; it ought to be resisted as far as it possibly can. The very worst thing that you can do with a skeleton is to lock the closet door upon it, and try to think no more of it. No: open the door: let in air and light: bring the skeleton out, and sort it manfully up: perhaps it may prove to be only the skeleton of a cat, or even no skeleton at all. There is many a house, and many a family, in which there is a skeleton, which is made the distressing nightmare it is, mainly by trying to ignore it. There is some fretting disagreement, some painful estrangement, made a thousand times worse by ill-judged endeavours to go on just as if it were not there. If you wish to get rid of it, you must recognise its existence, and treat it with frankness, and seek manfully to set it right. It is wonderful how few evils are remediless, if you fairly face them, and honestly try to remove them. Therefore, I say it earnestly, don't lock your skeleton-chamber door. If the skeleton *be* there, I defy you to forget that it is. And even if it could bring you present quiet, it is no healthful draught, the water of Lethe. Drugged rest is unrefreshful, and has painful dreams. And further; don't let your diary turn to a small skeleton, as it is sure to do if it has fallen much into arrear. There will be a peculiar soreness in thinking that it is in arrear; yet you will shrink painfully from the idea of taking to it again and bringing it up. Better to begin a fresh volume. There is one thing to be especially avoided. Do not on any account, upon some evening when you are pensive, downhearted, and alone, go to the old volumes, and turn over the yellow pages with their faded ink. Never recur to volumes telling the story of years long ago, except at very cheerful times, in very hopeful moods :—unless, indeed, you desire to feel, as did Sir Walter, the connexion between the clauses of the scriptural statement, that *Ahithophel set his house in order, and hanged himself.* In that setting in order, what old, buried associations rise up again : what sudden pangs shoot through the heart, what a weight comes down upon it, as we open drawers long locked, and come upon the relics of our early selves, and schemes and hopes! Well, your old diary, of even five or ten years since, (especially if you have as yet hardly reached middle age,) is like a repertory in which the essence of all sad things is preserved. Bad as is the drawer or the shelf which holds the letters sent you from home when you were a schoolboy; sharp as is the sight of that lock of hair of your brother, whose grave is baked by the suns of Hindostan ; riling (not to say more) as is the view of that faded ribbon or those withered flowers which you still keep, though Jessie has long since married Mr Beest, who has ten thousand a-year : they are not so bad, so sharp, so riling, as is the old diary, wherein the spirit of many disappointments, toils, partings, and cares, is distilled and preserved. So don't look too frequently into your old diaries, or they will make you glum. Don't let them be your usual reading. It is a poor use of the past, to let its remembrances unfit you for the duties of the present.

I have been in a hurry, I have said ; but I am not
so now.   Probably the intelligent reader of the preceding pages may surmise as much.   I am enjoying
three days of delightful leisure.   I did nothing
yesterday: I am doing nothing to-day: I shall do
nothing to-morrow.   This is June : let me feel that it
is so.   When in a hurry, you do not realise that a
month, more especially a summer month, has come,
till it is gone.   June: let it be repeated : the *leafy
month of June*, to use the strong expression of Mr
Coleridge.   Let me hear you immediately quote the
verse, my young lady reader, in which that expression
is to be found.   Of course you can repeat it.   It is
now very warm, and beautifully bright.   I am sitting
on a velvety lawn, a hundred yards from the door of
a considerable country-house, not my personal property.   Under the shadow of a large sycamore is this
iron chair ; and this little table, on which the paper
looks quite green from the reflection of the leaves.
There is a very little breeze.   Just a foot from my
hand, a twig with very large leaves is moving slowly
and gently to and fro.   There, the great serrated
leaf has brushed the pen.   The sunshine is sleeping
(the word is not an affected one, but simply expresses
the phenomenon) upon the bright green grass, and
upon the dense masses of foliage which are a little
way off on every side.   Away on the left, there is a
well-grown horse-chestnut tree, blazing with blossoms.
In the little recesses where the turf makes bays of

verdure going into the thicket, the grass is nearly as white with daisies as if it were covered with snow, or had several table-cloths spread out upon it to dry. Blue and green, I am given to understand, form an incongruous combination in female dress ; but how beautiful the little patches of sapphire sky, seen through the green leaves ! Keats was quite right ; any one who is really fond of nature must be very far gone indeed, when he or she, like poor Isabella with her pot of basil, "forgets the blue above the trees." I am specially noticing a whole host of little appearances and relations among the natural objects within view, which no man in a hurry would ever observe ; yet which are certainly meant to be observed, and worth observing. I don't mean to say that a beautiful thing in nature is lost because no human being sees it ; I have not so vain an idea of the importance of our race. I do not think that that blue sky, with its beautiful fleecy clouds, was spread out there just as a scene at a theatre is spread out, simply to be looked at by us ; and that the intention of its Maker is balked if it be not. Still, among a host of other uses, which we do not know, it cannot be questioned that one end of the scenes of nature, and of the capacity of noting and enjoying them which is implanted in our being is, that they should be noted and enjoyed by human minds and hearts. It is now 11.30 A.M., and I have nothing to do that need take me far from this spot till dinner, which will be just seven hours hereafter. It requires an uninterrupted view of at least four or five hours ahead, to give the true sense of leisure. If you know you have some particular engagement in two hours, or even three or four, the feeling you have is not that of leisure. On the contrary, you feel that you must push on vigorously with whatever you may be about ; there is no time to sit down and muse. Two hours are a very short time. It is to be admitted that much less than half of that period is very long, when you are listening to a sermon ; and the man who wishes his life to appear as long as possible can never more effectually compass his end than by going very frequently to hear preachers of that numerous class whose discourses are always sensible and in good taste, and also sickeningly dull and tiresome. Half-an-hour under the instruction of such good men has oftentimes appeared like about four hours. But for quiet folk, living in the country, and who have never held the office of attorney-general or secretary of state, two hours form quite too short a vista to permit of sitting down to begin any serious work, such as writing a sermon or an article. Two hours will not afford elbow-room. One is cramped in it. Give me a clear prospect of five or six; so shall I begin an essay. It is quite evident that Hazlitt was a man of the town, accustomed to live in a hurry, and to fancy short blinks of unoccupation to be leisure,—even as a man long dwelling in American woods might think a little open glade quite an extensive clearing. He begins his essay on *Living to One's-self*, by saying that being in the country he has a fine opportunity of writing on that long-contemplated subject, and of writing at leisure, because he has *three hours good before him*, not to mention a partridge getting ready for his supper. Ah, not enough! Very well for the fast-going, high-pressure London mind; but quite insufficient for the deliberate, slow-running country one, that has to overcome a great *inertia*. How many good ideas, or at least ideas which he thinks good, will occur to the rustic writer; and be cast aside when he reflects that he has but two hours to sit at his task, and that therefore he has not a moment to spare for collateral matters, but must keep to the even thread of his story or his argument! A man who has four miles to walk within an hour has little time to stop and look at the view on eithei hand; and no time at all for scrambling over the hedge to gather some wild flowers. But now I rejoice in the feeling of an unlimited horizon before me, in the regard of time. Various new books are lying on the grass; and on the top of the heap, a certain number of that trenchant and brilliant periodical, the *Saturday Review*. This is delightful! It is jolly! And let us always be glad, if through training or idiosyncrasy we have come to this, my reader, that whenever you and I enjoy this tranquil feeling of content, there mingles with it a deep sense of gratitude. I should be very sorry to-day, if I did not know Whom to thank for all this. I like the simple natural piety which has given to various seats, at the top of various steep hills in Scotland, the homely name of *Rest and be thankful!* I trust I am now doing both these things. O ye men who have never been over-worked and over-driven, never kept for weeks on a constant strain and in a feverish hurry, you don't know what you miss! Sweet and delicious as cool water is to the man parched with thirst, is leisure to the man just extricated from breathless hurry! And nauseous as is that same water to the man whose thirst has been completely quenched, is leisure to the man whose life is nothing but leisure.

Let me pick up that number of the *Saturday Review*, and turn to the article which is entitled *Smith's Drag.*[*] That article treats of a certain essay which the present writer once contributed to a certain monthly magazine;[†] and it sets out the desultory fashion in which his compositions wander about. I have read the article with great amusement and pleasure. In the main it is perfectly just. Does not the avowal say something for the writer's good humour? Not frequently does the reviewed acknowledge that he was quite rightly pitched into. Let me, however, say to

[*] June 4, 1859, pp. 677-8.

[†] Concerning Man and his Dwelling-place.—*Fraser's Magazine*, June 1859, pp. 645-661.

the very clever and smart author of *Smith's Drag*, that he is to some extent mistaken in his theory as to my system of essay-writing. It is not entirely true that I begin my essays with irrelevant descriptions of scenery, horses, and the like, merely because when reviewing a book of heavy metaphysics I know nothing about my subject, and care nothing about it, and have nothing to say about it; and so am glad to get over a page or two of my production without *bonâ fide* going at my subject. Such a consideration, no doubt, is not without its weight; and besides this, holding that every way of discussing all things whatsoever is good except the tiresome, I think that even Smith's Drag serves a useful end if it pulls one a little way through a heavy discussion; as the short inclined plane set Mr Hensom's aerial machine off with a good start, without which it could not fly. But there is more than this in the case. The writer holds by a grand principle. The writer's great reason for saying something of the scenery amid which he is writing is, that he believes that it materially affects the thought produced, and ought to be taken in connexion with it. You would not give a just idea of a country house by giving us an architect's elevation of its *façade*, and shewing nothing of the hills by which it is backed, and the trees and shrubbery by which it is surrounded. So, too, with thought. We think in time and space; and unless you are a very great man, writing a book like Butler's *Analogy*, the outward scenes amid which you write will colour all your abstract

thought. Most people hate abstract thought. Give
it in a setting of scene and circumstances, and *then*
ordinary folk will accept it. Set a number of essays
in a story, however slight, and hundreds will read them
who would never have looked twice at the bare essays.
Human interest and a sense of reality are thus com-
municated. When any one says to me, " I think thus
and thus of some abstract topic," I like to say to him,
" Tell me where you thought it, how you thought it,
what you were looking at when you thought it, and to
whom you talked about it." I deny that in essays
what is wanted is results. Give me processes. Shew
me how the results are arrived at. In some cases,
doubtless, this is inexpedient. You would not enjoy
your dinner if you inquired too minutely into the
previous history of its component elements before it
appeared upon your table. You might not care for
one of Goldsmith's or Sheridan's pleasantries if you
traced too curiously the steps by which it was licked
into shape. Not so with the essay. And by exhibiting
the making of his essay, as well as the essay itself when
made, the essayist is enabled to preserve and exhibit
many thoughts which he could turn to no account did
he exhibit only his conclusions. It is a grand idea to
represent two or three friends as discussing a subject.
For who that has ever written upon abstract subjects,
or conversed upon them, but knows that very often
what seem capital ideas occur to him, which he has
not had time to write down or to utter before he sees

an answer to them, before he discovers that they are unsound. Now, to the essayist writing straightforward these thoughts are lost; he cannot exhibit them. It will not do to write them and then add that now he sees they are wrong. Here, then, is the great use— *one* great use—of the Ellesmere and Dunsford, who shall hold friendly council with the essayist. They, understood to be talking off-hand, can state all these interesting and striking though unsound views; and then the more deliberate Milverton can shew that they are wrong. And the three friends combined do but represent the phases of thought and feeling in a single individual : for who does not know that every reflective man is, at the very fewest, " three gentlemen at once ?" Let me say for myself, that it seems to me that no small part of the charm which there is about the *Friends in Council* and the *Companions of My Solitude* arises from the use of the two expedients : of exhibiting processes as well as results, of shewing how views are formed as well as the views themselves ; and also of setting the whole abstract part of the work in a framework of scenes and circumstances. All this makes one feel a life-like reality in the entire picture presented, and enables one to open the leaves with a home-like and friendly sympathy. Do not fancy, my brilliant reviewer, that I pretend to write like that thoughtful and graceful author, so rich in wisdom, in wit, in pathos, in kindly feeling. All I say is, that I have learned from him the grand principle, that abstract thought, for ordinary readers, must gain reality and interest from a setting of time and place.

There is the green branch of the tree, waving about. The breeze is a little stronger, but still the air is per·fectly warm. Let me be leisurely; I feel a little hurried with writing that last paragraph; I wrote it too quickly. To write a paragraph too quickly, putting in too much pressure of steam, will materially accelerate the pulse. *That* is an end greatly to be avoided. Who shall write hastily of leisure ! Fancy Izaak Walton going out fishing, and constantly looking at his watch every five minutes, for fear of not catching the express train in half-an-hour! It would be indeed a grievous inconsistency. The old gentleman might better have stayed at home.

It is all very well to be occasionally, for two or three days, or even for a fortnight, in a hurry. Every earnest man, with work to do, will find that occasionally there comes a pressure of it ; there comes a crowd of things which must be done quickly if they are done at all ; and the condition thus induced is hurry. I am aware, of course, that there is a distinction between haste and hurry—hurry adding to rapidity the element of painful confusion ; but in the case of ordinary people, haste generally implies hurry. And it will never do to become involved in a mode of life which implies a constant breathless pushing on. It must be a horrible thing to go through life in a hurry. It is highly expedient for all, it is absolutely necessary for most men, that they should have occasional leisure. Many enjoyments—perhaps all the tranquil and enduring enjoyments of life—cannot be felt except in leisure. And the best products of the human mind and heart can be brought forth only in leisure. Little does he know of the calm, unexciting, unwearying, lasting satisfaction of life, who has never known what it is to place the leisurely hand in the idle pocket, and to saunter to and fro. Mind, I utterly despise the idler —the loafer, as Yankees term him, who never does anything—whose idle hands are always in his idle pockets, and who is always sauntering to and fro. Leisure, be it remembered, is the intermission of labour; it is the blink of idleness in the life of a hard-working man. It is only in the case of such a man that leisure is dignified, commendable, or enjoyable. But to him it is all these, and more. Let us not be ever driving on. The machinery, physical and mental, will not stand it. It is fit that one should occasionally sit down on a grassy bank, and look listlessly, for a long time, at the daisies around, and watch the patches of bright-blue sky through green leaves overhead. It is right to rest on a large stone by the margin of a river; to rest there on a summer day for a long time, and to watch the lapse of the water as it passes away, and to listen to its silvery ripple over the pebbles. Who but a blockhead will think you idle? Of course blockheads may; but you and I, my reader, do not care a rush for the opinion of blockheads. It is fit that a man should have time to chase his little children about the green, to make a kite and occasionally fly it, to rig a ship and occasionally sail it, for the happiness of these little folk. There is nothing unbecoming in making your Newfoundland dog go into the water to bring out sticks, nor in teaching a lesser dog to stand on his hinder legs. No doubt Goldsmith was combining leisure with work when Reynolds one day visited him; but it was leisure that aided the work. The painter entered the poet's room unnoticed. The poet was seated at his desk, with his pen in his hand, and with his paper before him; but he had turned away from *The Traveller*, and with uplifted hand was looking towards a corner of the room, where a little dog sat with difficulty on his haunches, with imploring eyes. Reynolds looked over the poet's shoulder, and read a couplet whose ink was still wet :—

> By sports like these are all their cares beguiled ;
> The sports of children satisfy the child.

Surely, my friend, you will never again read that couplet, so simply and felicitously expressed, without remembering the circumstances in which it was written. Who should know better than Goldsmith what simple pleasures 'satisfy the child ?'

It is fit that a busy man should occasionally be able to stand for a quarter of an hour by the drag of his friend Smith; and walk round the horses, and smooth down their fore-legs, and pull their ears, and drink in their general aspect, and enjoy the rich colour of their bay coats gleaming in the sunshine ; and minutely and critically inspect the drag, its painting, its cushions, its fur robes, its steps, its spokes, its silver caps, its lamps, its entire expression.   These are enjoyments that last, and that cannot be had save in leisure.   They are calm and innocent ; they do not at all quicken the pulse, or fever the brain ; it is a good sign of a man if he feels them as enjoyments ; it shews that he has not indurated his moral palate by appliances highly spiced with the cayenne of excitement, all of which border on vice, and most of which imply it.

Let it be remembered, in the praise of leisure, that only in leisure will the human mind yield many of its best products.   Calm views, sound thoughts, healthful feelings, do not originate in a hurry or a fever.   I do not forget the wild geniuses who wrôte some of the finest English tragedies—men like Christopher Marlowe, Ford, Massinger, Dekker, and Otway.   No doubt *they* lived in a whirl of wild excitement, yet they turned off many fine and immortal thoughts.   But their thought was essentially morbid, and their feeling hectic : all their views of life and things were unsound. And the beauty with which their writings are flushed all over, is like the beauty that dwells in the brow too transparent, the cheek too rosy, and the eye too bright, of a fair girl dying of decline.   It is entirely a hot-house thing, and away from the bracing atmosphere of reality and truth. Its sweetness palls, its beauty frightens ; its fierce passion and its wild despair are the things in which it is at home. I do not believe the stories which are told about Jeffrey scribbling off his articles while dressing for a ball, or after returning from one at four in the morning : the fact is, nothing good for much was ever produced in that jaunty, hasty fashion, which is suggested by such a phrase as *scribbled off.* Good ideas flash in a moment on the mind : but they are very crude then ; and they must be mellowed and matured by time and in leisure. It is pure nonsense to say that the *Poetry of the Anti-jacobin* was produced by a lot of young men sitting over their wine, very much excited, and talking very loud, and two or three at a time. Some happy impromptu hits may have been elicited by that mental friction ; but, rely upon it, the *Needy Knife-Grinder*, and the song whose chorus is *Niversity of Gottingen*, were composed when their author was entirely alone, and had plenty of time for thinking. Brougham is an exception to all rules ; he certainly did write his *Discourse of Natural Theology* while rent asunder by all the multifarious engagements of a Lord Chancellor ; but, after all, a great deal that Brougham has done exhibits merely the smartness of a sort of intellectual legerdemain ; and that celebrated *Discourse,* so far as I remember it, is remarkably poor stuff. I am now talking not of great geniuses, but of ordinary men of education, when I maintain that to the labourer whose work is mental, and especially to the man whose work it is to write, leisure is a pure necessary of intellectual existence. There must be long seasons of quiescence between the occasional efforts of production. An electric eel cannot always be giving off shocks. The shock is powerful, but short, and then long time is needful to rally for another. A field, however good its soil, will not grow wheat year after year. Such a crop exhausts the soil: it is a strain to produce it; and after it the field must lie fallow for a while,—it must have leisure, in short. So is it with the mind. Who does not know that various literary electric eels, by repeating their shocks too frequently, have come at last to give off an electric result which is but the faintest and washiest echo of the thrilling and startling ones of earlier days? *Festus* was a strong and unmistakable shock; *The Angel World* was much weaker; *The Mystic* was extremely weak; and *The Age* was twaddle. Why did the author let himself down in such a fashion? The writer of *Festus* was a grand, mysterious image in many youthful minds: dark, wonderful, not quite comprehensible. The writer of *The Age* is a smart but silly little fellow, whom we could readily slap upon the back and tell him he had rather made a fool of himself. And who does not feel how weak the successive shocks of various eminent authors are growing? They strike out nothing new. Anything good in their recent productions is just the old thing,

with the colours a good deal washed out, and with
salt which has lost its savour.   Poor stuff comes of
constantly cutting and cropping.   The potatoes of
the mind grow small; the intellectual wheat comes
to have no ears; the moral turnips are infected
with the finger-and-toe disease.   The mind is a reser-
voir which can be emptied in a much shorter time
than it is possible to fill it.   It fills through an
infinity of small tubes, many so small as to act by
capillary attraction.   But in writing a book, or even
an article, it empties as through a twelve-inch pipe.
It is to me quite wonderful that most of the sermons
one hears are so good as they are, considering the
unintermittent stream in which most preachers are
compelled to produce them.   I have sometimes
thought, in listening to the discourse of a really
thoughtful and able clergyman—If you, my friend,
had to write a sermon once a month instead of once
a week, how very admirable it would be!

Some stupid people are afraid of confessing that
they ever have leisure.   They wish to palm off upon
the human race the delusion that they, the stupid
people, are always hard at work.   They are afraid of
being thought idle unless they maintain this fiction.
I have known clergymen who would not on any
account take any recreation in their own parishes, lest
they should be deemed lazy.   They would not fish,
they would not ride, they would not garden, they

would never be seen leaning upon a gate, and far less carving their name upon a tree. What absurd folly! They might just as well have pretended that they did without sleep, or without food, as without leisure. You cannot always drive the machine at its full speed. I know, indeed, that the machine may be so driven for two or three years at the beginning of a man's professional life; and that it is possible for a man to go on for such a period with hardly any appreciable leisure at all. But it knocks up the machine: it wears it out: and after an attack or two of nervous fever, we learn what we should have known from the beginning, that a far larger amount of tangible work will be accomplished by regular exertion of moderate degree and continuance, than by going ahead in the feverish and unrestful fashion in which really earnest men are so ready to begin their task. It seems, indeed, to be the rule rather than the exception, that clergymen should break down in strength and spirits in about three years after entering the Church. Some die: but happily a larger number get well again, and for the remainder of their days work at a more reasonable rate. As for the sermons written in that feverish stage of life, what crude and extravagant things they are: stirring and striking, perhaps, but hectic and forced, and entirely devoid of the repose, reality, and daylight feeling of actual life and fact. Yet how many good, injudicious people, are ever ready to expect of the new curate or rector an amount of work which man cannot do ; and to express their disappointment if that work is not done. It is so very easy to map out a task which you are not to do yourself: and you feel so little wearied by the toils of other men ! As for you, my young friend, beginning your parochial life, don't be ill-pleased with the kindly-meant advice of one who speaks from the experience of a good many years, and who has himself known all that you feel, and foolishly done all that you are now disposed to do. Consider for how many hours of the day you can labour, without injury to body or mind : labour faithfully for those hours, and for no more. Never mind about what may be said by Miss Limejuice and Mr Snarling. They will find fault at any rate ; and you will mind less about their fault-finding if you have an unimpaired digestion, and unaffected lungs, and an unenlarged heart. Don't pretend that you are always working : it would be a sin against God and Nature if you were. Say frankly, There is a certain amount of work that I *can* do ; and *that* I *will* do : but I *must* have my hours of leisure. I must have them for the sake of my parishioners as well as for my own ; for leisure is an essential part of that mental discipline which will enable my mind to grow and turn off sound instruction for their benefit. Leisure is a necessary part of true life ; and if I am to live at all, I must have it. Surely it is a thousand times better candidly and manfully to take up *that* ground, than to take recreation on the sly, as though you were ashamed of being found out in it, and to disguise your leisure as though it were a sin. I heartily despise the clergyman who reads *Adam Bede* secretly in his study, and when any one comes in, pops the volume into his waste-paper basket. An innocent thing is wrong to you if you think it wrong, remember. I am sorry for the man who is quite ashamed if any one finds him chasing his little children about the green before his house, or standing looking at a bank of primroses, or a bed of violets, or a high wall covered with ivy. Don't give in to that feeling for one second. You are doing right in doing all that; and no one but an ignorant, stupid, malicious, little-minded, vulgar, contemptible blockhead will think you are doing wrong. On a sunny day, you are not idle if you sit down and look for an hour at the ivied wall, or at an apple-tree in blossom, or at the river gliding by. You are not idle if you walk about your garden, noticing the progress and enjoying the beauty and fragrance of each individual rose-tree on such a charming June day as this. You are not idle if you sit down upon a garden seat, and take your little boy upon your knee, and talk with him about the many little matters which give interest to his little life. You are doing something which may help to establish a bond between you closer than that of blood; and the estranging interests of after years may need it all. And you do not know, even as regards the work (if of composition) at which you are

busy, what good ideas and impulses may come of the
quiet time of looking at the ivy, or the blossoms, or
the stream, or your child's sunny curls. Such things
often start thoughts which might seem a hundred
miles away from them. That they do so, is a fact to
which the experience of numbers of busy and thoughtful men can testify. Various thick skulls may think
the statement mystical and incomprehensible: for the
sake of such let me confirm it by high authority. Is
it not curious, by the way, that in talking to some
men and women, if you state a view a little beyond
their mark, you will find them doubting and disbe-
lieving it so long as they regard it as resting upon
your own authority; but if you can quote anything
that sounds like it from any printed book, or even
newspaper, no matter how little worthy the author of
the article or book may be, you will find the view
received with respect, if not with credence? The
mere fact of its having been printed gives any opinion
whatsoever much weight with some folk. And your
opinion is esteemed as if of greater value, if you can
only shew that any human being agreed with you in
entertaining it. So, my friend, if Mr Snarling thinks
it a delusion that you may gain some thoughts and
feelings of value, in the passive contemplation of
nature, inform him that the following lines were
written by one Wordsworth, a stamp-distributor in
Cumberland, regarded by many competent judges as
a very wise man :—

Why, William, on that old gray stone,
  Thus for the length of half-a-day,
Why, William, sit you thus alone,
  And dream your time away?

One morning thus, by Esthwaite lake,
  When life was sweet, I knew not why,
To me my good friend Matthew spake,
  And thus I made reply:

The eye,—it cannot choose but see;
  We cannot bid the ear be still:
Our bodies feel, where'er they be,
  Against or with our will.

Nor less I deem that there are Powers
  Which of themselves our minds impress:
That we can feed this mind of ours
  In a wise passiveness.

Think you, 'mid all this mighty sum,
  Of things for ever speaking,
That nothing of itself will come,
  But we must still be seeking?

Then ask not wherefore, here, alone,
  Conversing as I may,
I sit upon this old gray stone,
  And dream my time away!

Such an opinion is sound and just. Not that I believe that instead of sending a lad to Eton and Oxford, it would be expedient to make him sit down on a gray stone, by the side of any lake or river, and wait till wisdom came to him through the gentle teaching of nature. The instruction to be thus obtained must be supplementary to a good education, college and professional, obtained in the usual way;

and it must be sought in intervals of leisure, inter-
calated in a busy and energetic life. But thus inter-
vening, and coming to supplement other training, I
believe it will serve ends of the most valuable kind,
and elicit from the mind the very best material which
is there to be elicited. Some people say they work
best under presure : De Quincey, in a recent volume,
declares that the conviction that he *must* produce a
certain amount of writing in a limited time has often
seemed to open new cells in his brain, rich in excellent thought ; and I have known preachers (very poor
ones) declare that their best sermons were written
after dinner on Saturday. As for the sermons, the
best were bad ; as for De Quincey, he is a wonderful
man. Let us have elbow room, say I, when we have
to write anything ! Let there be plenty of time, as
well as plenty of space. Who could write if cramped
up in that chamber of torture, called *Little Ease*, in
which a man could neither sit, stand, nor lie, but in a
constrained fashion ? And just as bad is it to be
cramped up into three days, when to stretch one's
self demands at least six. Do you think Wordsworth
could have written against time ? or that *In Memoriam*
was penned in a hurry ?

Said Miss Limejuice, I saw Mr Swetter, the new
rector, to-day. Ah ! she added, with a malicious
smile, I fear he is growing idle already, though he
has not been in the parish six months. I saw him,

at a quarter before two precisely, standing at his gate with his hands in his pockets. I observed that he looked for three minutes over the gate into the clover field he has got. And then Smith drove up in his drag, and stopped and got out; and he and the rector entered into conversation, evidently about the horses, for I saw Mr Swetter walk round them several times, and rub down their fore-legs. Now *I* think he should have been busy writing his sermon, or visiting his sick. Such, let me assure the incredulous reader, are the words which I have myself heard Miss Limejuice, and her mother, old Mrs Snarling Limejuice, utter more than once or twice. Knowing the rector well, and knowing how he portions out his day, let me explain to those candid individuals the state of facts. At ten o'clock precisely, having previously gone to the stable and walked round the garden, Mr Swetter sat down at his desk in his study and worked hard till one. At two he is to ride up the parish to see various sick persons among the cottagers. But from one to two he has laid his work aside, and tried to banish all thought of his work. During that period he has been running about the green with his little boy, and even rolling upon the grass; and he has likewise strung together a number of daisies on a thread, which you might have seen round little Charlie's neck if you had looked sharply. He has been unbending his mind, you see, and enjoying leisure after his work. It is entirely true that he did look into the clover field and enjoy the fragrance of it, which you probably regard as a piece of sinful self-indulgence. And his friend coming up, it is likewise certain that he examined his horses (a new pair) with much interest and minuteness. Let me add, that only contemptible humbugs will think the less of him for all this. The days are past in which the ideal clergyman was an emaciated eremite, who hardly knew a cow from a horse, and was quite incapable of sympathising with his humbler parishioners in their little country cares. And some little knowledge as to horses and cows, not to mention potatoes and turnips, is a most valuable attainment to the country parson. If his parishioners find that he is entirely ignorant of those matters which they understand best, they will not unnaturally draw the conclusion that he knows nothing. While if they find that he is fairly acquainted with those things which they themselves understand, they will conclude that he knows everything. Helplessness and ignorance appear contemptible to simple folk, though the helplessness should appear in the lack of power to manage a horse, and the ignorance in a man's not knowing the way in which potatoes are planted. To you, Miss Limejuice, let me further say a word as to your parish clergyman. Mr Swetter, you probably do not know, was Senior Wrangler at Cambridge. He chose his present mode of life, not merely because he felt a special leaning to the sacred profession, though he did feel that strongly ; but also because he saw that in the Church, and in the care of a quiet rural parish, he might hope to combine the faithful discharge of his duty with the enjoyment of leisure for thought; he might be of use in his generation without being engaged to that degree that, like some great barristers, he should grow a stranger to his children. He concluded that it is one great happiness of a country parson's life, that he may work hard without working feverishly; he may do his duty, yet not bring on an early paralytic stroke. Swetter might, if he had liked, have gone in for the Great Seal; the man who was second to him will probably get it; but he did not choose. Do you not remember how Baron Alderson, who might well have aspired at being a Chief-Justice or a Lord Chancellor, fairly decided that the prize was not worth the cost, and was content to turn aside from the worry of the bar into the comparative leisure of a puisne judgeship? It was not worth his while, he rightly considered, to run the risk of working himself to death, or to live for years in a breathless hurry. No doubt the man who thus judges must be content to see others seize the great prizes of human affairs. Hot and trembling hands, for the most part, grasp these. And how many work breathlessly, and give up the tranquil enjoyment of life, yet never grasp them after all!

There is no period at which the feeling of leisure is a more delightful one, than during breakfast and after breakfast on a beautiful summer morning in the country. It is a slavish and painful thing to know that instantly you rise from the breakfast-table you must take to your work. And in that case your mind will be fretting and worrying away all the time that the hurried meal lasts. But it is delightful to be able to breakfast leisurely; to read over your letters twice; to skim the *Times,* just to see if there is anything particular in it (the serious reading of it being deferred till later in the day); and then to go out and saunter about the garden, taking an interest in whatever operations may be going on there; to walk down to the little bridge and sit on the parapet, and look over at the water foaming through below; to give your dogs a swim; to sketch out the rudimentary outline of a kite, to be completed in the evening; to stick up, amid shrieks of excitement and delight, a new coloured picture in the nursery; to go out to the stable and look about there;—and to do all this with the sense that there is no neglect, that you can easily overtake your day's work notwithstanding. For this end the country human being should breakfast early: not later than nine o'clock. Breakfast will be over by half-past nine; and the half hour till ten is as much as it is safe to give to leisure, without running the risk of dissipating the mind too much for steady application to work. After ten one does not feel comfortable in idling about on a common working-day. You feel that you ought to be at your task; and he who would enjoy country leisure must beware of fretting the fine mechanism of his moral perceptions by doing anything which he thinks even in the least degree wrong.

And here, after thinking of the preliminary half hour of leisure before you sit down to your work, let me advise that when you fairly go at your work, if of composition, you should go at it leisurely. I do not mean that you should work with half a will, with a wandering attention, with a mind running away upon something else. What I mean is, that you should beware of flying at your task, and keeping at it, with such a stretch, that every fibre in your body and your mind is on the strain, is tense and tightened up; so that when you stop, after your two or three hours at it, you-feel quite shattered and exhausted. A great many men, especially those of a nervous and sanguine temperament, write at too high a pressure. They have a hundred and twenty pounds on the square inch. Every nerve is like the string of Robin Hood's bow. All this does no good. It does not appreciably affect the quality of the article manufactured, nor does it much accelerate the rate of production. But it wears a man out awfully. It sucks him like an orange. It leaves him a discharged Leyden jar, a torpedo entirely used up. You have got to walk ten miles. You do it at the rate of four miles an hour. You accomplish the distance in two hours and a half; and you come in, not extremely done up. But another day, with the same walk before you, you put on extra steam, and walk at four and a half miles an hour, perhaps at five. (*Mem.:* People who say they walk six miles an hour are talking nonsense. It cannot be done, unless by a trained pedestrian.) You are on a painful stretch all the journey: you save, after all, a very few minutes; and you get to your journey's end entirely knocked up. Like an over-driven horse, you are off your feed; and you can do nothing useful all the evening. I am well aware that the good advice contained in this paragraph will not have the least effect on those who read it. *Fungar inani munere.* I know how little all this goes for with an individual now not far away. And, indeed, no one can say that because two men have produced the same result in work accomplished, therefore they have gone through the same amount of exertion. Nor am I now thinking of the vast differences between men in point of intellectual power. I am content to suppose that they shall be, intellectually, precisely on a level: yet one shall go at his work with a painful, heavy strain; and another shall get through his lightly, airily, as if it were pastime. One shall leave off fresh and buoyant; the other, jaded, languid, aching all over. And in this respect, it is probable that if your natural constitution is not such as to enable you to work hard, yet leisurely, there is no use in advising you to take things easily. Ah, my poor friend, you cannot! But at least you may restrict yourself from going at any task on end, and keeping yourself ever on the fret until it is fairly finished. Set yourself a fitting task for each day; and on no account exceed it. There are men who have a morbid eagerness to get through any work on which they are engaged. They would almost wish to go right on through all the toils of life and be done with them ; and then, like Alexander, "sit down and rest." The prospect of anything yet to do appears to render the enjoyment of present repose impossible. There can be no more unhealthful state of mind. The day will never come when we shall have got through our work: and well for us that it never will. Why disturb the quiet of to-night by thinking of the toils of to-morrow ? There is deep wisdom, and accurate knowledge of human nature, in the advice, given by the Soundest and Kindest of all advisers, and applicable in a hundred cases, to " Take no thought for the morrow."

It appears to me, that in these days of hurried life, a great and valuable end is served by a class of things which all men of late have taken to abusing,—to wit, the extensive class of dull, heavy, uninteresting, good, sensible, pious sermons. They afford many educated men almost their only intervals of waking leisure. You are in a cool, quiet, solemn place : the sermon is going forward : you have a general impression that you are listening to many good advices and important doctrines, and the entire result upon your mind is beneficial ; and at the same time there is nothing in the least striking or startling to destroy the sense of leisure, or to painfully arouse the attention and quicken the pulse. Neither is there a syllable that can jar on the most fastidious taste. All points and corners of thought are rounded off. The entire composition is in the highest degree gentlemanly, scholarly, correct; but you feel that it is quite impossible to attend to it. And you do not attend to it; but at the same time, you do not quite turn your attention to anything else. Now, you remember how a dying father, once upon a time, besought his prodigal son to spend an hour daily in solitary thought: and what a beneficial result followed. The dull sermon may serve an end as desirable. In church you are alone, in the sense of being isolated from all companions, or from the possibility of holding communication with anybody: and the wearisome sermon, if utterly useless otherwise, is useful in giving a man time to think, in circumstances which will generally dispose him to think seriously. There is a restful feeling, too, for which you are the better. It is a fine thing to feel that church is a place where, if even for two hours only, you are quite free from worldly business and cares. You know that all these are waiting for you outside: but at least you are free from their actual endurance here. I am persuaded, and I am happy to entertain the persuasion, that men are often much the better for being present during the preaching of sermons to which they pay very little attention. Only some such belief as this could make one think, without much sorrow, of the thousands of discourses which are preached every Sunday over Britain, and of the class of ears and memories to which they are given. You see that country congregation coming out of the ivy-covered church in that beautiful churchyard. Look at their faces, the ploughmen, the dairy-maids, the drain-diggers, the stable-boys: what could *they* do towards taking in the gist of that well-reasoned, scholarly, elegant piece of composition which has occupied the last half-hour? Why, they could not understand a sentence of it. Yet it has done them good. The general effect is wholesome. They have got a little push, they have felt themselves floating on a gentle current, going in the right direction. Only enthusiastic young divines expect the mass of their congregation to do all they exhort them to do. You must advise a man to do a thing a hundred times, probably, before you can get him to do it once. You know that a breeze, blowing at thirty-five miles an hour, does very well if it carries a large ship along in its own direction at the rate of eight. And even so, the practice of your hearers, though truly influenced by what you say to them, lags tremendously behind the rate of your preaching. Be content, my friend, if you can maintain a movement, sure though slow, in the right way. And don't get angry with your rural flock on Sundays, if you often see on their blank faces, while you are preaching, the evidence that they are not taking in a word you say. And don't be entirely discouraged.   You may be doing them good for all that.   And if you do good at all, you know better than to grumble, though you may not be doing it in the fashion that you would like best.   I have known men, accustomed to sit quiet, pensive, half-attentive, under the sermons of an easy-going but orthodox preacher, who felt quite indignant when they went to a church where their attention was kept on the stretch all the time the sermon lasted, whether they would or no.   They felt that this intrusive interest about the discourse, compelling them to attend, was of the nature of an assault, and of an unjustifiable infraction of the liberty of the subject. There feeling was, " What earthly right has that man to make us listen to his sermon, without getting our consent ?   We go to church to rest : and lo ! he com-pels us to listen ! "

I do not forget, musing in the shade this beautiful summer day, that there may be cases in which leisure is very much to be avoided.   To some men, constant occupation is a thing that stands between them and utter wretchedness.   You remember the poor man, whose story is so touchingly told by Borrow in *The Romany Rye,* who lost his wife, his children, all his friends, by a rapid succession of strokes ; and who declared that he would have gone mad if he had not resolutely set himself to the study of the Chinese language.   Only constant labour of mind could " keep the misery out of his head."   And years afterwards, if he paused from toil for even a few hours, the misery returned. The poor fisherman in *The Antiquary* was wrong in his philosophy, when Mr Oldbuck found him, with trembling hands, trying to repair his battered boat the day after his son was buried. "It's weel wi' you gentles," he said, "that can sit in the house wi' handkerchers at your een, when ye lose a freend ; but the like o' us maun to our wark again, if our hearts were beating as hard as my hammer !" We love the kindly sympathy that made Sir Walter write the words : but bitter as may be the effort with which the poor man takes to his heartless task again, surely he will all the sooner get over his sorrow. And it is with gentles, who can "sit in the house" as long as they like, that the great grief longest lingers. There is a wonderful efficacy in enforced work to tide one over every sort of trial. I saw not long since a number of pictures, admirably sketched, which had been sent to his family in England by an emigrant son in Canada, and which represented scenes in daily life there among the remote settlers. And I was very much struck with the sad expression which the faces of the emigrants always wore, whenever they were represented in repose or inaction. I felt sure that those pensive faces set forth a sorrowful fact. Lying on a great bluff, looking down upon a lonely river ; or seated at the tent-door on a Sunday, when his task was laid apart ;—however the backwoodsman was depicted, if not in energetic action, there was always a very sad look upon the rough face. And it was a peculiar sadness—not like that which human beings would feel amid the scenes and friends of their youth : a look pensive, distant, full of remembrance, devoid of hope. You glanced at it, and you thought of Lord Eglintoun's truthful lines :—

> From the lone shieling on the misty island,
>   Mountains divide us, and a world of seas :
> But still the blood is strong, the heart is Highland,
>   And we in dreams behold the Hebrides :
> Fair these broad meads, these hoary woods are grand,—
> But we are exiles from our fathers' land !

And you felt that much leisure will not suit *there.* Therefore, you stout backwoodsman, go at the huge forest-tree ; rain upon it the blows of your axe, as long as you can stand ; watch the fragments as they fly ; and jump briskly out of the way as the reeling giant falls ;—for all this brisk exertion will stand between you and remembrances that would unman you. There is nothing very philosophical in the plan, to "dance sad thoughts away," which I remember as the chorus of some Canadian song. I doubt whether that peculiar specific will do much good. But you may *work* sad thoughts away ; you may crowd morbid feelings out of your mind by stout daylight toils ; and remember that sad remembrances, too long indulged, tend strongly to the maudlin. Even Werter was little better than a fool ; and a contemptible fool was Mr Augustus Moddle.

How many of man's best works take for granted that the majority of cultivated persons, capable of enjoying them, shall have leisure in which to do so. The architect, the artist, the landscape-gardener, the poet, spend their pains in producing that which can never touch the hurried man. I really feel that I act unkindly by the man who did that elaborate picking-out in the painting of a railway carriage, if I rush upon the platform at the last moment, pitch in my luggage, sit down and take to the *Times*, without ever having noticed whether the colour of the carriage is brown or blue. There seems a dumb pleading eloquence about even the accurate diagonal arrangement of the little woollen tufts in the morocco cushions, and the inter-laced network above one's head, where umbrellas go, as though they said, "We are made thus neatly to be looked at, but we cannot make you look at us unless you choose ; and half the people who come into the carriage are so hurried that they never notice us." And when I have seen a fine church-spire, rich in graceful ornament, rising up by the side of a city street, where hurried crowds are always passing by, not one in a thousand ever casting a glance at the beautiful object, I have thought, Now surely you are not doing what your designer intended! When he spent so much of time, and thought, and pains in planning and executing all those beauties of detail, surely he intended them to be looked at ; and not merely looked at in their general effect, but followed

and traced into their lesser graces. But he wrongly
fancied that men would have time for that; he forgot
that, except on the solitary artistic visitor, all he has
done would be lost, through the nineteenth century's
want of leisure.   And you, architect of Melrose, when
you designed that exquisite tracery, and decorated
so perfectly that flying buttress, were you content to
do so for the pleasure of knowing you did your
work thoroughly and well; or did you count on its
producing on the minds of men in after-ages an
impression which a prevailing hurry has prevented
from being produced, save perhaps in one case in
a thousand? And you, old monk, who spent half
your life in writing and illuminating that magnificent
Missal; was your work its own reward in the pleasure
its execution gave you; or did you actually fancy
that mortal man would have time or patience—
leisure, in short—to examine in detail all that you
have done, and that interested you so much, and kept
you eagerly engaged for so many hours together, on
days the world has left four hundred years behind?
I declare it touches me to look at that laborious
appeal to men with countless hours to spare : men, in
short, hardly now to be found in Britain. No doubt,
all this is the old story: for how great a part of the
higher and finer human work is done in the hope that
it will produce an effect which it never will produce,
and attract the interest of those who will never notice
it! Still, the ancient missal-writer pleased himself

with the thought of the admiration of skilled observers in days to come ; and so the fancy served its purpose.

Thus at intervals through that bright summer-day, did the writer muse at leisure in the shade ; and note down the thoughts (such as they are) which you have here at length in this essay. The sun was still warm and cheerful when he quitted the lawn ; but somehow, looking back upon that day, the colours of the scene are paler than the fact, and the sunbeams feel comparatively chill. For memory cannot bring back things freshly as they lived, but only their faded images. Faces in the distant past look wan ; voices sound thin and distant ; the landscape round is uncertain and shadowy. Do you not feel somehow, when you look back on ages forty centuries ago, as if people then spoke in whispers and lived in twilight?

CONCLUSION.

AND such, my friendly reader, are my RECREA-
TIONS. It was pleasant to me, amid much work
of a very different kind, to write these essays. I trust
that it has not been very tiresome for you to read
them.

There is a peculiar happiness which is known to
the essayist. There is a virtue about his work to
draw the sting from the little worries of life. If you
fairly look some petty vexation of humanity in the
face, and write an account of it, it will never annoy
you so much any more. It recurs: and it annoys
you: but you have a latent feeling of satisfaction at
finding how exactly accurate was your description of
it; how completely your present sensation runs into
the mould you had made. It is a curious thing, too,
that there is a certain pleasure in writing about a
thing which was very unpleasant when it happened
to one. You know how an artist makes a pleasing
picture out of a poor cottage, in which it would be
very disagreeable to live. You know how a great
painter makes a picture, which you often like to look

at, of an event at which you would not have liked to have been present. You pause for a long time before the representation of some boors drinking; or of a furious struggle in a guard-room; or of a murdered man lying dead. Now, in fact, you would have got out of the way of such sights: the first two would have been disgusting: the last, at least "a sorry sight."

It is not quite a case in point, that we look with great interest and pleasure at the representation of a sight which it would have been no worse than sad to see. Such a sight may have been elevating as well as saddening. I see a figure laid upon a bed: you know it is stiff and cold. It is a female figure: there is the fixed but beautiful face. And through the open window, I see in the west the summer sunset blazing, and the golden light falling upon the pale features, and the closed eyes which will never open more till the sun has ceased to shine. I do not wonder that the exquisite genius of the painter fixed on such a scene, and preserved it with rigid accuracy, and wrote beneath his picture such words as these :—

The sun shall no more be thy light by day; neither for brightness shall the moon give light unto thee : but the Lord shall be unto thee an everlasting light, and thy God thy glory.

Thy sun shall no more go down; neither shall thy moon withdraw herself; for the Lord shall be thine everlasting light, and the days of thy mourning shall be ended.

But there is in this one respect an entire analogy between the feeling of the artist and the feeling of the essayist: that to both, this world is to a certain extent transfigured by the fact, that to each, things become comparatively pleasing if they would please when described or depicted, though they might be unpleasing in fact.   Not merely are those things good which are good in themselves: those things are good which, though bad, will please and interest when re-presented.   It is extremely certain, that there is a pleasure in writing about what there is no pleasure in bearing: and here is a happiness of the essayist. You are grossly cheated, my friend, by a man of most respectable character.   You are worried by some glaring instance of that horrible dilatoriness, unfaith-fulness, and stupidity, which come across the suc-cessful issue of almost all human affairs.   You are vexed, in short, at seeing how creakingly and jarringly and uneasily the machine of life and society manages to blunder on. ·Well, you suffer; and you have no relief.   But the essayist's painful feeling at such things is much mitigated when he thinks that here is a subject for him : and when he goes and describes it. Once, it was to me unrelieved and unalloyed pain to be cheated : or to listen to the vapouring of some silly person.   Now, though still I cannot say I like it, still I dislike it less.   I make a mental note.   It will all go into an essay.   One gets something of the spirit of the morbid anatomist, to whom some peculiar phase of disease is infinitely more interesting than commonplace health.   Interesting wrong becomes (must I confess it?) a finer sight than uninteresting right. You know how country servants rejoice in coming to tell you that something is amiss: that a horse is lame, or a pig dying, or a field of potatoes blighted. It is something to tell about. Perhaps the essayist knows the peculiar emotion.

I sometimes have thought that the writer of fiction is to be envied. He has another life and world than that we see. He has a duality of being. He sits down to his desk; and in a little he is far away, and away in a world where he is absolute monarch. It has not been so with me. In writing these essays, I have not been rapt away into heroic times and distant scenes, and into romantic tracts of feeling. I have been writing amid daily work and worry, of daily work and worry, and of the little things by which daily work and worry are intensified or relieved. I cannot pretend to long experience of life; nor perhaps to much. But from a quiet and lonely life, little varied, and very happy, I have sent out these essays month by month; and I hope to send out more.

THE END.

Printed by Ballantyne, Roberts, & Company, Edinburgh.

A PLEA FOR THE QUEEN'S ENGLISH.

By HENRY ALFORD, D.D.,

Dean of Canterbury.

Tenth Thousand. Small 8vo, 5s.

" A volume full of lively remark, amusing anecdote, and suggestive hints to speakers and writers. The Dean's stray notes are very amusing, and very instructive too."—*Guardian.*

" There are very few persons, even among those who would be shocked at being told they were not well educated, who might not read these lectures with profit. Every person who truly respects himself endeavours to perfect his mastery over his mother tongue. Nevertheless, vicious forms of speaking and writing abound in society and literature. Dean Alford has collected a larger number of these for discriminating censure than were ever before brought together, has shown in what respects they offend, and explained the principles on which better forms of expression may be constructed. It is of some importance that this work should be performed by a competent author, because there is a great deal of false criticism current. Nonsense now-a-days cannot be content to be itself; it puts on serious airs, and is nothing if not critical. This volume will be useful, because it will give the thoughtful reader insight into the spirit of thought which determines the form of language."—*Daily News.*

LETTERS FROM ABROAD.

By HENRY ALFORD, D.D.,

Dean of Canterbury.

Second Edition. Crown 8vo, 7s. 6d.

" Well worn as is the subject of Italian travel, Dr Alford has managed to produce a work of great freshness. . . . He is aided by his really remarkable power of description; and his first letter, describing the famous coast road from Nice through Genoa to Pisa, is a very charming specimen of easy, unaffected, yet picturesque writing. Of the present state of Rome and of religion there, Dr Alford gives a striking account, and not, as we believe, the least over-coloured."—*Spectator.*

MEDITATIONS:

IN ADVENT, ON CREATION, ON PROVIDENCE.

By HENRY ALFORD, D.D.,

Dean of Canterbury.

Small 8vo, 5s.

THE POETICAL WORKS OF HENRY ALFORD,

DEAN OF CANTERBURY.

Fourth Edition, Enlarged. Small 8vo, 5s.

MAN AND THE GOSPEL.

By THOMAS GUTHRIE, D.D.

Author of "The Gospel in Ezekiel," &c.

Crown 8vo, 7s. 6d.

"This volume exhibits very forcibly the characteristics of Dr Guthrie's mind. There is a broad and simple and faithful enunciation of gospel truth, an ardent and affectionate earnestness of expostulation, a wide and generous sympathy with good men and good deeds wherever they are found, and a felicitous and most exuberant flow of choice and accurate illustration of the subject in hand."—*Weekly Review.*

"In point of striking thought, as well as apposite and beautiful illustration, this work will bear comparison with any which bears Dr Guthrie's name."—*Edinburgh Courant.*

THE ANGELS' SONG.

By THOMAS GUTHRIE, D.D.

Uniform with "The Pathway of Promise."

Cloth antique, 1s. 6d.

SPEAKING TO THE HEART;

Or, SERMONS FOR THE PEOPLE.

By THOMAS GUTHRIE, D.D.

Crown 8vo, 3s. 6d. Pocket Edition, 2s.

"Dr Guthrie never speaks without speaking to the heart; but these discourses seem to bear with unwonted vividness the impress of his great emotional nature. They glow, they sparkle, they burn with intense feeling. We have seldom looked into a more fascinating book."—*English Churchman.*

LAZARUS, AND OTHER POEMS.

By E. H. PLUMPTRE, M.A.,

King's College, London.

Second Edition. Small 8vo, 5s.

"Out of a whole pile of religious poetry, original and selected, which rises like a castle before us, only one volume—Mr Plumptre's Poems—demands that particular attention which is due to merit of an uncommon order."—*Guardian.*

"Professor Plumptre's freshness and originality of thought in treating familiar subjects give a great charm to what we may term his Biblical Idyls."—*Churchman.*

PROFESSOR PLUMPTRE'S TRANSLATION
OF THE
TRAGEDIES OF SOPHOCLES.
WITH A BIOGRAPHICAL ESSAY.
Two Vols., crown 8vo, 12s.

"There is much in Professor Plumptre's English Sophocles which satisfies a high critical standard. . . . . He is evidently gifted with a poetic perception which tells him how much may be done by a happy boldness in reproducing in English, Greek phrases of singular and pregnant beauty. . . . . His biographical essay is a distinctive feature of this work, and is particularly valuable for its elaborate notice of the parallelisms between the contemporaries, Sophocles and Herodotus. The subject is very fascinating, as is the discussion which relates to the moral and religious teaching of one of the most genuine 'schoolmasters to bring men to Christ' that heathen literature can boast."—*Saturday Review.*

"Let us say at once that Professor Plumptre has not only surpassed the previous translators of Sophocles, but has produced a work of singular merit, not less remarkable for its felicity than its fidelity; a really readable and enjoyable version of the old plays."—*Pall Mall Gazette.*

THEOLOGY AND LIFE.
SERMONS CHIEFLY ON SPECIAL OCCASIONS.
By E. H. PLUMPTRE, M.A.
King's College, London.
Small 8vo, 6s.

SIX MONTHS AMONG
THE CHARITIES OF EUROPE.
By JOHN DE LIEFDE.
Two Volumes, post 8vo, with Illustrations, 22s.

"Mr De Liefde's book is readable, interesting, stimulating. It shows how moral energy will overcome obstacles that seem enormous, how faith and enthusiasm move mountains. It has pretty little biographical sketches, and conveys a general idea of the objects and plans of the various institutions."—*Fortnightly Review.*

"This book is excellent. It will be eagerly read by persons of practical benevolence. It shows how much can be done by determination and singleness of purpose to diminish the sum of human suffering, and to promote the happiness of mankind. The author writes conscientiously of what he has observed, and gathers together an immense amount of experience and history relating to various kinds of charities. Such a work cannot fail to be extensively appreciated."—*Daily News.*

THE COLLECTED WRITINGS OF EDWARD IRVING.

EDITED BY HIS NEPHEW, THE REV. G. CARLYLE, M.A.

Five Volumes, demy 8vo, £3.

"The greatest preacher the world has seen since apostolic times."—*Blackwood's Magazine.*

"Irving, almost alone among recent men, lived his sermons and preached his life. His words, more than those of any other modern speaker, were 'life passed through the fire of thought.' He said out his inmost heart, and this it is that makes his writings read like a prolonged and ideal biography."—*Saturday Review.*

"It was time that one who cannot be forgotten should possess some worthy monument; and nothing more fitting could be built up for him than these memorials of his genius."—*English Churchman.*

"Edward Irving had the power of reaching the true sublime, and the English language can show no more magnificent specimens of religious eloquence than those which are contained in his collected writings."—*Times.*

"No one can read these volumes without being impressed with much more than the eloquence of Edward Irving. Eloquent he was, with a rich and stately eloquence, rising at times to the height even of those great models—Taylor, Hooker, and Barrow—from whom he seems to have sought his inspiration."—*London Quarterly Review.*

MISCELLANIES FROM THE COLLECTED WRITINGS OF EDWARD IRVING.

Post 8vo, 6s.

"It is by such a volume as this, we are inclined to think, that Irving will come to be widely known to general readers. There are passages of a purely theological character which, we think, display profound wisdom, and are models of clear, strong, living utterance. They are practical and ethical 'sayings,' that are as gold and rubies and diamonds. We entirely approve the principle of its compilation, and welcome it as fitted, in a very remarkable manner, to quicken genuine and deep religious feeling, and to impart earnestness and force to the religious life."—*Nonconformist.*

THE VICARIOUS SACRIFICE,

GROUNDED ON PRINCIPLES OF UNIVERSAL OBLIGATION.

BY HORACE BUSHNELL, D.D.,

Author of "Nature and the Supernatural," &c. &c.

Crown 8vo, 7s. 6d.

CHRIST AND HIS SALVATION,

IN SERMONS VARIOUSLY RELATED THERETO.

By HORACE BUSHNELL, D.D.

Second Edition.   Crown 8vo, 6s.

" These sermons are distinguished from the ordinary discourses of the pulpit by being the product not merely of religious faith and feeling, but of religious genius."—*Atlantic Monthly.*

NATURE AND THE SUPERNATURAL,

AS TOGETHER CONSTITUTING THE ONE SYSTEM OF GOD.

By HORACE BUSHNELL, D.D.,

Author of " The New Life," &c.

In Crown 8vo, cloth, 3s. 6d.

" It is a work of great ability, and full of thought, which is at once true and ingenious."—*Edinburgh Review.*

" We have not had in our hands, for a long time, a book from which so many beautiful and powerful passages could be selected. . . . . The book is a remarkable one, and deserves to be widely known and read."—*British Quarterly Review.*

THE RECREATIONS OF A COUNTRY PARSON.

FIRST SERIES. POPULAR EDITION.

Crown 8vo, 3s. 6d.

" It is impossible not to be pleased with the ' Recreations of a Country Parson,' or to feel otherwise than on the best possible terms with the author."—*Saturday Review.*

THE GRAVER THOUGHTS OF A COUNTRY PARSON.

BY THE AUTHOR OF " RECREATIONS OF A COUNTRY PARSON."

Crown 8vo, 3s. 6d.

" This volume will be a permanent source of recreation and refreshment. There is, throughout these papers, a genial, cheering, manly, and healthy spirit, which acts as a tonic to mind and body."—*English Churchman.*

COUNSEL AND COMFORT,
SPOKEN FROM A CITY PULPIT.

BY THE AUTHOR OF " RECREATIONS OF A COUNTRY PARSON."

Crown 8vo, 3s. 6d.

" Here there is evident heart-work—an earnestness that ought ever to be apparent in those seeking to guide, counsel, and comfort. We have perused the volume with pleasure, and so commend it to the notice of our readers, certain they will indorse our opinion as to its merits."—*Saturday Post.*

OUTLINES OF THEOLOGY.
BY ALEXANDER VINET.

Post 8vo, 8s.

OUTLINES OF PHILOSOPHY AND LITERATURE.
BY ALEXANDER VINET.

Post 8vo, 8s.

" These volumes are of great merit and extreme interest. The editor, M. Astie, has done his work with remarkable skill, and has succeeded in giving us a remarkable embodiment of M. Vinet's thinking on the several subjects that pass under review. . . . . Our readers will find in these volumes a rich vein of vigorous thought, extremely suggestive, and always pervaded by a devout and reverent spirit."—*British Quarterly Review.*

CHRIST THE LIGHT OF THE WORLD.
BY C. J. VAUGHAN, D.D.,
Vicar of Doncaster.
Small 8vo, 4s. 6d.

PLAIN WORDS ON CHRISTIAN LIVING.
BY C. J. VAUGHAN, D.D., VICAR OF DONCASTER.
Small 8vo, 4s. 6d.

" There is a self-controlled abstinence from rhetoric in Dr Vaughan's sermons, accompanied by a power and freshness of thought, which gives them the reality that other writers sometimes seek through a strained ' unprofessionality' of tone."—*Guardian.*

PERSONAL NAMES IN THE BIBLE.

BY THE REV. W. F. WILKINSON, M.A.,

Vicar of St Werburgh's, Derby, and Joint Editor of Webster and Wilkinson's
Greek Testament.

Small 8vo, 6s.

" Mr Wilkinson's illustrations of the ' Personal Names in the Bible'
will be found useful and interesting by many readers. . . . . No names of
importance appear to have been omitted, and there is subjoined a useful
and indeed absolutely necessary index."—*Westminster Review.*

" This is a book for all who would wisely, justly, and usefully study the
sacred volume."—*Homilist.*

SERMONS AND EXPOSITIONS.

BY THE LATE JOHN ROBERTSON, D.D., GLASGOW CATHEDRAL.

Crown 8vo, 7s. 6d.

" Dr Robertson had not a superior among the Scotch clergy : for manly
grasp of mind, for pith and point in treating his subject, he had hardly
an equal.   Let it be added that a more genial, kindly, liberal-minded, and
honest man never walked this earth."—*Fraser's Magazine.*

Popular Edition.   In One Volume, 6s.

STUDIES FOR STORIES,

FROM GIRLS' LIVES.

THE CUMBERER.	DR DEANE'S GOVERNESS.
MY GREAT-AUNT'S PICTURE.	THE STOLEN TREASURE.

EMILY'S AMBITION.

" Simple in style, warm with human affection, and written in faultless
English, these five stories are a real source of great delight for all who
can find pleasure in really good works of prose fiction."—*Athenæum.*

" Each of these studies is a drama in itself, illustrative of the operation
of some particular passion—such as envy, misplaced ambition, sentiment-
alism, indolence, jealousy.   In all of them the actors are young girls, and
we cannot imagine a better book for young ladies."—*Pall Mall Gazette.*

" There could not be a better book to put into the hands of young
ladies."—*Spectator.*

STORIES TOLD TO A CHILD.

BY THE AUTHOR OF "STUDIES FOR STORIES."

With 14 Illustrations by ELTZE, HOUGHTON, and LAWSON.

Cloth, gilt edges, 3s. 6d.

THE LIFE OF OUR LORD,

IN ITS HISTORICAL, GEOGRAPHICAL, AND GENEALOGICAL
RELATIONS.

BY REV. SAMUEL J. ANDREWS.

Second Edition. In Crown 8vo, cloth, 6s. 6d.

"There has been great need of a life of Christ in our language, which should present attractively the best results of modern investigations of the subject. Mr Andrews has given us a book very carefully made, full of the results of patient investigation, with thorough knowledge of the literature of the subject, clearly presented and very succinctly, without dogmatism, and in a spirit of reverence, both for the subject treated and the inspired record in which it is contained. There is no book on the subject in English so well adapted both for purposes of instruction and for private reading."—*Princeton Review.*

"A sensible, thorough, and impartially written harmony of the Gospels. The book will be found very useful to divinity students."—*Guardian.*

IDYLS AND LEGENDS OF INVERBURN.

BY ROBERT BUCHANAN,

Author of "Undertones."

Small 8vo, 5s.

"As far as my judgment goes, this is genuine poetry; very sweet and noble in its feeling, very true and simple in expression."—*From Article on Robert Buchanan, by G. H. Lewes, in the Fortnightly Review.*

"We do not call to mind any volume of modern poetry so rich in tenderly-told story, beautifully-painted picture, and abundant spontaneous music."—*Illustrated Times.*

"A volume of genuine poetry of distinguished merit."—*Pall Mall Gazette.*

UNDERTONES.

By ROBERT BUCHANAN.

Second Edition. Revised and Enlarged. Small 8vo, 5s.

" Poetry, and of a noble kind."—*Athenæum.*

"The offspring of a true poet's heart and brain, they are full of imagination, fancy, thought, and feeling—of subtle perception of beauty, and harmonious expression."—*Daily News.*

THE FOUNDATIONS OF OUR FAITH:

TEN PAPERS.

By Professors AUBERLEN, GESS, and others.

Second Edition. Crown 8vo, 6s.

CONTENTS.

INTRODUCTION. By Professor Riggenbach.

WHAT IS FAITH? By Professor Riggenbach.
NATURE OF GOD. By Wolfgang Friedrich Gess.
SIN; ITS NATURE AND CONSEQUENCES. By Ernest Stahelin.
THE OLD TESTAMENT DISPENSATION AND THE HEATHEN
 WORLD By Professor Auberlen.
THE PERSON OF JESUS CHRIST. By Professor Riggenbach.
CHRIST'S ATONEMENT FOR SIN. By Wolfgang Friedrich Gess.
THE RESURRECTION AND ASCENSION OF JESUS CHRIST. By
 Professor Auberlen
THE HOLY SPIRIT AND THE CHRISTIAN CHURCH. By S. Preiswerk.
THE DOCTRINE OF JUSTIFICATION BY FAITH. By Dr Immancel
 Stockmeyer.
THE FUTURE. By Ernest Stahelin.
 Part I. The Immortality of the Soul.
 Part II. Eternal Life.

" We know nothing that can compare with this work for completeness, wisdom, and power."—*Nonconformist.*

TANGLED TALK.

AN ESSAYIST'S HOLIDAY.

Second Edition. Post 8vo, 7s. 6d.

"'Tangled Talk' is the work of a true essayist. . . . It is a mosaic of suggestive bits; or, since mosaic is a false image, let us say it is a skein of bright and broken threads, every one of which may readily be woven into the reader's own thoughts, adding colour and strength to them for the future."—*Illustrated Times.*

HENRY HOLBEACH:

STUDENT IN LIFE AND PHILOSOPHY.

A NARRATIVE AND A DISCUSSION.

WITH LETTERS TO

MR MATTHEW ARNOLD,	REV. H. MANSEL,
MR ALEXANDER BAIN,	REV. F. D. MAURICE,
MR THOMAS CARLYLE,	MR JOHN STUART MILL,
MR ARTHUR HELPS,	REV. DR J. H. NEWMAN,
MR G. H. LEWES,	

AND OTHERS.

Two Volumes, post 8vo, 14s.

" Mr Holbeach's volumes have remarkable merits, nor are the volumes like so many books of the kind, dull and wearisome. The writer can enliven his subject, and possesses some quiet humour."—*Athenæum.*

"The brave manner in which mere utilitarianism, materialism, positivism, and authority are grappled with, convinces the reader that he is in the hands of one who has read extensively and thought profoundly on all the terrible questions of the day. . . . We think that the book is worthy of some of the themes which it discusses, and will compel the distinguished men who are addressed to listen, and perhaps reply."—*British Quarterly Review.*

"The author seems to be a man of sweet and serious mind, quick to be moved by great ideas, and with native affinities with what is delicate and exquisite. The book is one which will speak pleasantly to the cultivated reader."—*Pall Mall Gazette.*

"The book is not only a book of thought—honest, earnest, conscientious thought; but it is emphatically a thought-suggesting book. Higher merit than this could not, perhaps, be exhibited by any work of the sort." *Illustrated Times.*

" In the picture of the obscure Puritan colony there are touches worthy of George Eliot."—*Spectator.*

DREAMTHORP.

A BOOK OF ESSAYS WRITTEN IN THE COUNTRY.

BY ALEXANDER SMITH.

Crown 8vo, 3s. 6d.

"A capital pocket companion to carry into the many quiet Dreamthorps of our native land—a book to be read in the spirit of lazy leisure to the sound of babbling brooks and whispering woods. It is exquisitely printed, handy, handsome, and cheap."—*Athenæum.*

"Mr Alexander Smith comes to us with more natural vitality, with a culture that is rarer, and with a broader, deeper range of sympathy, than any one who has attempted essay-writing, in the proper sense, in his own day."—*Nonconformist.*

A SUMMER IN SKYE.

By ALEXANDER SMITH.

Two Vols., post 8vo, 16s.

"Mr Alexander Smith speaks of Boswell's Journal as 'delicious reading;' his own work, though after a very different fashion, affords delicious reading also. The food provided is unlike that provided by the guide writer. Here you will gain more wisdom than knowledge, more suggestions than facts, more of what is felicitous in expression than of what is precise in detail. Mr Smith can, when he pleases, describe Highland life and Highland scenery with considerable f licity, but he likes best to relate the impression made upon his own mind by what he heard or saw. His egotism is never offensive; it is often very charming. If the traveller is sometimes lost in the essayist, who will not prefer an Elia to a Pennant?"—*Daily News.*

"There is in this work so much excellent writing, good thought, and picturesque description, that it must rank among the very best books of the season. . . . Since the great Professor Christopher North's time, there has been no greater landscape-painter in words than Mr Smith, and the 'Summer in Skye' is by far his best effort in this branch of literature."—*Inverness Courier.*

PRAYING AND WORKING.

By the Rev. W. FLEMING STEVENSON.

Crown 8vo, 3s. 6d.   Pocket Edition, cloth, 2s.

"The Bishop of Argyll begs to inform Mr Strahan that he thinks so highly of the book 'Praying and Working' that he intends presenting each of his clergy with a copy. The Bishop would like to see this work largely circulated at the present time, as he is persuaded that much good would result."

"Since Dr Guthrie published his celebrated 'Pleas for Ragged Schools,' no book has appeared which is so calculated to touch and quicken the public mind."—*Caledonian Mercury.*

"Mr Stevenson's book comes to us at a period of suffering to thousands—of anxiety and suffering to all. It will prove a source of strength to the active, and an incentive to the indolent."—*Manchester Examiner.*

GOD'S GLORY IN THE HEAVENS.

By WILLIAM LEITCH, D.D.,

Late Principal of Queen's College, Canada.

Crown 8vo, cloth extra.   With Illustrations.   Price 6s.

"We cannot conclude our notice of Dr Leitch's book without dwelling upon the admirable manner in which the astronomical facts contained in it are blended with practical observations and the highest and most ennobling sentiments. It is thus that books on popular science should ever be written."—*Reader.*

The Ninth Thousand is now ready of

BEGINNING LIFE:

CHAPTERS FOR YOUNG MEN ON RELIGION, STUDY, AND BUSINESS.

By JOHN TULLOCH, D.D.,
St Mary's College, St Andrews.

Crown 8vo, 3s. 6d.

"It is gratifying to see one whose office connects him so closely with the intellectual and religious interests of the country, and whose name is now so well and widely known, coming forth to address a larger audience of young men than he can gather in his own classroom, and speaking to them frankly and faithfully about the great religious truths which he believes lie at the root of all excellence in life. He speaks as a friend to friends, with hearty sympathy for every difficulty, and with a clear insight of the truth that will resolve the difficulty."—*Sc. tsman.*

"Principal Tulloch's excellent book for young men."—*Edinburgh Review.*

A YEAR AT THE SHORE.

By P. H. GOSSE, F.R.S.

With 36 Illustrations by the Author, Printed in Colours by LEIGHTON BROTHERS.

Crown 8vo, 9s.

"The volume before us sustains Mr Gosse's reputation, both as an observer and as an illustrator. It is a truly handsome book, and we know not which to admire the most, the easy and felicitous style in which the writer conveys us over sands and seaweeds, into creeks, bays, and caverns, making the commonest thing almost romantic in its new attire of interest, or the charming and life-like engravings which make present, indeed, to the eye what description had before made very distinct to the mind."—*Eclectic Review.*

"A delicious book, deliciously illustrated. The study of natural history is always interesting, and Mr Gosse is a genial and enthusiastic instructor."—*Illustrated London News.*

THE AUTOCRAT OF THE BREAKFAST-TABLE.

By O. W. HOLMES.

With 24 Woodcuts by LINTON, from Drawings by J. GORDON THOMSON.
Small 8vo, 6s.

"I would rather be the author of 'The Autocrat of the Breakfast-Table,' than of all Shelley's writings put together."—*A. K. H. B. in Fraser's Magazine.*

PAPERS FOR THOUGHTFUL GIRLS.

WITH SKETCHES OF SOME GIRLS' LIVES.

By SARAH TYTLER.

With Illustrations by MILLAIS.

Crown 8vo, cloth, extra gilt, price 5s.

"One of the most charming books of its class we have ever read. . . . Miss Tytler has produced a work which will be popular in many a home when her name has become among her own friends nothing more than a memory."—*Morning Herald.*

"Here we have one of the best books that ever was written for a purpose. There has recently been no lack of books on the whole duty of women; but in none of them has there been so catholic a spirit, so just an appreciation of all the adornments of the feminine character."—*Scotsman.*

"We wish that half the novels of the day were as wholesome and suggestive as these 'Papers for Thoughtful Girls.'"—*Economist.*

"We cordially advise those who have girls to put Miss Tytler's 'Papers' into their hands."—*London Review.*

HEADS AND HANDS IN THE WORLD OF LABOUR.

By W. GARDEN BLAIKIE, D.D., F.R.S.E.,

Author of "Better Days for Working People."

Crown 8vo, 3s. 6d.

"I have read 'Heads and Hands in the World of Labour' with the liveliest interest. Its curious and entertaining details, the kindly and Christian tone which it uses both to masters and workers, the examples which it holds up both for imitation and warning, the sagacity and prudence which characterise its practical suggestions, and the exceedingly attractive style in which the whole is set forth, leave nothing to be desired but that every buyer and seller of labour in the country had a copy of it, and imbibed its spirit."—*Extract from a Letter of the Rev. Dr Guthrie.*

BETTER DAYS FOR WORKING PEOPLE.

By W. GARDEN BLAIKIE, D.D., F.R.S.E.

Crown 8vo, boards, price 1s. 6d.

"I lately read a book which I would strongly recommend to your attention. It is an excellent book, on every part of the working man's fortune and labour, and is called 'Better Days for Working People.' In this small volume I find the best rules on everything relating to the working man, on everything which relates to the improvement of the mind."—*Lord Brougham at Working Men's Meeting, Edinburgh, 9th October* 1863.

THE WORKMAN AND THE FRANCHISE.

CHAPTERS FROM ENGLISH HISTORY ON
THE REPRESENTATION AND EDUCATION OF THE PEOPLE.

By FREDERICK DENISON MAURICE, M.A.

Demy 8vo, cloth, 7s. 6d.   People's Edition, 1s. 6d.

ESSAYS ON WOMAN'S WORK.

By BESSIE RAYNER PARKES.

Second Edition.   Small 8vo, 4s.

" Every woman ought to read Miss Parkes' little volume on ' Woman's Work.' "—*Times.*

WOMAN'S WORK IN THE CHURCH;

BEING HISTORICAL NOTES ON DEACONESSES AND SISTERHOODS.

By JOHN MALCOLM LUDLOW.

Small 8vo, 5s.

" We recommend this work to the careful study of all who are anxious for the full development of Church work."—*Clerical Journal.*

Books Preparing.

LIVES OF INDIAN OFFICERS;

FORMING A BIOGRAPHICAL HISTORY OF THE CIVIL AND MILITARY SERVICES OF INDIA.

By JOHN W. KAYE, Author of " The Life of Lord Metcalfe," &c.
In Two Volumes, Demy 8vo.